You're Clear

JL LeGerrette

Printed Edition June 2017
ISBN 978-1548489250
Printed in the United States
Digital Edition June 2017 Febronia Publishing
Contact the author at Jerilynn@JLLeGerrette.com
or visit her blog site www.JLLeGerrette.com

Cover and interior book design by Cheri Lasota
www.CheriLasota.com Cheri@CheriLasota.com

Dedication

To the ones who loved me most and taught me how to love

To the one whose blood lives within me,
Mickey Jean Dodson-LeGerrette

To the one who loved me as if hers did,
Matilda Jane Dodson-Costa

And to the one whose blood lives within my children,
Theresa "Marie" Irwin-Fontyn

I hope I've made you proud . . . on the other side.

Chapter 1

The Beginning . . .
of the Best, Worst Day of Her Life

JAHNNI PULLED OUT of her driveway, popped in a CD, made the familiar turns out of her neighborhood, and cruised down the freeway—not thinking about anything in particular, just whatever came to mind. She liked the sweet respite of time alone with her thoughts before work.

She'd set the clock on her dash five minutes fast to fool herself into never arriving late for anyone or anything. She'd also drawn a red line on her gas gauge at the one-third mark in permanent red marker. She had never run out of gas before and she didn't plan to . . . ever. A little box in the center console held a journal with extra pens and sticky notes to record reminders and thoughts. Her glove compartment was stocked with a flashlight, a fog rag, deicer spray, a tire gauge, and winter gloves (with matching scarf), plus a small expandable umbrella. The trunk held a plastic roadside emergency kit she'd owned for years but never had a need for.

Maybe it's time to recheck it and get ready for winter, she noted to herself since the trunk popped into her mind. *Summer is a great time to buy winter items, before supply and demand cause the price to go up.* Another sticky note was added to the journal. Everything in her life was orderly, just how she liked it.

An old CD of Jack Johnson sent notes dancing into her soul while the sun sparkled happiness into the car. The window was rolled down halfway, and she breathed in the fresh scent of another new, summer day. She smiled as she felt the gentle, rhythmic, ticking of life keeping time like a grandfather clock in the sky.

Jahnni happily checked off her pending to-do list in her head. Her weekly supervisor report would be ready to submit after logging today's events however they played out. The roster for the upcoming end-of-summer music bookings was ready for final approval with the Port of Portland. She enjoyed being on the committee that booked local musical talent to entertain passengers as they scurried through the airport. Four baby grand pianos were placed in different concourses, and there were stages for soloists, duos, and full bands who played classical, jazz, or even light rock. Jahnni was on the committee every season. Music in her ears was like blood to the veins. Life flowed and healed because of it.

She loved her job and appreciated being at the airport with all its ever-changing, daily airline events. Every day was different and started out with controlled promise, but things always changed and Jahnni felt she couldn't leave work on any given day if she wasn't caught up, or if she was being honest, ahead of things.

Jahnni parked in the airport employee parking lot and caught the employee bus to the terminal. When she arrived, she immediately exited the bus and walked briskly across the little roadway that lined the airport entrances. Before she entered the rotating doors, she paused to glance around and gauge the passenger loads by the number of cars and people-traffic hugging the curb. She wondered what fast-paced adventure they all might be embarking on.

Jahnni felt proud that Portland International Airport, better known as PDX, was a favorite airport among travelers. Conde Nast magazine had named it the "favorite airport among business travelers" in the U.S. for several years in a row. Although part of the reason was the easily navigated concourses, she knew the real reason was that it was a beautiful airport. It was designed above a former underground water purification system, which incorporated the original skeletal framework into the airport's underlying structure. This allowed the architects to design a beautiful, enormous, outdoor fountain that erupted, sending water into three cascading waterfalls that fed into three ponds. As did others, Jahnni liked to sit by the fountain during her breaks to take in the serene peace of the falling water.

Jahnni started to walk past the Cart Man as he stepped toward a cart that had been left on the sidewalk. Called that because of his job tending the carts at the airport, Carlton was always dressed neatly in his uniform, and his kind gestures made him seem almost regal yet also approachable. She usually noticed him by the fountain in the early morning or late afternoon after his "cart runs." Throughout the day, he always seemed to have a cart ready for some hapless person burdened by overstuffed bags, though his real job description was to gather up previously rented carts to return to the kiosk for the next number of passengers to rent.

"How are you today, Carlton?" Jahnni asked, glancing at her watch as she slowed down to talk to him.

Carlton smiled and ran his fingers across the escaping ribbons of salt and pepper curls, trying to push them back into the ponytail secured at the back of his neck. He used his kerchief to wipe the perspiration off his forehead.

"I'm at the top of my game. The sun is gracing me with its company, and I can smell the bacon cooking in the food court," he chuckled. "Why are you in such a hurry?"

"I'm always in a hurry it seems," Jahnni answered. "But, I'm loving the sunshine today too." She squinted as she glanced up at the warm sun. "Hey, remember that story you were telling me about—the big airport renovation in the '70s, and how the huge water fountain in the outdoor part of the food court was a result of what remained of the previous company that owned the land?"

Carlton answered with an even bigger smile than he greeted her with. "Of course, what's on your mind?"

"Well," Jahnni said, "I was thinking about that guy you mentioned, Zale Baptiste, the guy who owned the water purification plant that was first built here. It seems strange he isn't mentioned in the chronological PDX transitions over the years. I stopped to look at the mural in the food court more closely, and in the first photos of just the land purchase that guy isn't mentioned at all, yet there's a picture of his water plant. If he was so important in the beginning, especially since it's because of him we have the fountain's plumbing, why would they leave that information out? Seems odd."

"There is always more to any story, Miss Jahnni. After working here and watching people day in and day out, you should know that!" He winked, his deep chuckle bubbling up and infecting people around them like a virus. Carlton continued, "At the time, the system was developed to run the water from the Columbia River, or use the water from the nearby underground well-field being tapped and developed. These waters were pumped directly into his underground water system. By the time the water snaked through the plant until it reached the final testing and containment site, a mere day could produce enough water to send out to all of Multnomah County and keep storage tanks filled, and he wasn't even operating at capacity at the time."

Carlton dabbed at his forehead again and continued. "His long-term plan was to produce enough purified water to send shipments to areas in the United States that were perpetually hit by drought, or to areas with contaminated groundwater. As a follower of the Austrian naturalist and inventor Viktor Schauberger, he believed he could someday purify severely contaminated waters as well."

Jahnni glanced again at her watch. She looked up as another employee bus pulled up across the roadway and watched airport and airline employees spill out as they began their march through the crosswalk like busy ants with purpose. Her mind began to wander, *I better tell Tammy she has a run in her tights. Oh look, the bus driver is changing buses. Hmmm . . . he must be taking the Long-term parking lot run now. I should ask Carolyn if she still needs me to write up the new security updates for the employee bulletin. I forgot my lunch! I can't believe that! I forgot my lunch! I guess I'll just grab something in the food court.* Jahnni popped to attention when she realized Carlton was still talking.

". . . wanted to heal. Most poverty, he felt, could be eradicated, starting with clean water technology. You may have noticed that every nation mired in poverty does not have clean water," Carlton finished saying as the words just now began to float into Jahnni's ears.

"Oh, yes, clean water. Always important," she added. "Wait, I thought you said last week he was creating water for joggers? You know, because the 70's were the enlightened era of jogging . . . and Jazzercise." Jahnni swirled her hands in front of her like a dancing marionette and they both laughed.

"Yes, that was his first level of business. But long range, he wanted to help resolve some of the water issues here in this country and then he hoped to, over time, export his water or the technology to other countries that had a shortage of healthy drinking water, but politics and greed forced his company to shut down." Carlton explained further, "But what he truly wanted was to teach the people in these impoverished countries how to purify their own water, empowering them to build, and be self-sustaining. And then . . ."

Jahnni started to worry about the time. She raised her arm and glanced at her watch. The to-do list in her head was growing longer, the closer she got to the airport door. Her foot began tapping with the tempo she used to alphabetize and memorize things until she could get to paper and pen. She noticed once again Carlton was still talking. "I'm sorry Carlton, I better get going. My mind is a flood of lists and the sooner I get started, the sooner I will complete every dot and tittle."

"Every dot and tittle?" Carlton asked teasingly, cocking his head forward, "That sounds like something from Sunday School."

Jahnni had turned to walk away but stopped and answered with jovial seriousness, "So that's where I got that saying. You know me, dot every i and cross every t." Jahnni enjoyed talking to Carlton when she had the extra time, which she really didn't have right now. She often wondered why such a knowledgeable man spent so much time tending carts for the airport.

Chapter 2

And the Day Begins . . .
Rather Normally

JAHNNI WAVED GOODBYE to Carlton then resumed her fast-paced stride into the entrance of the airport. As soon as the rotating door plunged her into the lobby, she hand-pressed her shirt, checked her belt, I.D. badge and work keys. Jahnni always presented herself with polished finesse. Her dad had always told her, "To be successful, you must dress the part," and his advice, now that she was older and could appreciate it, had never let her down. *I sure miss them,* she thought, as the twang of their wonderful memory floated to the surface.

She enjoyed all the perks that working at the airport gave her. Even though the free travel was available to her, there was always some reason or another why she wouldn't follow her deepest longings and travel to the destinations she watched others embrace. Oh sure, she took the occasional hop to Disneyland for the day with a friend, or a quick jaunt to San Fran or Reno for a day or two. But not the long getaways that made you forget about the difficult things in life so a person could refuel. She longed to hop a plane, and go away . . . far, far away. She always told herself there would be other opportunities, and she would go soon enough. Besides, she couldn't go alone, and all her friends were married or attached to work, kids or relationships. So, who could she go with anyway?

She walked toward the ticket counter and glanced at her watch, again. She still had about ten minutes to spare to get clocked in for her last shift of the week. Suddenly, she found herself dancing back and forth to avoid being run over by a cart piled high with boxes labeled with the owner's name and addressed to Taipei. She cleared the cart, only to look forward as another man in front of her pivoted in place, reversed his direction, and plowed right into her chest, head first. Caught unaware, it knocked the wind out of her for a moment and she staggered a bit to catch her balance. It surprised her when a loud breathy *Ooof* blasted out of her.

They both started muttering 'excuse me' as she watched him step back. "Oh, my goodness. Are you okay?" she laughed as she backed up slightly. She extended her hand in case he needed support while he too caught his balance.

"Ah, no. I mean yes. Of course, I am fine, thank you. I, ah, did not see you . . . or rather I did not know anyone was behind me when I realize I was going wrong direction. Please excuse me. I beg your pardon," he stammered, a foreign accent revealing itself.

And there he stood, in his brown-plaid suit, mumbling

under his breath as he stepped back and forth trying to avoid another dance with her. His eyes wore the signs of anxiety, she thought. It was hard to tell. The lines in his face looked as though he used to smile and smile often, but time and age must have erased the opportunity for such a festive emotion. His silver hair was perfectly groomed as if he'd just returned that day from the barber. It was slicked back with pomade that was only slightly detected under his brown hat he was quickly replacing on his head.

She couldn't help but notice that the top of his head barely cleared her chin. Then again, she had been a little taller than most girls all her life. Glancing down before they waltzed apart, she noticed his highly polished brown leather shoes. She watched him hurry away and wondered about the slight twitch in his shoulder. *A nervous traveler?* she wondered. She turned and walked towards the offices behind the ticket counter to 'clock in.' Being the next supervisor coming on duty for First Class Air, tardiness won't be tolerated. Especially in herself. Jahnni believed that she was tardy if she wasn't ten to fifteen minutes early.

As she walked through the door into the break room, she heard her name being called.

"Oh, Jahnni," Samantha screeched as she shuffled quickly toward her. Her eyes were sparkling and her lips were closed so tight, Jahnni wondered if a bird would fly out if she opened her mouth. "Guess what I'm going to do when I get off and get cleaned up tonight at 1700? Oh, don't bother guessing," Samantha said with a wave of her hand, dismissing the opportunity to play the guessing game. "I'm going on a date and I have to be ready by 1830. I think I've met the one."

Jahnni laughed as she glanced up and down at Samantha's perfectly curled long blonde hair, fitted uniform and expensive work shoes. *Like she needs to get cleaned up. She already looks like a perfect replica of Barbie,* she noted. She looked at Sam's pretty smile and sunshine eyes then answered teasingly, "Gee Sam, you've really managed to morph into an airline geek and wear the verbal uniform very quickly." They both smiled, remembering the struggle Samantha had learning military time. "So, is this the pilot you rode with when he taxied the plane to the hangar last week?" Jahnni added.

After thinking for a few moments to place his name, she began to explain, "Oh. No. That was, ahh . . . he was . . . hmm . . ." Samantha thought as she rolled her fingers across her chin several times before she gave up and said, "not Mr. Right after all. We just didn't, I don't know, click."

"Wait," Jahnni said when something jogged her memory. "Is this the guy you dumped because he had a big . . . big toe?" Part of her didn't want to know, but the curious side of her wanted to know everything. Jahnni knew Samantha always found something wrong with every guy she dated. Tonight, would be no different. She was sure of it. Since she had started working here about a year ago, her accumulative date total had more digits than a math test. Samantha was desperate to find Mr. Right. Jahnni worried that someday it was Sam that was going to get hurt instead of being the other way around. She only hoped Sam would find *the one* soon, so that 'getting hurt' didn't happen to such a great person.

Samantha continued her plea, "I'm looking for someone to cover the last part of my shift so keep me in mind if someone asks you about picking up hours."

Jahnni answered, as she signed into the computer to check the company bulletins, "Sure kiddo. I'll keep that in mind. How much of your shift did you need covered, in case someone mentions they need hours? I haven't looked at the schedule yet."

But she was half listening as she started reading the latest company news and security directives.

- *Uniforms are ready.*
- *Hearing tests due.*
- *Reminder, NO escorting people around the security checkpoint or through bi-pass doors.*
- *Challenge anyone not wearing their PDX badge in complete view when in a secure area.*

This one is interesting, she frowned. *Police are looking for two people who broke into the office of the City of Portland Development Services offices and are now in possession of a large collection of archived historical blueprints from Resources/Records. Under the assumption that they may be trying to travel, because of the odd nature of the break-in, this information has been released to all the airlines, train stations and bus depots.*

Jahnni noted their pictures were captured by the security cameras. Even though their faces were covered by stocking caps with just their eyes showing, they looked surly. *What would anyone want those things for?* Still, she printed out the pictures for her agents, and planned to post them at the ticket counter at each computer station, below the public view.

"What a waste of manpower," Jahnni whispered, with an air of incredulity. Then she became aware Samantha was still chattering at her.

Samantha squealed with glee at whatever she was saying to Jahnni, threw her head back as if she was going to faint, and began to back out through the door to head to the boarding gates.

"By the way, what position are you working today?" Jahnni called out as she jogged to the door to catch Samantha before she was out of range.

"UML," Samantha said, as she glanced back over her shoulder, trying to sound like it was no big deal. "It will be easy!"

Easy means either boring or frantic in airport language, Jahnni thought.

Jahnni used to like to work pretty much every position *but* being the Unaccompanied Minor Liaison and taking care of the unaccompanied minors. It was either crazy busy or slow and boring, but it was an important position so she always tackled it with her usual due diligence.

After she signed out of the computer, she walked over to Maggie, one of the 'new hires' and reached out her hand, introducing herself. "Hi Maggie, I will be the mid-day Supervisor on Duty. How are you?"

"Great! Oh, ya, I remember you. You were in the interview meeting," Maggie said with the sweetest southern drawl Jahnni had ever heard. It matched her delicate features that had soft wisps of hair framing her face while the rest of her hair was pulled back in a simple barrette. She reached out to shake Jahnni's extended hand.

"First day jitters? Look, I'm heading down to the gates," Jahnni informed her. She looked at the daily schedule on her clipboard and added, "I'll take you down with me so you can meet up with Tina since you're doing the airport tour today. By the way, did you understand the UML position when you were in Seattle for training?"

Maggie's eyes darted back and forth between Jahnni and the girl she was talking to before Jahnni walked up. "Uh, yes? As much as possible until I'm done with OJT. Theory, I guess, but I am nervous about it. Why?" she warily responded.

"I just wanted to mention a few important details for you to understand when Tina gets to that portion of your training. It's a critical position and you don't want to be lax with it."

Jahnni noticed the deer in the headlights look and explained, laughing a little, "I am not sending you to the UML position if that is what you are worried about. I just want to prepare you for a couple of things. You see, one of our agents was let go because she was in such a hurry to get off work, she told the agent boarding the flight she was taking her UM out to the plane. Then she put the wrong UM on the wrong flight. Theodore Gomeau was supposed to be going home to Burbank. His father is the famous movie director, Thierry Gomeau. Theodore ended up in Billings Montana, and Teddy Gomez ended up in Burbank. It was in all the papers around the nation. Possibly even the world. The Weekly Inquisitor had it headlined as 'Baffled Babysitter Bungles Billings and Burbank Boarding.' It was so embarrassing for the airline, and the thought that someone could have somehow showed up and said they were sent by the parents in the other city, well, you can imagine the horrible fears it can cause. It worked out in the long run for the boys, but there is still an ongoing court matter because of it."

"Man, I hope I can master this. There is so much to learn," Maggie said.

"Trust me. Your mama bear senses come alive. You will be awesome," Jahnni promised. "The main thing is that you don't leave them alone or let them out of your sight. Follow the paperwork. Here, you see this form? It has a section for everything. Even their assigned seat numbers, gates, special notes, parents and pick up adult . . . everything. It's your map to the child's safety."

They walked out the office door, passing the ticket counter and then picked up their pace on the carpeted mezzanine. Maggie was looking over the form as they walked. In the short, wide corridor that led to the food court, outdoor patio, and waterfall, Maggie stopped for a few seconds to look at all the flights displayed on the FIDS. "Wow, I never really knew before, that so many flights came and went every day."

"Yep, after a while, you'll have the major flights of the other airlines memorized as well as our own," Jahnni said, matter-of-factly. "You get to know what goes on at the airport and what airlines you can reroute your passengers on, if needed."

Jahnni let out a hum then walked on, assuming Maggie would follow. She did.

After passing the long lines for the security checkpoint, they turned down a hallway leading to a security door. Jahnni showed her the process to swipe her badge, key in her secret numbered code and place her finger on the print pad. She added, "I'll go first. If you don't come through behind me in about thirty seconds, I'll key back through to see what the problem is. Oh, you can just tap your badge on the pad or swipe it like a credit card. Both ways work, but you still need to add your personal code and print." They were through the first door in fifteen seconds.

"Okay, these stairs lead up and down behind the scenes," Jahnni began to explain, "but you don't need to worry about that right now. This next door here will take us out into the concourse. Key yourself through before me, and be sure that the door closes securely behind you after you pass through."

Maggie was waiting for Jahnni when she came through the door. They walked across the concourse to the other side, weaving between passengers coming and going along the walkway. They entered a wide gated area consisting of two boarding podiums for two different flights.

"We have lots of gates!" Jahnni said as she pointed down the concourse. "You'll work many of them during training. Each gate area has a permanent numbered gate sign by the entrance, and above each boarding podium inside the gate will be the flight numbers and city destination that directs passengers to their correct waiting area with their correlating cities.

The scrolling bright red neon words should minimize confusion, but even with that, some passengers will walk up to a podium with a big C-3 above it, stare at it and ask the busy agent, 'Where is C-3?'" They smiled at each other with Jahnni shaking her head in exaggeration, then she waved Tina over when she saw that she was finished speaking with a passenger.

"Now, here you are. I am turning you over to your trainer." Jahnni motioned as Tina approached the gate podium. "Tina, this is Maggie, the new-hire assigned to you for the next two weeks. She already has the security doors mastered. I was explaining some of the details about the UML position. Sam is the UML today if you want to point her out later." After Tina and Maggie walked on, she smiled at the other nearby agents, and turned to leave.

Jahnni walked down the concourse to check on the agents at each gate. She dropped off the updated gate sheets, and headed back up the concourse to go back to her office.

Chapter 3

It's All About Customer Service, Right?

AFTER SHE WENT over the day's schedule and made notes to herself, Jahnni noticed that the line at the ticket counter was long, so she decided to step in and get people checked in to prevent them from missing their flights. She clocked into an empty computer and changed the overhead sign to show she was open for check-in. Then she motioned to the first person in line. "I can help you over here, sir. Welcome to First Class Air. Where's your destination today?"

"I am going to San Francisco and I already check in, but I have lost my bag I was to carry on plane. It have my medicine."

And there stood Brown Plaid Man, the man who ran into Jahnni when she arrived to work. As he rattled off his story, she wondered if her shirt was becoming a familiar sight to him because his words were starting to slow down at the end of his story. His face seemed to redden as he stared, his eyes lingering on her badge. One hand rested on the counter and the other was shaking as he took his handkerchief out of his pocket and dabbed his forehead.

"I am so sorry to hear that Mr. . . . ?" Jahnni inquired.

"Tropopoulis. Mr. Arnad Tropopoulis." Although he spoke excellent English, she could not help but pick up that Mediterranean accent. *Possibly Greek?* she asked herself. *His accent reminds me of the father in the movie, My Big Fat Greek Wedding.*

"No, I am sorry Janie. I did not mean to crinkle your shirt earlier," he answered back, slight embarrassment on his face. He took his hat off and bowed slightly before returning it to his head. He thought her name tag said Janie, instead of Jahnni, but she was not willing to take the time to correct him.

"Again, Mr. Tropopoulis, I am sorry about your bag," Jahnni offered as she reached for the phone. "Let's call the Port Police and start a report for your lost or stolen bag."

"No need!" he quickly said, almost cutting her off. "I mean no thank you, Janie. I would like to just look further for it myself. I come up here again to see if possible, someone turn in a suitcase to your counter-place here. I did have my old information on it from when I last fly, many years ago. I thought, maybe it was here," he explained. Jahnni heard a little strain in his voice.

"Well, no Mr. Tropopoulis. If someone found your bag, provided it was lost and not stolen, it would have been picked up by the Port Police and searched. Is the medication in your bag something you can readily get from home? Should I call someone for you?"

"I have much time until my flight with your airline is to depart, so I will look more and let you know if I need further assistance. I carry full week of medicine in this little pill holder. Very tight lid. Has rubber seal." He partially pulled it out of his inside jacket pocket so she could see it in full view, before adding, "I have enough, but I do not want to lose expensive medicine. It help me with, shaky nerves."

Feeling a bit sorry for Brown Plaid Man, Jahnni watched him walk away. He seemed to walk with such bravado for a man of smaller stature. Even his nervous tic had a slight elegance to it. After searching it out, she added some comments to his reservation for the next agent who may end up helping him, then looked up to see how long the line was.

She needed to tend to other matters as the Supervisor on Duty. But the lines were so crowded and long. Four people were out sick and there weren't any more 'on-call' agents to fill the empty slots. She decided to stay at the ticket counter for a while longer to help get the lines down, then she would head back to the office before going to the gates.

Jahnni looked up at the line of passengers waiting to check in. *Why don't they just do the self-check-in? It's not difficult. Maybe I should mention to the head office that we need another marketing gig on all the newer tech options.*

"I can help you over here ma'am. Here, let me help you with that bag," Jahnni offered as she climbed over the scales to help the elderly lady pull forward her tangled bags. "Are you traveling alone today, or is there someone to help you?"

The little lady seemed a little flustered as she tried to

straighten up her little case that fell sideways off the handles of her big suitcase. She brushed the wisps of hair from her face and walked the rest of the way to the counter with Jahnni. "Oh, yes," she answered Jahnni. "I mean, I am traveling with my friends but I'm early. I'll be fine once I check in big Bertha here. This suitcase is too big, but it's all I have."

Jahnni asked for her name and ID, finished checking her in, tagging her bag after noticing that it was not overweight, and sent her on her way. She watched her walk away but as she looked past her, she could see several Port Police fanning out and walking through the lobby. They seemed to be scanning the passengers and their bags, but a little too casually, she thought, for it to be urgent. They split off and some went through the revolving door to continue what she assumed was a visual scan of the curbside area. *I wonder what they are looking for? Must not be too important if they aren't contacting us, or making announcements. Uh, oh, the dogs are here now. What the heck?* she wondered as she watched the dogs walking and sniffing bags, garbage cans, and people.

She watched them walk past the First Class ticket counter and down to the end of the lobby, accessing the last bypass door. She looked back down the lobby for any activity, but everything appeared calm, or rather as calm as a busy airport can be. Jahnni called the next person up and began checking him in. Every ten to fifteen seconds she glanced up at the area and did a quick scan for anything that might catch her eye. Still, she saw nothing but the bustle of people and business travelers. *It was probably just a drill,* she told herself.

"I can help the next person over here," she called out. "Welcome to First Class Air. Where is your destination today?"

"Oh, hello Jahnni!" one of the airline's regular travelers said as she approached the ticket counter. Her colorful bohemian skirt and long flowing scarf swirled around her as she hurried towards Jahnni. "You are just the person I was hoping to see today!"

"How are you Annabelle? How was your trip to Mexico? Did you find more information about your genealogy?" Jahnni inquired.

"Oh, it was fabulous. And yes! I met some delightful distant relatives who, believe it or not, remember my great-grandmother. They were elders in the tribe. Beautiful souls. Anyway . . . I brought you back this handwoven basket that was crafted specially for you. I just told her the size, and colors I wanted and when I came back the next day, I was stunned with the intricate weave patterns and hand stained grasses she used. I have never seen these weave patterns before."

"This is for me? It's so beautiful! Thank you so much! What did I do to deserve this?" Jahnni said breathlessly. She turned the basket around and around to look at the detailed design, stopping only to wipe the tear from her cheek that breached the rim of her watery eyes.

"Your airline always goes above and beyond. You especially, have helped me so many times when things go upside down with my reservation. I just thought of you when I was going through their market. Thank you for all that you do," Annabelle said as she placed her hand over her heart. With that, Jahnni climbed over the bag scale to the other side of the counter to draw Annabelle to her in a big hug. Annabelle released Jahnni and smiled. She waved goodbye as she walked towards the escalators to the baggage claim. Jahnni stood watching her go, waiting for the chance to wave one last time before she watched her disappear in the crowd.

Time was flying by. They were very busy at the counter today. Some passengers would make demands of the agents, and not accepting no for an answer, Jahnni had to go over and 'back up' the agents and explain why rules had been implemented concerning whatever situation was at hand. She was just getting ready to take a ten-minute break when she decided to waive one more person up to the ticket counter.

She waved over the next person in the Special Services line. "Welcome to First Class Air, I can help you over here."

Like a slow-motion entrance from a soap opera, he walked the few steps to the counter, and now stood before her. His dark jeans and form-fitted Henley hugged his muscular body yet hung looser on his waist like a model in a GQ ad. She waited impatiently for his answer, ready to pin to memory, every syllable that breached his lips.

"I am on the San Francisco flight and I am traveling armed . . . oh, and I would like to check a bag also," said the tall, dark haired, handsome, green eyed Adonis standing before her. His face appeared chiseled; his eyes freezing the part of Jahnni's brain responsible for forming complete sentences. All sorts of electrical short circuits were going off in her head . . . and elsewhere. He was sublime; a beauteous specimen of maleness.

Absolutely worth the embarrassing open mouthed drool that was beginning to form on her lips. His dark hair glimmered with a few patches of sun kissed caramel, the sign of an outdoors adventurer. Her imagination detoured to a sunset beach as they walked hand in hand along the edge of the water, the soft waves lapping at their bare feet. He stopped and pulled her close to him as the glow of the setting sun warmed their embrace. He leaned forward to whisper a vow of eternal love as he gazed into her wanton, longing eyes. Slowly, with a tempo of measured pause, he tilted his head to offer her a supple kiss that would pledge his love forever . . . when suddenly she heard him say, "Excuse me? Can . . . I check this bag?"

"Oh yes. Whew. It must be hot in here. I feel a little warm suddenly. I think the air conditioner is pfftt," she said as she waved her hand in an arching, sliding motion up to the ceiling. A nervous giggle flew out her mouth like a sly burp. *I cannot believe . . . I just spaced out like that,* she moaned queasily in her head before recovering enough to continue.

"Let's see your I.D. and credentials. Okay. Well, your flight doesn't leave for a little while," she offered. "There is still plenty of time." Little trickles of sweat were forming on her forehead as she tried to cram several pieces of extremely important information into her brain at the same time. His flight number, the time it left, his name, was he wearing a wedding ring . . . check, check, check, and no. *It's all about customer service,* she noted to herself.

"I need you to fill out the Armed Individual paperwork and sign please," Jahnni said, handing him the AI form concerning his armed status as an FBI agent and adding, "you'll need to show this paperwork at security and when you introduce yourself to the gate agent. I can get you checked in. What is your last name sir? Oh yeah, I just memorized it, I mean . . . saw it. Would you like a window or an aisle today?" she asked as she handed his badge back to him.

"Harleyman. Beau Harleyman. I'll just take the seat reserved in my name. Thanks." He smiled as he filled out the Armed Individual form, glancing up at her every few seconds. When he had finished, he handed it back to her, still smiling, which caused his green eyes to burn a fever into hers.

She reached for his credentials again because he was standing there with his badge still in hand, added edits to the flight info, and continued the check-in process with all the pertinent steps for an AI.

His bag tag popped out of the machine and eager to be efficient, she immediately strapped it around the handle. The fold of the name tag holder was slightly lifted and she could sort of make out a faded image of the name TROPOPOULIS barely showing under the flap but it appeared to be scribbled over. Above it, the name BEAU HARLEYMAN was written in a bolder ink. Tires screeched a warning in her head. She looked at his boarding pass, and then looked at the name tag once again.

"This is your bag, Mr. Harleyman?" she quizzed as she slowly looked up at him.

He had started to put his badge away but flipped open his wallet once again to show an official badge stating Department of Investigation, FBI, Special Agent Beau Harleyman. "Sure is," he answered in a matter-of-fact tone.

She needed to stall while thinking through the situation, so she reverted to the old security questions from years gone by.

"Has anyone unknown to you asked you to carry an item onboard this flight today?"

"No."

"Have any of the items you are traveling with been out of your immediate control since the time you packed them?"

"No."

"Do, do, do . . . any of your items contain firearms, knives or sharp cutting instruments of any kind?"

"No. That is except the firearm at my side," he reminded her.

Duh, she thought to herself, *we already did the paperwork for that.* "Dangerous, flammable materials or explosive devises of any kind?" she rattled off.

"No," he answered while breathing his words out as she received them like warm pudding being savored on her palette. *If I could listen to his voice the rest of my life, I would die a happy woman,* she told herself.

She gazed at his smile resting between his dimples, again, and she slowly let out the breath she realized she'd been holding. Her toes gripped the inside of her shoes so she didn't lose her balance as her heart rode the wave brought on by cupid's arrow. Something was quivering somewhere in her body whenever she looked at him, but she was unsure from where.

It seemed as if everything—everywhere was. Even her voice.

Back on track, Dawson, she ordered herself. *Pay attention. Why would an F.B.I man have Brown Plaid Man's bag? Why the apparent name change, and why does the bag appear to match Brown Plaid Man's jacket?* Another realization popped into her head. *Ah, nuts, pinecones and sap. Just my luck. I knew he was too good to be true.* She decided she didn't want to walk on the beach with a thief after all.

She watched Mr. Harleyman as he left the counter, and took note of his self-assured gait. When he was out of sight, she turned and set the bag onto the bag belt where she knew it would be scanned by the CTX machine once it landed in TSA's hands behind the scenes.

She was just getting ready to pick up the phone to call the Port Police to ask their advice on the situation when up walked Mr. Tropopoulis. He seemed quite a bit calmer as he announced, "Please do not worry, Janie. I have found my bag. Someone turn it in to the Pizza A' Plenty and they were just getting ready to call someone to come get it when I show up and claim my bag. Very nice pizza people."

"Are you sure it is your bag, Mr. Tropopoulis?" Jahnni blubbered out.

"Oh yes, Janie." He held it up, showcasing the fine woven details of the browns, oranges and shades of yellow lacing their pattern throughout his brown prized possession. "Thank you for, well for . . . uh, well, just thank you anyway."

"You are sure this is your bag? I mean, many bags look alike," Jahnni reminded him. *Well, most other bags, usually not*

32

this one, she thought.

"Yes." Then he slowed his speech a little while staring at his bag, but nodded and offered with possessive pride before walking away, "Yes, it is mine."

Maybe he is lying about something. Or maybe it was not his bag he recovered, Jahnni thought as her curiosity was ignited. *Could someone have traded his bag with the other one? This is a serious matter of cosmic proportions! How could there be two ugly brown plaid bags in this universe?*

Something is just wrong here! How can there be two bags . . . like that? And why would someone like Mr. Harleyman have one . . . like that? Who would even want to steal a bag . . . like that? And for what? Travel fashion tips? Hardly. She felt there must be an explanation. She looked up the seat assignments for Brown Plaid Man. *Tropopoulis. Yes. Here it is. 3A. Okay . . . Harleyman. Hmm . . . 3C. Side by side in First Class. Too weird. But they aren't in the same reservation. Maybe I need to talk to the screeners to see if they had any reason to pull the bag,* she thought. *After all, the Port is either doing a drill, or they are looking for something. While I don't want to cause unnecessary trouble, it's best to be cautious.* Jahnni signed out of her computer, grabbed her clip board, then scurried through the bypass door next the ticket counter by swiping her badge, entering her private code into the security panel and placing her index finger on the pad for print analysis. The door buzzed and she walked through it and directly over to the elevator.

When she arrived at the next floor down, she exited the elevator into the secure area under the airport and walked over to the screening area. Jahnni watched the screeners grab and run several bags through CTX. The large x-ray machine was at the base of the bag belts that wound down from the ticket counters via a side belt altering the route. She watched the TSA agents grab the screened bags and place them back on the conveyor belt, and she smiled to herself at how lonely the bags looked as they continued their journey to the airline's bagwell.

She remembered when the bags simply rode down from the ticket counters after the passengers took their tagged bags to the large CTX machines in the lobby. But now, she liked the ease of simply throwing the bags on the belt behind her at the ticket counter so all the bags went through the CTX machines behind the scenes. With the flip of a switch, the bags traveled directly to the bagwell, or were intercepted and rerouted to the screeners, which of course, is how it was set up as a permanent change . . . until methods are changed again at some future date in time. Things were ever-changing and fluid at an airport.

"Hey Danny," Jahnni said. "I need to ask about a bag that I just sent down."

After she pointed out the bag and asked a couple questions, he replied, "Nothing unusual in the bag. It just had clothes, I think a book, shoes, a Dopp kit, you know, the usual."

"A what? What's a Dopp kit?" Jahnni asked.

"You know," he answered. "A man's toiletry bag. Holds his manly-man stuff. The cologne and woo-woo magic that attracts the ladies."

"Oh. Right. The magic," she mumbled as she rolled her

eyes in fake boredom. "But if there was nothing on the x-ray to peak your interest, why did you do a physical search?"

"Oh, it was just random. We must randomly select bags throughout the day, to do physical searches. You know . . . national security and all," one of the other screeners answered.

"But how do you remember what was in that particular bag?" Jahnni grilled him further.

"You are kidding, right? Who wouldn't remember the bag that looks like my great-grandma's sofa?" he chuckled. Then everyone around them began laughing.

Noting that she had no concrete evidence yet to be able to confront Mr. Harleyman, because everyone used friend's suitcases, she told the TSA worker, "I'm just double-checking security measures for Carolyn, the station manager."

Jahnni decided that since she was already half way there, she would go down to the gates to check on her staff. May-be she would see something. Hear something. Feel something . . . other than that annoying quivering every time Mr. Harley-man's face jumped into her memory.

Chapter 4

The Sum of all Things Is Planning

JAHNNI WATCHED AS other employees passed each other in the hallway chambers or roadways under the main passenger area of the airport. They were either working in the bagwell or circumvented the corridors. Things banged, pipes clamored and she could hear the bag belts humming around and above, attached to the floor, walls or ceiling, carrying bags into the web of transfer belts. The belts went forward in a straight line, or curved up and over other belts, and some wound through passageways only to exit and careen down to a transfer area. Bag carts were being driven through the tunnels by several different airlines as they dropped off transfer bags and exchanged loads whenever possible to save a trip to the other side of the airport.

She smiled at the collection of boxes, suitcases, golf bags, sleeping bags, car seats, wheelchairs, walkers, guitar cases, and a couple dogs in crates. She remembered when she started working for the airlines, a passenger had checked in a ninety-nine-pound floor sander. It was amazing all the things she learned that people checked.

As she walked along and looked all around her, she remembered the longstanding rumor that these tunnels also had an access point somewhere that led to a dungeon, as many called it. She had never met anyone who had been down there, if 'there' even existed. Some people jokingly called it the mine shafts. Jahnni had never tried her badge in any secret-looking door. In fact, she had never even seen a secret-looking door.

She turned once more to walk the underground shortcut to the First Class Air's gates. Music was blasting away and sunglasses were perched on top of heads after the tug drivers entered the tunnels, bringing newly unloaded bags to be dropped at the carousels or sorted for transfer to other flights. Other drivers donned their sunglasses as they pulled out of the bagwell, headed out to load aircraft, or meet incoming flights. She walked out the large tunnel door that led outside to the cargo loading area for the aircraft. Jetways reached out overhead, connecting the inside airport areas with the airplanes. The airplanes sat stoically on the pavement, waiting to be loaded with people from above and cargo down below. *Such magnificent beauty,* she thought. Being so close to them made their enormous size even more majestic. *I'll never understand how they stay in the air.*

The sound of the planes taking off and landing caused a stir in her chest that welcomed adventure, but usually only in her imagination. Although there were other ways to stay indoors while traversing the underground maze, Jahnni preferred this route. She was very mindful of security and safety and stayed within the painted areas that allowed for airport employee foot traffic. Exhaust and jet fuel mixed with fresh air smelled like Freedom. Escape. Adventure. Maybe even a little trouble. Just a little.

After breathing in one last fill of adventure, she climbed the metal grate stairs that led to the door, which gave access to inside the airport. She keyed herself in. The door unlocked and she proceeded into one of the boarding areas for First Class Air.

Once inside, she waited for her eyes to adjust from being in the bright sunlight. Jahnni turned to approach the boarding area for Brown Plaid Man's flight . . . when she crashed head on with Mr. Harleyman.

"I think we must have a special connection, you and me," he chuckled.

Jahnni was about to say she has no connections with thieves, nor did she desire to kiss them when she heard herself say, "M-m maybe we do. I would accuse you of following me, but I suppose that would have been impossible, given our location." She smiled, wondering if, or more like hoping, he wasn't a thief and they did have some kind of connection. *After-all, the bag went through CTX, so it's really a non-issue at this point,* she tried to assure herself.

"True, true. A mere impossibility seeing as I came in through that area," he agreed as he hooked a thumb over his shoulder, pointing to the security checkpoint, "and you came in through that area." He pointed around the corner to the door with the big 'Employees Only' sign emblazoned across it. "I actually watched you walk up from outside while I was standing here admiring the view from these big windows. You look like you really know your way around this massive airport," he added.

His gestures caused his arms to flex. This caused her to be unnecessarily sidetracked while imagining the feel of his bulging arms as they wrapped protectively around her, shielding her from all forces of ill-will. She recovered from her momentary sidetracked imagination by saying, "Well, I have to check on my staff and tend to some important tasks. You'll have to excuse me, Mr. Harleyman." She smiled as she backed away to go to the podium, too embarrassed to look him in the eyes. *I know he knows what I'm thinking. He can probably read my mind, or my body language, gestures, who knows! I've read about these FBI types. They have secret training. I bet he has lots of secrets.* She took a deep breath and sighed, *I hope any future secrets include me.*

When she was halfway to the podium, she turned again to see if he was watching her walk away. *Yep. I hope he likes the view. I need to think of what information I need,* she thought to herself. *One, find out why he is flying . . . for business or pleasure? Two, official FBI business? Oh, he wouldn't be allowed to tell me that. One thing for sure is number three. I need to find out if he is married,* she reasoned.

Jahnni tried to keep her mind focused so she started checking the computer for the daily flight loads. She knew that long eastbound flights, or flights heading to the sunshine tended to be booked to capacity if not over-booked. She called OPS, "I need the updates on inbound and outbound expected delays that haven't been put in the computer yet. Are there any mechanicals or other issues that you foresee causing a delay?"

Jahnni was always one step ahead. Actually, two or three steps ahead if possible. She liked a smooth operation because there were issues that popped up all day long, every day. Planning reduced the stress on her staff, as well as the passengers. Her team always worked better if they were on the same page, and had access to the same tools. She was determined to always provide that.

There is so much to think about all day long, she reminded herself so she would stay focused. *Sick calls, staffing, backups at the ticket counter, did he notice me? I mean really, really, notice me?* Her mind tried to stay on task but it continued to sidetrack her thoughts when she thought of Mr. Harleyman. Once the bank of flights went out later, she decided that she'd check FLIFO to look at the flight ETA's and ETD's for the rest of the evening. *That will keep me busy. That's what's wrong. I just need to stay focused, stay on task. Make plans . . . to get to know Mr. Harleyman.*

Chapter 5

A Hiccup in the Day

SUDDENLY THE SUP phone was chiming. "First Class Air Supervisor Jahnni. May I help you?" She already knew that the call was coming from the Operations Department when she saw the caller ID. *There must be an issue with a flight,* she wondered.

"Hey Jahn, a flight from Denver is diverting to PDX, flight 198. A winglet was hit by lightning and the captain is going to set down. They will be on the ground in 18 minutes. Spot C-2. Can you meet the plane and let the passengers know that we will have an ETD within a half hour? There is a plane at the hangar that we will use for the swap-out. It was here for scheduled maintenance and was released into service just a couple hours ago," Pablo explained.

Jahnni called down to the RAC Room to have everyone reseated if the seat configuration was different. She knew they would ensure the SSR's like wheelchair passengers and UM's were taken care of. They would retag bags for any rebooked passengers and the ground agents would rally to transfer any cargo and bags in a timely manner. The Ramp Action Center, also referred to as the Re-accommodation Center, has been a superb behind-the-scenes office in First Class Airline's bag well. Not every airline had a RAC Room but because of the size of First Class Air and the size of PDX, the added support their airline depended on streamlined so much work behind the scenes.

Basically, at First Class Air, OPS handled the planes and the RAC room handled the behind-the-scenes issues with passengers and their bags. Having worked both of those positions herself, she knew the departments stayed in contact to make decisions that kept the passengers moving forward, and sometimes checking on the same things. *Redundancy reduces calamity and that makes me happy,* Jahnni reminded herself.

When the diverted plane arrived, Jahnni met the plane at the end of the jetway and boarded to make the announcement that once they deplaned, they were to remain in the gate area because their plane was being swapped out while this one is sent over to the hangar for an LSP check. Since they were hit by lightning, Lightning Strike Protection had to be checked and verified or the plane would remain grounded until the LSP on the plane was operational. They would be on their way with a new plane in short order.

A few minutes later, Jahnni noticed the plane swap had been entered into the computer so she printed out a list of the passengers that had new seat assignments and planned to call up only the ones who had been reassigned. A second list was printed for the passengers whose seat assignments remained the same. She knew it would be a few minutes while the planes were swapped. She stopped and looked out at the passengers waiting for their flights. *Another busy day filled with changes.*

While she waited to hear that the new plane was ready, Jahnni glanced out to the concourse to watch the passenger flow. Some people appeared to have just arrived and some looked like they were getting ready to depart, holding their boarding passes in their hands as they turned in circles scanning the boarding gate signs, or stood staring up at the FIDS checking the airline, flight number and gate locations. Other people were casually strolling about and some were sitting, perusing books, magazines or other items. Everyone seemed to have a drink of some type in hand: coffee, soda, or water. She always wondered where people were going.

She realized she had been staring at a service member walking by the gate as she stood near the entrance. She broke her gaze and watched two Port Police pass him, walking as if on their way to the B gates but they accessed a bypass door in quite a rush. Movement caught her eye and she turned to her left to see two more Port Police rush past the gate and access the same door, disappearing behind it. *Something is going on.* She decided to call the station manager to see what she knew.

After hearing her station manager hadn't heard anything yet either, Jahnni finished the conversation by telling her boss, "Well, if you find out anything, please call me right away. This doesn't feel right." With so much to do with so many flights about to depart, and agents getting off and agents coming on, her focus changed to the litany of tasks that ruled her day. Her auto-pilot kicked in, knowing it would be interrupted many times, but realizing by now that you just rode the wave and made the best choices from what were available. After about twenty seconds, a sideline thought burst forward, *Why are there so many Port Police scurrying about? This is lasting longer than their normal drills. Are they looking for someone? Was there a threat called in? Why haven't they let all the airlines know what they are doing? I better put that thought back on a shelf for now until I hear something. A front shelf, but* . . . She remained alert while going about her duties.

Chapter 6

Whatever Works

JAHNNI SAW THAT one of the flights at another gate became oversold in the last sixty minutes. She sent an agent over to the other gate to help with the oversold flight and took this agent's place to board up the diverted flight. She checked all the flight information and got ready to make her announcements once she heard from the ground crew.

"Seattle to C-2, ready to board."

"Copy that . . . here they come," Jahnni called back, speaking into her radio. She began her boarding announcements.

Everyone applauded when they had heard the radio squawk to life, mentioning Seattle. There was a special service request for a Spanish-speaking-only passenger, so she had brought it to Jorge's attention earlier so he could make her announcements in Spanish, just as he had done when she met the plane to explain why they were diverted. Jorge was at the next gate podium, boarding another flight, but grabbed his PA mic and repeated Jahnni's boarding announcement in Spanish for the passenger, Mr. Rodriquez. When all the passengers had boarded, she looked up as a little bundled up lady came shuffling up with her arm extended and the boarding pass limply hanging off the end of her fingers. Thinking that she must have missed someone somehow, Jahnni started to ask her name and reach for her boarding pass when she noticed that it indicated that she was going to Vancouver, Canada.

"Oh, THIS IS NOT YOUR FLIGHT."

"Yes," she smiled back, bobbing her head up and down, up and down.

"NO, I MEAN, YOUR FLIGHT IS AFTER THIS ONE . . . LATER," she tried to express, pointing her hand toward the ceiling and the wall to indicate 'away . . . later.' Jahnni looked at Jorge when he approached her podium to grab another pen and he began to softly chuckle. Without looking up at the little passenger, he said in a low voice, "You know Jahnni, talking louder doesn't translate what you're saying into their native language."

Jahnni didn't want to look at her either because she didn't want to laugh in front of her. She was laughing at herself and didn't want the passenger to think they were laughing at her.

"Yes," she affirmed again as she bobbed her head. Jahnni motioned graciously for her to go sit down and she seemed to understand. So, she sat. Jahnni turned and grabbed her radio.

"C-2 to Seattle."

"Go ahead."

"You're clear. Everyone's onboard. I'm coming down to

clear the count with the flight attendant. Did you transfer all the bags?"

"Affirmative. All onboard," the ground agent assured her.

Jahnni disappeared down the jetway corridor, in-flight papers in hand. She gave the flight attendant a verbal passenger count with her paperwork. The flight attendant smiled and gave Jahnni a 'thumbs up' concerning the passenger count. The flight attendant closed the plane door, and Jahnni pulled the jetway back away from the plane. After waving to the captain and first officer as the tug began pushing the flight out, she walked back up to the boarding area away from the tin city of people finishing their journey to Seattle.

She now stood at the large window and watched the plane get pushed back by the ground agents to the taxi area. The sunlight was gleaming onto the plane and sending shards of light bouncing into the window. Jahnni smiled, wanting to wave goodbye to her metal friend. She then turned and walked over to the boarding area to check on everyone else when she bumped into a wall of muscle. Again. "Super job there . . . with the flight and all," Mr. Harleyman acknowledged. "I'm impressed. You have a cool head."

Jahnni was a little rattled as she tried to think of a professional response. What she had in mind to say was still muddled and she was pretty sure that asking permission to pet his muscled arms would be considered harassment. "Well, not really. I tend to think methodically. People call me a control freak. The flight was supposed to be boarded up by one of my other agents, but I wanted to get it done fast, and out of here in time for them to make their connections in Seattle. Plus, I needed my agent to help with another flight at C-10."

"Are you always this . . . organized and methodical?" he asked.

"Only when I need to be," she said after a pause, then admitted with a jovial laugh, "well, pretty much all the time . . . unfortunately. I get teased a lot about it and I do have to make myself slow down and not be too serious all the time." She waived her arms out away from her body to emphasize slowing down. "I like having things work out . . . smoothly . . . and if there is any way to prep for that, then I'll find it." They both laughed and Mr. Harleyman shook his head 'yes' so Jahnni thought he understood.

She didn't want him to think she just wanted to get away, but she had things she had to get done. "Well, I really must be going. I should, uh, I need to, do stuff. You know. Important stuff. Really, really, important airline stuff," she stuttered. She wanted to continue her work pace, but her feet felt cemented in place and her mouth kept speaking with no brakes in sight. "So much to do and so little time."

Finally, she paused, drawing a complete blank about what to do and how to do it, and she shook her head slightly to wake up her brain. She moved one foot to try to break the hold the floor had on her.

"Well, I'm sure you'll figure it all out, sweetheart," Mr. Harleyman added.

Eerrrrk. What did he call me? She crisply snapped her ears to attention. *Well, will he still call me that after we walk down to the altar? And what kind of invitations will I need to create? Romantic ones that evoke a feeling of unguarded emotion? Or a modern design of mysterious, blurred-edged color suggesting intrigue about the romance of an FBI agent and the woman who stole his heart? Actually, maybe something official looking to create a sense of secrecy would be good. Wouldn't a floral watermark overlaid onto the invitations be absolutely lustrous! I hope he likes lime, plum, and champagne for the wedding colors. Or maybe . . .*

"Uh, are you okay?" Mr. Harleyman asked with raised eyebrows that accentuated his seductive green eyes. "You seem . . . lost in thought."

"Um . . . Ya. I was, um, collecting my thoughts for the tasks ahead," she responded.

Then she began lecturing herself, *Wedding invitations? Are you nuts? You're putting the cart before the horse Jahnni! You don't even know him . . . yet. You haven't even spent five minutes alone with him much less on a date. Get it together girl. Get it together and get back to work.*

Chapter 7

Check and Recheck

WALKING PAST THE boarding area, she looked around for Samantha. When she didn't see her, she went back to one of the podiums to use the computer and check the SSR's of a few flights and saw that one UM was scheduled to leave on flight 991 to SFO (San Francisco). She looked up his reservation and saw that he was inbound from JFK first. *That must be where Samantha is, picking him up from the JFK flight that just got in,* Jahnni thought.

Jahnni looked up as Samantha walked into the gate area with a UM, papers in hand. She realized that she could disconnect from worrying about the connecting UM on the SFO flight after-all. Samantha had it under control. Since there weren't any other UM's on the current flights, she could doubly disconnect from her mothering nature.

The boarding process would soon begin for SFO991 and she knew that Samantha would walk the UM for this flight to the Flight Attendant. Jahnni always cross-checked that papers were signed off and made sure the times recorded for every transfer of supervision was properly documented. UM records were researched every month for accuracy. If not completed accurately, employees received reprimands and in the worst cases, lost their jobs if following the safety procedures were not adhered to. Jahnni didn't want that to happen, so she followed up every day on that paperwork to be sure the records were accurate. The child's safety always took precedence.

Every day something happened that required notations in the daily log. This day was no exception, so Jahnni added notes to the papers on her clipboard. She'd enter them in her daily report at the end of the day.

Jahnni decided to look around to see if Mr. Tropopoulis had arrived at the gate for his flight. SFO991 was going to board up in about twenty minutes. *Which means that I only have a few minutes to think of a way to either get Mr. Harleyman to give me his phone number or get him to ask for mine. It's in his reservation, but I don't dare use that information for personal intrigue. Think. What can I say to get him to know I'm interested? Maybe something clever will come to mind before too long. In the end . . . Mr. Harleyman will just have to buy new luggage when we get married because I will not be caught dead traveling with that ugly brown tweed plaid bag on my honeymoon. Ugh.*

Chapter 8

UH-OH

SUDDENLY, AS SHE was mid-stride into the boarding area to help with the SFO flight, the terminal alarms started sounding. She grabbed her cell phone and speed dialed OPS to see if they knew what was happening. Passengers started getting up and wandering over to the opening for their gate, trying to get a glimpse of the action. Jahnni spread her arms, and forcefully told people to hold back and wait for direction. Samantha stood by the podium with her UM that was connecting on the SFO flight and held the shoulder of his light jacket. Jahnni blocked the way so no one could leave while she waited for OPS to answer. The degree of the emergency dictated the path of escape.

She paced across the opening, waiting for some communication, but she knew she had to keep everyone contained a few seconds more, at least until she had more information. She just wanted to know which direction to take, or where to send the people who were in the boarding area. Exiting to the tarmac was not the first avenue of escape, but was a viable option if the emergency dictated that route. No one was picking up the phone in OPS. She hung up and dialed the back line. No one picked up. She dialed the station manager's number. No one picked up. She dialed again, and then all the lines were busy. *No time for panic. Think. I need to take care of these passengers.* She set her panic aside and she went into automatic pilot. Her mind began to run options across the chalkboard of her memory. Different training scenarios popped forward as she looked around the boarding area to see how many people there were. She looked down the terminal walkway at the other First Class gates and was just beginning to motion to the agents that stood at their openings, to move the passengers to scenario two. She was going to hold up two fingers and wave her hand in the air for her agents to see the known code and for them to send passengers to exit the checkpoint. The booming recording that began, validated her choice. Overhead, an announcement began. The ear-blasting authoritative male voice made the announcement that blared on again and again.

"PLEASE IMMEDIATELY PROCEED TO THE NEAREST SECURITY CHECKPOINT AND VACATE THE CONCOURSE. PLEASE IMMEDIATELY PROCEED TO THE NEAREST SECURITY CHECKPOINT AND VACATE THE CONCOURSE."

She motioned to all the passengers and told them to grab their belongings and leave the area. She was trying to get them moving so she could run over to the next boarding area for First Class Air to be sure everything was under control there as well, but was stopped by a barrage of voices.

"What is going on?"

"Will we miss our flight?"

"Can you call my husband if I give you the number?"

"I knew it! I told Fred I hate flying and this just proves my point!"

"Should we wait in the airport or outside?"

"Is the airline gonna buy us something to eat?"

The questions were coming faster than she could answer, so Jahnni said quickly, "I know just as much as you right now. Just leave the concourse and listen for direction on the other side of the security checkpoint. Someone will direct you when you get outside security. Just please, hurry. Samantha, you and your UM come with me, we will take him out with us so he doesn't get lost in the crowd. Don't let go of him," she said with a firm tone. Jahnni looked around to motion the passengers towards the checkpoint. She ran her arm like a windmill and pointed her other arm in the direction of the checkpoint. She looked around the now empty boarding area to check for left-behind bags or suspicious looking items. Relief washed over. *Good, nothing . . . one less thing*, she reassured herself.

She heard the boarding doors clicking shut, and when she glanced out the large windows, she saw all the occupied planes being pushed back 50 yards from the jetway for security purposes. Anyone who was enplaning or deplaning on the various flights, and stuck in the jetway when the doors locked, were rushed back on the plane by the Flight Attendants if they were observed not exiting the jetway into the terminal. In an emergency EVAC, passengers cannot be stuck in a freezing or a stifling jetway. Unoccupied planes were already locked down, so they were not a priority to move away from the terminal.

Everyone knew their job, and carried out emergency procedures as they were trained to do. If an inside agent wasn't available to pull back the jetway for the pushback, then the ground agents could do that. It all transpired and was completed within three minutes.

Jahnni waited briefly to see that her agents had cleared their own boarding areas, having received a thumbs-up as they passed or a verbal yes if they were close as they passed her. This meant that all of First Class Air's passengers had evacuated their gates. She nodded to Samantha that they were going to exit as well, the UM between them.

The last of United's passengers were running for the checkpoint and their agents were trotting in a group behind them. What looked like two Port Policemen, were running in the opposite direction towards the end of the concourse, hands on their guns. The employees that were still left split their ranks down the middle and plastered their backs to the wall when they saw their hands on their weapons, but continued towards the checkpoint as soon as the police flew past.

At first, everything seemed so quiet and echoing as the concourse emptied so quickly. All employees everywhere had to evacuate. She hadn't ever realized how quickly the concourse could be evacuated. She briefly wondered about the restaurants and grills and food orders. *Why am I thinking of that at a time like this? That's silly.* Although the next thought was, *No it isn't silly. It could pose a fire hazard!*

Jahnni turned to head toward the check point with Sam and the U.M. to vacate the area when they thought they heard what sounded like a couple gun shots. It startled her and she crouched slightly, not knowing what direction they were coming from. She and Samantha both grabbed the U.M. by the shoulders of his jacket and pulled him down to the ground, leaning to cover him. Jahnni noticed that her fingers felt numb when she held a hand down on the floor for balance. She shivered suddenly, like ice water had been poured down her back. At first, everything went silent for about three seconds, but immediately the roar of people fleeing and screaming from the other side of the security checkpoint landed on Jahnni's ears and she went into survival mode.

She was just about ready to stand up and pull them toward the checkpoint opening, when they heard another 'pop, pop' and what sounded like glass shattering. Her eyes searched the area as far as she could see without moving. She was frozen in place, her heart pounding through her chest. It felt as if it would shatter her rib cage like ice breaking on a frozen lake. They slowly stood and she motioned them back the few steps into the boarding area to take cover until they knew it was safe to proceed out in the open to the check point again. She knew that all the doors to the jetways were automatically secured by a computer program. This protected the planes at the end of the jetways from being hi-jacked. So, they couldn't go through those doors. She looked at Samantha and they locked eyes. They both knew that they were among the last ones who needed to evacuate. They could hear radios squawking, and shouting getting closer. They crouched behind a podium but realized they might be seen if someone came into the boarding area they were in. Jahnni scanned the area and desperately searched for an escape.

She realized her own radio was on but people talked over each other and their voices were muddled as they were interrupted. She tried to cut in and state her position, but she was drowned out by other talkers on the radio. She just couldn't make it out. What were they saying? She looked at Samantha's dilated eyes and could only assume she was also filled with the worst fear as well. Jahnni reached over and touched the UM's arm, then tried to pat it for comfort but her hands felt numb to her touch and hoped she wasn't patting too hard.

Jahnni saw the larger podium and fell to both knees and crawled to hide behind it, motioning Sam and the UM to follow her. She turned her radio down because she didn't want anyone else to hear it. Then she began racing through options in her head. She briefly closed her eyes and tried to will their bodies invisible while she came up with a plan.

Jahnni heard noise like shuffling feet, getting closer. She peeked carefully around the corner. Slowly, two people in white hooded masks attached to white clothing resembling overalls, made their way into the boarding area. They looked like they were preparing to decontaminate something. One was crouched down and the other one was crawling on the ground towards the rows of chairs. They had what looked like machine guns slung around on their backs as they clamored toward the back of the boarding gate.

Although there was a tremendous amount of noise collecting on the other side of the checkpoint she could hear at least one helicopter coming in to land, and possibly one still in the air further away. By now, the security checkpoint gates were locked down, so she knew she had to think of another way to get out of there. Jahnni kept peeking around, trying to understand what was happening. She tried to control her breathing to calm her racing heart and hoped it would settle the whooshing sound in her ears that every beat of her heart created. Jahnni slowly turned to Sam and the UM and placed a finger on her lips, as they locked eyes. It sounded like one of the gunmen jiggled the door handle that led to the jetway from the other boarding podium. She heard shuffling, like they were crawling on their bellies, or scooting, and they were getting closer. Jahnni knew that in seconds they could be face to face. She felt ice fill her veins and had to make a conscious effort to stop her body from jumping up and running. Her joints felt like rubber, and a cold sweat was now accumulating on her back. *Are they one of us or are they part of a terrorist situation?*

The gunmen stopped moving about a row of chairs away. Then she heard them just around the corner of the podium. Jahnni held her breath, and closed her eyes briefly. When she realized she was holding her breath much too long, she let it out slowly then took in a big, deep intake of air slowly through her mouth, so more air could quietly fill her lungs. In just about four to five more feet, and one more corner, they would be inches away from each other.

She looked down and saw her radio had fallen off her waistband sometime during the commotion. She motioned for Sam and the UM to slowly crawl around to the back of the tall cabinet. They backed around the corner and she followed them, crawling so quietly, she was afraid they were moving too slowly. They knelt on their knees, frozen like statues. No words were needed between them. The two people whom she could only assume were the bad guys, began fumbling with Jahnni's radio she had dropped. She heard the volume being turned up and down and channels clicking. If any sound came out of a channel, it was only static.

Her ears perked up when they whispered a quick interchange. She heard them moving and held her breath as she waited for them to come around to the back of the tall cabinet. But the rustling of their clothes sounded like it was moving away from them. Still, she didn't move. When they sounded further away, she slowly moved her head to barely glimpse where they were. A shock of white fabric caught her eye and then another patch of white entered her line of sight. The two gunmen were crouched at the opening of the gate area. Jahnni remained still, afraid that any more movement would garner their attention. She watched as they scanned up and down the concourse.

In a sudden flurry of movement, they ran across the concourse aisle-way to the other side. Jahnni heard a verbal warning for the people in white to stop. It came from further away in the concourse and the order was obviously not heeded. Whoever shouted to them sounded far away, but loud running and stomping was getting closer. The guys in white disappeared through the bypass door; the one she used earlier to bring the new-hire to the gates. When their pursuers got closer, she saw what looked like the same two Port Policemen who had run up the concourse when this all started. Something didn't look right, didn't feel right. She wanted to wave them over for help but a nagging fear kept her silent. She slowly moved her head to look at Samantha and with the smallest of perceptible movement, motioned her head no.

She watched who she assumed might be two Port Police officers talk on a radio of some type. They were describing the situation, telling who she assumed was dispatch, which door the gunmen accessed. Their radios didn't look like the ones all the airline employees used, but she assumed, again, they possibly had a newer model. But as before, something was off. For some reason, they didn't access the doors themselves and this made Jahnni leery and confused. *All Port officers have badge access to bypass doors,* she reminded herself. *Why did the guys in white have access but these two policemen-looking people didn't?*

Whoever was on the other side of the radio was yelling orders at them. "You should have grabbed them. Shoot them if you must. Don't let them get away!"

Jahnni felt her mouth go dry. Even her eyes felt dry. Now, after hearing they were told 'to shoot them if you must,' she wondered why they would be given an order like that. That didn't sound like something the Port Police would be told to do.

She heard the order for them to go back down to the end of the concourse again "to keep watch," although she had no idea what they were looking for. Frozen in place, she watched them start trotting briskly back, and they were soon out of sight.

Should I have flagged them down and let them know we are stuck in here? But why couldn't they access the bypass door? Maybe they aren't Port Police. Who are they then? This made Jahnni reluctant to come out of hiding. *How long can we stay here?* she asked herself.

So much confusion. *If we run out will WE be mistaken for the gunmen?* she wondered to herself. *Should we stay here and wait it out? Or should we try to access a bypass door to get out of the concourse?* She had to think. Samantha whispered something.

"What?" Jahnni whispered back with a capitalized question mark in her voice. "You're hungry?" *What a silly thing to be concerned about at a time like this,* she thought to herself.

"No. The masked guys. They're from Hungary," Samantha corrected, whispering a little louder.

"The masked guys, those masked guys are hungry? This is no time to worry about their diet schedule!" Jahnni snapped, although she was trying to hold back her pessimistic feelings about such nonsensical information.

"No! I said . . ." Samantha whispered as loud as she could, "They. Are. From. Hungary." Then she said, "My grandmother and grandfather are from Hungary. It is the only language spoken in their home."

"And you understood them? What were they whispering about?"

"I think they said something about keeping them from getting to the fountain's pipes first," Samantha interpreted using air quotes when she said the words, 'they,' and 'them.'

"Why in the hell, oops, sorry kid, what's your name again?" Jahnni whispered.

"Crutch."

"I'm Jahnni, Crutch, nice to meet you," Jahnni said then added, "I'm sorry we are in this situation. Don't worry, honey. We'll take care of you."

"Anyway," Jahnni continued as she turned back to Samantha, "Who in the heck would they be preventing from going to the fountain? There is nothing but water down there. And fish. Someone is after something, obviously. But at this point, I don't care what it is. We just need to get out of here and get Crutch to safety."

"I don't know if you noticed Jahn, but the first guy in those odd white suits just used a badge and coded them through the security door."

Jahnni mumbled, "Yes. I noticed. There are cameras all over the property. And the Port can check to see whose badge is scanned in and out of the bypass doors. Oh wait, maybe someone else besides the Port Police are monitoring things. Man, I don't know! For now, be still and let's stay hidden for a bit more while we figure out what to do. I don't want a trigger-happy person shooting us."

Jahnni lowered her whisper to finish, "Do you think the masked guys in white are like some sort of SWAT? Or are they the bad guys? Maybe we could just walk slowly to the check point with our hands up? Except the security screens at both checkpoints are probably down and locked now. Even the concourse connector to the D & E gates is closed. I can't see around the corner, but I'm sure I heard the rolling chained dividers being lowered soon after the concourse emptied. So, we can't even get out that direction anymore either."

Samantha appeared just as confused. "I don't know. Maybe the masked guys are looking for the people responsible for a security breach. But that wouldn't make sense for them to be the ones hiding and being shot at while the guys in uniforms chase them. Would it? Hey Jahn, what about the door between the restrooms? Maybe we can get over there and snake our way down to the bagwell. Then, get to the last door in the bagwell that will spit us out by the baggage service carousels. We'll be in the common area and by the doors that lead to the street!"

Jahnni was silent then said, "I'm not sure yet. That door is too far away. We'd be out in the open too long and what if the doors are locked down? We saw what happened to the guys in white when they ran out there. But at least we saw that particular door can be badged through. That one is probably our best option with a direct exit out of the concourse. Once we go through the door we'll be in the stairwell, but only a few steps to the next door that leads us into the public area. We have to do something to get out of here, as opposed to simply waiting it out though."

All she was concerned about was getting Sam and Crutch to safety and not get shot in the process. Things seemed to have fallen silent, at least in this part of the airport. She tried to use her cell phone one more time, but service was still disrupted.

She assumed that the uniformed gunmen had made their way back down the concourse where they initially ran to in the beginning. She decided to crawl out and check out their options. She crawled past Sam and Crutch and slithered around the large free-standing cabinet they were hiding behind, motioning to Samantha and Crutch to stay where they were, and she crouched behind the podium. Slowly, she reached above her head for the phone that was at the center point of the podium. Jahnni hoped she could call someone from the podium phone, if it still worked. She pulled the handset down and shakily started dialing. Nothing. *Maybe I forgot to wait for the dial tone.* She listened and was ready to dial again. Nothing. No dial tone. Jahnni decided to crawl back to Samantha and Crutch behind the cabinet. She began crawling slowly to come around the other side, arriving behind Samantha and Crutch once again.

She looked at them, and saw they had turned and were staring at her with their mouths open. Crutch had a wide-eyed look frozen on his face as he stared behind Jahnni. Time seemed to stand still. No one spoke. She felt the hairs on her head tingle when she searched their faces. Crutch was still wide-eyed but silent. Then she clearly heard it. She heard her name being whispered by her shoulder. It was clearly a voice of authority. It made a shiver run up her spine. She knew she had to face whatever, whoever it was and get it over with. Slowly, she turned.

"Mr. Harleyman? What are you doing here? Where have you been all this time?" Jahnni stammered out in a most flabbergasted, breathy voice.

"When the announcements started, I saw him going the wrong direction and by the time I worked my way back through the crowd, I couldn't find him. Then when I did, he was back there in that alcove and it was too late to exit the concourse through the checkpoint. I decided to wait with him until things calmed down. We waited back there," he said as he pointed over his head to the long corridor that led to another jetway. "I couldn't just leave. And there were too many lives at risk to just start waving a gun at no one in particular when we heard the commotion. Plus, I had this guy to worry about, so this was the next best idea when they closed off the gates at the checkpoint before we could get there. I thought I could just call someone but my phone is inoperable," he added.

Jahnni opened her mouth to say something, but he interrupted to finish explaining.

"You all showed up right after we made the decision that we couldn't make it out in time, and when I saw the others . . . you know the ones in white, I watched the situation. I was ready, if things went south. You're safe, at least for now."

"Okay . . . this is nice. Who is 'him'?" Jahnni said in a whisper that got louder and firmer as she ended her sentence.

"Ah, hi Janie. Nice to see you. Beau here is very smart boy.

He will know what to do." And without a shiny hair out of place, Brown Plaid Man was poking his head out from around the corner of the corridor that led to the locked-down jetway door.

"So, Jahnni, what do you think? Can we go through that security door, across the way there?" Mr. Harleyman whispered as he pointed to the door Jahnni and Samantha saw the masked gunmen had gone through.

After taking a little bit to decide whether to trust him, Jahnni realized she didn't have much choice. *I mean after all; trust is a very important issue in a relationship. Or Marriage.*

She shook her head, hoping it would stop the stuck recorder playing in her mind then explained, "Well, first, we thought if we could make it about fifty feet down the wall to a bypass door by the restrooms, we could wind our way down to the bagwell then eventually exit that area into the passenger pick-up and baggage carousel area.

"Okay, that sounds viable," Mr. Harleyman agreed.

"Of course, because it's so far away, and I don't know if the bypass doors are locked down, I would rather go through that door you pointed at right over there to get on the other side of security. I now know that access door works. It also has a stairwell that leads down to the bagwell, you know, the entire basement floor where every airline here handles all the baggage behind the scenes. I don't want to go down there, so we'll then access the bypass door just a few feet on the other side of that door, to enter the common area," Jahnni explained. "Basically, the stairwell is a secure area between two bypass doors.

Mr. Harleyman listened with an intent look on his face as he glanced from Jahnni to the other door. When Jahnni was finished talking he added, "All I want to do is get us to safety. If that door leads immediately to another door, then let's do it."

"Fine by me. It's just a couple swipes of my badge and safety is on the other side. To be honest, I'm a little confused about who the good guys are and who the bad guys are. The gunmen in the white hazmat-looking suits just went through that bypass door with a badge, but the two guys who kinda look like Port of Portland Police officers don't even have a badge," Jahnni added.

"Is that so? Considering our group here, getting to safety is number one. I'm not concerned with who they are or where they went. I have one intention and that's to get us on the other side of this locked down concourse. We don't have any other choices now but that one," as he pointed to the door across the concourse walkway. "Like I mentioned already, I did try to make a call to my office with my cell phone, but the signals are blocked. They could be using an SK-4 but that would only block a radius of 60-70 feet. The airport is pretty large so they could possibly be using a TRJ-89. That is pretty strong and can keep signals blocked for about five miles."

"Who would block the signals like that?" Jahnni asked.

Mr. Harleyman answered, "Hopefully, people from my agency in the Portland Division would have arrived quickly once the call went out. It's a basic security sweep to block terrorists from communicating or using their cell phones as a detonation device. It doesn't matter who set up the block at this point. Blocked is blocked."

Jahnni was enraptured by every word he spoke. She watched his lips move as he contemplated the situation, *probably analyzing details only he could understand.*

"Back to getting out of here. It shouldn't be that hard. Let's do it," he whispered in a low gravelly voice that made Jahnni want to be stuck here with him forever.

Sizing up her options, she decided to do what she shouldn't ever do . . . escort an AI, armed Individual, or even passengers through a bypass door. It was a major security breach and she could lose her job. *I suppose Mr. Harleyman is right. I should trust him. And of course, hope the consequences aren't too severe when this is over. I mean, what could possibly go wrong just going through one or two bypass doors to get out during an emergency?*

Chapter 9

How Hard Can It Be?
Just Open the Door

THE REST OF them crawled slowly and quietly from behind the podium. They huddled and waited. Mr. Harleyman motioned for everyone to wait there as he crawled towards the gate opening. Not being one to be told to wait, Jahnni crawled right behind him. She carefully peeked around the corner after he did. She could see a couple guys in uniforms at the complete end of the concourse. They appeared to be waiting for something, or someone, and it appeared like they were looking out the large plate glass windows that overlooked the runways. Then they would walk briskly over to the windows that gave them a glimpse at the Mezzanine. Back and forth they paced, like they knew what they were looking for. They were about twenty-four gate areas away, twelve if you figured that the gates were also numbered two at a time across from each other. The concourse was lined on both sides with food establishments and specialty shops, sometimes breaking up the flow of the gates. Jahnni thought that everything looked like a small abandoned city.

She looked up the other way to see what Mr. Harleyman saw. She saw no one, only the cavernous space where travelers first entered the concourse and gathered their belongings after clearing the TSA checkpoint. The FIDS still glowed with flight information as if life at PDX was still flowing with a measured cadence. Looking up, she froze; the security cameras. She was just about ready to wave at the one almost facing their direction when she remembered the gunmen in white had access to the security door.

"Could someone have taken over security access or the entire airport? Could the Port Police have been taken hostage themselves? I mean, something doesn't seem right if these guys in white have badging access and the police-looking guys don't," she noted to Mr. Harleyman. She just couldn't be sure who was in charge. The only reason it concerned her was the mystery of who to trust and who could be monitoring things. They crawled back to the group who remained gathered behind the large podium.

"Okay, I know we are probably going to be seen by the Port Police looking guys," Jahnni whispered. "But, here is the best way I can think of. We'll go through that bypass door across from us. Then the bypass door into the common area is right there as well, on the other side of that door. We'll be done with this in a few minutes. If we are seen, then we won't have time to bring each other over one at a time. Not even two at a time."

"Right, Jahnni, so you'll lead and access the door. I'll follow at the end of the line," Mr. Harleyman instructed as he pointed and gently guided everyone into their positions. "I think Crutch should be right behind you and then Samantha will be third. Pops will be right behind Samantha. Stay tight."

Jahnni looked right at Crutch and asked, "Are you scared?"

"Are you serious? I'm having the time of my life!" Crutch whispered a squeal of delight that revealed a crackling squeak in his voice as he looked up from playing his hand-held game.

"Okay then. Now that I don't feel brave anymore, let's proceed," Jahnni said.

"Are you ready, Mr. Harleyman?" Jahnni asked, noting that everyone was in line. He nodded yes.

"Don't worry. You have the access and I have your back," he promised as he held her gaze a little longer and smiled. There was something about the confidence in his voice and the way he looked at her that made Jahnni know she could trust him.

"On the count of three, know where you belong, and follow me as fast as you can. Mr. Tropopoulis, are you ready?" Jahnni asked while motioning to him. He gave her a quick nod yes. She looked at each person in the group. "Okay . . . 1 . . . 2 . . . 3 . . . GO!"

They didn't look for cameras. They didn't look again to see if anyone was crouching nearby. They only ran—ran as fast as they could. Everyone forgot to slow down before they got to the other side, and slammed into the back of Jahnni as she reached to swipe her badge and put in her code. The numbers went in wrong and she had to start over. She hit 'cancel' and swiped her badge again and started putting her code in. She heard voices on the other side of the door. She stopped and looked at the others. They heard them too. Noise from her left made her whip her head around and she saw what looked like uniformed police running towards them from the bottom of the concourse. Before she could finish adding her code, the 'uniforms' shouted for them to stop. Suddenly the security door swung open apparently of its own volition before she even finished keying in. She scooted in first, pulling Crutch in with her. Everyone else filed through after her. Mr. Harleyman pushed Mr. Tropopoulis in then secured the door shut after he followed. As they tried to regroup and continue their journey, Jahnni looked up to see the two people dressed in white, wearing hooded masks, pointing their machine guns, or whatever kind of gun they held, one on Samantha and one on Mr. Tropopoulis. Then the banging on the other side of the door began.

It sounded like someone was talking into a radio. "They went through this door." Then a voice answered back, "Clear the way. I have you on camera. I can access you through remotely." Jahnni was confused. After a brief pause, she realized that she could just key her badge in the other door in front of them. In the sudden confusion, it took her a few seconds to realize that these people in white suits stood between them and the last door they needed to go through. Direct access to the other side of security was right there. A couple more feet. She looked at the door, looked at the people with the guns, then glanced at Mr. Harleyman. Escape into the common area was a mere arm's length away.

Jahnni looked again at Mr. Harleyman, wondering why he didn't pull his gun out and start ordering these people around. He nodded almost imperceptibly, lifting his chin towards the people with guns as if he wanted her to listen to them. Then the tall, more muscular gunman quickly grabbed Jahnni by the armpit and started pulling her up the stairs, motioning for everyone to follow. The smaller gunman lifted his gun at the same time and pointed for Mr. Tropopoulis to follow them up the stairs, waving the weapon like it was a pointer stick. He looked at Mr. Harleyman and pointed the way with his weapon, and Jahnni watched him nod in agreement and begin climbing the stairs behind Mr. Tropopoulis. She turned back to watch where she was going but after rounding the third curve on the stairwell, Jahnni slipped and fell up the stairs. The man grabbed her again and yanked her up, trying to hurry as they continued climbing.

Below, the 'uniforms' had made it through the door. They sounded like cattle being rustled into a bull pen, as they started clamoring up the stairs after Jahnni and her little posse. The gunman shoved Jahnni forward to motion for her to keep going up. Then he pulled something out of his jacket. The rest of them kept running up the stairs behind Jahnni. The smaller gunman motioned for Mr. Harleyman and Mr. Tropopoulis to follow the rest of them on their ascent, then scurried past them. Mr. Harleyman had hold of Mr. Tropopoulis's arm to keep him steady as he tried to keep up. The first gunman took the item he had pulled out of his jacket, pulled on it with his teeth and threw it down the stairwell.

"Oh! No!" Samantha said too loudly. "A grenade!" Everyone hit the floor, cowering under their arms, and covering their heads.

Some were on a landing between floors. Some were crumpled on the stairs. The pop sounded, but not as loud as Jahnni had imagined it would sound.

"What is that smell?" Jahnni demanded as smoke started filling the stairwell from below. "I can't breathe! I can't see!"

"Just get up! Now!" her captor screamed when he turned back to pull her forward. "Keep moving!"

So, she complied. "But really!" she complained as she gasped for breath. "I can't breathe! I can't go any further." She collapsed on the stairs, coughing into her sweater as she held her arm to her face. Everyone fell down on the landing by the door. They were all coughing as the cloudy stench hovered in the air. The 'uniforms' were slowly gaining on them but were slowed down by their own coughing and gasping for fresh air.

Jahnni didn't understand why, but felt that these white gunmen were trying to slow down the uniformed cops for them. The smaller gunman, who helped push them forward up the stairs before climbing over them to get ahead, had already accessed the security door for them and started to pull on their arms, and push them through it. Then the two gunmen in white continued bounding up the stairs to the roof, leaving Jahnni and her crew to fend for themselves on the other side of the security door.

Jahnni's group were coughing and wiping their eyes. The

noise of the 'uniforms' getting closer, confirmed them doing the same. Mr. Harleyman was the last one through the door after Mr. Tropopoulis. The commotion was heady with the door alarm now dinging and she wondered how close they were as she pushed the door to shut it behind them. But just as Jahnni was pushing the door shut, a hand reached out through the last sliver of a crack, and grabbed onto her arm. He tried to pull her back through the door. He wedged his foot between the door and the door jamb to keep it from closing, holding firm onto her arm. His grip was heavy and binding and she screamed out while she twisted and pulled to get away. She felt the strain in her muscles because she was pushing on the door, and pulling on her arm, but she continued to hold the door while she braced her own foot against it. She didn't look behind her, but felt Mr. Harleyman's weight against her, beside her, holding the door from opening further, and pulling on the fingers that gripped her arm.

Jahnni lowered her head and bit into the hand that held onto her arm, hoping he would release his grip. He did, screaming out in pain just as Mr. Harleyman kicked at the man's knee causing his foot to slide out of the way of the door and they both pushed it shut. On the other side of the door, moaning and yelling and barking orders seemed to add to the confusion. But the five of them had made it through. Jahnni looked around at them watching as they sucked the fresher air into their heaving chests, wiping strange tears off their cheeks.

With red eyes, Samantha glanced over, then grabbed Crutch and hugged him tight, wiping his face with her sleeve.

She brought his chin up so she could look into his eyes. "It's okay, sweetie. We aren't going to give up. We will keep you safe!"

"I know. I know you will. I'll be okay," Crutch stammered. Then after a pause, "Wow, that was one heck of a trip!"

Chapter 10

Let's Play Hide and Seek

"I DON'T THINK I have ever been here," Jahnni said, still out of breath as she turned circles to get her bearings. She went into the nearest room and noticed its configuration. "Look in this room. I have an idea. Everyone . . . hide in this room. I can see an alcove around the corner in here. I don't think they will see us until they are right up on it. I'll be right back. There's another door at the end of the hallway . . . but, Sam . . . whatever you do, don't let go of Crutch."

"We just need to find our way to the other side of security, don't we?" Samantha said, pleading with her eyes as she continued looking around the room and over Jahnni's shoulder.

"I realize that, but we have to lose these guys that are chasing us first. Then we can get back down to that floor and walk out to the open area. I don't want to get shot before we reach safety to explain who we are . . . Or who we aren't. And they are probably going to get electronically scanned through this door any minute, so hurry . . . I don't know where that door at the end of the hall even leads to, so I'm thinking, we should go back the way we came up and then go back to our original plan to get to the other side of the secured area. We could be in worse shape trying to scan through up here. We just need to go back down the stairwell. Hurry and get to the alcove there on the right!" Jahnni whispered loudly, pulling on Sam and Crutch, and motioning for Mr. Tropopoulis and Mr. Harleyman to go around the corner and into the alcove.

Crutch put his hand on Mr. Harleyman's arm and asked, "Why don't you just wait for them to come through the door, then hold them with your gun and get us to safety that way?"

"There's many reasons," Mr. Harleyman said as he looked around the room before continuing. "The main reason is you. I'm not here right now to catch these guys. I'm here to help get everyone to safety. Bullets flying will not accomplish that. Right now, I don't care who they are. I'm not risking your lives." Mr. Harleyman smiled, patting him on the shoulder and held out his arm to guide him to the alcove. Crutch nodded okay.

There were so many areas that were off limits to the public. They couldn't just go screaming through a security door when she didn't know who to trust. In fact, Jahnni wasn't sure who was in the control rooms at the Security or Port Police offices. On one hand, she had accessed a bypass door and brought others through it during what she assumed was an Imminent Threat. With the old codes, it would be considered a code red. Part of her feared that a move like that placed her in a position of being an assumed terrorist, or may implicate her in some way. Possibly even put her in a 'shoot first, ask questions later' predicament. But another part of her was twisted with doubt. *They expect us to use our judgment in precarious situations . . . and I just need to get everyone to safety, especially Crutch. So, wouldn't there be leniency once they reviewed the circumstances . . . if we live to tell our story?*

Mr. Harleyman's face was stoic. His eyes moved like he was accessing different compartments of his brain. She hoped that between the two of them, they could keep everyone safe.

The group gathered behind Mr. Harleyman who kept putting his arm behind him as if it encircled them into an invisible shield. They craned their necks, listening intently. Jahnni hesitated a moment, looked around, then hurried away.

She ran down the long hall as she peeled off her sweater. She threw it right up next to the other access door, partly touching the door and partly skewed against the door jamb. She doubled back to hide with the others in the room with the alcove. She heard the stairwell door's lock click and feared that the two police-looking gunmen were being remotely keyed in already. Panic set in when she realized she wouldn't make it to the room where Mr. Harleyman and the others waited. She reversed direction again to head back and swung herself around the large pillar at the end of the hallway, near the small open area where she had thrown her sweater against the other bypass door. She stood frozen, flattening herself against the wall, knowing they could see her if they turned at just the correct angle once they arrived in the small open area. She began to breath as slowly as she could, silently trying to calm the nerves she knew could cause her knees to buckle in fear.

Her mind was roiling like a wave, trying to understand what was happening. Frankly, it bothered her that they never identified themselves as Port Police. In fact, they never had identified themselves as anyone who should be waving a weapon. They were either running, yelling, and from the sounds of it, shooting things at the end of the concourse. Her intuition said not to trust them.

She heard the stairwell security door fully open and the 'uniforms,' neither of whom Jahnni had recognized before, lumbered down the hall, still clearing their throats. She listened for a scuffle or argument, had they found the others, but she heard nothing but their rustling clothes, heavy breathing, and foot falls moving through the area. They began trotting down the rest of the hallway towards where Jahnni was partially hidden behind the large pillar.

"So, what do we have here?" one of the 'uniforms' said to the other. He let out a cough, cleared his throat, then began to reach down.

He picked up Jahnni's sweater, tossed it to the other 'uniform' and called in on the radio.

"We need to be scanned through #3929," the big one spoke. Then what felt like quite an undue amount of time to wait for it to take place, she saw in the corner of her eye, the light turn green and they both grabbed for the handle to pull it towards them. They clamored through the door and it smoothly swung closed and clicked as it locked behind them.

Oh, my God. My heart is going to pump out of my chest. Just breathe. Just breathe, Jahnni told herself. The hall was empty. Jahnni waited. She made sure she didn't hear anyone lingering on the floor or listening from the other side of that door. When she felt it was safe, she hurried back to the conference room where the others waited. Mr. Harleyman met her at the conference room door first, weapon in hand.

He glanced back and forth then motioned for the others to hurry. He motioned for them to follow Jahnni as she accessed the stairwell bypass door and held it while they all hurried back through. Jahnni quickly pulled the door shut, cutting off the immediate threat of the door dinging from being held open too long. They beat the five second timer. She leaned against it and looked at the group, smiling that they got away . . . until she heard voices in the hallway they had just escaped.

"Sir," the voice said, "We were already here."

"I know you already went through it. I scanned you through, idiot! That's why I sent you back! Pay attention! I'll scan you through #3927 When I checked the camera, I saw the door closing. I am having trouble seeing who last keyed the door because my security computer keeps freezing up. Wait . . . here it is, Jahnni Dawson. We'll call it a security breach when the time comes. I want them in my office."

Jahnni and the rest of the group began rushing down the stairwell, letting their hands slide over the handrail as they ran. *One more door. One more door,* she told herself as they followed her back down the stinky stairwell.

Jahnni and Samantha were leading the way back down the

stairwell with Crutch between them. She reached out and put her ear to the security door that led to the main floor of the airport. "This door leads to the common area of the airport. That door there," she said as she pointed behind them, "leads to the boarding gates that we first escaped from."

She quickly scanned her badge and began the process to access the door. Nothing happened. She hit cancel and started over. Nothing happened. Wide-eyed, she looked at Samantha. Sam pushed forward and tried to scan through using her badge. Nothing. Not a green light nor a red light. It was like the door was dead. Jahnni paced in place, trying to decide what to do. Above them, they heard voices and the footfalls of the 'uniforms' began their descent.

"You said there's a way through the bagwell from here, right? Take us there. Now. Hurry!" Mr. Harleyman said as he pushed them one by one towards the stairwell that continued down.

She kept looking back to see if Crutch and Mr. Tropopoulis were keeping up. She saw Mr. Harleyman following at the back . . . appearing a little too calm, but noticed that he continued to look behind, and up the staircase between the floors. *One more stairwell landing and we will be on the bag-well floor in the basement,* she thought, as she tried to envision any other routes.

Jahnni froze as they made it to the door that leads into the bagwell. Her hands shook as she tried to untangle her badges to try the bypass door. *Will it even work this time?* she asked herself, noting that minutes ago, the last door was dead to her.

The familiar sounds of pursuing footsteps, made all of them look back and forth at each other.

"Here," Mr. Harleyman said as he pointed, and they all jumped to follow his instructions.

Jahnni hurriedly scanned the door with her badge while the others jumped into action. *Yes!* She screamed in her head. Her badge worked this time. Then she pulled the door wide open, hoping it would ding to mislead their pursuers into following through the door. She then joined the others as they all had leapt into the two dumpsters used for recycling paper. Mr. Harleyman had rolled Mr. Tropopoulis in then smoothly pulled himself over the edge of the container, reaching his hand out for Jahnni to join them. Just as Jahnni's foot cleared the air, and the lid was lowered at the same time by Mr. Harleyman, the uniforms came around the last bend on the stairwell and burst into the small area that held the large commercial recycling containers. They caught the door before it closed all the way and they clamored through and took off at a dead run down the little roadway that the tugs drove on to deliver bags.

Jahnni and her group leapt out of the containers and quickly started picking pieces of shredded paper out of each other's hair and clothes. After Jahnni opened the secured door again, she peeked around the corner to see that no one was near. They went through the door into the bagwell together, but not until the door alarm began its security dinging once more. Realizing that their pursuers might very soon figure out that they had been tricked again and may have heard the door, Jahnni decided on another escape.

Sure enough, the far away footsteps started getting closer. Louder and louder they pounded until they came around the last corner. Their shoes squeaked to a stop.

"We've lost them. I don't think they came this way," reported the 'uniform' who seemed in charge of the radio.

"This is the only way they could have gone. Keep looking," ordered the voice on the radio.

"Did the cameras pick something up?" the winded 'uniform' said.

"They are there somewhere, I'm telling you. I am looking at the camera-feed replay that faces that door. Hold on . . . Not only are we looking for an airline employee named Jahnni, Arnie is in the group. Ha ha! I repeat. Arnie is with Jahnni. Keep looking. Bring them all to me!" the voice ordered.

"Boss says we are looking for a guy named Johnny now and this Arnie he's been searching for all day. We need to find these guys!" ordered one of the uniformed guys to the other.

"Did you see the photos he said he was going to show us, of this Arnie?" the other 'uniform' asked.

"No. I think he forgot when he set off the plan too soon. We'll worry about that later. Let's keep looking."

Jahnni had been holding her breath, while trying to listen to their conversation. She heard the footsteps of the 'uniforms' as if they scurried, looking around every crevice and nook. Their voices faded as she continued her last-second journey with Sam, Crutch, Mr. Tropopoulis, and Mr. Harleyman until the only sound she could hear was the whirring of bag belts and clanging of metal rollers as their bodies hit a curve in their path. Once on a moving, flat, rubber conveyor belt, she rested momentarily and listened to the pulse in her ears that echoed her heartbeat.

Chapter 11

I'm Not Having Fun Anymore

THE BAG BELTS were still running in some areas and making all sorts of racket. It was a virtual freeway of belts and rollered conveyors. Off to the west end of the first transfer belt, one that all the airlines use to send the bags transferring to other airlines, were five clumps coming around the bend. They were laying down and riding the night train into the darkness and out again before being dumped onto the main loading belt for American Airlines. The bag carts were parked in rows and half loaded, obviously abandoned as the emergency went into effect. All the employees had evacuated the area after they had secured the aircraft and the nearby wide access doors that led out to the planes. The bags were going around and around the circular belt with no one to sort them into their respective carts for loading.

"Ouch!"

"Weeee."

"Ahh."

"Umph."

"Mffff."

All five bodies slid out the bag shoot and tumbled onto the final carousel belt for sorting, had they been bags destined for an American Airlines flight. Jahnni was the last one, watching the others arrive ahead of her. She thought they all looked like overstuffed luggage. Mr. Tropopoulis went feet first and appeared to slip down the shoot onto the belt ending in a standing position, before hurriedly sitting down on the circulating belt. Samantha and Crutch slid down like they were on a playground slide . . . backwards and landing in heap. But Mr. Harleyman . . . Jahnni was sure that she saw him tuck and roll, then land onto the transfer belt in a squatting position. *Impressive,* she thought.

They sat frozen on the moving rubber landing, like monkey statues on a conveyor belt, churning around in a circular motion. Their eyes darted everywhere as they looked around. Jahnni listened intently, checking to hear if they were still being pursued. But there was silence; except for the churning of the motors and belts which usually carried bags through their galactic-appearing routes. After they jumped off the circulating belt, they ran to the nearby carts and hopped into them. They rested to let their breathing calm down while they tried to figure out their next move.

Mr. Harleyman lifted his shirt and tucked his weapon back in the black leather holster. He scanned the area then whispered to Crutch, "Okay, Geronimo. Enough fun already?

Why did your parents name you Crutch anyway? That is one weird name, if you don't mind me saying."

"It's . . . my nickname. Everyone calls me that at home. It's a complicated story. Maybe later, I'll tell you the story when we have more time," Crutch whispered back without looking up. He was still playing a hand-held game that he'd had since Samantha picked him up from his inbound flight.

"Hmmm. Okay, buddy. I expect to hear the full version very soon," Mr. Harleyman said with a smile, then looked over Crutch's shoulder. "By the way, you have to hit jump two times before you try to jump over the volcanic magma that's trying to destroy that bridge. If you only click once, you will miss the hanging rope that swings you to the cliff's edge where you can find the hidden stairs when you hit jump two times again."

"How did . . . you've played this before?" Crutch asked, looking up at Mr. Harleyman before shifting his eyes at Jahnni. She smiled and shrugged her shoulders.

"Men are just taller boys," she said, speaking in a low tone as she looked out of the cart she was in, to address them in the next cart.

Mr. Tropopoulis was sitting next to Jahnni. They were both leaning against some medium size animal crates. She let her head fall back against the crates as she looked up, trying to think. She held back tears, refusing to give up. *How difficult can it be to just get to a door? If I knew where the 'uniforms' were, we could simply run to the door at the other end of the bagwell, badge through, and be done with this nonsense.*

She turned her eyes to see that Samantha seemed distract-

93

ed; *probably mooning over the fact that her big date wasn't going to happen tonight,* Jahnni thought. Crutch kept playing his little electronic game, with the sound turned off. She was glad he had it to keep him occupied. Mr. Tropopoulis sat smiling as he looked around at the entire baggage area, his eyes following the walls and vents and pipes. He looked like he was in his own world.

Jahnni glanced over at Mr. Harleyman and wondered what he was thinking. He sat still and somber, tapping his index finger against his leg while looking around the bagwell. Jahnni could only assume his mind was churning out ideas.

She studied his chiseled features and once again, noticed his lips, wondering . . . well, just wondering. She closed her eyes, only briefly of course. Her mind wandered as she imagined his touch. She thought about the moment he walked up to the ticket counter, the beach fantasy playing in slow motion over and over in her mind. Then he was smiling at her as sand kicked up behind him with each running step. He ran to her with his hands outstretched to catch her when she flung herself into his arms. The soft sand of the beach was warm on her bare feet as she threw herself into an embrace. He swung her around in the air, trickles of water splashing with each step. She felt him softly nudging her shoulder and sliding what felt like his wet sensuous lips on her neck, his warm breath blowing softly, no panting, as he ran his face up to her ear and then across her cheek, and . . . *What am I thinking? This isn't the time to day dream, girl! We are in trouble here. Focus!*

Jahnni immediately turned to look behind her where she

and Mr. Tropopoulis were sitting. Her mouth fell agape when she saw the sight that had caused her so much imaginary happiness. Poodles. Two, furry, fluffy, panting, poodles; crated and marked for shipment. One huddled close to the edge of the cage still trying to give her more puppy kisses; its tongue licking the air between the metal bars of the crate. She slowly reached over and patted the little guys through the bars with her fingers, making kissing noises to them so they'd stay calm . . . And to give herself time to let her heartbeat get back to normal.

Crutch looked up and smiled, shook his head and then went back to his game. Mr. Harleyman got up and moved the kennels further to the back of the cart.

"It's okay, Pops. You're kinda silent over here. We'll figure this out and get out of here," Mr. Harleyman said, giving him a one-armed hug.

Wow, thought Jahnni. *Warm and consoling too! What more can a girl ask for?*

"Hey, Mr. Harleyman," Jahnni whispered suddenly. "What kind of guns were the two Port cops waving around? That is, if they are Port cops. And what were the guns that those people in the white overall looking suits carrying? Not that I plan on being on the other end of one, but, I'm just curious."

"The Port Police, again, I'm not sure yet if they are Port Police but I doubt it . . . were carrying a Glock 22. Same as I'm carrying. I used to carry a Sig Sauer, but I've been carrying this one for about a year. Very Reliable." After pausing Mr. Harleyman went on, "and the two guys in the waterproof hazmat-type suits are carrying M4's. They are becoming standard issue in the military, replacing the M16a2's. Haven't worked out who they could be yet. You have any ideas?"

But before Jahnni could answer, he touched her arm as if to tell her to not talk. He looked at the others and held his finger to his lips. Voices. Or was that the whirring of the bag-belt? No . . . Jahnni definitely heard voices. They all quietly and slowly pulled their legs back up into the carts and moved to hide behind the bags that were already in the carts. About this time, Jahnni wished they wouldn't all have jammed together in the same two carts.

The two guys in the white hazmat suits slithered around the corner, backs to the wall. *What are these guys? Who are these guys?* Jahnni thought, still puzzled. They were jabbering in a language she couldn't understand, even though she continued to eavesdrop. After talking, one motioned his head towards the main tunnel.

They pulled up their M4's and started winding around the walls and carts. They stopped by the Coke machine to look around the corner for clearance, and then took off running for the main tunnel.

The main tunnel, Jahnni thought. *That leads to the mezzanine where the fountain is.* "Where the fountain is," she whispered out loud, looking at Samantha.

"Uh, Jahnni? Remember when I told you I understood the masked guys?" Samantha said, more like a question.

"Ya. What did you hear?" Jahnni said before noticing Mr. Harleyman's mouth half open as if he was going to ask the same thing.

Samantha added, "Right before they left, I am sure that I heard one of them say that they should have grabbed them before, since they already knew who they were. Then the other one said that they couldn't yet because it wasn't clear if they even had the plans to know how to get down there, under the fountain." She paused as she added air quotes around the words, "down there."

"You must have ears like a bat. I couldn't make out a thing they were saying even if I spoke Hungarian," Jahnni commented.

Samantha went on, "Then the tall one said, 'They are here in the airport somewhere,' then the other one whispered back, 'I still think we could have stopped this entire debacle long before it got this far if he would have listened to us.'"

Samantha stopped speaking briefly to look at each one in the group before finishing what she had to say. "It isn't so much what they said, but who said it. I just realized that the smaller guy . . . well isn't a guy. He's a her. A she. A lady. She said they had to block the other route to the fountain's pipes, and stop them from getting to it. But, I don't know who the 'them' is. It can't be us because they already had us . . . briefly, remember? And I don't know why someone is going through all this just to get into a stupid fountain."

"By chance, did you ladies see the lovely ornaments on their neck?" Mr. Harleyman asked, even though he didn't look over at them. He was watching the tunnel.

"Well, now that you mention it, I wondered about that

when we saw them the first time. I saw something that looked like a small swim mask or rubbery looking thing around their necks. But I was a little too preoccupied to give it much more thought," Jahnni answered.

"Well, those little swim masks are tethered to a very small underwater breathing device that holds crystals. It is a new concept that is being developed for underwater divers, rescuers, treasure hunters and the like. It's now being called the Aquatic Vent, but it is still in development. The small t-shaped device the small mask is tethered to holds the crystals. You can breathe underwater using it. Like a fish. Our Dive Teams at Quantico are testing them." He looked over at Jahnni after scanning the area. Jahnni met his gaze then looked away towards the tunnel that the gunmen exited as she tried to process the meaning of this new information. Plus, she was trying not to look too long into Mr. Harleyman's eyes because it made her lose her train of thought. *Not good at a time like this,* she reminded herself.

"The Columbia River is quite a walk from the airport. The only other water I can think of is the fountain's pools and they are not very deep, maybe two to three feet at different places. And they are stocked with fish. A few sockeye or chinook salmon, steelhead trout. Oh, and the Japanese-looking one has huge Koi," Jahnni said as her eyes searched up, down, and around at nothing in particular while she tried to think if any other water was nearby. "I did learn when I started working here, that the currents produced by the waterfall had been engineered to create the optimum oxygen levels for each of the species. So, it would seem like there is too much . . . engineering? to mess with to try and climb backwards in the fountain. And for what?" After no one had any more input, she sighed, realizing that there were so many questions and not enough answers.

Jahnni reminded everyone, "If something is going to happen at the fountain, then we need to go the other direction to get out of here. I don't want to even know what is going to transpire there. I just want to get us out of here and safe! The closest access door from inside here to the passenger bag carousels was taped over with caution tape. I got a brief glance at it when we were riding the bag belts here. Not sure what that is about. So, we need to alter the plan a bit. There are more doors that lead out to the baggage carousel, but a little further away. And there's also the large openings that the tugs drive in and out through. Oh, wait, those are closed and locked down now, so I guess one of the other carousel access doors is our best option."

"Well, I think Beau will get us safely out of here. He is good boy, this fellow. Good boy!" Mr. Tropopoulis said with such fervor. "I go where he goes."

"Okay Jahnni, how do we get to the First Class Air's bagwell?" Mr. Harleyman said before adding, "If it's not far, we can get there quickly and maybe check the phone lines again."

At this moment, he could demand to be taken to Cuba and Jahnni would comply. *Tropical. Caribbean waters. Soft sand that trickles between our toes as we run in slow motion toward each other to embrace. If he were to ask that,* she thought, *it would be wise to inform him of the new political climate and suggest we visit Jamaica or possibly, even the Dominican Republic.* "But I'd like Bora Bora . . . I hear the sand is luxurious between the toes . . . So many choices!" she blurted out before she realized the words were falling from her mind and out her mouth. "I mean, I, uh, um, there are a couple ways to get to our bagwell." *What is wrong with me? Do your job!*

"Jahnni? Are you okay?" Mr. Harleyman asked, to get her attention. "So, it's close? Can we go there now?"

"Oh," she blushed, "I don't think this is the time to plan a tropical excursion like this, but we could possibly . . ." she stopped talking when she noticed his confused look when his eyebrows arched up. "I mean, oh yeah, sure, our bagwell is not too far and it is on the way to the other exit doors to the bag carousels." *Okay, that's enough! She lectured herself. Stop daydreaming. You're not going to Cuba . . . or Bora Bora.*

She listened to see if it was safe to re-enter the tunnel.

"You guys need to stay behind me. I'll make sure it's safe. Just guide me," he told Jahnni.

She nodded and they started walking very quickly, stopping only before each corner for Mr. Harleyman to check that the 'uniforms' were not nearby. They dodged traffic cones, abandoned tugs, and followed a path that Jahnni knew well. She had worked just about every position from ground agent, or stocking food and beverages in planes, to working inside the airport. Her well-rounded experience was what got her the supervisor position she held now. Not to mention her penchant for mastering everything her job title called for. She didn't want bragging rights, she just didn't like to not have the answers to important questions. She studied anything and everything to gain any knowledge she might possibly need. Now, some of that knowledge was proving more useful than she imagined.

They didn't stop until they rounded the last corner and started to enter the First Class bagwell. They slid to a stop, bumping into each other. Had the bag belt not been whirring and clanking around and around, the uniformed guys would have heard them and they would have been caught.

Samantha motioned with her finger to her lips as she looked at Mr. Tropopoulis and Crutch. Then she pointed across the cemented bagwell area. Slowly, they backed against the wall and looked for a way to escape, in case they were indeed heard.

The 'uniforms' were in the bagwell ripping open bags, dumping them out, and riffling through the belongings. Peering through the gape in the bricks, Jahnni could not understand. To comprehend what was being done was not something she could grasp. *All the bags had already been scanned. What are they looking for? If they knew the name of the person whose bag they were looking for, why didn't they just read the names on the bag tags?*

"Hey, isn't that your bag he has now?" she whispered to Mr. Harleyman.

"How dare that man!" Mr. Tropopoulis whispered angrily. "He is holding my bag that I was to carry on plane. I leave it at gate area when all this trouble happen! I have much important things in there!"

"Maybe, Pops. Or it might be mine. It's okay. We will get your bag back and everything in it. Mine too. We will get both bags back," Mr. Harleyman vowed.

Jahnni just stared in amazement. *What is it about these bags that have these two so worked up?*

Chapter 12

Dear Whoever:
I Think We Need Some Help

THE FIVE OF them huddled in silence. They all watched the bumbling security guards, or whatever they were, look for something that seemed of great importance. Hearing new instructions on their odd-looking radio, they abandoned the shambles they had created and grabbed the brown plaid bag they already had in their possession and started running out of the baggage area towards the main tunnel. They began weaving their way away from Jahnni and her friends. Thinking that they might possibly return, Mr. Harleyman motioned for them to stay put for a while longer. When the 'uniforms' passed Southwest's area, and kept going at a brisk pace towards the main area under the mezzanine, Jahnni looked at him and raised her eyebrows, nodding slightly as if asking if they should proceed into the First Class Air's baggage area. Besides, she had an idea. *One that doesn't include beaches,* she noted sadly.

They all ran around the little wall towards the belt in First Class Air's bagwell and cautiously walked against the inner walls and around the carts behind Mr. Harleyman, who had his shirt pulled up slightly on the side and his hand on the gun in its holster. They proceeded to check for unwanted company. Seeing none, they all crawled up onto the nearest cart, positioning the bags in front of them in case someone else came into the area as well. They sat in silence looking at each other and looking at all the mess that was strewn around. Clothing, deodorant, shoes, magazines, blow-dryers, toys, blankets. Anything you could possibly expect to find in a traveler's suitcase, was on the floor. It looked like a battlefield of colorful fabric carnage. Jahnni wondered what Mr. Harleyman was thinking as he sat there silent. *Always thinking, never sharing. Typical,* she thought.

Mr. Tropopoulis sat still and stared at the walls and ceiling. His head was tilted slightly and one ear turned toward the floor. He glanced down, and then up at the walls. Samantha sat next to Crutch. Crutch just sat, leaning back onto a large bag, lounging and playing his game, apparently, no worries in the world. Jahnni on the other hand had lots of worries. She was down in the bagwell, with an old man, a co-worker, a UM and a man that made her feel like she just ate chili peppers for lunch. Her body temperature rose with each passing minute she spent near him. Her palms were sweaty, and her face was flushed. She tried to keep her mind on their situation, but every time they stopped to rest, and things felt slightly calm, her mind would wander to him. *Was he married? Did he have a girlfriend? Did he even notice me as anyone more than his baggage checker? Oh, what am I thinking? I need to stay on task! Get us out of here!* Then she watched him as he slowly breathed in and out. *Obviously, he must be calculating his options, and weighing the pros and cons of each decision he might need to make. That's what I would be doing if I was a highly-trained FBI Agent . . . with secrets,* she noted to herself. His jaw was set, and she could almost see his heartbeat echoing in his neck. His lips were full and pouty and curved slightly upwards at the edges in a slight smile that evoked confidence at every moment. *And cuteness. Definitely, cuteness. If we get out of this,* she thought, weighing her options to herself . . . *I am for sure . . . going to kiss those lips someday. Maybe. I hope.*

"Uh . . . Mr. Harleyman?" Jahnni whispered

"Look, at this point, you can call me Beau," he answered. "I think we have passed the introductory phase." He chuckled slightly and then turned to face her.

"Okay . . . Beau? I'll unlock the bagwell office door. Inside, there is a system called Flight Navigation Monitor from which I can get all sorts of information. I can track flights for any airline, any city, and I can pull up a flight manifest for all our own planes today. It can show us fuel logs, cargo load, pretty much anything. I wonder if that will help us figure anything out?" Jahnni asked.

"Not unless I recognize any names on a manifest. Or if there is any way that someone has posted or sent information about this emergency. Maybe, this doesn't have anything to do with flights. I wonder . . ."

"Well, the sooner you brief me about what you are wondering, the better, don't you think?" Jahnni asked.

After giving him a bug-eyed, *Well?* look, Jahnni told everyone to stay together and follow her. She used her keys to open the door and with the lights off, proceeded over to the computers. She checked to see if she could access the internet, and sure enough they were online, so First Class Air's private satellite service hadn't failed them, just like the software engineers had promised. They were the only airline to have invested in the expensive system. Instead of investing in First Class Air's technology, the other airlines were vehement about developing their own so they didn't have to pay royalties to First Class Airlines. *Whatever,* she thought. *Their loss now, obviously.*

She could see all the flights grounded at PDX. She saw their IN times, and saw that for the next few hours at least, all other inbound planes had been diverted. She made some entries and saw they were headed back to their origins, or were being rerouted, mostly to Seattle. There were some planes that had taxied out to the runway, before this all started, and here at PDX they were on a compete ground stop, loaded with angry passengers no doubt. All their planes were on an interactive program with a satellite process that "read" the planes data. It showed what time they were "out," but it also showed what time they chocked the brakes once they were told to stop. It showed which had passengers and crew still onboard. *The crew must have accessed the satellite system and posted a new passen-*

ger count and names when some were forced back onboard from the jetways during the initial lockdown, she thought. Jahnni and Beau looked at the names on all the outbound passenger lists. Nothing looked familiar to Beau so far. They looked at the names on all the inbound flights for the day. Nothing seemed of any importance to Jahnni. She didn't even know what she was looking for.

"What are you even looking for? How would you know any of these people?" Jahnni asked.

"I hoped I would see a name on our wanted list," Beau mumbled.

Jahnni then pulled up the first inbound JFK that landed earlier that morning. "What about this name here?" Samantha interrupted, reaching over Jahnni's shoulder and pointing. "And what about this one . . . here also?"

Jahnni looked at the names. Looked at the seat numbers, but didn't know what she was driving at. Before Jahnni spoke, Beau asked, "What about them?"

"Well, remember when I said that the two gunmen in white were from Hungary? Well, the two gun-*people*," Samantha added haltingly, "I mean, I knew, because I speak Hungarian. These two names here, although they are not seated together, are Hungarian. Oláh and Horváth. Not that it means anything, but I just thought . . . maybe it might? And look, one is a man, and one is a woman." She looked back and forth between Jahnni and Beau then wiped her hands in the air as if she had solved the entire case.

"I don't know. It seems like a long shot. Can you pull up

their reservation Jahn?" Beau asked.

"I can do that, *and* tell you when they bought their ticket, where the reservation was made and how they paid for it . . . and even who they spoke with them to make it if they called the reservation line. I can even tell you what computer checked them in and what agent checked their bags, if they had any," she added as she pulled up the PNR.

"Now this is confidential information Beau. I mean, we are only trying to ascertain what kind of situation we are in, and how to get out of it, right?" Jahnni said. "You have to forget anything you see here. I am not supposed to let you see anything in here. Geez, I'm in so much trouble already, bringing you all down here, hauling a UM into danger. I'm going to be fired, poor, and homeless. I'm really, really, gonna be in so much trouble!"

"Look Jahn, everything that got us down here was survival. If there is nothing in this record that appears pertinent, then we can back out of it and go to plan B, C or whatever. Do we have another plan?" Beau laughed under his breath as he looked out the window into the bagwell. After a few moments, he looked back at Jahnni. She was staring at his chest.

"What?" he asked

"What do you mean, 'what'?" she answered

"What? What are you staring at?" he asked again as he glanced down at his shirt. "Is there something on my shirt?"

"Oh, uhhh, nothing. Let me look at this res." She turned her pink face towards the computer, knowing that it wasn't what was on his shirt so much as how nice his shirt looked on him. *What is wrong with me? Concentrate!*

"They flew in from JFK on our early morning inbound. I don't show them on us before that. Oh wait. Their electronic tickets show they flew in to New York from Frankfurt yesterday on Lufthansa. They were on our first flight out of New York early this morning, which is why, with the time change it looks like they got here in about 2 hours, but it really takes about 5. They didn't check bags, but these guys here in PDX had machine guns, or rifles or . . . whatever they are called." She was muttering as she read everything that even appeared pertinent. "You can't sneak those through customs. So, someone had to supply those once they landed."

"You mean M4's. Those aren't machine guns," Beau whispered behind her ear to correct her. His breath moved across her skin and she shivered from her ears to her toes. She reminded herself once again, *focus.*

She went on, "But this is weird; their tickets were purchased here in Portland. Yesterday, right before they checked in, in Frankfurt. Man . . . they paid enough for last minute tickets! Who has that kind of money for last minute International flights? These tickets cost like a couple month's salary for me! And together in First Class from Frankfurt? Make that six-month's salary . . . each! But they were seated apart, from New York to Portland. Maybe there weren't any seats together at the last minute. You suppose, Samantha?" Jahnni said. Samantha shrugged affirmatively.

"Who is seated next to them from New York?" Beau asked.

Jahnni pulled up the passenger manifest again, choosing

to send it to the second monitor next to the first one that they were initially using.

"Pull up that reservation again," Beau said.

Jahnni saw his eyes scanning the history and waited to hear what conclusion he came to . . . about anything.

Running his finger down the screen, he breathed out a sigh and finally spoke while pointing to the payment information in the reservation. "You know, I don't think we need to worry. If these are the masked guys in white, then these guys aren't the enemy. So, who are the 'uniforms' then? And why do they look like the Port police, but they can't badge their own way into each area?" he asked out loud then turned to Jahnni. "You said you didn't recognize them, right?"

"No, I don't, but maybe they are new, or maybe they always work the property and not the terminal. I don't know, but it is weird," she offered then added, "Their uniforms are slightly different too."

"How do you know this?" Mr. Tropopoulis asked with eagerness. "How can you know that these two guys, I mean people, from Hungary are not 'bad guys?' I feel much concerned that someone have my bag. It is much important to me! That is MY bag and no one has right to steal it. It is good thing pizza people find it for me . . . when I forget it under table." Then he turned to Jahnni and said, "remember Janie?"

"You know, Pops, I'll explain later. Please, trust me. I just know. But let's hurry and get out of here safely. In the meantime, once you all are safe, I will . . ." Silence fell around them before he continued in a lower voice, "I will do what I have to do to make sure we get the answers we need." Pausing, then looking down at Mr. Tropopoulis, he added, "and your bag and everything that is in it too."

Jahnni stared at Beau, and then she looked at the reservation again. She tipped her head to the side while she scanned the room, the computer screen, the desk and everything on top of it, and then stared blankly at the computer. A jumble of thoughts rolled over and over in her mind but the connections were not making a conclusion. *When, how, who* . . . she couldn't even put her questions in her mind into a complete sentence. Finally, she thought to herself, *why does he think everything is going to be okay? And what did he see in the payment info?* She examined the payment info he momentarily pointed at.

"Okay then," Samantha sighed. "Can't we just call someone from here, or fax someone, or email someone, or . . ."

"SAM! I can't believe you thought of that! The computers are not on the phone's cable line system during an outage, but as we can see, I still have updated access to flight status. The phones and regular cable are still out, and the cell phone and radio reception is blocked. But our computers are on the new satellite system! So, bingo! We can put an email to someone in the queue via this system," she said as she thought through the complexities of the satellite linkage. She looked at Beau and tried to break it down as she remembered the details of it. "When it kicks into emergency mode, it can accept inbound info, and queue outbound at thirty minute increments. It has something to do with a different type of wave length, satellites, transponders, and expense but . . . I don't truly understand it all. Our shortest flight is forty-five minutes, that is why they set it at thirty. That still gives the outstation enough time to work with an inbound from an emergency coded airport. When not in emergency mode, everything is in real time."

"Well, for whatever reason, let's get some info to someone, then we are getting out of here," Beau said. "Draw me a sketch of our location and the direction we are headed when we leave here. We are going straight to the carousel door and ending this crazy cat and mouse game. At least now, we are only looking to avoid the two in police-looking uniforms. The guys, or rather guy and lady in white, are not an issue."

"I knew I should have pressed the issue about having Skype and Facetime allowed on our computers!" Jahnni said with fake anger. "They blocked those programs so the employees wouldn't play on them. We sure could have used something like that right about now! Wait . . . maybe that wouldn't work though, since you'd have to wait thirty minutes between sentences," she added as she realized it still couldn't just live-stream during the curtailed access during an emergency.

Sam looked quite perplexed. "Wait, then why do those police looking guys have radios that work?"

Beau spoke up, "That's not a radio. Per se. When phone lines are down, and cell reception and two-way radio is blocked . . . SAT phones will work. They are using a SAT phone . . . they're directly linked to satellites bypassing the ordinary communication devices. Because PDX is dense, there is a PBX, I mean, private branch exchange, system located on site to allow a broader range of reception. Otherwise service is limited to direct satellite view by the phones. There is probably more than one and they are linked. The PBX is like those operators from the old days that would find out who you wanted to call, then plug you into the right line. Like a relay system. But now, it's all computerized of course. In fact, now that you mention it, law enforcement here has probably switched out to SATs as well. That could pose a problem for the bad guys if they are on the same PBX. But with what is going on, I imagine that there must be a secondary PBX system located somewhere. Some models have the capacity to use text messaging. Those two amateurs act like they aren't familiar with using a SAT phone. I get the idea that they were hired for their brawn, not their brains," Beau quipped as he chuckled under his breath.

"So, they work sort of like our satellite system here then? We must have our own PB whatever it's called, too. But, let's stay on topic here. Who can we send an email to?" she asked as her fingers signed into her personal company email. *Better make it official,* she thought to herself. *Not to someone that could be at the airport cuz they can't check their email on their phones.*

Her fingers waited as the cursor blinked in the 'TO' section of the email. They all stared at the blink as if it was a secret message waiting to be interpreted. Blink, blink, blink. She nervously waited as her fingers twitched. Everyone stared at the empty email. No one said anything. "It doesn't have to be the president, guys. Just think of someone important." Then, after much thought, she remembered the email address that she saw in the reservation. Beau had pointed at it, with a slight smile on his face.

It also seemed to be a familiar name to her at this point as well.

Thanks Carlton, she thought, thinking back on their conversations over the last couple weeks. Carlton's voice echoed in her head, '*I feel that everyone needs to know who to believe in,*' she remembered him telling her. Pieces were coming together and pieces were falling apart. The talk about the fountain, the name in the reservation, some type of breathing device on the people in the white jumpsuits. She couldn't yet figure out how or why they were all thrown into this bizarre chain of events together, but somehow, she felt it was meant to be. Who was who, and what was what, was all part of this big mystery, but she vowed to get to the bottom of it. She hated missing pieces to a puzzle and this was no exception. She glanced over at Crutch. *He is my first priority no matter where this day leads,* she thought. *I will keep him safe even if I have to give my own life to do it.*

Focusing again on her twitching fingers, she began to type the email address she and Beau saw in the PNR. Then she added a couple more addresses to the Bc portion of the email. The First Class CEO in Seattle, a friend who was a station manager in another city for her airline, and one to her own station manager even though she wouldn't see it until she left the area. *Best to let more people know what is going on, and cover our bases,* she figured. Who knows when they will get them, but at least it will be some type of a trail.

TO: Zale.Baptiste@rebornorganic.com
Subject: HELP

She only hoped he checked his email as often as she checked hers, especially considering the recent events in which they found themselves. She summed up who she was, and who was with her and that his name was pointed out to her in someone's PNR when she pulled up the flight manifest. She tried to give a quick synopsis of their predicament and asked if he knew what was happening and why. And to please follow up with the FBI and let them know that Beau Harleyman, one of their agents, was with her, but they would be sending an email with similar information to the FBI in hopes that someone would read these emails in time to help them.

After she reread it, she sent it and drafted another email for Beau to finish to those above him at the Bureau. He stood there waiting before clearing his throat and asking, "Are you going to take dictation, or are you going to let me sit there and type it myself?"

"Oh," Jahnni said as she realized she was hogging the space, "just pull up a chair." When Beau squinted at her, she realized he wanted to type his own email so she stood up and gave him the chair. Hope was mixed with fear while she waited for Beau to finish his email. She thought to herself, *here goes. I hope we made sense.* She looked at Beau when he seemed finished and he nodded. She nodded ascent also and he clicked SEND.

Chapter 13

Foiled Plans, Again

JAHNNI SKETCHED A map for Beau. He studied it for a bit, looked out the window that faced the bagwell, then set it back down. Jahnni herded them out of the FC bagwell office and pulled the door shut behind her.

She paused and offered a thought, "Maybe we should consider just waiting back in the bagwell office and locking the door. Shouldn't we wait for a reply to the emails? If we leave the lights out, and stay close to the floor, we can just wait for this all to die down and someone can rescue us."

"No. We can't wait that long. We don't know how long until they will get it, if they get it, and by then, we could be out of here. We are heading to the door you said connects to the baggage carousel and exiting the area," Beau answered. "First though, if you want, you guys can wait in there and I can just poke around out here looking for my bag. With them rummaging around earlier, I need to see if it was my bag or Pop's bag they had."

"No can do, Tonto. You cannot have access to all those bags. It's another security breach if I allow it," Jahnni insisted.

"Wait. Are you saying that you don't trust me? You think I'm hiding a bomb in my back pocket or something?" He shook his head slightly.

"Well, no. Of course not, Beau. I'm just saying, that we may be in a bad situation, but it doesn't give me permission to throw caution to the wind and let people gallivant around the airport in a secured area," Jahnni snapped back.

"Good Lord Jahn, we are in this together. What possible motive could I have to even be interested in someone else's luggage?" He stood there with an exasperated look on his face. Then he raised his eyebrows while he waited for an answer.

"Look, just stop," she said as she held her hand up in front of her like a stop sign. "You are so used to calling all the shots that you aren't looking at this from my perspective. I have a security clearance that . . ."

"Oh," he said as he interrupted her, "and I don't have any sort of special government clearance . . . which I might add allows *me* to carry a *weapon* into a secured area *and* onboard an aircraft? So . . . do you have that kind of clearance? Hmmm?" He paused as he turned his head a little sideways and tilted his chin up at her. He continued, "Besides, technically, I AM in charge now. I just depend on you because you know the layout of the airport."

Jahnni glared at him for a moment then answered in a calm, but terse tone, "Not that you don't have a valid point about a broad sense of security, but the point I am making, Batman, is that this is my job. This is where I work and this is where the airport expects me to follow every protocol accurately, when possible. I've already broken enough rules to get fired, or arrested. When this is all over, you will walk away and still have your job. I might never be able to work in the airline industry, or even get a security clearance for any type of job that needs one, ever again. You will probably leave here after today and forget all about me . . . I mean us . . . I mean this." As she opened her arms to add the group situation into her meaning she insisted further, "I can't lose this job. Besides, don't think I don't understand that you are trained for all this. We need you, and you need us because we know the airport. I'm not trying to tell you how to do your job, as much as I am being . . . torn about where the line is between what measures I should have followed and what ones I won't be crucified for breaking."

Beau stared at her for several seconds, processing everything she said. He then calmly and succinctly answered her in a low, reassuring tone. His lips curled up at the corners and dimples popped into his cheeks when he smiled and summarized, "I see your point. I was looking at the whole picture and not your internal struggle with your responsibilities. I assumed because we were sitting in the carts before, that it made them more accessible for me in your eyes. I also assumed that you would know that you could trust me, but I see now that you are indicating that it isn't about trust as much as it is about our different expectations of security procedures as this drama has unfolded. And . . . that you are trying to walk the line . . . with what is expected of you in your position concerning security directives . . . but also to keep us safe while trusting me to do my job. I shouldn't make assumptions. But, I would hope that you would understand that my security clearance does give me clearance to do whatever is necessary to do my job. On the clock or not. And by the way, not to push any buttons, and not to make light of your job, but during this emergency, I trump you."

Jahnni held her breath as she realized that this lug not only knew his job but he knew how to communicate clearly. It made her, once again, a little weak-kneed although she was seeing that she needs to try to let go of the things that don't matter right now. "Okayyy," she cautiously mumbled, "I'm sorry that we didn't understand each other, but as long as we can work together, we will get out of this safely. And I won't lose my job . . . if possible . . . if they believe me . . . and we don't get shot in the process." She locked the door as they walked away from the RAC room.

Jahnni followed Beau as he walked cautiously around some carts, weapon in hand, leading them out of the bagwell. *I still think we should have waited in the RAC ROOM, but I guess it wouldn't get us out of here fast enough,* she thought. The half-filled carts were only a few feet away. No one talked until they came to a corner that Beau stopped to look around.

"You know Jahn, I'll never forget about this." He looked behind himself at her, and gently touched her shoulder. He blinked slowly, searching her eyes as he started to say more, then paused. "What I mean is, I'm sorry we misunderstood each other. When this is all over, I'll never forget about any of this . . . or you."

For a moment, Jahnni was stunned. She tried to break every word and every letter down to understand his exact meaning. *Was he being polite? Was he just being nice? Did he want to let me know that he will never forget about this airport drama? Or is it me? Maybe he wanted to be friends? Or maybe . . .?*

"Jahnni, I don't feel so good," Samantha whispered. I think I need to sit down for just a bit before we go any further. Please?" She looked at Beau for permission since he was leading the way now.

Beau nodded and they jumped into some nearby carts to stay hidden while Samantha rested. Everything was silent except for the usual whirring and banging from other bagwells that didn't get shut down. Jahnni looked over at Crutch to see how he was doing, but he seemed calm, once again biding his time by playing his handheld game. Mr. Tropopoulis sat stoically with a soft smile on his face while his eyes took in every nook and cranny of the walls and ceiling. Beau watched the entrances to the bagwell they were in, glancing back and forth at them. He looked at the closed door that led out to the planes but after a contemplative look, nodded to Jahnni.

"Can we raise those doors? Will that get us out of here any faster?" Beau asked.

"I don't think I can override the lock," she answered him.

"That's probably not an option anyway," Beau added. "I'm not sure that being anywhere near a plane during this emergency would be a safe idea with possible snipers and other law enforcement around in the distance."

Samantha moaned as she suddenly remembered her hot date that she wasn't going to go on. "Man!" she whispered loudly, mostly to Jahnni, "I was so excited to go out with that guy again! There is probably no way that his flight made it in before all this happened. And we had so much fun together last week. It was like, what is it called? Serendipity. Ya, that's it. It was like we just clicked. Like meeting him was meant to be. I am majorly bummed!" After she paused, she added, "Carter. Carter Laurent Mercier. He's French. You have no idea how he melts me." Then she sighed as she stared up in the air.

Jahnni took in Samantha's admission of her disappointment. *Maybe she finally met someone she wasn't willing to toss away because of some manufactured slight or imperfection.* Jahnni knew all too well that it was probably Sam's way of convincing herself that the wrong one's were truly the wrong ones. *I hope this Carter guy is going to be worth it and treats Sam well.*

Jahnni suddenly sat up straighter, narrowed her eyes in deep thought and said, "I wonder if they remembered, or had time to lock the bag belt door at the ticket counters?"

"You mean the opening that your bags disappear into when you check in?" Beau asked eagerly.

"That would be the one," Jahnni replied as she shook her head yes very slowly. "In fact, I actually had to climb up it once when a trombone got stuck."

Beau beamed as he added, "I'll climb up and lead Crutch and Pops out of here. They can explain everything to the first official person they see. We three can stay down here, find my bag, then we'll climb out too. That way we won't feel like mallards on opening day hanging around while we head to the carousel door." Then his stomach let out a hungry sounding gurgle.

Crutch looked at Beau and added sheepishly, "Sounds like you could use a BK Whopper about now. I'm trying not to think about being hungry, but sometimes it's hard cuz my stomach keeps reminding me too."

Beau's hand touched the front of his shirt then answered Crutch, "In due time, kiddo. We aren't going to starve."

Who could think of eating at a time like this, except a kid? Jahnni said to herself as she reached over and patted Crutch's knee. "Soon, sweetie. I promise."

Jahnni looked at Beau and explained, "I can't send Crutch out there without me or Samantha. He must be with one of us always. And I certainly don't want to split up. Officially, I also can't let anyone stay down here rummaging around screened bags, much less wandering around unaccompanied. I know . . . I know . . . I remember the last conversation we had. But think about it. I can't leave anyone down here. I need to decide who to bring up first if it's open."

The route wasn't exactly obvious from where they sat and she knew that Samantha had never had reason to climb the belt routing. The maze would have to be crawled, and hopefully, the exact belt they needed to crawl on was turned off or they wouldn't be able to crawl fast enough to traverse it. Jahnni envisioned someone like Mr. Tropopoulis trying. *It would be like walking 'up' a 'down' escalator, especially with the rollers.* She thought about it and decided that maybe they did need to split up somehow.

"Sam, if I take Crutch up first, I'll have to stay with him. Can you help Beau and Mr. Tropopoulis?" Jahnni whispered, then added in surrender, "and help Beau find his bag, I guess?"

"Sure. Will it be obvious where to go?" Sam asked. "Are we going to wait a little bit and then follow you up the belt to the ticket counter?"

Jahnni nodded yes, "Once I get around that bend up there, you'll barely be able to see me up higher, at the top. I'll wave before I go around the bend. We'll have to climb over the diversion arm that sends the bags to the CTX instead of shooting them directly to the bagwell carousel for loading. Give us enough time to have a conversation with the police, maybe 10 minutes, I suppose, and then head up. By then, I will have them waiting for you guys. So, you'll be safe."

She peeked out from the cart she was sitting in, scanned the area and listened for footsteps. Seeing and hearing nothing other than the whir of belts that were still rotating and the clanking that haunts the bag-well, she climbed out and went over to the wall and punched the big red stop button. Then she froze. She thought she heard something. *Uhhh . . . it was probably the belt shutting down,* she decided. Everything seemed silent now.

She carefully climbed onto the carousel belt and walked over to the opening that normally shot the bags down. She grabbed the corners of the framed opening and hoisted herself up. She glanced up and her eyes followed the path of the overhead belt to gauge the distance then looked down at the rest of them sitting in a couple carts. She motioned for Samantha to send Crutch up. Samantha hesitated and pointed to Mr. Tropopoulis. She made hand signals like she would keep Crutch next to her, but motioned she felt Mr. Tropopoulis should go first because of his age. Beau nodded in agreement. Leaving Crutch with Sam was fine and since they were with an FBI agent that seemed safe. She backed down the short distance she covered already.

Mr. Tropopoulis cautiously traversed the same path that Jahnni just climbed and grabbed the metal edge with one hand, and extended the other hand to Jahnni. She pulled him up and onto the upper belt. She glanced back at Sam and understood Sam meant she should get Mr. Tropopoulis to the top, and then Sam would follow with Mr. Harleyman and Crutch in a few minutes. When Sam shrugged her shoulders, and shook her head like they weren't going to look around, Jahnni took that to mean Beau and Sam must have decided that just getting out was more important than a scavenger hunt looking for his bag at this moment.

They began to crawl on their hands and knees up the long rubber belt. They'd gone about five feet when Jahnni heard the definite sound of a slide release on a gun. They both froze. She slowly turned and looked over the metal sides of the belt and saw that the two 'uniforms' were pointing their weapons at her and Mr. Tropopoulis.

Jahnni saw in the corner of her eye that Beau moved like

he was going to jump out of the cart, but he must have second guessed his decision. She assumed it was because he could see that they were pointing their guns at their heads. She knew he couldn't chance it. *He probably doesn't trust them to not shoot us by accident. Maybe they will take us upstairs to the police and we can tell them the whole story. Or, if we don't come back soon, Sam can chance it and take Beau and Crutch to crawl up the belt and out to the ticket counter themselves. Beau could explain everything.*

Chapter 14

Do I Know You?

"THAT'S FAR ENOUGH lady! You two can just scuttle back down and come with me," the portly cop said. "Is there anyone else with you?"

"Oh, my family decide not to come on this trip," Mr. Tropopoulis offered loudly with a friendly smile, as if he was being interviewed by a friendly source. "It is just me and Janie here trying to find our way out of airport basement place here. See Janie! These nice police people will help us now!" Mr. Tropopoulis was obviously playing a part, but Jahnni was sure that it was very convincing to the uniformed guys with the big guns pointing at her face. The chubby cop and the tall skinny cop looked at each other and nodded before turning back to Jahnni and Mr. Tropopoulis.

"Whatever, old man. Just get down here. Now!" The tall skinny cop shouted as he waved the gun in his hand back and forth at the wrist, motioning the direction she was to take.

Jahnni paused to think, then she motioned that they were coming down. When they jumped, and slid onto the lower belt, they were each grabbed by the arm and told to walk. Jahnni's eyes darted to Beau, squatted behind a pile of bags in a cart with his gun pointed towards the men behind her. She nodded her head no, back and forth very slowly and slightly, hoping that he would not do anything to spook the guys with the guns pointed at them. The fear coursing through her was second to the fear she felt for Crutch. Then she moved her eyes to Sam and Crutch, then up at the top of the bag belt. She barely moved her eyebrows, asking if he understood. Again, she moved her eyes to look at Sam and Crutch then up at the top of the belt. She hoped he understood to take Samantha and Crutch out after they were taken away. She felt a gun near the back of her head and could see out of the corner of her eye that Mr. Tropopoulis had one pointed at his back.

"Where are you taking us? I imagine we'll be able to talk to someone and explain everything…so waiting and staying calm is what everyone involved right now should do," she said to Mr. Harleyman while seeming to speak to her new captors. "What is happening here at the airport anyway? We have been trying to find a way to get upstairs. I was, uh, giving my grandpa a tour of the bag-well and the education offices. Everyone was evacuated while I waited for him by the bathroom. You know . . . weak bladder and all at his age," Jahnni sputtered.

"Ya. Well, no one belongs down here right now, so you need to go see the boss," the skinny cop croaked out in a low baritone voice as his Adam's apple bounced with every word he spoke. She had glanced at his badge and saw Charlie Benson on it. She thought his voice didn't match his looks.

"You have a badge hanging off your neck chain there. Why didn't you just use that to get through the doors?" the portly cop asked. Jahnni looked at his nametag and the name Eric Craigs was pinned to his chest pocket. She knew these were the same two that had followed them earlier, but they didn't seem to recognize her and Mr. Tropopoulis. Her eyes roamed down at his hand and she noticed a big red swatch of swollen skin with teeth marks embedded in it. She realized that if he did recognize her, and that she was the one who bit him, he may not take them to their boss at all. He may have his own idea of justice. She swallowed and calmed her voice before she spoke.

"Oh . . . well . . . I tried, but there must be some kind of lockdown or maybe the computers are down? I, uh, can't get it to work anymore," she mumbled.

The big guy grabbed his radio, or rather SAT phone, now that she knew what it was. He hit a few keys and after a brief wait, spoke into it. "Boss, Craigs here."

Jahnni was thinking that he probably failed the Police Academy a few times before he finally made it, *if* he made it. She couldn't imagine him flipping over that tall barricade that you see them climbing over in movies about the academy. In fact, she wasn't all that convinced that he was a real cop. He seemed more like a mob boss than a civil servant.

"Go ahead Craigs . . . please tell me you have something for me," the voice answered.

"Ya, uh, well we have a lady with a Port badge and her grandfather. We haven't been able to find those other people. They must have figured a way out, and . . . we haven't found that John guy . . . yet," Craigs reported.

"Bring them to me," the voice at the other end demanded.

"You got it boss. We are at the central elevator downstairs, below you."

They walked a little way, and then stood by an elevator door. She glanced up at the camera, wondering who was watching them. Jahnni turned to keep her head facing the other direction. The elevator door light turned green, seemingly all by itself, but Jahnni knew they were being watched on the camera that faced the elevator door and that they were scanned in remotely. They were pushed and nudged into the elevator, probably for the sole purpose of being bullied. By the look on their captor's faces, she could tell it made them feel important to bully a lady and her 'grandpa.' She felt the elevator going up and her stomach lurched, trepidation replacing hunger. She was trapped in this tin box with these two bullies. Suddenly, a raw sense of protectiveness melted over her when she looked at Mr. Tropopoulis. She leaned toward him gently, and smiled when he looked up. She wanted him to feel safe, even if she wasn't sure they were. He smiled at her, his head held high and confident like he was trying to make *her* feel safe. They rode the rest of the way up, both slightly smiling the angst away.

After exiting the elevator, they stood in the hallway near the main office, the Port of Portland PDX office. She glanced out the tinted one-way window that was in front of them, and saw very official looking people milling around the mezzanine and lobby areas below them. From where she was, she could see over the tops of the backs of all the ticket counters and out onto the roadway too. That was the passenger drop-off area. FBI, TSA, Homeland Security, Port Police, and even guys in yellow jumpsuits. *What is going on?* She wondered. The upstairs offices were fronted by a wide 180-degree arced one-way window spanning the entire length of the offices. She knew that they would still be able to see out, but no one could see back through the windows at them. Red, blue, and yellow flashing lights were everywhere, bouncing their vibrant warnings into the airport through the tall glass windows that overlooked the curbside.

She felt a big thud in her chest at the sight of it all. *This is really one of those things we all trained for, but hoped would never happen. I am in the middle of it, and I don't even know what 'it' is.* Her heart started to pick up speed again and her face began to feel the damp chill that moistened her warm face. She didn't see a way out and felt like a trapped animal in a small cage.

The office door dinged as the four of them went in. It sounded more like the chime you heard when a someone walked into a clothing store, letting the employees know they had a customer. Along one whole wall to the right and forward, were systems with large monitors. They were obviously security cameras, congregated among the desks, with computers and various equipment. One person sat studying them, without looking up even though he could not help but hear them come in. Buttons and switches were being punched and twisted. One camera was trained exactly on the front of the fountain. Another was zeroed in on the back of the of it. Police dogs were sniffing every square inch of the area the fountain was in, but the dogs didn't seem to be interested in stopping to warn their partners of anything. Jahnni was still perplexed about the involvement of the fountain. *It's just a bunch of concrete blocks and water! What was the big deal?* she asked herself. She thought of the Cart Man and stories he had told her about something that included the fountain but nothing specific was coming to mind to explain the intense interest that she was seeing. She came back to the present when she felt Craigs grab her arm. Then he pushed her forward.

Benson grabbed Mr. Tropopoulis's arm and pushed him also, standing them to face another door connected to this office. They knocked and waited for an invitation to enter. Craigs entered first with Jahnni and Benson pushed Mr. Tropopoulis in next.

The man behind the desk stared at everyone, his mouth turned down in a large frown. He then stood, walked around the desk with his hands in his pockets and sauntered over to the four of them. Jahnni stood icily still. *Wait . . . this is the Port Manager's Office. Does he have the power to fire me right here and now? Should I try to explain? But, what would I say? Where should I start?* She tried to gather all the information she had so far from the beginning of all this, this . . . this . . . whatever this is. Her mind was jumbled and she couldn't get her thoughts to line up in any kind of comprehensible order. *Should I talk first and tell him to let me explain?*

Wait a minute, this is a good thing, she told herself. *Finally, finally! I can explain this whole debacle to someone who will understand and this will be all over. We're safe!*

She turned to tell Mr. Tropopoulis that everything was going to be fine. It was just one big misunderstanding with these two . . . these . . . Then she saw that Mr. Tropopoulis just stood there staring right at the airport manager.

"Well, hello Arnie," the airport manager said mockingly, then raised his eyebrows as if he was waiting to be acknowledged.

Chapter 15

You Must Be Crazy

Mr. Tropopoulis nodded his head slightly at an angle and returned the greeting. "Hello. Why you bring me and nice Janie here to this place?"

He didn't answer him right away. Jahnni looked at his Port badge because she couldn't remember his name. She had seen him at Port Security meetings for years but her mind was solid stone, unthinking, frozen like an ice block. She even saw his face in the monthly newsletters. But his name escaped her at this very moment. *His name is . . . as she squinted to read the moving display . . . is . . . Perry. Mr. Perry . . .? Of course, Prattle, Perry Prattle. How did I draw a blank on that? Wait, how does he know Mr. Tropopoulis?* She wondered, looking back and forth between the two of them.

Perry walked 3 steps to a table. Jahnni and Mr. Tropopoulis followed him with their eyes. She gasped. *The Brown Plaid Bag! But? How did he get it? Which, whose bag was that? Huh?*

He opened it slowly and then turned to look at Mr. Tropopoulis. "Where is it?" he asked him.

"Where is what?" Mr. Tropopoulis asked in return with innocent looking raised eyebrows.

"Come on Arnie! After all this time, I know you have it. Why else would you be traveling to San Fran during this very timely couple of days? Who were you going to pass it to? I've been watching the flights, looking for you. Just in case, of course. I had you placed on the secondary screening list that requires extra clearance. More importantly, I put you on a level that would give me an alert about the person the airline was attempting to check in. How was security? Extensive?" Perry laughed.

Jahnni could not make the puzzle pieces fit in any kind of picture. She was more confused now than a couple minutes ago, when she began to assume that they would be safe now. She turned to Craigs, the Port cop who was squeezing her arm even harder now, like it would squish the information Perry wanted, right up and out of the top of her head. She twisted away and said between her teeth, "Let me go! You big . . . BISON!"

The Port Manager, Perry, nodded to Craigs that it was okay to let loose now.

"What is happening here? You know each other? Why are we here? I am so confused!" Jahnni breathed out as she turned her head back and stared into Perry Prattles eyes.

Perry turned to the large flat screen on the wall and clicked the remote that was in his hand. He glanced at Mr. Tropopoulis without moving his head, and then looked back at the large TV that began playing what appeared to be a recording of the 6:00 news from a few days ago. In fact, Jahnni recognized this broadcast. She slowly stepped closer to Mr. Tropopoulis. He was still standing there all stoic; just a small smile on his lips. She thought he still looked so well-groomed for all they had been through. His hair was still slicked back in place. His shoes barely had a scuff on them except for small smudges on the toe's tips from the brief crawling on the rubber bag belt. She had spent so much time today with him that she even forgot he walked with a slight little shoulder tic. *I love this little guy,* she thought. *What a nice man.* Then the voice of the KATU News Anchor brought her mind back to the moment. Perry turned up the volume on the video.

"Yes, you heard it right folks. The winner of the Portland Water Festival's purified water contest is . . . an anonymous person! Every one of the 47 entrants brought with them a sample of their most recent thirst quencher for testing. They were all tested for over 182 different water contaminants. Some are organic compounds; some are inorganic and believe it or not, even things that go bump in the night. Well, at least wiggle day and night! Oh please! Test away folks," she announced as she shivered. "All the samples that were tested came back with unbelievable scores. Consider this . . . only one rated so pure, it won the Blue Ribbon. But officials don't know who to congratulate! He or she left instructions saying, and I quote, 'I just want everyone to know . . . it can be done.' Then finished his note with, 'If I win, I will attend the San Francisco Water

Festival for the big reveal.' Apparently, he left a secret code on the message that was left with the container for the judges that will confirm his identity in San Francisco . . . as the . . . water-istas?"

The co-anchor looked to her in mock confusion. "Is that what you'd call these . . . water purifier people?" she chortled. "And where do these water aficionados go from here?"

"Well," she answered, "the top winners from all over the nation are headed to San Francisco for this weekend's Bay Area Water Works Days. You know, I shouldn't be presumptuous, the mystery person could be a her, not necessarily a him."

The co-anchor then looked to the anchor and said, "True. Sounds like this anonymous water master could change life across the globe! You know, I think they could be called wateristas, like a barista is for coffee? Water-tenders? Water-purifiers? Hmmm . . . Up next . . . Have you ever wondered . . ."

Then another news feed was spliced in saying, "City of Portland Development Services is asking the public for their help. Some thieves have broken into the offices overnight, and besides making a mess of things, escaped with some old archived city blue prints. They are not sure why they would want these outdated prints. If you or anyone you know has any information concerning these stolen blue prints, you are asked to call the Portland Police Department, at 800-555-0199 to share your information."

Perry began walking back towards his desk, before looking at Craigs and Benson. "Well, you can scratch that plan. You guys got the wrong ones," he said with a grimace as he glared at the two of them standing behind Jahnni and Mr. Tropopoulis.

Then Perry said matter-of-factly, almost like a side note, "Nice contest, huh, Arnie? I used my dad's research papers. Surprised even myself! I'm astonished you or your brother didn't enter this year. Biggest prize ever. So, where is he?"

Jahnni was now quite sure Benson and Craigs were not Portland Airport Police, but possibly armed security guards or something like that. She watched and listened as Perry continued speaking directly to his two hired goons. "You stole the ones that PDX used when they moved the airport and built over the top of the previous buried tunnels!" Then Perry added, "I specifically said I wanted the 'original' originals."

They looked at each other. Benson shrugged his shoulders. "You said grab the originals, so we found the ones that were listed as the originals."

"No, you didn't. You got . . . oh never mind. How many times must I explain how this system used to work? Forget it. Arnie here can help me . . . or else," he said as he turned and bore his eyes into Mr. Tropopoulis's. "You know Arnie, no matter how thorough we searched, we could never find, or understand how this piping system could ever have done more than water the garden, or give us such a beautiful waterfall display. It is so basic, what was left buried, that it just didn't make sense. Dead ends everywhere. No access. Just your basic plumbing. Sort of. The pipes were an odd size, but extremely useful with the basic system. All I wanted was the original blue prints. Is that so much to ask Arnie? Is it?" he asked sternly as he paced back and forth behind his desk.

He turned back to look at Mr. Tropopoulis again before continuing, "One night I sat struggling over the fact that my dad mentioned a long time ago that everything was hidden; buried; concealed. I mean, I was just a kid, really. But I knew it meant something. It dawned on me the blue prints that were handed over to the Port were specially designed to conceal the underground web that was really buried *under* the ones that were *shown* to be buried! Or rather, there was at least another level, possibly more . . . Who would even know? Don't get me wrong, the simple water purification allowances make for a spectacular waterfall. But let's be honest Arnie, we both know that you are the key to this dilemma. So where are the prints Arnie?"

Jahnni was more confused with the added information she gathered. *Mr. Tropopoulis is involved? I mean, how can this quiet man have anything to do with any of this?*

"Were you going to meet Zale, in San Fran Arnie?" Perry leaned forward to ask. "Is that where he lives now?"

"I really don't know what you want from me. I no see Zale for many, many years. You have my bag right there. If I have anything to give someone, wouldn't you find it in my suitcase?" Mr. Tropopoulis offered in a low innocent voice. "Why do you want these old things?"

Perry paced while staring down Jahnni and Mr. Tropopoulis. He stopped for a moment then slowly started speaking in a calm sing-song manner. "You do remember me, right Arnie? You aren't so old you could have forgotten such important people in your life?"

Mr. Tropopoulis squinted his eyes like he was trying to decipher hieroglyphics, and then said, "Yes, I do."

"I am Perry Prattle," he said, pronouncing it Prawtlay as if he was a French Dignitary. Jahnni assumed he wanted to impress people with a French sounding name. "My dad worked with you and Zale. He was one of the original scientists that developed the water purifying process alongside good ol' Uncle Zale. I am the head of the Port now, as you can see of course. I thought this position would allow me to freely comb the underground area once I figured out how to get down there. I knew the original development would still be there, because I just didn't believe Zale would destroy his baby completely. I'm going to have my own blue prints developed, once I find it, match it with my father's work, and sell the unparalleled water purification to China for more money than Bill Gates is worth. Yes, I knew this was my fate, my calling, you might say." He stared at them with unfocused eyes.

Jahnni caught her breath and said, "This sounds like an impossible plan, Mr. Prattle," pronouncing his name to rhyme with rattle. "You can't just dig up the ground under an airport."

"No," he offered, "not just anyone could, but the right people could be working on the plumbing for the sake of the Port. If I need to go that far, that is. I'll just get the right people who will follow directions and shut up about it. I don't believe there needs to be any digging . . . so to speak. Just access. So, the original plans would be better." He paused to make sure he had their full attention. "And once everything is in place, I can rebuild it on a much smaller scale, and then sell everything.

The Chinese like techie stuff you know. Even they didn't have this water technology down. They're probably still working on it using shells, sand, charcoals and hope. They still depend on chlorine, large amounts of chlorine, and we all know that isn't a good idea. The world needs me and I plan to be their hero. Zale was way ahead of his time. Pity he got shut down and disappeared. Probably in hiding all these years from embarrassment. Right Arnie?" Perry laughed and laughed but no one else was laughing.

"If this is true, you don't have the methods and all the scientific data, or anything yet," Jahnni noted. "Why now? Why all this?" she asked as she waved her arm motioning to the entire airport dilemma.

"No, but I have my father's work that is clearly documented. Each scientist worked on a different portion of the water study. And each person had a hand in the original construction. I will have more of the pieces when I have Arnie's plans, and Zale Baptiste's underground safe . . . or rather underground vault," Perry answered like he was adding up a 'to-do' list.

This made Mr. Tropopoulis's head jerk up and he asked, "Underground what?"

"Oh, so you do know about the vault, Arnie?" Perry asked. "I always wondered why my dad said no one could find Zale. No one would find his work. Then when my dad . . . passed, I found this odd, misshapen rock alongside his original scientific contributions to the project. Etched in it was the number eleven. I pondered this for many years. Then when I was watching the Pope on TV one day, for some reason, it all came to me! Roman. Roman numerals. It wasn't an eleven. It was the Roman numeral two. Due, as the Italians say."

He traced the air with his hand to form the number two. "If this was so, then there must be a number one. And together this would open . . . what? Made from a rock, a shape that looks like it is one half of another rock. You have no idea how this puzzled me and how much sleep I have lost for many years. Oh, the secrets that my dad took to the grave with him when he, well, so unexpectedly . . . passed." He paused to let that sink in as he sneered. "Passed, and so untimely," he added, a fake frown adorning his chin.

"You killed your own dad?" Jahnni whispered with more sadness than fear.

"Let's just say he had a drowning accident on the De-schutes River," Perry corrected, "while collecting water samples." He added, "how else was I going to get access to his Will and safety deposit boxes?"

Jahnni was beginning to feel fear creeping up and clinging to her back. The hair on her arms stood up and she felt chills go up her neck, into her hair. She shook it off with a shiver. "All this for water?" she asked incredulously.

"No," Perry answered. "All this for what's owed me! For all the years my dad spent developing a water purification system with good ol' Uncle Zale . . . I hated calling him that!" Perry raised his voice in anger and slammed his hand on his desk. "He wasn't my uncle! But he may well have been with the amount of time they spent together. It was always Uncle Zale this and Uncle Zale that—he was always working with Uncle

Zale. My dad couldn't make a single one of my ball games! Didn't have time to take me to the father/son boy-scout camp outs. Never came to my piano recitals." He was now pacing and sweating. His jaw moved back and forth like he was grinding his teeth. "I WAS ROBBED OF MY CHILDHOOD BY THIS, THIS, WATER!" He then coughed and gathered himself together, realizing that Jahnni was staring at him in his moment of lost control, and Mr. Tropopoulis was looking at him with sad eyes. He continued, "And now . . . I believe, I deserve to . . . own it. At least until I sell it for more money than you can even possibly imagine in your little brains."

Jahnni didn't know what to say. This seemed so bizarre to her. Sharing long held plans about what he would do about everything in the future was risky. Jahnni knew that she now knew too much, especially about Mr. Prattle's father's death. Mr. Tropopoulis knew even more. She asked Perry, "So, what now, I mean right . . . now?"

"I have waited a long time for this very day," Perry mumbled with a monotone voice. Then, he stared at Mr. Tropopoulis, "This very unfolding of such grand exposure. I knew he would come for the vault eventually. I put the pieces together and I know the vault is below . . . somewhere. When I finally figured out what the rock was for, I knew there must be another one, and once I have them together, I could open the vault. He needs me just as much as I need him now. If Arnie doesn't have it, then obviously, Zale does."

Silence settled in the room. Craigs and Benson didn't even seem to flinch. *He must have included them in his plans,* Jahnni thought. But, Jahnni bet that soon Perry would make sure that they would have an 'accident'. He didn't appear to be the type to share.

Chapter 16

Never Underestimate the Old Guy

Very calmly, Mr. Tropopoulis asked, "May I use the facilities please?"

"No!" Perry snapped.

"I am old Perry, and have need to relieve myself immediately. Please sir."

Perry nodded at the portly Craigs. "Go with him. Two minutes!"

"What are you going to tell the news crews, and FBI? What about TSA and Homeland Security? They are down there waiting." But what Jahnni really wanted to ask was when he planned to get rid of her and Mr. Tropopoulis, and how he planned to do it. *Maybe we could escape,* she realized, but the thought seemed unlikely as her eyes landed on Craigs and Benson. *Maybe Beau would figure out something and rescue us. Ya . . . maybe that's what is going on right now. Beau is probably figuring this all out and is going to help us somehow, but I'm not waiting on anyone. We'll have to find a way to get away from this deranged maniac on our own.*

"Well, funny you should ask, doll. I have security data showing you, yes you and Arnie, accessing bypass doors. And it appears that you have three other accomplices. Why Benson and Craigs didn't find them is just a trivial matter. I have all the proof I need. Sounds like you are in big trouble, missy! Your other friends I saw on camera earlier; well as soon as we catch them too . . . gee . . . I'm sorry to say that you won't live long enough to make a conflicting statement," Perry calmly shared.

"You're going to KILL US?" Jahnni said breathlessly, leaving her mouth open and her eyes wide with fright. Her knees felt rubbery, barely able to keep her standing. Her mind was a screen of flashes, pictures from yesterday, last year, her youth. *It's not time! I . . . I . . . don't know how to be nothing. I didn't do anything to deserve this! And I can't marry Beau if I'm dead! What is wrong with this guy? He's ruining everything!* She looked at Perry's mouth as more words spilled out.

"Eventually," Perry said, taunting her with the unknown time frame. "But for now . . ." he stopped to watch Mr. Tropopoulis and Craigs come back into the room, "I have a statement to make to the press and I have an official meeting to ascertain how to capture those other two terrorists that are roaming the airport to make things difficult for me. You see, being the Port Manager, if I call them terrorists, that is all I'll have to say. The word alone will make them want to shoot first and ask questions later when they corner them."

Perry stared back and forth between Mr. Tropopoulis and

Jahnni. His eyes seemed to dart around like his brain was on overdrive. "It was quite fortuitous of me to think to tell the Port Police earlier today that I received a call threatening our precious fountain. Did you hear my fake gunshots and shattering glass sounds I played over the intercom in the C concourse after the EVAC message played? That was my beautiful theatrics to get the concourse cleared if anyone was still milling around." He laughed out loud a little too long, as if he was the best comedian anyone had ever heard. After glancing at himself in the mirror and adjusting the top of his hair and sweeping the sides back with his palms, he added, "That should keep anyone else away from my favorite bypass door at the end of the concourse. If I need it later. And, once I gather up your other three friends that have been frolicking through the airport bypass doors with you . . ." Perry paused to glare at Craigs and Benson and asked, "So tell me why you didn't find the other three and bring them too?"

But Craigs and Benson both shrugged and looked at each other, not understanding who he was talking about. Craigs answered him after extending a palm up and motioning to Jahnni and Mr. Tropopoulis, "We thought we happened upon this employee and her grandpa while we were looking for 'Johnny.' We didn't see anyone else."

"What? Don't you get it? This. Is. Jahnni!" Perry growled while opening his hand and extending his arm like he was introducing them. "You still didn't figure it out when I spoke to Arnie here?"

Jahnni interrupted the ongoing side-conversation Perry

was having with Benson and Craigs to protest, "Wait. One is just a kid! He, in fact all of us, are innocent! We haven't done anything to deserve to be treated like this! We are simply trying to get out of here! You have to at least leave the kid alone. He is just a U.M.!"

"Not likely. We can't be responsible if your airline lost a kid in the confusion, and someone else, someone unscrupulous probably, found him with all the other passengers being shuttled away from the airport," he said, taunting her with fake concern and laughing at his own wit. "Such bad publicity for First Class Air . . . again. And you being a terrorist and all, trying to plant a bomb in the fountain. I mean, what a great asset you have become to me. I couldn't have planned it any better. While the Port is guarding the fountain upstairs, we will be opening up the wall and finally gaining access to the previous system down below. I know it's there. I know it."

By this point, he was sitting down in his chair, leaning back and watching them for a reaction. "See here!" he added, "While you were gallivanting around the airport, I already started working on your suicide confession they will find in your pocket when they find your body. Your conscience will get the best of you and you won't know of any way to make amends so you'll . . . you know . . . check out. In fact, as soon as I realized that you had devious plans, I . . ." at this he made some key strokes and deactivated her access to any part of any secure area in the airport. "I will inform the authorities that I was able to track you by your badge. I'll let them know how I cornered you by allowing your badge to stay activated temporarily. Craigs here will be more than happy to do the job. And now, I will also deactivate our other little friends in white, now that I figured out who they are. I can't believe I didn't figure this out sooner; working here in my airport, under my nose as baggage handlers," he mumbled. "Oh, and your friend Samantha. I recognized her from the PDX Customer Service team meetings too. I am deactivating her also. If they're still down there, they're stuck until we find and eliminate them as well. You have really made my plans difficult, but at the same time, oddly improved."

"Wait, why would I commit suicide? That doesn't make sense," Jahnni asked, puzzled with his ramblings. "Why would I call in a bomb threat?"

"I don't know! You are the one who did it, and is going to have regrets. Who knows what the mental ramblings of a lunatic mean. Let them figure that out," Perry snapped back. "You're probably upset about something. I'll just blame everything on you."

"Whatever. Anyone who knows me knows that I would never do something so stupid. You aren't going to get away with any of this. Besides, if you can see us on the cameras then the Port can see us as well. So, they are probably looking for us already," Jahnni said hopefully, to call his bluff.

"Nope! Everything was shut down . . . for them . . . during that time. I am the only one who had access. Even the doors are deactivated for everyone else. For everyone . . . except me and the few doors that I have released," he said, his pride in himself beaming like a child. "That's the only reason your

151

badge worked anywhere. I still control a specific portion of the security doors."

Any hope Jahnni had suddenly began seeping away. Her mind was numb with the thought that maybe no one else even knew she, Sam and the others were missing. The more she let go of hope, the worse she felt. She asked if she could sit. The rubbery knees were back and her heart was pounding, sending the beat whooshing in her ears. She realized Beau must be right. *The masked gunmen, or rather gun people, were really the good guys. The Port Police, or rather these security guys, Craigs and Benson, were the bad guys. This all must have played out sooner than they expected and these new guys hadn't gotten back their SIDA and Customs clearance for their badges yet. Or maybe they are just security and not hired at the Port? That must be why he was remotely scanning them in each door. I wonder how he finagled private security guards for himself . . . and what reason did he give to have it okayed?* she asked herself. *Somehow, we need to get to Beau, Samantha and Crutch. Then maybe we can go to whomever . . . the Police, TSA, and FBI, whoever will listen and protect us while we try to tell our story. Hopefully, they went ahead and crawled up the bag belt to get help.* She lifted her head and stared straight ahead.

"Craigs, Benson," Perry ordered.

"Ya boss," they said in unison.

"Benson, you come with me. Craigs, keep an eye on them until I get back from my meeting. Then I'll decide when to . . . just keep them here until I get back."

Perry shrugged his jacket on and tightened his tie in the

mirror. Benson stood at attention. Craigs stared at Jahnni and Mr. Tropopoulis like he wanted to be the one to deliver the fatal blow. She was marked as already "guilty" but she knew the truth. She wasn't going to give Craigs the benefit of thinking she was afraid him, even though she was. Her eyes met his and she told herself, *hide all emotion on my face, but look at him blankly, holding his gaze until he turns away. I refuse to cry. I'm stronger than this. Mr. Tropopoulis needs me.*

Jahnni slowly reached over to Mr. Tropopoulis and held his hand. She watched as Perry grabbed a pile of papers off the printer, then he reached for the door. Perry and Benson walked out the door without looking back.

Mr. Tropopoulis sat upright and appeared calm. He looked all around the room slowly, like he was admiring the décor. He smiled at Jahnni and winked before turning his head to speak to Craigs. "May I choose a book off the shelf to read? To pass the time until Mr. Perry Prattle return?"

Craigs snarled, then slowly walked toward them. He nodded and walked with Mr. Tropopoulis to the bookshelf, keeping Jahnni in his sights and himself between the door and them both. He waved his hand to indicate to *go ahead.*

"Janie, would you like a book also?" Mr. Tropopoulis asked innocently. "There are so many to choose from. Even classics. See?" He pointed directly to a spot on the shelf.

"Huh?" she said as she looked up. "No, no thank you. I couldn't make sense of the words at a time like this."

"Sure, you do Janie . . . Choose book from these right here," he pleaded politely as he pointed again at the same spot.

"I choose one that is good for . . . the noggin," Mr. Tropopoulis said as he smiled and tapped his head. "Unless, uh, you are . . . still having tummy ache?"

"No really, I'm . . . okay, maybe I will." She had changed her mind when she looked at the area on the bookshelf that Mr. Tropopoulis was pointing to. "Maybe it will help take my mind off . . . my stomach ache too."

All three stood at the bookshelf. Jahnni and Mr. Tropopoulis perused the many books like they just couldn't decide which one to choose. She held her arm across her belly, making a light, painful moaning sound every few seconds, wincing enough for Craigs to see it.

"Janie, I just cannot decide! I believe I will choose . . . two . . . right now," Mr. Tropopoulis said as he smiled.

Suddenly Jahnni doubled over and started making slight gagging noises and seemed to be holding back from hurling all over Craigs' shoes. She covered her mouth as if that would hold it all in. Craigs looked down at his new shiny shoes and grimaced. While his head was down, looking between Jahnni's gagging and lurching, and his shiny shoes, Mr. Tropopoulis grabbed the rock. *The* rock. Number II. The bookend that was holding up a row of classic literature. Then with a swift swipe, he reached up and whacked Craigs on the back of the head. He fell forward and crashed into Jahnni just as she was raising back up. She tried to hold him up with her arms, but she couldn't, and she fell to the ground with him. He was now on top of her as she struggled to get out from under his large menacing frame. She scooted her lower body out from under him but every time she tried to raise herself up, her head was yanked backwards. She stopped struggling to reassess how to get free of Craigs and realized her hair was simply caught on his watch. She finally just grasped the lock of hair and yanked it free, breaking it off mid-shaft. She raised up, checked the back of his head and noted that he wasn't bleeding too much. Still, she checked his pulse. She wanted to escape, but she didn't want to add manslaughter to her activities today.

She looked at Mr. Tropopoulis and asked breathlessly, "How did you get up the nerve to do that?"

"Oh . . . Well . . . I needed to rescue you. So, I did." He stepped over the big lump on the floor.

Jahnni lurched behind the desk and saw that the security program that controlled the employee badges was up and running. She saw that her name as well as Samantha's had been moved over to the "EXCEPTION-FULL BLOCK" side of the page. *Great airport security, leaving the program open you idiot,* she thought. She clicked on her name and moved it to "FULL ACCESS." She didn't know what category she was in before, as there were several categories depending on where people worked and what their title was. But full access was fine with her right about now. Next, she moved Samantha's name over to the full access side. While she was at it, she saw the two foreign names that she couldn't pronounce, but recognized on the flight manifest, and moved their names back to full access as well. *These must be the two in those weird white hazmat- looking suits. I hope Beau is right cuz I just gave them permission to chase us if he isn't. Or do something horrible if they are up to no good.* She then clicked SAVE, and exited the program. In the flurry of the mayhem, she realized that the security badge program wasn't supposed to be run out of Perry's computer.

He must have created some type of access because the Port Badging Office controls the authorization of badges, she thought. *I have no idea what is going on here, but at least I can slow him down for a while.*

She reached to begin the process to completely shut down the computer but on a whim, right clicked the program's shortcut that was on Perry's desktop on his computer screen and deleted it, sending it to the recycling bin. Then she held the start button down until the computer just shut down completely. She glanced around trying to figure out how else to slow him down when he returned, then she just pulled the plug out of the wall. Not feeling satisfied, she yanked the plug out of the back of the computer and shoved it into the large potted plant over by the book shelf, practically shoving it into the dirt. "Happy hunting," she said under her breath. Then looking at the computer tower, she thought, *I should have thrown his name into the NO ACCESS side. Damn! There's no time now.*

"Janie . . . hurry! We must get away!" Mr. Tropopoulis begged.

They both crept to the door to try to hear what was on the other side. Although she wasn't sure who may be there, besides the one security guard monitoring the screens, she decided to slowly open the door and check. Again, it was only the one deeply concentrating security guard staring at the monitors and busying himself with computer clicks. She brushed back her hair with her hands, smoothed her clothes and arranged her badge. They walked out the door quietly, but with their heads up as if they were supposed to be leaving. He didn't look up.

Mr. Tropopoulis had the rock, number II, in his right hand and he was grasping it firmly. Under his left arm was his prized Brown Plaid Bag that he had scooped up as they walked to the door.

Jahnni and Mr. Tropopoulis opened the main office door and glanced out before fully accessing the hallway. They started to head for the elevator when they heard it faintly ding as it left one of the floors below. It was heading straight for this floor. Jahnni spun back and forth as she looked around for another way out. Her arms swung left, then right, her head searching for an escape. Then she saw the security door about 20 feet away. Slightly closer was a snack machine. She didn't know if her badge would even work that fast after being re-activated, so she decided that the door was not an option. She pointed to the corner for Mr. Tropopoulis and made her own decision. The elevator dinged twice as it arrived at their floor. She scrambled to hide on the other side of the snack machine, her back boring into the wall. Mr. Tropopoulis froze with his back to the wall by the big silk tree that sits to the right of the elevator when exiting it. Perry Prattle waited for the elevator doors to fully open, then walked directly out of the elevator, turned to the left, and walked towards his office. Jahnni heard his door pushing open and the rustling of clothes following him in. The elevator doors began to close.

At the last second, as Perry Prattle and Benson crossed into the office, Mr. Tropopoulis took two strides to the elevator, knocking the plant into a swirl as if it was trying to fall. He blocked the door open with his foot and the doors reversed from closing in time for him and Jahnni to scurry in. Jahnni quickly scanned her badge, put her code in, and then she placed her print on the pad. She started banging on the "door close" button repeatedly. Then she kept pushing the 'B' for basement. Her fingers were shaking, as her mind kept flashing a picture of Perry's door only a few feet away. Too fearful to even look toward it, she kept her focus on the buttons and willed the metal doors to begun closing. Mr. Tropopoulis stood between Jahnni and the door, with his hand against the frame. She closed her eyes to scream in her head, *please badge, work! Please be online already!*

The office door banged open and pounding feet lumbered toward the elevator. At the same time, the elevator doors began to move towards each other. Perry ran towards the door, lunging his arm forward but his fingers missed blocking the closing elevator doors by a hair's breadth. Jahnni kept pushing the close button, hoping to override the button commands on the outside of the elevator door if Mr. Prattle tried to punch the down button over and over. When the elevator began to move downward, she leaned back against the wall of the elevator, saying nothing, but smiling in relief as she felt her pounding heart begin to slow its rhythm.

The elevator seemed to be moving in slow motion. Jahnni's mind raced as she reached to comfort Mr. Tropopoulis.

She thought she could feel Mr. Tropopoulis's heartbeat as she took his hand into hers. Or was it her own pulse keeping rhythm? She kept thinking over and over she must get to Beau and the others, although she wasn't sure if they would still be there waiting.

Mr. Tropopoulis just stood there with a smile on his face. "Don't worry Janie. They will not find us. I can get us out of airport now, and we will be safe. Please trust me. I am old man now in body, but my mind is alive and very well! I know . . . what you call . . . cool shortcut!"

With that, Jahnni decided to trust him. She saw it in his eyes. She saw it in Beau's eyes too. She could trust them. She would trust them. Together, they'd find safety and figure out who to trust "out there." The only thing she thought to do when they reached the bagwell floor, or basement as the elevator called it, was to grab something to wedge in the door so that the elevator doors won't be able to close. If they couldn't close, the elevator wouldn't operate and return to the floor where they just escaped from. She thought that might buy them some more time before Mr. Prattle realized that the elevator was not coming back.

Chapter 17

Meanwhile, in the Bagwell

"How long should we wait here, Mr. Harleyman, I mean Beau? And why didn't you do something? You have a gun. You could have stopped them from taking Jahnni and Mr. Tropopoulis," Samantha demanded.

"First, a gun doesn't mean you are the automatic winner. They had guns too. Brains before brawn. I had to choose between hope that I could take over the situation, and knowledge that possibly you, Jahnni, Crutch or Pops could have been shot. We have time. Patience and time wins before guns and confrontation sometimes. As for how long to wait, if they don't come back in the next few minutes, I'll grab the bag those security-looking guys missed and we'll crawl out through the opening up there at the ticket counter and get help for Jahnni and Pops," Beau answered Samantha before adding, "If something happens to Pops, I will spend my life hunting down everyone who is responsible."

Samantha and Crutch looked up at Beau, a confused look on their faces. Sam began to ask, "Why do you feel so responsible for . . ."

"Okay, here's what we're going to do," Beau said at the same time that Sam started speaking, but stopped and lifted his head up to the sound of light footsteps running in their direction. It sounded like someone jogging softly . . . on tip toes. The three sat back in the cart. Beau released his weapon from his side and faced the area where he heard the footsteps echoing. He waited, his gun a last resort if the same uniformed guys that took Jahnni and Pops saw them in the carts.

Closer and closer the footsteps sounded before they stopped. In the new silence, Beau listened more intently. Sam held onto Crutch, pulling his head into her shoulder, and burying her face into his hair. No one moved. They waited.

"Whirrrr . . . reep, reep. Whirrrr . . . ah ah ah ah reep reep," came the sound of a bird somewhere near.

"Whirrrr . . . reep, reep. Whirrrr . . . ah ah ah ah reep reep," Beau answered in half whistle, half throated answer.

Samantha whipped her head up and stared at Beau with her mouth hanging open. "What the . . .?" she mouthed with wide eyes, as he in turn smiled back at her.

Crutch simply whispered very low, "Cool bird call."

Beau put his weapon back in the holster and started to climb out of the cart. Sam grabbed his arm and shook her head in a wide-eyed silent protest.

"It's okay. Jahnni and Pops are back. It's safe," he said as he touched her arm to assure her.

Jahnni came around the corner, holding Mr. Tropopou-lis's hand. She had led him into the bagwell where they all embraced. Beau hugged Pops and kissed the top of his head when his hat fell off, but then reached down, picked it up and placed it back on Pop's head. Beau made eye contact with Jahnni, narrowed his eyes a bit and smiled, shaking his head with relief. They didn't say anything, but Beau felt the weight of the world fall off his shoulders, if only momentarily.

Finally, he reached for her hand, and rested his other hand on her shoulder and whispered, "Thanks. I won't forget this." Then he brought her to him in a relieved embrace, still holding her hand to his chest.

"I won't either." But after an awkward pause, Jahnni pulled away and looked up at Beau, shook her head and then added, "Especially once I find out how you two know the same bird call. Plus, we have so much to tell you. Mr. Tropopoulis says he knows a shortcut to get us out safe. But first, I still want to try again to go up the belt to see if it is open at the top because that still might get us out. Those security guys, Benson and Craigs, will undoubtedly be back here soon, so we need to hurry. They are crazy and dangerous! Well . . . maybe not Craigs, the big one, he probably won't be back. Mr. Tropopoulis kind of rendered him useless, but I will explain that later."

"No," Crutch interjected as he paced in place. "What hap-pened Mr. Tor . . . Torpop . . . Troppelupagus? Tell us what happened."

Mr. Tropopoulis looked at Crutch with a gentle gaze, "It's no important right now. But we tell you soon. Oh, you can call me Mr. T. I think it easier to say than confusing me with big furry elephant." He chuckled, almost in a whisper then nodded to Jahnni and Samantha also.

Chapter 18

So Much to Say
So Little Time

After they listened for anyone coming, and checked around the corner, Jahnni moved quickly to the bag carousel and pulled herself up through the first opening that normally would be spitting bags out onto the carousel belt. Then she began crawling on her hands and knees toward the curve up near the ceiling, knowing that she would be able to get a better view of the ticket counter opening, up above; if it was not shut and locked that is. *It's a long shot, but just maybe the counter agents forgot to secure the bag belt gate in all the commotion before they evacuated. Certainly, a major security breach, but in the pandemonium, someone could have made a mistake.* She glanced down at the knees of her pants, and paused long enough to glance at her hands. *Ugh! I look like I have been crawling through pencil lead, and chalk!* she thought. Jahnni decided there wasn't any time to worry about that now, so she continued crawling up and around the corner. *There's too much light coming through the rubber PVC curtains. That's a good sign,* she told herself. *That means the belt door is open.*

When Jahnni got to the top, she peeked through the heavy strips to see where she could go to. There was a gap in the counters between First Class Air's ticket counter and Southwest's that was to the left of this bag gate. It gave her a view of some of the area in front of the ticket counters. She could see a bomb sniffing dog leading its handler. Homeland Security agents or FBI she wasn't sure from this vantage point, were gathered about 20 feet from her. Since the tall ticket counters were directly in front of her, she imagined that if they all hurried, they could exit together and approach the police to explain what has happened to them. She couldn't believe her luck that safety was only a minute away, or rather however long it took Mr. T to crawl up the belt. *Maybe I should go out now and let them know that there are four people still left down there that need protection. And I'll be able to let them know about the FBI agent with us and tell them about Perry Prattle.* She put her hand on the rubber curtains, ready to part them and stick her head out as the next pair of officials started walking towards the ticket counter. *It is now or never,* she convinced herself. She had just decided to go for help first. Help was only a few feet away. She leaned forward and started to part the rubber curtain to climb out.

That voice! I know that voice! Jahnni thought as she slowly set the rubber PVC curtain back so it wouldn't sway. *What is he doing?*

"Yes! He's right over there by the public elevators sirs. He is resting an ice bag on his head. Quick! He needs to be taken to the hospital!" Mr. Prattle ordered as the EMT's pushed what sounded like a squeaking gurney past the ticket counter. "Officers, I would like to wait until the FBI gets done with those people over there so I can explain this to you all. Oh, never mind, here they come now . . . Okay, I am Mr. Perry Prattle, the Port of Portland Manager here at PDX. Like I just told one of our Port Police officers, there were originally two employees that I had identified by their badge access who I believe are heavily involved with this situation. They even had the audacity to access my office and accost one of my security guards when he challenged them. That's him right over there, officers," Mr. Prattle said breathlessly as he pointed to the big menacing Mr. Craigs. "They said something about a bomb, and blasting the water fountain in the food court. Then something or other about hearing them talk about some other accomplices . . . having help on the inside . . . and about their accomplices wearing some type of white over-garment and carrying big firearms of some sort. He was a little rattled trying to get his bearings and give me a report when I found him on the floor."

Mr. Prattle stumbled over the words motoring off his tongue. "I pulled up security footage and thought I recognized the two in white, so I pulled up their badge access of the security doors and then their badge photos . . . along with these other two. Basically, they are sick individuals. I can barely piece this all together. They need to be captured because the airline agent held a device in her hands that I can only imagine is a bomb activation device. And she bragged to my officer, right before she assaulted him, that she is armed so he better not follow her. She has a gun, officers . . . In a secured area . . . She has sneaked in a weapon . . ."

His story seemed to grow as he talked on and on. Jahnni was beginning to get confused herself, listening to his concocted tale of woe.

"The entire area has been locked down but I bet they will try to activate their plans by accessing the water fountain. Take no chances at apprehending the lunatics! I am very concerned that we need to finish doing a complete evacuation of the building now. Not just passengers and most employees, like we have already done." Then he finished passing out copies of their pictures to everyone there. "Here, this is their official badge pictures and descriptions. These two are holding three other passengers as hostages, but I am not sure of the hostage's names yet. I do know that one is an innocent child. A U.M. You know . . . an unaccompanied minor whose parents entrusted the airline to care for him during his travels. Poor family. They must be distraught. Maybe I can get the U.M list from the First Class Air Station Manager and we can have them begin calling to see which U.M. hasn't been accounted for yet. This one here," he pointed to Jahnni's photo, "she is the one who is armed and has some type of device in her hand. You'll probably have to shoot her at first sight, before she fires on your own officers first," he offered.

It sounded to Jahnni as if he was hoping that they would do just that. *What should I do? What if they believe him and shoot us!* She searched her mind, racing through options, but with everything she thought of, she kept imagining them all being shot before they could explain. She craned her head a little closer without disturbing the curtain.

She could see the side of the FBI agent as he held his hand up and said "Let us do our job and you do yours. Thank you for this critical information. We'll get it to the special agent overseeing this investigation here at the airport right away." Then the FBI agent began talking into his SAT phone and waving his arm, shouting directions to other people somewhere. Everyone began moving away from the counter and their voices began fading. It was pandemonium that Jahnni had never heard, or seen before. Her mouth hung open in complete shock. She could only see visions of running for help, only to be shot for approaching an officer. *Oh, my gosh, how are we going to survive this mess?* she cried in her head. *That liar! There must be a way to safely get out of here. Maybe once we're safe, we can negotiate and get them to listen to us . . . maybe they will believe us and see that Mr. Prattle is the one who is lying! But why would they believe US? How can we prove that HE is the one that is behind all this? Maybe they'll believe Beau. Ya, Beau can talk to them! I need get back to the others. I hope they're still safe.*

Before Jahnni backed away, she saw Mr. Prattle standing there alone, looking around with a worried frown on his face. *Probably wondering if they bought his convoluted story. Faker,* Jahnni thought. *I hope they didn't believe you.*

Jahnni started to quietly back down and away from the opening, fearful that someone would hear her. Mostly, she feared the dogs being sent to get her. Once she got to a section that was wider, and no longer a flat rubber belt, she turned around to face the direction she could start rolling in a sitting position. The rollers sped up her descent and she came around the bend to another rubber belt that she had to start crawling on again. When she had previously climbed up, she straddled the rollers by placing her feet on the outer edges. Before coming around the last bend of the belt, she waited and listened. Not hearing anyone, she finished her descent and dropped onto the bagwell's carousel belt. After a long five seconds, Beau walked out from behind a cart, put his arm around her and held his other arm out to the others.

Sam whispered in a pleading voice, "You took forever! We were beginning to think that something happened to you! I thought maybe you got caught by those two guys again!"

"No. Well, one of those guys is on his way to the hospital thanks to Mr. T. He saved us! But we have to get away from here!" Jahnni whispered quickly. Then after a short pause to stare into Beau's comforting green eyes, she let out a calming breath and went on, "The Port Manager is the one who held us upstairs. And not because he is a good guy. He has some weird plan I don't understand, and he said, because we got in his way, he planned on . . ." she paused when she looked at Crutch but finished the other part of her story, "but we got away! There is so much we need to tell you. He is up there telling the police that we are the ones who have a bomb and we are crazy and he is so worried for everyone! Can you believe that? *He* is blaming all of this on *us*! Mainly me. He told them that I had a gun and was also going to blow up the fountain . . . I mean . . . what an evil man this guy has turned out to be," Jahnni whispered so loud, her voice began to crack. Tears sprung up in her eyes even though she told herself she wouldn't cry. She was beginning to feel void of hope, but as she started to tell Beau that, she looked at him and realized that even though she didn't know what to do, that he certainly would. She gazed into his eyes again and felt that calming sense of safety, which was exactly what she needed.

Beau turned to Mr. T. "So, you said you know a way to get us out of here? You really know a secret way, Pops?"

"Yes! You must trust me, Beau and Janie! I can help," Mr. T pleaded, looking at Beau and then turning to Jahnni before adding, "I used to, uh, work here many years ago, when I was a younger man."

"That's good enough for me. Okay, lead the way Pops. Oh wait . . ." Beau said as he reached into the cart they sat in before. "This . . . is a family heirloom. This bag comes with us!" And the scratchy, itchy bag that bled oranges and browns together into a woven pattern of obsolete fashion was now in the possession of Beau. He started walking with this bag, and Mr. T held the other one that he had grabbed from the Port Office. He clutched it close to his chest and started walking towards the corridor, as if he really did know where he was going.

"Wait," Jahnni said in a very loud, demanding whisper. "I'm sorry. But rules are rules and sometimes you have to figure out a way to follow procedures the best way possible."

They all looked at her, and turned to look at each other.

"Huh?" they said in unison.

"I need to do a security search on your bags," she said with authority. "I'm sorry, but this one," pointing at Mr. T's bag, "came down after being in someone else's possession and had not cleared security at all. And this one," she added as she pointed to the one Beau was holding, "a passenger accessed after the bag cleared CTX screening and a hand search after it was in a secured area."

"Wait, what, huh? How do you know if my bag was actu-ally hand searched?" Beau asked confused.

"Oh, I meant, uh, possibly searched," Jahnni said, cover-ing the fact that she did go down and talk to the screeners about Beau's bag. But her reasons were blended. It was a cross between security and romantic intrigue but there was no time to explain that. Like ever.

"We don't have time for this Jahn. We are not waiting to have these bags searched. You need to let go of this need to fol-low every rule that pops up," Beau began lecturing. He looked at her face as he finished telling her what was going to happen . . . and not happen.

Jahnni bit the side of her bottom lip, torn between know-ing he was right and worrying that she would be in more trou-ble for what would normally be an incident that would get her immediately fired. She looked around, rubbed her lips togeth-er and tried to explain. Her eyes darted back and forth from one bag to the other as she tried to just let it go. She started to say something, then closed her lips again.

Jahnni hurriedly grabbed Mr. T's bag, mumbling about

security, bad guys, directives . . . "I, I, can't lose this job. They are going to shoot me, they think I'm the terrorist, I need to make sure, be sure, tell them, let them see . . ." Then starting with Mr. T's bag, she blurted out, asking if there were any sharp items, open razors, or needles in the bags. No one answered, just stared at her. She kept her head down, and continued to check the bag as if her life depended on it. Her moves seemed exaggerated and purposeful.

She ran her hands around the outer edges, bottom, explored the handles, and then ran her hands around the inside edges as well as the entire inside bottom, and inside top. She squeezed all the crumpled and folded items and unraveled them if they felt 'odd.' Flipping the clothes over and then pulling out the shaving kit, she checked every item for secret compartments, even attempting to quickly unscrew the bottom of cans, if it were possible, and checking liquid contents. Any electric razors were thoroughly examined for false bottoms and any other items that appeared alterable were focused on as well.

She began sniffling, keeping her head down but mumbling to Mr. T, "Why do you have these big hard envelopes of papers hidden in the top inside lining of your bag, Mr. T?"

"I just have important things that I do not want to lose, Janie. I keep them there for many years. Like a safe," Mr. T answered. "I think it was good that Mr. Perry Prattle no find them. My personal things. Some of my brother's things. Stuff I keep forever."

She went to grab Beau's bag as she continued her narrative

about getting out of there, stopping Perry before he lies about her to more people, losing her job, people not trusting her ever again . . . when Beau grabbed her by the shoulders and turned her around to face him. Tears were flowing down her cheeks and he looked down at her shaking hands. He grabbed them both, and pulled her close to him first, then enveloped her in a hug saying, "Shhh . . . shhh . . . shhh . . . It's okay Jahnni. You're going to be fine. I promise I will make sure that no one thinks those things. I'll vouch for you. You don't have to do this. It's okay. Shhh . . . It's okay. Please, trust me."

Jahnni muffled her cries into Beaus chest as she tried to calm down. After a couple minutes she finally said, "I, um, still should tag Mr. T's bag for his flight so he can leave it here, and not drag it around though. That's okay, right?"

She pulled away from Beau and glanced around at the others, embarrassed for her lack of self-control at a time when they all needed her. She looked at Samantha.

"Jahnni, Beau's right. You'll be fine. He's got this, because he's right," Sam said as she reached to touch Jahnni's arm.

"Ok, ok," Jahnni said, wiping her cheeks one more time before adding one more teensy thing she needed to do. "I'll just put a quick tag on this and put it in the bagwell office. It'll be secure in the locked office here. I mean, it sounds like we need to keep this bag safe for Mr. T but it's too bulky to drag around. And yours is already tagged, so I'll just . . . you know . . . leave it where it was. Okay?"

"Sure. But we need to go, Jahn," Beau said in a tone that came out gentle, but definitely wasn't a request. Jahnni understood and began moving again in her brisk flow.

"I'm on it, see?" Jahnni said as she hurried her movements. "By the way . . . what is so important about your bag? I get that Mr. T is worried about his private paper stash, but all yours had was basic travel items."

"How do you know what's in…oh never mind," Beau responded, shaking his head like he was confused. "The eternal question. Why does a big guy like me travel with such a . . . an . . . uncomely, old fashioned bag? Well, it belonged to someone close to me a long time ago. It's just a way to remember her."

Hmmm . . . that's odd he would have the same bag as Mr. T. Maybe it was a fashionable bag many years ago, and lots of people had them. Not me. Once I say, 'I do,' I'm not using that bag, she promised herself.

Mr. T had a worried look on his face. "I can take a little extra medication out and carry with me, right?" he inquired. "But I would like to keep this rock, number two, with me instead of packing it."

Jahnni had already turned the thing all over and searched for any way that it could have harbored something internally. Plus, the look on Beau's face said, hurry . . . and yes, he can take it. It apparently had something to do with their predicament so she shook her head yes. It was the size of a small grapefruit, but it shouldn't pose too much trouble carting around with them. *Besides,* she thought to herself, *if it gets too much for him, we'll just pass it off to our group muscleman.*

She accessed the office and put a special expedite tag on the bag. Beau, Mr. T, and Crutch were fortuitously booked on

175

the same flight to SFO. She didn't need to see their reservation to know what flight and city pairs to insert on the tag as she had Beau's itinerary memorized . . . accidentally of course . . . after checking him in. She locked the office door and then turned to the group, nodding to Mr. T that he was up. It was his turn to show them that cool shortcut.

No one questioned anything at this point, and simply followed Mr. T. They maneuvered their way past several other bagwells, always peeking around corners before walking on. He led them behind a section of rollered transfer belts, and then he motioned for them to enter a wide door that was marked "Hazard Zone-Authorized Personnel Only." Jahnni hoped her badge was still live, and had the full access she gave herself right before she and Mr. T escaped Perry Prattle's office. She lifted her badge to access the door, and she noted to herself that this was a maintenance door that only the Port maintenance workers ever had access to. She thought it was plumbing or electrical, but she never really had paid attention.

The green light beamed at her. Mr. T smiled and swung his arms forward like he was directing traffic. Jahnni understood, opened the door, and motioned for them to get going. She gently pushed on everyone's back to move them along as they passed by her, entering the room. They obeyed, although the frowns on their faces revealed their combined confusion as they looked up, down, and around the little maintenance room. Beau was the last to back into the room, after keeping watch while they scurried in. He checked the door, pushing and pulling on it roughly after he closed it then turned and winked at Pops. It was a very tight room with so many people huddled together.

Mr. T wiggled his way to the back of the group and asked Beau to help him. "This whole electrical box must be . . . pulled out . . . forward," Mr. T mentioned confidently, with one hand on his hip and the other hand wiggling a finger towards the big box.

"Uhhh . . . are you nuts? We will all be electrocuted if I yank on this and pull live wires out of the wall," Beau stammered.

"No, there is panel . . . right here . . . and if I pull on this point . . . and you pull the box toward you . . . then it slide forward to you, but stay on own platform," Mr. T explained. "They use this box to control electrical here in bagwell. They don't know what else . . . it does."

Beau paused, then took a couple deep breaths and readied his arms to pull out the large panel. He felt around the sides until he found some indentations just large enough along the sides to slip his fingertips into. Pops slid his hands down the side of another panel and pushed down on a hidden lever. He nodded to Beau to begin pulling and slowly, the electrical box slid towards him. It kept coming, and coming until it was sticking out of the wall about twelve inches. It was seated on a platform like a shelf that obviously could be pushed back, as easy as it came out. The entire back appeared to be coated in some type of water resistant foam or rubber material that completely encased the back of the box, but this was not visible to anyone from the front if they had to work on it. Still, Jahnni didn't yet understand what they were doing.

"Stand back a bit please," Mr. T ordered as he patted the wall nearest him. "This wall going to move. Here comes cool shortcut!"

They all shuffled . . . slowly . . . and looked at each other for some type of explanation. Even Beau didn't seem to know what Pops was doing. It was silent in the little room as Mr. T then walked over to the electrical box and pushed on the right side of the unit until it pivoted to the left out of the way of his reach. All the wiring that fed into the back of the rubber casing was wrapped in a type of insulated tubing that ran upwards out of the way. Above the top of the box, inside the wall, was a rubber coated handle hanging downward. He pulled it towards him and stepped back immediately. The concrete wall to the right of where everyone was standing began to slowly move back. It inched its way further and further away from them until it had created a large opening. Mr. T's eyes sparkled and his mouth gave way to a large smile that tried to breach the limits of his cheeks. He looked like a kid who found his long-lost toy.

"What in the world is THIS?" Jahnni asked. "How did you know this was here?"

Mr. T didn't speak right away. He just smiled, beaming with a look of pride then said, "I tell you that I know shortcut. And here is shortcut."

"I certainly realize that this is something . . . but a shortcut to where? And you didn't answer me. How did you know this was here?" Jahnni panted out like she couldn't get the words out fast enough.

"Because . . ." He breathed in like he was filling his lungs before answering, then held his head high when he proclaimed, "I design this. I design all this." Mr. T arced his arms as if he meant to include the universe. For the first time, Jahnni was beginning to see there was something to know about why Perry Prattle kept demanding to know information from Mr. T. *Mr. Prattle must know that he used to work here when this was designed? Or built? Or?*

"You were what, a construction worker for the airport relocation in the 70's?" Jahnni asked.

"No, I was lead engineer. I have much to show you. Much to show you all. I get us safe," Mr. T said, nodding up and down. He pointed to the opening and motioned for everyone to follow him.

Chapter 19

Cool Shortcut

"ALLOW ME," MR. T said with a bow, his hand folded at his waist. "I must be sure it is safe time to enter system."

Beau had already motioned his arm forward when Mr. T first indicated he was going first, *so who am I to argue?* Jahnni thought. *Mr. T sure seems to be able to handle his own and more than once had the wits about him to think and perform his way in and out of situations that I'm grateful for.* So, she waved her arm toward the opening and calmly said with a fake smile on her face, "Absolutely Mr. T. Just let us know what to do." A little trepidation had begun to creep up her back. *There better not be any spiders. I hate spiders.*

"Let me go first, Pops. I can ascertain the safety of the environment down there." Beau insisted as he looked down into what Jahnni could only describe as an abyss.

"No, my boy. I am the one who needs to check couple things. I can tell if it is safe. I climb all my life. I never forget.

What do you call it? Like riding bike," Mr. T said with pride in his voice.

"He'll be fine Beau. I trust him," Jahnni blurted out a little louder than a whisper. She waited for Beau to look at her then added, "Like I trust you. With my life. We are a good team." Of course, her head was talking about the current situation but her heart was thinking of so much more.

"I'm good with it too," Sam threw in.

Mr. T grabbed the handrail for the stairs with his left hand. With great agility, he slipped his right foot onto the first metal stair. That appeared to surprise the new fast friends because they opened their eyes wide and smiled at each other before turning back to watch him further. He looked down, then to the left. After glancing to the right, he let his right foot slide over to the edge of the first stair as he pulled his left foot onto the railing. Then he let his right hand grab the other side of the handrail in an old but familiar movement. His joy was evident in his smile. He raised his eyes to Beau, made jumping motions on the stair rails and announced, "See! Good as new. No problem." He nodded his head to the group to follow.

Their preassigned order was now out of synch. Generally, Mr. T was next to last. They didn't know who should go next as they shuffled forward, then back, bumping into each other. Beau stepped forward, and poked his head into the opening. He didn't act like he saw any type of imminent threat so Jahnni decided that the words *harmless so far,* came to mind. After all, she was sure that Pops wouldn't take ladies or a child into a dangerous situation on purpose, would he? Beau motioned for

Jahnni to go next, then moved Crutch into the next position. He pointed for Samantha to head down the stairs after Crutch. He would obviously be last.

Jahnni looked back up that ladder after she climbed down. She watched Beau reach out and climb onto the stairs, the last person to leave the maintenance room. After he accessed the top of the stairs, he reached back and grabbed onto the panel and pulled it towards him, causing the edges to become flush with the inside wall. He stared at a lever next to the panel for a few seconds, then pushed it up. Jahnni could faintly hear a dragging sound that she attributed to the concrete wall in the maintenance room, sliding back into place.

Once gathered together on the floor, Beau asked Pops, "What is this round room? And why do I feel like a bug in the pipe under the kitchen sink, waiting to be flushed away when the water is turned on?"

Crutch was turning circles, with an awestruck look on his face. "Hey, why is that copper ridge coiled like a fat hose along the length of this cartoon size pipe we are in?" Pausing to look around, he added, "I saw a movie once where all the people were very small and they had to make everything on the movie set ginormous so it made the actors look like they were really small. This is SO COOL."

Jahnni tipped her head as she studied Crutch. "You don't seem very rattled by everything that's been happening kiddo. Are you sure you are okay?"

"Well, not too much rattles me. I always just go with the flow. Watch everyone else. Figure things out as I go along. I'm not a planner so this is more like an . . . adventure. We'll be fine. You guys will get us out of here," Crutch answered. "My parents play a new game where they try not to ask me yes or no questions because they want more than a two or three letter word answer. They say I'm too quiet most of the time."

"I'm a little worried, if anyone wants to know. Where are we going?" Samantha asked in a quivering squeak. "But more importantly, where are we?"

"This is a pipe. A big, big, pipe! First, I already check before we climb down. This part is dry and still sealed off from water system that goes to pretty fountain and the other pipe that gives water for nice roses," Mr. T said. Then after he looked around, he added, "Second, the curling copper slat is part of old water processing plant. Help with centrifugal movement of water. Just watch step Mr. Crutch or you trip. I can still take you to more exit. Not sealed from . . ." Mr. T stopped to stand tall, looked at each of them and said, "me."

"Do we move this way Pops?" Beau asked, more like a suggestion as he started walking forward. He already saw the end of the pipe near where they were and Jahnni watched him as he had canvassed every inch with his eyes. Jahnni looked around as well and didn't see a place that appeared to harbor what could be an exit. Not even a hidden one.

"Yes. We go that way with Beau," Mr. T confirmed, pointing forward.

Beau walked towards the curve of the pipe. He was now in the lead yet he continued to look back at them. Jahnni kept walking forward, keeping everyone together, and she herself kept glancing forward to watch Beau, feeling her heart melt every time she looked at him. The feeling got worse if he was looking at her when she glanced at him. *What is he thinking? Does he think he can get us safe once Mr. T shows us the way out? It shouldn't be too long I suppose. I wonder if he is going to get my number. Maybe I should get his, even though it is in his reservation. It will be better if he gives it to me so I don't look like a stalker . . . which I'm not . . . I don't think. That way he'll know I'm interested. Then I'll call him in a couple days to see how he's doing. Maybe he will call me back next time he is in town. When he comes over, I'll leave the Bridal magazine on the coffee table, then if the topic comes up . . .*

Jahnni realized she wasn't walking. She focused and noticed that he wasn't walking anymore either. He was looking at her. He tipped his head sideways and asked, "Deep in thought or is your mind wandering aimlessly about nothing?"

"Oh, I'm just, uh . . . making plans for when we get out of this outlandish situation," she answered with pink rushing to her cheeks. "Just trying to keep my thoughts clear . . . to be open."

"Be careful. Watch your step," he said with a tenderness that made her heart skip a beat.

Beau turned and walked on with a confident gait. His footsteps carried an echo that bounced off the walls with a slight ping which made him look down and check his boot. Jahnni watched him walk in a smooth rhythm as he stepped over the twirled copper slats that encircled their current 'room.' The spacing was almost perfect for his pace, but each step for everyone else was longer then shorter as they approached each copper coil. *This twirling thing inside this pipe reminds me of a candy cane. Or a barber pole,* Jahnni thought.

They trudged on, running on adrenaline. Crutch seemed to be playing less and less of his game. "Where's your earbuds?" she asked.

"I took them out so I could make sure I didn't miss anyone talking to me," he answered.

"Are you doing okay? What's going on in your head?" Jahnni said, trying to make conversation so she could get a feel of his anxiety level.

"I'm good. I've been afraid before and this isn't even a close comparison. I'm just going with the flow, you might say." Then after he walked a few more steps, added, "I hope my mom's not worried. My dad too. I wish I could let them know I'm okay."

"I know. As soon as it's possible, we'll make sure they know you are," Jahnni said, almost in a whisper.

The walls were cold. "The steel reminds me of an underground bunker at a training ground I stayed at a couple years ago," Beau began sharing. "Steel has a way of talking to you. You feel it, weird as that sounds. It's stoic, firm, inflexible so that outside forces would have a difficult time getting past them . . . or destroying them. As brutal as it would be for this pipe to fall on you, once inside its round encompassing form, you feel enveloped in safety. A dichotomy of purpose," he said without looking up.

Jahnni turned around to look behind them and her eyes followed the coiling copper as it circled and circled in a never-ending pattern from one end of the pipe to its conclusion, where they started from.

"Mr. T," she summoned ahead of her, "why is the other pipe, copper I think, spiraling around the steel pipe again? I've tripped on it a couple times so I don't think this big cavernous pipe was meant to be walked in, right?"

"It is scientific method. When water pushed through this portion of process, it keep water spinning. Like I tell young boy. Centrifugal. Very fast centrifugal," he clarified . . . sort of. "It help clean water . . . like nature."

Then he stopped and pointed up. "Okay, here we are. Once I climb ladder, I see handle for next place we must go," Mr. T declared. "This fun, yes?"

"Well, I'm not quite sure I would use the word . . . fun . . . exactly," Jahnni replied. "Maybe, rousing. Or possibly motivating, in a survival sort of way. Probably electrifying, but not necessarily a good spine tingling, more like being hit with lightning and living to tell about it," she muttered to whoever wanted to know how she felt.

"Ah . . . I have not been down here in a few years . . . no . . . decades! We will be safe as soon as I help us get out. You will see Miss Janie." He assured her.

They stood at the bottom of another metal stairway that was secured to the walls of the pipe. Mr. T put his hands on the railings and pulled to check the strength. "Beau, could you please double check for me . . . these railings? I see some worn places on brackets up higher. I'm sure okay, but just want to be sure for everyone else," he requested.

"Sure Pops. I'll climb up to the top first, too. You can just tell me what to do when I get there." Beau added.

They waited patiently as Beau climbed the ladder, checking the security of the brackets. "It's fine up here Pops. The brackets are very secure. Once I open this lid, what should I expect? Is there anything I need to look out for?"

"Not . . . yet. We will come up when you get it open," he answered.

Jahnni thought it seemed simple enough. Beau grabbed a rubber-coated handle that was like a left facing paddle and flipped it up and around clock-wise. Everyone heard the door's release on the oval shaped door.

Jahnni noticed the shape and thought to herself, *hmmm . . . this is kinda shaped like a plane door that they swing out, or in, depending on the type of aircraft. Or maybe a door one might find in a submarine.*

After Beau pushed the opening forward and to the side, he poked his head through the opening. He climbed the last few railings and stepped onto a platform that sounded like grated steel when his boots landed on it, "Come on up guys! How about Pops first, then Jahnni, Crutch, and then Samantha can be the caboose!"

Mr. T started climbing first. As soon as there was enough clearing from his feet, so she wouldn't get smacked in the head, Jahnni started climbing too. Crutch grabbed the side railings to pull himself up but froze. He snapped his head to the right and whispered to Sam, "Did you hear something? I heard something back there."

Sam looked that direction but shook her head, *no*. She let out a loud *Shhh* to those above her. They froze also and looked down to see what the problem was.

"What?" Beau whispered down. "What is it?"

"Crutch thought he heard something," Sam whispered up then turned back to listen. "Oh . . . Oh . . . I hear it too!" she answered in a loud whisper to Beau. "It's voices. Yes . . . I can hear it! Oh, my gosh! Someone's coming! I think they are coming down the stairs back there!" she shakily whimpered. "Crutch, go, go, go . . . quick. Don't look back. Just climb!"

Beau had just helped Pops through the opening when he reached down and grabbed Jahnni's hand. Then he just grabbed her other hand, practically pulling her up to the scaffolding through the air. She shuffled to the side but kept peeking down to see what was happening.

"Ahhhh . . . hurry Crutch! I think they are running this way! Up, Up, Up!" Samantha whimpered again as she climbed up right behind him.

Crutch jumped through the opening and Beau immediately reached for Samantha. She tripped on the last rung that her foot tried to catch and started sliding down a few feet before she caught her grip. She started the climb again, but she was shaking as the foot falls coming from the other direction were getting louder. "Give me your hand, Sam!" Beau ordered in a firm whisper.

Sam reached up and Beau reached further down and grabbed her other hand as he did with Jahnni and hauled her up through the air. She bumped her knee on the edge of the landing as she was clearing the opening but she didn't seem to notice. Jahnni stood and anxiously spun left and right, seeking an escape route. She pleaded with Mr. T with her eyes, as if to say, *what now,* but he had not noticed she was looking at him yet. He too was looking around.

Jahnni asked Mr. T, "What should we do? Where should we go?"

Beau quickly, yet carefully started to close the hatch opening. "GO! Pops . . . take them and go!" The rubber casing made a sucking sound like it sealed when he pushed it closed.

Jahnni heard them on the other side and froze while the others ran with Mr. T. She stood a few feet from Beau, but waffled back and forth a few steps trying to decide whether to wait or go. It was muffled but she could clearly hear them slamming into the staircase as they started climbing.

Beau grabbed the handle and locked it into place.

He scanned back and forth from the door to the wall . . . then quickly whipped off his belt and wound it around the handle's post. He then looped the other end of the belt through a ring on the wall and pulled it tight, bringing it towards the buckle end that was wound around the handle. Pounding came from the other side as someone tried to move the handle and push on the door. He pulled the buckle end as tight as he could, trying to make it reach and finally got the buckle clasped. It was stretched across the door so it held it from being pushed forward and opened from the other side.

He turned around to see where the others had gone and saw them on the other side of the large cavernous room on the scaffolding. Mr. T waived at Jahnni and Beau to hurry and was also motioning Sam and Crutch to go through the door he was holding.

Beau grabbed Jahnni's hand and started running; his boots so noisy as they clanked on the open grates. He ran around a piece of machinery situated in the bend of the corner, careful to maneuver Jahnni around it. Jahnni was glad for the help as he pulled her along. Her mind rushed through scenes of shooting, bullets bouncing and pinging off all the metal she saw around them. She imagined someone getting shot, possibly Crutch. She thought of the possibilities if Beau shot first. None of the scenes flashing in her head led to a good feeling. Now that the thoughts were rumbling through her head as they ran towards the door, she realized that it was Pops that was leading the way. *I guess it's still going to be a group effort.*

Mr. T had climbed through the door with the others by the time Jahnni and Beau reached it. So many doors around here. How did he know which one to choose? Beau slowed their pace and practically pushed her through the door as he grabbed the door casing to swing himself in.

He paused next to Jahnni before he began closing the door, then turned to look back at the other opening that was being slightly secured by his belt. Jahnni leaned under his arm to see what he was looking at. He left the door open about two inches as they quietly watched the door that Beau tried to secure after they all made it up out of the pipe. They saw the door being shoved over and over from the other side, and the belt finally unraveled and fell from the handle. They were coming.

"Well, it held long enough, I guess," Beau whispered for Jahnni to hear. "Shoot, that was my favorite belt." They pulled their heads away from the crack of the door as fast as they could, then quietly shut the door, not waiting to see who it was that forced their way past the door.

Mr. T led them through this big office room that appeared ghost-like, like no one had been there for many years. Large and small monitors were embedded into the walls, switches and knobs in different colors were obviously in a designated pattern near each screen. The screens had a greenish color to them. The walls were painted an ugly shade of yellow that Jahnni was sure hadn't made a comeback yet in DÉCOR, or House Beautiful . . . much less Architectural Digest. Chairs were pushed up against the desks like a school room from yesteryear.

Turning the corner and heading towards the back wall, Beau said to Jahnni, "This room is probably like all the surrounding rooms, in relation to the inner area with the scaffolding. I noticed that there were no windows, except on each door that faced inward. I also noticed, there may be approximately 3-4 floors below this one of similar resemblance to this floor. I don't know what this building is. Below the airport is obvious. Accessed through that gigantic water pipe was odd, but obvious. But why?"

"This way Miss Janie. I take you all to safer place, so we . . ." Mr. T stopped mid-sentence to listen to the banging noise in the near distance. "Uh oh. Follow me," he ordered, instead of asking.

He pulled open a door on the outer wall and Beau held it open for the rest to go through. Mr. T already began trotted forward along the scaffolding which appeared to surround this commodious mysterious structure. They shut the door behind them and ran to catch up, which wasn't that difficult, given his age. He darted to the left down a skinny hallway after glancing behind them. Quietly, he pushed a door open and motioned for them to follow and silently they entered the door he was holding open. Once inside, with no lights turned on, they just stood silent in the dark only hearing each other's nervous, unsteady breathing. Jahnni heard Beau's gun scuff against its leather holster. She assumed he was still against the door, weapon in hand, the first encounter if someone came through.

Faint running footsteps could be heard coming closer, and closer, the banging of their feet reverberating through the walls. Then the footfalls faded as their pursuers continued forward in an obvious attempt to catch up to them, not knowing that the group had taken a side route. Once it felt clear that they were much further away, Mr. T flipped up a switch and lights randomly blinked and flickered on until the room was lit with a brighter, but still dim light. Although still frozen in place, they looked around to get their bearings.

"Is this . . . a bathroom?" Crutch asked.

Jahnni piped up first after looking around, "Yes, we are in a restroom. A lady's restroom."

Mr. T was already walking across to the other side of the row of sinks and motioned with his arm to follow him. Still trying to make their footsteps light, they gathered towards him and waited for him to explain where they should go next. He pointed forward to another door and pulled on the handle.

"Wait a minute," Samantha whispered, "Isn't this the big room that we just came out of?"

"Yes, yes, it is," Mr. T confirmed. "And now, we go back in it this way."

Beau let everyone go in front of him as he kept an eye on the door they entered, that led them into this bathroom. He glanced around and flipped a switch to turn the lights off.

Back they went to get to the inner scaffolding that they first came to when they crawled up out of the large pipe. Mr. T kept up a brisk pace as he kept looking back to check if they were still there. He stopped momentarily to glance down before swinging his leg over and down onto a metal ladder. After nodding for them to follow, he went down and down until his feet hit the next floor. He glanced up again and nodded as he saw them also climbing down and glance toward him once they also touched the floor. He swung his foot over and started climbing down another metal ladder. Once again, glancing to be sure they were following, and nodding to them with an encouraging smile to keep following. Down he went, carefully, but as fast as his aged legs could move. They followed him again, to a floor, then after gathering there, down one last stair rail. Once on the bottom floor, he waited for the rest.

"This place is eerie, Jahnni. Have you ever been down here?" Samantha whispered, hoping Jahnni could hear her. "Where are we?"

After about 10 seconds, Jahnni whispered back, "Not only

have I never been here, but I didn't even know this place was down here. You'd think that maybe, if it was somewhere that someone could stumble upon, that we would have heard about it. It looks old, like it's been here awhile too. Maybe it's some kind of underground emergency bunker or something."

"Oh Janie," Mr. T interjected, "no one could, how you said, stumble . . . on this place. To get here is big secret. I don't know who follow us but I think we should not wait to ask their names."

"You're right, we need to go. Whoever that is, they may have decided to back-track by now Pops," Beau interjected, with a voice that Jahnni could tell was meant to stress the need to keep moving. "Where do we go now? All I'm interested in right now is getting us out of here safely. No bullets. That's a last resort, as I've said before. Once we get out, I'll explain everything to the teams."

Chapter 20

Above the Fray

"LET ME GET this straight," Carolyn, the station manager for First Class Air said as she raised one eyebrow and tilted her head forward. "You're telling me, that my best agent, one of my supervisors, is a terrorist? And she has one accomplice and possibly three hostages . . . three passengers and one is a U.M? I'm sorry, Perry. That does not sound like Jahnni. She is as steady as a rock and probably one of the most trusted people in this entire airport!"

"I'm so sorry to be the one to give you this news, Carolyn," Perry Prattle said in an airy half-whisper. "I am just as shocked as you are. But we have been following up on some leads and had been tracking her. It seems that she has threatened to blow up the fountain . . . with a bomb!" Perry rushed the words out even faster now. He spoke as if he was trying to shove the words into her head. "Oh! In fact, she left a suicide note that must have fallen out of her possession when she attacked one of my men. He's in the hospital right now getting checked out," Perry said as he rummaged through his pockets for the note. Carolyn watched his face as he unfolded it and handed it to her like he was revealing a secret weapon.

Carolyn shook her head in disbelief as she reached for the note and held it by the very tip of a corner, trying to keep her fingerprints off the body of the note. Her other finger gently opened it. She scanned the room, then looked back down at the note. She didn't say anything or make any noises while she read it. Perry waited. Finally, after standing silent for 30 more seconds, she looked up at Perry.

"This note doesn't say why she is doing this. There are no demands. Why would she take hostages if there isn't a trade? There is always a trade to get demands met. And why would she take hostages if she takes the time to write out a suicide note? This isn't something Jahnni would do."

"Well, I don't know, Carolyn! I'm not the one who orchestrated this! I only know so much. She attacked one of my men! That's a criminal assault right there. She's dangerous, I tell you. Oh, and she bragged to my man that she is armed. She is carrying a weapon, Carolyn! I don't think you know her like you thought you did." He finished his speech then stood there like a mix between a victim and a man who thought he was in control of his own chaos.

Carolyn stood there for a few more seconds as she pondered something. "Why haven't you given this to the Homeland agents or the FBI inside? This is evidence . . . don't you think?"

"Oh, uh, I, well, uh, I forgot I had it in my pocket. I was going back to my office to get it and hand it over," Perry answered. "I mean this is a disturbing situation. I simply forgot at first. In fact, hand me that back so I can give it to them right away." He reached out to pluck it from her grasp.

Carolyn shrugged her shoulder to the side to keep him from taking the note out of her hands. He grabbed for it again but she turned her shoulder away from him once more. He tried to reach around her the other way, but she stepped back, faced him with the note held behind her back and said, "Hey! I just want to get a picture of this for my records. Stand back from me!"

"That isn't yours, Carolyn. Give it to me! Give it back!" He panicked. He looked around then nodded his head. "Then hurry. I need to give this to the authorities. I, uh, already told someone that I was, um, gonna bring it to them."

She turned her body halfway away from him as she took out her phone and quickly snapped a couple pictures of it for her records before it got 'lost and forgotten' again. Then she handed it to him, watching him stuff it into his front shirt pocket under his suit jacket, using no care to keep it protected or clean for examination.

"Oh, uh Perry, how long have you been following Jahn?"

"Following? What do you mean . . . oh, you mean since we were tipped off? Uh, probably about a month. Yes, I am sure of it. It's been a month."

"And in this whole month, concerning an agent with security clearance, here at the airport, which is under Homeland

Security directives and the TSA, you never thought to come to me, or anyone else about this possible security breach?"

"I couldn't yet Carolyn. I, uh, had to figure out this situation and decide the best course of action."

"Perry, there isn't any 'deciding' that was needed by you. There are directives that we are held to with absolutely no wiggle room. Protocol has already been established. We have trained for this for how many years together? Are you a one-man army? Basically, by not bringing this to my attention, everything that was done on Jahnni's shifts are now considered a security breach. Every single flight and transaction done while Jahnni had access to ANYTHING concerning our airlines is now considered suspect. I'm very surprised, that if you thought there was cause for concern, that you didn't give me time to pull her off the floor, and start an investigation. This is a pretty significant security breach. Every branch of the law should have been notified and Homeland should have told YOU what the next step was."

"Carolyn! It was top secret! I couldn't let you in on it yet. I am just as surprised by her actions as you are!" he said with exasperation in his voice.

Carolyn squinted her eyes at Perry then asked, "What do you mean top secret? By whom? Who notified you and why wouldn't they notify me, the First Class Station Manager? I'm sorry Perry. But I am not surprised at her actions like you think I am. I find this extremely difficult to believe. And don't change the subject. We were discussing your inept ability to follow emergency security protocol."

Perry Prattle was sweating under his suit coat. He loosened his tie and moved his neck side to side, making popping noises. He extended his arms as if to adjust the fit of his clothing and shrugged his shoulders up and back. He looked at Carolyn with a distant, detached stare. He just stood there, not answering. Carolyn stood there as well, not saying anything either, waiting until he answered her last question.

He pulled out his cell phone and acted like he was getting a call. "I have to take this Carolyn. We will talk soon." Then he walked back across the lanes that carried cars, taxis, buses, and foot traffic on a regular day. He held his mobile phone to his ear and his mouth was moving and his head bobbing like he was in deep agreement with someone. He continued into the airport, with his cell phone to his ear.

Carolyn stood there in a total shock. Not about the sui-cide/terrorist note, not about the lockdown, and certainly not about whether Jahnni was guilty of these heinous accusations. She glanced around and finally saw who she needed to talk to. She waved him over from where he was guarding the entrance to the parking garage, keeping unauthorized people from sneaking into the mix. He then motioned to another person on his team with the Port of Portland Police Department, and pointed to the area he was leaving so he could walk towards Carolyn. She began walking towards him too, and they met half-way.

"Jake, how long have you been with the force?"

"Gee Carolyn, probably almost as long as you have worked here. Maybe 15 years give or take," Jake said.

"Any complaints here? Problems with anyone, behavior that piqued your interest?" she queried.

"Hell, no Carolyn. I love this job! Best place to work ever. My wife complains that I help a little too much by picking up shifts for the guys . . . oh and gals," he assured her.

"I assume I can trust you to be open with me?" Carolyn asked further.

"Of course, well, except for our own NTK, but what can I help you with?" Jake said with furrowed eyebrows of concern.

"Ya, um . . . didn't you just tell me that there is a 5-mile wireless phone and radio blocker down by long term parking, behind the garage?"

"Yes. That was one of the first positions that were set up when this situation presented itself. But immediately, before that, they called the wireless carriers to activate the kill switch for the cell towers in this zone of the city. Wireless phones lost their connection to the towers that service this area first. But the zone had to be expanded with this type of situation. That's why the larger radius block is set up. We are all using the Port SAT phones, if that is what you are worried about."

"No, no, I know about the SAT phones. I'm using one. But you are absolutely sure there is no cell phone access at all, right?"

"Like I said, none. The cable lines are down inside the air-port also. That was standard for the emergency. I mean, the land lines are connected through the cable so they are out as well. The computers will work individually off-line, but they can't talk to each other or go out into the internet while they are down. Why?"

"Grab those Homeland guys standing by the Max, and the FBI gal over there. Find out who is in charge. Homeland or FBI. Tell them I want to talk to them. We need to have a conversation. Thanks."

Chapter 21

Self-Importance is Blinding

PERRY CAME BACK to his office to think. As he passed the first room in his office, he was oblivious to the fact that the tech who was monitoring his cameras before, was gone and replaced by Port tech support. They too didn't hear him slip in the door and access his private office, as he shut the door quietly behind him. His darting eyes slowed to a stare. He paced between the door and his desk, running his hands through the top of his hair. He patted it down then smoothed his hands back over the sides of his hair to erase his disheveled appearance. He whispered to himself, "There's no time. I need to find Arnie. I need to find him and make him use the key to . . . Hey wait! What the . . ."

Perry started rummaging through everything in his office as trickles of sweat began to bead up and roll down the sides of his face. His hands moved over the shelves and touched every dusty corner like they were thirsty, seeking to find the one thing that would quench their anxiety. He stood on a stool to brush his hands over the top of the bookcase, hoping that possibly, he moved his prize during the frenzied activity today. His eyes bulged and frown lines dug into his face. He turned in circles, swinging his head back and forth, up and down, trying to see every possible place it could have gone. Not only was it not here, but Arnie's bag was gone as well. "I didn't notice that before when I found Craigs! Aaaarrrgh! What have they done?" he whispered loudly to himself. "I'm going to find those sleazy miscreants and kill them myself after I get that key back. In fact, I'm not even going to kill them fast. I'm gonna drag it out until I get bored with it."

Perry Prattle turned nervously to his desk. He saw the dark screen on his computer and his anxiety soared even higher. After wiggling the mouse to wake up the screen, he noticed that it was turned off. He began to pound on his keyboard before the realization that it would not respond started to sink in. Realizing the on-off button wouldn't respond, he started crawling on the floor under his desk and patting the floor at every corner. Then he crawled to the side of his desk looking everywhere for the cord. It was nowhere. Still scrambling, he shoved stacks of boxes, books, and small storage shelving out of the way, searching frantically for the missing cord. He found it, wadded in the plant's pot. His fingers fumbled to plug it in the wall socket before shoving it into the back of his desktop. His hands were shaking as he pressed the power button to get his computer powered back up. Now, it appeared to be in a long reboot mode, the screen stating that it is applying updates. The clock on the wall was ticking louder and louder with each passing second. Perry knew that he wasn't going to get his computer back up in time because he had to move fast. He pounded on the desk in frustration and looked around the office, realizing he had to devise another course of action.

"I don't have time for this!" he grumbled out loud to no one, but himself. A thought entered his head, *Maybe I'll use the computers in the badging office.*

He calmed his demeanor before he left his office, now noticing the techs working on the camera feeds in the next room he was passing through. As if it had no bearing on his situation, he turned his head back to the door, ignoring the fact that his own tech was not sitting in the main seat. *No time to think about that. I need to bypass the Port computers to re-gain access to mine.* He wound his way down the three floors towards to the Badging and Port Police offices and pulled up short when he saw who was there. Homeland Security agents were mingling with the FBI agents and the Port Police as some were huddled around the Airport Badging Office Manager's computer. She looked very intent as she typed away. They all seemed to be waiting for whatever information she was accessing. Perry slid back behind the pillar he was by to watch from a distance. He could see through the office windows to watch what was going on. He could not hear their conversations but he knew it wasn't good. He had to accomplish his plans today or there would never be another time. Changing plans, people interrupting, glitches. Nothing was going as he planned. He still needed to re-craft his cover-up with all these pieces falling apart. *The last thing I need is to lose my job. What will this airport do without me?* he grumbled in his mind to himself in his normal grandiose, self-appreciative way.

Chapter 22

Technology on the Heels of the Mayhem

THE PRINTER THAT was directly connected to the computer kept spitting out pages and pages of information.

"Thank you for staying and helping us out, Doris," Special Agent Delaram Pahlavi said after she had introduced herself. "This is my partner Special Agent Liam Anthony. He is headed over to the food court right now to speak with the remaining TSA agents. I have many questions, but you can interrupt me if I miss anything."

"No problem, Ms. Pahlavi. I am happy to help in any way that I can," Doris answered her.

"Okay." Agent Pahlavi asked Doris, "Can you tell me which agents accessed the security doors today? Like . . . times and badge numbers. I understand that the list will be quite long, but we'll have a starting point, and a possible end point when compared to the time that access was shut down." She wanted to compare the information that the Station Manager for First Class Air had confided to her, minutes before, along with the information and photos that her other FBI agents had passed along to her.

"Well . . . yes is the short answer, but it will take a little more research. Just a few minutes to match up badge numbers to security clearance because it comes in like a list of data with a time stamp and I need to convert it. Do you need that right now?" Doris asked, trying not to show her curiosity.

"Yes . . . is *my* short answer," Agent Pahlavi replied with a smile on her face. "And . . . are all the security doors locked down? Are they all on one grid, or divided into sections? I understand that some doors shut down automatically and no one can override the lock with badging, so which doors can still be accessed in this exact emergency? What about the fountain? Does anyone else have access to the workings of the fountain, apart from, Port Police that we have there right now?"

"All doors are secured and no one can enter or leave through a security door. In the event of an airport emergency, certain doors are automatically sealed when it throws itself into no-access. Airport employees have about three minutes to exit the secure area through the interior doors to access the public area. Five, to make it through the gated checkpoints," Doris began explaining. "And when all the cable lines and intranet go down, for whatever reason, all access is severed for safety after that three-minute window. Here, I'll show you," she said as she accessed the program she needed that showed a colored grid on her computer. "This is the last live feed to my computer. But keep in mind that at this point, even if I wanted to, I can't release anyone's badge to access the doors because my computer can't communicate outside of itself . . . except to the printer that we hard wired to it. We will need the cable, or intranet back up for me to release egress and ingress for one, twenty, or all previously cleared employees."

Doris pulled up the program through which all security doors were monitored, then turned to Agent Pahlavi to explain, "Normally, I can grant or retract authorization through various areas, doors, and even private offices. While we wait, I can still pull up history. I can pull up information based on different search parameters. This information was already in my program before access shut down. For example, do you want to know access by clocked time, today or another date? By names under each airline, or other airport employees, Customs agents, Port Police, etc . . . I can even delineate the list to show you when someone accessed the employee parking lot coming or going."

"Hmmm," Agent Pahlavi said, "Instead of the entire day, I would like to start by time. Start with about an hour before the airport went into emergency protocol and forward to now. I will eventually throw the net out further, but I am looking for something in particular first. What about any other persons that have access to this program? Someone who may be able to grant or remove access to anyone."

"Well yes, the Port Manager here at PDX has that authority, but he always goes through us for transparency. With the protocol in place, no one can override the shut-down. Like I said, the entire airport is . . . oh," Doris said under her breath as she stared at the image on her screen. Pahlavi stood behind her, watching the screen also.

A quadrant of the airport had a green section that indicated that the security doors were active. The other quadrants were ensconced in red showing that no access was available through any doors within its parameters.

"I'm a bit confused," Doris said slowly. "There must be a glitch in the color coding or something because it's not supposed to be accessible. It should have shut down when the other sections shut down access. I need to get a message to the tech team. They were headed upstairs not too long ago, so let me send a runner with a message. Hang on."

As soon as she handed off the message, she began working on the list of information from the history that Agent Pahlavi had asked for. Then the printer fired up and paper after paper started feeding into another agent's hands. As it was handed back, Doris accessed another part of the program to narrow down the information.

Agent Pahlavi was looking out the office window into the baggage pick-up area, thinking about the conversation that she just had with Carolyn, the First Class Air manager. Carolyn said she knew where every one of her remaining agents were stationed around the airport before the emergency but now had concerns because of the information that she garnered from Perry Prattle. *So now . . . who else is still inside? And how do they plan on exiting the premises?* Agent Pahlavi wondered.

"Doris, could you print out the parameters of the green

section you just noticed? Like a screen shot or use a snipping tool. It seems odd that if you look here . . ." Agent Pahlavi said as she pointed to a couple spots on the grid, "and here . . . these doors are like a mere few feet apart yet one is accessible and one isn't. And if you look at the elevation view, it appears that an entire floor is operational and certain doors are randomly arced into this green area. The pattern is extremely random. I realize that it could be a technical glitch in color coding, but I would like to know what access doors are in that zone . . . and if possible, to see who accessed them. Just in case. Also, what about the cameras? Are they accessible? How are those configured into the security system?"

"You can go to the Port of Portland Police office right around the corner, and down that hallway. They can help you with that," Doris said without looking up from her computer as she printed out what Agent Pahlavi requested. "As far as the grid, there are so many doors in the airport that they had to draw the lines somewhere. It is weird though . . . how these doors here...and here, don't follow the regular grid pattern. More importantly, there was a reason the grid was built a certain way when it was compared with continuing security and safety. Still, I'm not sure how this green zone that forms a pocket down the center of the airport is . . . well . . . green. The techs will check it out."

Agent Pahlavi pointed to two other agents to stay with Doris and then motioned to one other agent to come with her. They walked out of the Security Badging office and turned down the hall. The carpeted hallway kept the noise to a minimum but with no passengers anywhere, it was mostly quiet at this end of the airport. No baggage carousels were spinning; no announcements were being made. No carts clinking and rolling around. Just the sound of footsteps seeking answers.

The door to the Port Police office was already open so they walked right in and identified themselves. There was no need, Delaram had already spoken with most of the officers that remained in the office when she had consolidated information between the chief of the Port Police, TSA and Homeland Security. She looked directly at the chief, Officer Chet Boulder, and made her inquiries, "Do you still have access to the Port cameras? Are they connected wirelessly, wired in, what?" she asked.

In a low, gravelly southern drawl, that reminded Delaram of a bass guitar, Officer Boulder answered her. "They are both. Wired for constant delivery but wireless access takes over if there is a problem with the cable delivery system. In this case, the wireless went down so the wired system took over. Our entire camera system is on its own cable protocol not associated with the main cable that enters the property. Which is a good thing since all the wireless signals have been severed. The mainframe is locked and located near the PBX system for our emergency SAT phones. The phone you are holding is on that PBX system. We have internal and external antennae that are interfaced with our facility's PBX. Of course, the cameras do not communicate with the SAT system. I was simply giving you a mini lesson on where the mainframe for them are located. They're near each other if we need to access them for any reason. What can I get for you?" Then Officer Boulder motioned for them to follow him into another room.

"There seems to be an issue with who is, or is not, still on the property behind the security doors," Agent Pahlavi said. "Doris, around the corner, is gathering some additional data for me, but I would like to know if you have been able to ascertain if any individuals, identified or not, have been noticed or monitored with the cameras in an area what should have been closed off. I'm specifically interested in badged employees." Then she waited anxiously for his response.

"To our knowledge, no," Boulder answered. "We have checked every corner, path, doorway, elevator, and circumference of the airport and there has not been any unauthorized activity that we have seen. But . . ." he started in, "There was a small 38-minute glitch where our inside cameras went offline because they are normally set to switch to wireless monitoring when an "event" presents itself. Our cameras went into back-up mode because the wireless signals were shut down. The technicians immediately started tracing back trying to figure out what caused the outage, and that is when they were informed that all the nearby wireless towers had been deactivated per emergency protocol, which explained the phones. The routers inside the airport were automatically shut down as well. With cable and other wireless signal access down, it did take a while for the camera system to get linked back into its own emergency cabled network."

Delaram was silent for a few seconds before she responded, "I'm confused. I thought that all the cable and phone lines were down, as well as radio and cell phone transmission."

Officer Boulder replied, "Yes. That is true. But, like I said, the cameras are all wired-in completely different from the rest of the airport operations. It is a security feature that remains in progress during an emergency. Normally, switching over to wireless is a smooth transition that is automated if the cable signals are interrupted. But since all wireless has been shut down . . . well, we are checking into it." He thought some more then added, "We still had visuals on the entire property but unfortunately, they were delayed for that thirty-eight minutes. The cameras still record. They each have their own drives. The transmission from our cameras to here was what was delayed. Sorta like when a cell phone monitors itself and switches from wireless access to data and then back again if it detects wireless access available again. In fact, electrically, it is also backed by a generator here at PDX, should the property lose electricity. You'd have to talk to the techs about how those specifics actually work with the recording, transmissions, delays etc . . . all I know is my job and I depend on them to make it happen."

He took out his notepad and checked his notes. "We have our techs checking on the cameras right now to be sure. Cameras are currently online over here." He pointed with his arm as he started walking over to the desks against the walls. He nodded with his head to a set of cameras that were being monitored by two other people slightly to the left of the others. "Those Port officers are reviewing the history that was suspended for that thirty-eight minutes I mentioned."

"Okay, I see. Even though the cameras may have been

down for your immediate remote viewing, the cameras are programmed to suspend transmission and save communication if their signal is broken. They will then send the video feed to the main hub and continue processing. Man, things are different from when I was monitoring cameras," Pahlavi summarized.

"We are isolating the history of that thirty-eight -minutes for you right now," Boulder assured her.

Delaram was glad he explained the camera situation in as much detail as he could. It gave her more info to go on and direction for her interviews. She started to walk away to confer with her agents when he touched her shoulder to get her attention quietly.

"Truth be told though," he began talking, almost in a whisper, "We cannot find the Airport Manager, Perry Prattle. That is a puzzling development for us. Our techs have a couple questions about the system set-up in his office. It doesn't appear that it is the same system that they themselves helped install."

"Why does he have monitors at his office location?" Agent Pahlavi asked.

"Oh, well, that was something he negotiated when he accepted the position. He said he wanted some cameras accessible to him for security purposes. The man seemed very knowledgeable with security needs and was a stickler for protocol and communication between the Port Police and his office. He can visually monitor the property as well. The system is quite a quagmire of interconnected capabilities and I would be lying if

I told you I could explain it, or understand it. My understanding begins with my job once the feeds hit my office. That is why we hire the best techs for onsite installation and support," he said. Then after a pause he questioned even himself by saying, "It is just that in all the confusion, we have not been able to contact him since he was in here last."

"Last? How long ago? What was the nature of his communication when he was here?" she inquired further.

"Oh, well, he said he needed to check the camera feeds and asked if we had any information deemed NTK for him. I explained that our cameras were offline for a slight bit but they were back up. He did say, as he came directly from Doris' office, that he was working on a lead of some sort and would be in touch soon. So, until the intranet in the airport comes back online, they can't give clearance to anyone else or remotely, access doors. It simply won't work," he explained. "He was here about 20-30 minutes ago, and said he was heading to his office first, but when I went up there, he wasn't there."

"Thank you, Officer Boulder. Doris already informed me that granting access to security doors has been down, because the airport is completely in lockdown mode, so I understand what you are saying, but we have garnered some new info about red and green coded areas that we are looking at. I'll be back if I need anything else. If you think of anything, hunt me down." *Now where is the Port Manager?*

Chapter 23

Where Still Waters Run Deep

MR. T LOOKED longingly at the huge structure in front of them and turned to the group and announced, "You know, this size not needed anymore. Only width of dime and length of straw needed now for some bad waters. Funny, huh?" Then he picked up his pace to walk around to the other side of it using the metal grated path that was under their feet. He stayed by the wall as he walked.

They stood there looking at a huge piped and glassed-in enclosure that practically took up the room. It also had large pipes leading to it, or leading away, Jahnni wasn't sure. Inside were thin, extremely thin drapes of some kind that were connected to the top and sides and bottom of the glass pipe enclosure. Jahnni thought the enclosure alone, was probably the width of a dump truck and parked three trucks deep in front of each other if that was any way to make an approximate measurement. There appeared to be several of these drapes, almost like a membrane of sorts, spaced about 6 feet apart. A type of coiling metal, much like the thick copper pipes they saw in the first big pipe, also ran the length of the glass enclosure along the inside walls of this . . . pipe structure? *What in the world? This must be the water purifying thing that Carlton said something about. It's huge! It's real! It's . . .*

"There they are," a voice bellowed from above. "Hey . . . Wait right there! We need to talk to you!"

Jahnni and the others turned to see who called out to them, but they had already walked too far under the scaffolding walkways to see who was up there. Jahnni's heart let out a startled electrical pulse that meant . . . get going! She froze and stared at Mr. T, waiting for him to tell them which way to go. She glanced back and forth between Beau and Mr. T, waiting for an answer.

"Pops," Beau interjected, "I need to know right now if you can get us out of here. If not, I am going to plan B. I don't want to have to, but if it's us or them, we are the ones who will come out of this on top. Not them, I guarantee it."

Mr. T waved them along. "Yes. Yes . . . I can get us out. We are near the exit. Or rather entrance. But we must hurry. What time is it, by the way?" he asked, eyes wide while he waited for an answer.

Jahnni looked at her watch. "It's almost 4:06, why?"

"We must hurry! The timer is set, and cannot be changed," he anxiously explained. Sort of.

"What time, for what timer Pops? What are you talking about? Where are we going?" Beau asked as he pushed everyone along trying to keep them protected from behind.

After a few seconds, Mr. T answered anxiously, "Where are we going, you ask? To get wet, that's where!"

Chapter 24

You Can Swim, Right?

ALTHOUGH JAHNNI WAS confused, he'd already proved invaluable in leading them from their pursuers. He knew where everything was and seemed to know exactly where he was going. But the sound of feet clattering on the metal stairs that they themselves had previously climbed down, was too unnerving to look back for. Jahnni watched straight ahead, keeping her eye on Crutch and Samantha foremost.

Mr. T opened another door and motioned his arms like a windmill, around and around, whispering for them to hurry. When they were all in, he turned to shut it tightly. He darted to a right corridor, and then followed that hall for about twenty-five feet then darted to the left. "What time is it now Miss Jahnni?" he called breathlessly from in front of them without turning around. "Exactly, what time is it?"

Jahnni could hardly get an accurate look at her watch with all the jostling and moving so she stopped to get an exact reading. "It is 4:09. Why Mr. T?"

"Does everyone know how to swim?" Mr. T called back to them as he kept up his trotting pace.

"Yes. Ya. Of course. Better than most," came all the replies.

"Good, we have no other choice, if we want to not be caught by those peoples behind us." He stopped to catch his breath and took several heaving lungs full of air before he went on, "It will start out slow at first . . . because the return is slower than the intake. It will be cold, but not too bad since it come from being warmed in the plant's pipe system." Jahnni had no idea what he was talking about, nor did anyone else by the looks on their faces.

"Pops! What are you telling us? Where are we going? You said you were getting us to a safe location . . . and of course, I believe you," Beau said as he turned Mr. T around to face him, "but we just need to know a little more information. I think you are scaring the ladies," he said. "Okay, I'll admit it . . . I'm feeling a little timorous about our situation. Skip to the getting wet part."

"Not much time," Mr. T began explaining a little more. "Old piping system. Was intake, but now is return for unused water. Had to hide original intake and create new one for simple looking airport water resource. Used to be feeding route of water over boulders that led to large purifying system that you see back there . . . before we run into last hallway. No time. No time. We run as fast as we can and we make the concrete observation landing. If not . . . we get wet. Remember, no worry! If water comes, let water carry you to landing. If water is high

224

enough and rushing fast, grab boulder hanging from pipe ceiling." He then got on his knees and put his ear to the floor, then pulled up on the large round access that they were unknowingly standing on seconds before.

Jahnni realized that they must be standing on the entrance to a pipe works of some sort. Mr. T opened the floor hatch with careful manipulation. It didn't look exactly like the other hatch doors they had climbed through, but when he pointed, they began to climb in anyway. One by one they all made it through and climbed down the metal stairs to the floor. Mr. T went in last and swirled the door lock to a clanking shut position. It was quite a few turns of the door wheel to get it shut tight, but once done, he climbed down the stairs.

"Double lock. That door is very good locked! Just in case," Mr. T mumbled, then shouted louder to them all as he motioned his arm, "Quickly! This way!" He took off in a trot . . . seemingly fast for him, but a fast walk for the others. The pipe was wet with dripping noises coming from behind, beside, and in front of them. Behind them there was a slight bend in the pipe that blocked their view of its origins.

Jahnni folded her arms around herself, feeling the draft of the wet environment in the pipe. She felt hesitant. "Is this safe enough for Crutch? Should we tie ourselves together or something? Maybe we should wait here until you send someone back for us."

"I'll be fine Jahnni! I can swim. Of course, I'll ruin my Vita but . . . at this point I don't think that matters, right?" Crutch replied. "I trust you. I trust everyone here. We can do this."

"Well, let's get going. What time is it now, Jahnni?" Beau asked, which was good because Jahnni assumed Mr. T would need to know that information anyway.

Jahnni answered, "4:14."

"What?" Mr. T said as he jerked up to look at her. He patted the inside pocket of his suit jacket. Jahnni made a mental note that the bulging rock, number II, appeared to be securely held captive inside the pocket along with his plastic pill holder.

"Mr. T? What should we do?" Jahnni pleaded.

"RUN!"

Without asking any more questions, they all took off— Beau waited for the rest to begin running. He came up behind Jahnni and Crutch and broke the hand link between them to hold tightly to Jahnni's hand. At the same time, he grabbed Crutch's hand and ran between them, pulling them forward. They caught up with Mr. T and Jahnni grabbed his hand as she began to pass him. Samantha had already been holding his hand since he told them to run. Then they heard it before they felt anything change. Water. It was coming. Fast. Pouring into the pipe somewhere behind them. They kept running as fast as the group could run without leaving anyone behind.

The water started swirling around their feet as it pushed past them quite quickly. It reminded Jahnni of how the tide felt when you were standing at the edge of the water at the beach when the tide begins to go out. Like it was tickling your feet as it pulled the sand out from underneath you. The tide pulled and pulled, begging you to follow it out to sea. It really could pull you out. Jahnni had made a note of this as a child when the neighbor boy drowned because he was knee-high playing in the water when the tide changed. She didn't see it happen, but she certainly heard the anguish that was left behind as the whole block and all his friends and family mourned his loss. *I will never do that to my family,* she had told herself, and added it to the many rules she followed in her life and reinforced it with years of swim lessons.

Their footsteps were splashing water as they ran. Seconds later they were pulling their legs up to run through the water as it crept higher and higher. They took larger, higher strides to stay balanced as they ran. Pushing forward, pulling up, and hanging on. Jahnni refused to let go of Beau or Crutch as they were pressed forward. The water was chilly as it slinked up her legs. She could feel her clothing absorbing the water as it snaked around them higher and higher. The water kept coming faster and with more force, creating a current that begged her to release the sturdy gait on the pipe below her feet.

Suddenly, the power of the current pushed Crutch's feet out from underneath him and his feet flew up to the top of the water. He rolled backwards, but before he flipped completely upside down, the water pressed all around him and immediately flipped him sideways, almost into a side-tumble. The intensity of the water pushed a current under Crutch's body that lifted him forward and in front of Jahnni and Beau. The tumble caused Beau's hand to release from Crutch, but he grabbed out at him so quickly, he caught the back of his belt. He yanked him upright and pulled him above the water's level. Jahnni's feet shot out from under her and she swung an arm out to stay upright in the roiling current. Chest deep, chin deep, then over their heads, the water had forged its own will against them.

Jahnni's left hand was still gripped tightly to Mr. T's. She tried to keep him close, but the deeper water rolled like a vortex spinning the friends to the point of exhaustion. He slipped quickly from her hand; although she continued to reach and extend her arm hoping to at least grab a piece of his clothing. But in the tempest, he disappeared and she lost him entirely as she too was being pushed and twirled like an underwater kite.

There was no time to think of anything but hanging onto Beau and try to go with the current that had risen so fast. They were at the mercy of the water whooshing them along. It was now more than half way deep in the large pipe and Jahnni couldn't touch the ground and keep her head above water. When she bobbed up, she barely had time to grab a breath before the water spun her back under. As she and Beau got popped up briefly, she saw the large boulders hanging from the ceiling by large steel rods. With a loud grunt of exertion, Beau pulled Crutch up and out of the water with his right arm. Just before he went back under, he shouted, "GRAB IT!" Then he sunk back under. All Jahnni could do was grab a breath every time she popped up. She felt helpless, mixed emotions screaming in her head. *Save yourself. No, save Crutch. Save Beau. Get to Samantha. Grab Mr. T.*

Her brief momentary solace was knowing that Crutch had grabbed the boulder. Her fear wouldn't let her open her eyes under the water. She didn't know which way was up in the tempest that tossed her like a leaf. She needed a breath.

Her lungs began to burn, and her mind urged her to open her mouth and breathe. She fought to hold on longer, and began to slowly let out the air in her lungs to possibly buy her some time. She stopped flailing, hoping that the water would push her upward.

Jahnni felt strong hands grab her, pulling on her then shoving her up out of the water, even though she could feel that it made him sink deeper into the dark churning water. She felt the cool air hit her face and gasped for the life-saving breathe that filled her lungs. She opened her eyes and saw that she was approaching another boulder. She grabbed onto the boulder, enough to get a hold from being washed further down the pipe.

In front of her, she watched as Samantha was swirled by the current as it pulled her under the water. She saw that Beau came up for air and reached out with both arms flailing, reaching in all directions for her. Then he was pulled under again, barely able to grab a quick breath. He was back under in the swirling white foam of water.

When he popped up, he had hold of Samantha, and pushed her upward. She grabbed the boulder above her and Beau grabbed the other end. Jahnni felt momentary relief as she watched her friends remain above the water, clutching the firm steadiness of a similar rock that she clung to tightly. The water still swirled around her body like a hurricane wind. Water splashed up around the pipe's edges and created chaos all around. She watched Beau whip his head all around. He called out, "POPS! POPS!"

There was no return answer.

Jahnni turned to look behind her and saw that Crutch was still clutching a boulder. She called to him, asking if he was okay.

Crutch called forward to Jahnni. "I'm okay. I'm okay! Don't worry Jahnni!" Then he cried out, "Where is Mr. T?"

She barely made out his words with the noise of the rushing water. But she understood. Jahnni called forward to Samantha a few boulders ahead, "Where is Mr. T.?"

Samantha couldn't answer just yet through her coughing. Beau appeared behind Samantha and helped her get a better grip, then after glancing at Jahnni and Crutch, he let go and allowed the water to take him away.

"What is he doing?" Jahnni screamed. "Beau! BEAU!"

She hoped the water would recede soon. She was exhausted. She could only assume that the others were as well. She didn't know what to do or where they were supposed to go next. *Where does this water go to? What are we supposed to do now?*

Her mind imagined the worst. She thought of the worst possibilities about Beau and Mr. T. *Stop it! Stop thinking that. They will be okay. Just believe it.*

"Oh, Mr. T," Jahnni whispered, although no one could hear her. Tears mixed with the water already dripping from her face. Then her breath escaped her lungs to breathe out . . . Beau."

Finally, she could feel the rush of the water getting slower and slower, but it was still too fast to let go of the boulders they clung to. The water started receding quite quickly and as fast as it rose, it turned into a slow-moving river. The three of them let go to drop into the calmer water and floated forward with the slow current. Jahnni and Crutch half paddled toward Samantha until their feet touched the pipe floor. They all stood, watching the water finally turn into a trickling stream that eventually turned to splashing puddles as they slogged along holding hands.

Jahnni refused to believe that Beau and Mr. T were gone. She called out their names every few seconds, "Beau! Mr. T ... Beau ... Mr. T?"

"Did you hear that?" Crutch laughed. "I heard him! I heard Beau! Hurry up! Let's run faster."

They ran around a large bend in the pipe and stopped in their tracks, dripping like cats pulled from a bath tub. Jahnni felt happiness flow onto her face and looked at Crutch and Samantha smiling back at her. They began running faster to the cement podium higher up towards the top of the pipe. It had an attached metal stairway leading up to it. They all grabbed the railing to climb the metal stairs at the same time, when Jahnni finally insisted that Crutch go first, then she stepped to the side to send Sam up next. She looked up and noticed that half of the narrow lighting system that ran down the middle of the ceiling of the pipe was out. In fact, every other tubular light was out, like a purposeful choice. The light was dim but useable, and at this point she didn't care. She was just glad to be alive, and that the others were safe.

When Jahnni got to the top of the staircase, Beau grabbed

her and hugged her to him as their wet clothes clung together like Velcro. She let the moment sink in as she wrapped her arms around his waist, leaning into his chest. He rested his chin on the top of her head as he breathed hard. The pounding of his heart and every rising chest movement was like a metronome to her own grateful heart. She only wished that this moment could last longer and under different circumstances. Everyone hugged and cried and hugged some more, elated that they were all safe.

Then Jahnni pulled her head away from Beau and posed the most important question of all to Mr. T. "How did you, when did, how, where . . . What happened? I was so filled with fear . . . that you had . . . not made it!"

Mr. T smiled a large grin that even showed the gold caps at the back of his teeth. They all looked eager, waiting for his paused response. "You have never heard of the saying, *hold your breath*?" he laughed.

"Pops," Beau whispered to him. "I thought I had lost you! I searched for you under water and when I couldn't find you I just knew that I had failed you! I love you so much Pops!" Beau bent and gave him a very long, gentle, loving hug.

Jahnni, Samantha, and Crutch looked at each other, then at Beau and Mr. T.

"Wait, Pops isn't just a nickname you gave him when you met him at the airport? You already know each other?" Jahnni and Samantha said that last sentence as a choir, then Jahnni added, "How could I have missed that?"

"What? You didn't know? Pops here is my grandpa. Wait

. . . you really didn't know that? I didn't tell you that already?"
Then looking at Pops, he said, "You didn't tell them that either?"

"Well, we have been so busy playing airport that I guess . . . I . . . forget!" Mr. T answered in a chuckle.

"Well, there is that. I don't understand how I didn't know this though. How I could not have . . . I don't know, put the pieces together," Jahnni said, shaking her head as if scolding herself. "It was so obvious. My mind must have been elsewhere, I guess."

"Oh! Then that explains the warbling bird language you spoke to each other back in the bagwell," Crutch said as a shiver started to run up his spine.

After looking around and watching each other begin a chorus of shivering, Mr. T said, "We are all cold . . . follow me. I know where we get dry clothes."

Mr. T reached up and took hold of another hatch-like opening that was on the concrete platform wall. They were all shivering at this point so when he opened the nearby hatch door, they seemed to gladly follow him in and waited as he closed the latch behind them. But when they turned around, Jahnni noticed that they were as confused as she was. This was a small room barely large enough for them to fit in. No furniture, no windows, no doors, except for the entry hatch. The floor had moved very slightly as they stepped in, but Jahnni didn't know what kind of room this was. There were slabs built into the wall of the strange room, obviously for sitting. On the forward wall, a large Red button was above a large green button. *What the heck?* Jahnni thought. *This looks like an elevator of some sort. Or, it reminds me of a windowless cable car.*

"What is this place? I thought you said something about clothes?" Jahnni asked as she continued to eye her surroundings while she shivered.

Beau motioned his arms to sit down and motioned for them to sit closely together. Jahnni knew it would preserve what body warmth they still had, so she was more than happy to comply. Beau wiggled between Jahnni and Pops and placed an arm around each of them and pulled them closer to help calm the shivering. Samantha sat on the outside with her arms around Crutch. She leaned both their bodies closer to the other three. Jahnni also draped her arm around Crutch to pull them closer as well. She could still smell Beau's cologne even after their trip through the human washing machine. *If only*, she felt her heart sigh. She couldn't tell the difference between the shivers and the quivers but they were both welcome; they warmed her.

Mr. T broke the new silence, except for the sound of chattering teeth, to proclaim, "Yes. I take you to clothes right now! But you must stay sitting down. It is not safe to stand . . . when I push that green button."

"You know, Pops. You could tell me to lay down and take a nap right now and I would, right here, right now!" Beau chuckled.

After a giggle, Pops said back to Beau, "Then why you not do that when you were young boy?"

"You got me there, Pops. I should have trusted and listened to you more back then." After thinking about it, he added, "I always trusted you. I should have obeyed more. And by the way, thanks for the swimming lessons when I was a kid," he added as they all laughed . . . until Mr. T stood up, grabbed hold of the nearby rail, and pushed the big green button.

Chapter 25

It's Really a Mission

THE TWO PEOPLE in white jump-suits that had chased after Jahnni and her group, came to a T in their path. They stopped to talk about whether to continue to follow them.

"Olah, if we continue pursuing them, we will miss our window and fail the mission. Too much training and planning has gone into this and we can't screw this up," he said before adding, "it's already been turned upside down, but I think we can salvage it. I can't believe he was able to sabotage that pipe! No one even knew how to get down to it that I know of."

"Come on Horvath, the guy's psychotic," Olah answered back. "I think our consensus is that he tossed or maneuvered a small explosive device down the fountain drain. Maybe he used a plumbing snake to drive it down far enough before it detonated. Who knows. Once we repair it, we can get out of here the long way and no one will even know we were here. I, for one, will be glad to stop schlepping bags. It's killing my back! We don't even have to quit in person. Leave a voicemail and let our boss know that our badges are in the mail. We can call it a, uh, family emergency. Oh, and you know, you can call me Mimi again."

"Olah, I mean Mimi, sorry. Being back home in Hungary, training for this, and then coming back here . . . calling everyone by their last names becomes an old habit. Anyway, please, don't call me Horvath either. It's so . . . impersonal." He chuckled and smiled at her. "Let's refocus, do our job and get out."

Mimi answered him, "You're right Addy. Our first sideways jump from the plan was letting Perry's goons see us. And what is with the fake gun shots over the intercom? Was he trying to . . . Oh wait, I get it. He was trying to create a diversion to empty the airport so he could have his goon squad get under the fountain and try to access the original pipe. Or maybe he thought they could guard it? I think their plan was interrupted, if you call it a plan that is. Real cops are guarding it now," she said then rolled her eyes and shook her head in mock disgust. "Like we would climb backwards against the water flow in that pipe. I mean, I'm not a big person, but even I can't climb down that pipe. He is such an imbecile. I don't understand his thinking. If he wanted to expose a water leak so he could send someone down to investigate any concealed pipes, wouldn't you think he could have just sent plumbers down to the exposed pipe that they already had access to?"

"I know," Addy said, shaking his head at the simplicity of it all. "He could've used slab leak detection. The sound sensors would have not only picked up the leak he caused, but had he known about electromagnetic pipeline locaters and a video feed, he probably could have found all of this. Thankfully, his secrets kept him from reaching out to the professionals."

Mimi shook her head in agreement. "Like I always say," she added as she took a bow, "Water issues should be left to the professionals."

"Well," Adrian, or Addy as his friends and family called him, said, "Since he made the statement in that one security meeting about pillars and walls concealing secrets, he is either figuring something out, or he is delusional."

Mimi said, "There's not enough time to try to analyze him."

After hearing Jahnni's and the group's voices disappear down a corridor, Addy turned back to Mimi and conceded, "You're probably right. We weren't hired to give psychoanalysis. Besides, Jahnni and them don't recognize us in our gear. I'm not even sure they've seen us this time. They seem to be running from the sound of our footsteps and voices. Let's get going. If we keep chasing them, they'll think we're doing it to catch 'em or to hurt 'em. I recognize that older man from our earlier briefings. He built all this and knows his way around. He'll get them out, we'll finish the mission, and hopefully someone can pin down Perry Prattle and expose him for what he is. And Jahnni, she is smart as heck. I've been on the airport security committee with her."

At his own statement, he laughed heartily. "That's funny, huh! Me, on an airport security committee. The duplicity of the situation did not go unnoticed by me! At least my motives are sincere, unlike Prattle's."

They moved at a measured pace, climbing the rest of the way down the metal stairs to reach the bottom platform. They arrived at the last place they saw Jahnni and the group and turned towards a different corridor than Mr. T had led the others down. Addy set out at a quick jog toward their final assignment. Mimi smiled as she ran, keeping pace next to her partner. She turned to share her thoughts with Addy, "After we weave our way to our destination and complete this task, we can get off the property."

A few turns through the underground maze, they arrived at their entry point for their mission. They had to wait for the water to recede on the other side of the pipe wall below them before the safety mechanisms allowed them to access the hatch. When they heard the familiar click, Adrian started rolling the circular airlock. Around and around it spun until it opened. They both climbed in and Mimi turned to reverse the door mechanism to relock it before she climbed all the way down the metal stairs. They began to run along the wet floor of the pipe towards the interior.

"We only have 4 more minutes, Addy." Mimi said with ease even though they were running.

"Yup. It's only a minute to the next hatch from . . . right about . . . here. The water just purged through the outflow pipe, and the intake is due for a new cycle in this pipe," he answered as they rounded another corner. "You got this. The equipment will be waiting for us at the site and ready to go. Just do what we practiced and we can be in and out. Once we seal the big leak in the pipe that feeds the fountain, we'll come back and catch the outflow pipe to make it off the property. Finally, we'll be able to walk away," he said as he picked up his pace. Then he added for clarity, "I mean, swim away, from life as Ground Service Agents."

Chapter 26

The Pieces Will Fall Where They May

Well, well. Would you look at that. I think Mr. Perry Prattle has been withholding information from us, Agent Pahlavi thought to herself. "Where is Carolyn? Have her come in here and ID someone for me," she ordered as she looked at one of her agents. "Take someone with you, preferably female."

"All of our female agents with the FBI are setting up their posts around the airport Ma'am." Agent Hartford informed her.

"Then grab that Port Officer over there." Agent Pahlavi pointed. "You know how I feel about women feeling strong-armed. I'd like her to feel comfortable with us so she'll share as much information as possible."

Carolyn was sitting next to the last baggage claim carousel, in the chair where she was told to wait. She was furious over the events that were playing out and was having such a difficult time controlling the rage that wanted to throttle

Mr. Prattle. She had explained what information she knew, or suspected, to the officers when they gathered around her earlier.

The FBI agent and a female Port of Portland Police officer went out of the room and soon returned with Carolyn.

"Agent Pahlavi? Is everything okay? Have you found my agents, or our U.M.? Do you know what's going on?" Carolyn rattled off, not waiting for an answer to any of the questions. Then she said, "I have something else I need to talk to you about. I just remembered something that happened during the Holiday party. It is probably nothing, but you might be interested."

When Agent Pahlavi nodded, and turned to give her, her full attention, Carolyn began telling her about the time that she saw Mr. Prattle in the fountain, late on the night of the airport Holiday party.

Carolyn said, "He told me that he must have had too many drinks and he accidentally fell into one of the ponds. But what was weird and I haven't been able to shake the mystery of it, was that after 'falling' into it, he climbed over the divider between the Koi pond and Salmon pond and then squatted down or bent over in the Salmon pond like he was looking for something. The fountain was turned off, which I thought was strange. He started to climb up the fountain, where the water normally flows down, when he saw me watching him and slid down into the trout pond. He laughed it off of course, saying that his watch fell in the water and he was looking for it. I laughed just because it was a strange encounter, but he seemed to be faking being drunk. I mean, at the time, I thought he was faking it. I was at the same party and I didn't see him drinking alcohol at all. In fact, alcohol isn't served at the Port's Holiday party. Not to mention, that would not be acceptable for the Port Manager to be imbibing."

"I didn't think the fountain was ever turned off," Pahlavi queried.

"Well, it never was, as far as I know," Carolyn answered. "The entire courtyard was cordoned off and the lights were off. It was very late and there are only a couple flights that come in that late. Everything is closed except for the one or two gates that these late flights come into. So, it wasn't too odd that the lights were off in the food court. I only saw him as I was walking by the big window and I wondered why everything was cordoned off. I also could see that the fountain lights were not on. I walked around the cones and yellow tape out to the courtyard and called his name. I was confused and thought he might be in some type of trouble or something. It was just so very strange."

"That is very interesting, this waterfall system and pipes. Do you have any idea what he could have been looking for, or why he would be looking for, whatever it was?" Pahlavi asked.

"Not really. Except the old rumors of a secret basement or something, having to do with the fountain. But I really don't think it's true. How could it be? I've always assumed it was folklore, exaggerated stories," Carolyn answered, shrugging her shoulders.

"Well, I'll put that on the back burner until I see how it

figures into something. In the meantime, could you look at some video feed for me and identify anyone in this section?" Pahlavi asked.

They rewound the video about twenty seconds and they started watching it together.

"OH, MY GOD! That's Jahnni! She is one of my best agents, the one I was telling you about," Carolyn said, pointing with her finger and tapping the screen. "Jahnni Dawson. Though, I don't know who those men are that are holding her arm and the arm of the older gentleman. I can't see their faces since they have their backs to the camera. Wait. Are they forcing her along? What's happening here?"

"Agent Pahlavi, come look at this. Here is one with the same lady but it appears that she is with another airline agent. Well, at least their uniforms look the same. Plus, a kid, an old man, and . . . Hey! Grayson! Come here! Quick! Who does that look like? Wait . . . let's rewind it a bit," he ordered the tech as he motioned his hand like he was trying to wind it up in the air. "Now look, watch this. Here she comes, and then the others, and then . . . Freeze it," the FBI agent monitoring the video yelled to the operator. "Right there. Who does that look like?"

In unison, Grayson and two other FBI agents said, almost in unison, "That's Harleyman! What the . . .? Why is he with them?"

Grayson stared at the screen then added, "He's one of us, ma'am. This keeps getting stranger by the hour, huh."

"Okay," Carolyn chimed in, "Then that's our AI from the SFO flight we were wondering about. The child must be our

U.M. we have been scrambling to account for. There is Jahnni, and it looks like . . . yep. That's Samantha. She is another good agent of mine."

Pahlavi looked around at the monitors that they were watching. "What's the time stamps on these? Start putting a timeline together so that we can see the order that these took place. Anyone else have anything?"

Pahlavi was beginning to form a plan when another agent monitoring a feed called out. "I found something you might be interested in Delaram, I mean Special Agent Pahlavi."

She hurried back through the room and had the tech re-play the feed. "Well I'll be damned," she said out loud.

Then, looking at the other agents said while tapping the screen on Craig's face, "Isn't this the guy that Perry Prattle said was attacked by Jahnni and her 'co-conspirators,'" she said while making tags in the air around the words co-conspirators, "when they burst into his office? That doesn't look like any bursting I have ever seen. More like they are the ones doing the dragging?"

Everyone stared at the screen. They were watching Jahnni and an older gentleman being strong-armed as they waited for an elevator door to open. Pahlavi wrote some notes on her pad then motioned for everyone in the room to stay put. "I'll be back in 10 minutes. I need to speak with Liam to see what he found out from the techs."

Chapter 27

Someone Always Knows Something

Agent Pahlavi went upstairs looking for Agent Liam Anthony, her partner. She was now standing before a large copy of the entire airport's blueprints using a restaurant table in the food court to lay out the different elevations. Crowded around the plans were FBI agents, electricians, plumbers, techs, and Special Agent Liam Anthony was taking notes. The Port Police officers who patrol the entire PDX property as well as inside the airport, were also waiting for Special Agent Pahlavi's update. The head of maintenance, was combing over the blueprints and marking various points of facts with small red removable arrow stickers as they identified the new assigned areas. They used yellow stickers to mark the areas that were already being monitored by the Port of Portland Police as possible areas of escape from behind security.

People stood staring at the blueprints, running their eyes all over the different elevations, pointing and discussing their different perspectives of knowledge. While they conferred in low tones, asking questions and answering others, a Port officer came to Agent Pahlavi and handed her a note. She unfolded it, read it, and then tapped it against her palm as she decided. "Okay, bring him up. Has he talked to anyone else about this?"

The officer shook his head no, and added, "Not that I am aware. He told me he hadn't when I asked him."

"Good, bring him up and of course, search him first. And if you don't mind, could you please bring us two cups of coffee. I am sorry to ask, but I don't know where they have set up the energy table," she said with a half-smile, knowing that he would understand the inside joke.

Delaram took out her note pad and added more notes. She walked to a table that overlooked the fountain out in the courtyard and sat down. The area by the fountain was cordoned off and guarded by two Port officers. Beside them walked two beautiful German Shepherds full of poise, continually watching every portion of the area, as were their handlers. If the handlers stopped, the dogs stopped and sat. If the handler started walking, the dogs would just start walking without being told what to do. They remained alert every moment. *Beautiful, intelligent creatures*, she thought, as she waited for the person who claimed he had some information about the Port, and the underground mystery that she needed to know.

She sat there, running the facts she had so far, around and around in her head. They were waiting for her back at the Port Office and she knew they would have the timeline of the videos for her. She squinted her eyes as she kept thinking about everything. It narrowed her thoughts so she could block out any interfering random ideas or pictures that wanted to sidetrack her. She had questions for herself. *Where is the tall guard that was with Craigs when they were forcing Jahnni into the elevator? Where is Mr. Perry Prattle? He is coming and going, yet no one sees him traverse the regular corridors, open areas, or even talking to the FBI, Homeland, or Port Police anymore. It must have to do with the green area on Doris' property security map. I bet that isn't a mistake. It was planned.*

She stood up as the Port Policeman walked the man towards her. Each were holding a cup of coffee. The man moved the coffee to his left hand then extended his right hand to introduce himself. She shook his hand, exchanging introductions, took her cup from the officer and thanked him before returning to her guest. She invited him to sit by pointing to the chair opposite of her then said, "Please. What can you tell me?" She sat back as The Cart Man began telling her the story about the acquisition of the Port of Portland property that now encompassed PDX.

She took notes as he spoke and answered her follow-up questions. After a while she turned the pad to him and he started perusing the account as she understood it. Then he signed it, noting that in the agreement she had offered her full support and his full cooperation would release him from liability in the ensuing investigation, provided he has been truthful and had not purposefully held back any pertinent information.

"You know, this is not a promise, as we may find that you are not telling me everything. But if you are, I will do what

251

I can to fulfill this agreement between you and me. I promise that if you are straight with me, I'll be straight with you."

"I fully understand. That is why I came forward. To help," he said.

She smiled, held out her palm in a gesture to ask him to wait, then suddenly jumped up and walked briskly over to everyone gathered around the blueprints. "Hey, the airport employees . . . you all have access badges, right?" she asked them all, and waited for whoever answered first.

"You," she asked Allen, the Port Policeman who escorted Carlton to her, "could you stay with Carlton until I say otherwise? Then she paused to listen to what they were talking about as they gathered around the blueprints.

"That's Carlton," someone in the group finally said. "He has worked here since, well for as long as I can remember. The guy just liked to be here. Nice man," he added.

"Why would anyone want to work in the same job for so many years doing the same thing over and over, day in and day out?" asked Mike, one of the techs in the group.

"Well, whatever he had to talk to her about, it must be important. Nothing gets past him," Rick mumbled, then nudged the person next to him and added, "We jokingly call him the walking check point. He has pointed out people to the screeners that he felt were sketchy and sure enough, he was right. Of course, now, the screeners are called T.S.A." Rick turned to the group to finish his story in case they may have overheard his brief factoid. "A few years ago, The Port actually caught an Al-Qaeda operative that had explosives strapped to him.

Carlton noticed him at his vehicle and followed him in the parking garage . . . at a distance, of course. Thanks to his quick thinking, it took the Port Police thirty seconds to get officers to the garage and they intervened before the guy accessed the airport. The fortunate point of the whole thing, is that the suicide bomber was doing a dry run and his explosive vest was not hot; totally fake and filled with kid's kinetic sand, playdoh, and fake wiring from stripped electrical cords. But no one had any reason to think it wasn't a live vest at first. Bomb squad and the robot came and everything. Even still, Carlton was a hero but refused to let us identify him to the press. He wanted no credit for it. Just said he is very observant and liked to help."

After a few seconds of silence, Mike looked around at everyone in the group and asked, "Have any of you ever had a long conversation with him? Smart ol' guy! Sometimes I think he should have been a professor. He's very intelligent."

Before she left the group, Agent Pahlavi looked at the Policewoman's badge, "Come with me, Officer Lansing. I need a female officer downstairs. And you too, Rick. As head of maintenance, I have some more questions for you." Then Pahlavi turned to the whole group. "Everyone else, wait here please, until I have confirmation on a couple things." She looked at the Port officers and added, "We may have to take new positions. I'll know more in a few minutes. Wait here."

Everyone was nodding at the appropriate time in answer to her fired off questions and orders. The others stayed with the blueprints and Agent Pahlavi took off at a quick pace back to the security office with Rick and Officer Lansing.

Chapter 28

Unraveling

PERRY PRATTLE WAS pressed against the walls of the bagwell as he wound his way from section to section, looking for Jahnni and her friends. He knew that he would find them. *I know you are here somewhere. You can't hide from me. I know every inch of this place.* "Stupid old man," he whispered out loud. "Arnie should have told me what I wanted to know when I asked him the first time." Then he crept further along the wall, now turning the corner to the actual roadway the tugs normally drove on when the place was used as an actual 'up and running' airport. "Now I'm just gonna kill him after I force it out of him. Oh wait. Silly me," he mumbled out loud. "I was going to do that anyway." He began chuckling under his breath like he was answering his own joke. He slowly pulled out a gun he had strapped to his side and noticed a sound behind a dumpster.

Perry crept towards the corner, stopping to listen, then

crept further towards the sound. He walked sideways with his back to the wall as he held his gun in front of him, faced up slightly so he was ready to move it in any direction should he need to quickly. *A little further. A little further, quiet now! I got ya. I know where you are hiding,* he was thinking in a sing-song voice in his head, all the while wearing an open-mouthed smile on his face. He swung his arm around the corner, holding tight to his gun and yelled, "I GOT YOU!" But only a couple little sparrows that had been feeding on tiny bread crumbs flew rapidly away from the danger.

He stood there for a few seconds before he jumped towards the dumpster and looked behind and beside it on the other side. Undeterred, he threw open the lid and pointed his gun inside the dumpster to catch whoever was hiding in it. But no one was there. Only some paper garbage, old lunch wrappings from the ground crews, and some old shredded up bag tags. *Okay, okay,* he thought. *I'm still coming for you. I will find you!* "I bet you are over by the fountain!" he whispered as he looked around to see that it was clear to leave the area the dumpster was tucked into. "Yes! That's where you are. You can't outsmart me. I knew the key was used there somehow. Ha, ha. I get it now. I get it," he added to himself, as it seemed to give him courage. He began slowly working his way towards the other side of the bagwell to get to the fountain area. He knew he could access the area. He would simply detonate the final distraction he planned so the ones guarding the fountain would run to help their buddies.

Wait, how am I going to do that if my cell phone is blocked from sending a wireless signal? Dammit! What was I thinking? Okay, I'll think of something else. I'll think of something really, really, good. I'm very smart! Don't, for a second underestimate me, you stupid people. You wait. By the time I'm done, you will think I'm the one that saved the day. I got this.

Chapter 29

Are the Rumorssssss True or Falsssssse?

AGENT PAHLAVI ENTERED the Port Security Office with the head of maintenance following close behind. She walked straight over to Carolyn first. She was standing by the wall but waiting to the side so she didn't interfere. Pahlavi asked her, "Does anyone know if the U.M.'s parents have been contacted yet?"

Carolyn bowed her head and then looked back up to answer her. "Yes. I sent word to the stations that were waiting for UM's later this evening, coming from us that is. Seattle has taken over the follow-up on all our SSR's. We now have our UM finally narrowed down to one young man coming into PDX who was supposed to transfer to a flight heading to San Fran. He's the one in the video. I told the San Fran station that our regular communications were down here, but if they can't get through to the SAT phone, they could send word through my liaison who will run back and forth off the property to relay messages. Our station manager in San Fran will not leave the parent's side. That is, until we can safely confirm his escorted arrival into SFO . . . once we have him again in our custody. I have not relayed details though. I am waiting for clearance once we know more.

"Okay, good. I need to send a team to them in San Fran. What do you know about him, like name, age, etc . . . I'll set that in motion right away." Pahlavi began taking more notes. Then she walked over to Officer Boulder.

"Tell me what you found with the time stamps on the videos. I just saw Doris and she told me she matched the agents with the badge numbers that had been used to access the doors. She also confirmed for me that the green area is indeed accessible. I sent two more techs back up to Prattle's office to try to confirm how he bypassed the system. The rest of the airport will remain in lockdown so spread the word. Here, she printed the security map showing the accessible points and the points of entry that were used. I'd like some of your officers to stay posted at these doors. My FBI agents will begin another interior team sweep. I need your officers to also continue patrolling the common areas this side of security here inside the airport and continue the entire property monitoring; except for the officers you chose to accompany my agents for the interior sweep, of course. I don't care what anyone says; if they manage to sneak out one of those doors, they are to be disarmed and detained until we can ascertain their identity and question them. I can confirm that we are looking for seven people for sure."

Agent Pahlavi turned to make eye contact with the team that was in front of her. "Now, besides Mr. Prattle and a possi-ble tall companion dressed as a security guard, name unknown yet," she said as she started handing out photos to help explain what they looked like, "we are looking for Jahnni Dawson, and Samantha Morrison-both agents for First Class Air. They are with an elderly gentleman who we haven't identified yet, and Beau Harleyman. Mr. Harleyman is an AI with the FBI, so he will be armed. We think he's caught up in this by accident, but still…disarm. They also have in their custody one UM, an Un-accompanied Minor named Eddie Link, traveling under the guidance of airline personnel. Again, disarm and detain. Re-member . . . There is a 13-year-old child somewhere on the other side of security. His safety comes first. Am I clear?" She spoke in exact words that would leave no question as to their orders. Everyone answered affirmatively.

"Good. Now," she pointed to two of her FBI agents, "I understand you know the AI involved. Tell me how you know him, for how long, and where is he stationed?"

She listened to them describe a very loyal team player with whom they trained at the Academy. They gave her what infor-mation they knew for sure and one of them ended with, "We went through the Academy maybe eleven, twelve years ago. With Harleyman, you never have to worry about your back."

Delaram Pahlavi looked at them and asked the obvious question. "Why is that? Isn't that a given?"

"Because he's not a hot-head," the blonde one answered.

"And he holds the highest score at the Academy, ever, for marksmanship," the red headed officer said with a cheesy grin. "He's very professional and focused. You may want to see about transferring him to PDX from Seattle when this is over. We'd love to work with him." He raised his eyebrows.

Agent Pahlavi regarded their words, then asked, "What do you mean 'holds the highest score?' You mean in your class at the Academy?"

The two agents looked at each other and then at her. The red-haired agent said, "Well, no ma'am. I mean yes, he holds the highest score, record, honors, whatever you want to call it, in our class. But the fact is, no one in recent history has outperformed him and until he joined the Bureau, there is no record of anyone with his marksmanship capabilities ever at the Academy."

"Interesting," Pahlavi said as she squinted to process their conversation. "I knew that there was 'someone' they called the Bullseye Messiah . . . but never even considered that I would encounter him. If this is him, that is. He's a good agent then?"

"Yes," they answered in unison.

"Harleyman has patience. He can defuse a situation without having to draw his weapon. But if he does, he'll win," The red-haired agent added.

The blonde agent cleared his throat and then in a serious tone added, "Call his SAC in Seattle, they'll pull his records anyway because of this incident. They'll tell you. You'll see."

Agent Pahlavi took in their brief but important conversation and made some notes. She glanced back up at them, nodded to convey her thanks, then dismissed them.

She turned to Officer Boulder and they began the process to pair up a Port officer with an FBI Agent and sent them as a group to access their assigned entry points in the active green sector that Doris found on the Port security map. Her agents needed the access and what better way than team them up with an officer from the Port. She gave each pair detailed plans to study while they waited to access the doors and actively pursue the seven that she was sure would be found on the 'other side.'

Pahlavi stood in one spot and turned to address the group. "We will access in thirty minutes from now. Heads up. I want our five brought out safe. Since the Port Manager is still unaccounted for, I assume, based on much information, that he is not friendly. I prefer he, and his cohort in the photo, be brought in alive for questioning."

The group broke and headed to their assigned places in the airport. Agent Pahlavi called to Rick, the head of maintenance, to follow her to the back of the office first. She intended to find out what he knew about the fountain access points and possible tie-in to the information, or rather rumors, that she gathered from Carlton. As bizarre as it sounded.

"So, is there another access point to the plumbing that feeds the fountain?" Pahlavi asked, getting right down to the question that was humming in her head.

"Well, I have never seen any other access, believe me. Because of the conspiracy theories over the years, it's not because I didn't search!" He laughed before he realized that he should remain somber. "There is a main access point for the plumbers, should they need to do repairs but it is an obvious system that runs from the water main. The largest inconsistency in the system from other commercial systems is that the pipes are rather large before the water meter. Then, the original large pipes from the previous construction site are still in use up to the water fountain. Once they hit the connection to the fountain, the plumbing is standard."

"So . . . how large is large? The original pipes that you are describing, that is?" Pahlavi asked.

"They are the size of a small culvert. A person could squat and crab walk through it as they do any repairs."

"So, let's just speculate that there could be some sort of wider or larger plumbing system somewhere else under here. Even larger than the one you just described. Like a pipe system that is possibly five times larger; in diameter, let's say? How would someone discover it? Or where would one do research to find it?" Pahlavi asked.

Again, Rick let out a chuckle. "I'm sorry, I don't t mean to laugh. It's just that . . . I uh . . . I've actually . . . okay . . . here's the truth." He nodded his head slightly up and down as he looked at Pahlavi with a grin. "I've actually done every search, in every city department, and every library looking for some sort of secret plans. I've even spoken with a historian trying to find or debunk this crazy theory that there is some sort of secret buried underneath PDX. There is nothing. Nada. Nein."

"So, if someone was on the other side of security, they wouldn't find any way to access some secret pipe chamber?" Pahlavi asked.

"Like a chamber of secrets? A basilisk roaming in our piping system?" Rick teased.

"Now you are making fun of me, aren't you?" Pahlavi said, breaking her serious tone with a small airy grunt. She wished she could have worded it differently, but it did sound Potterish now that she thought about it.

"No, I'm not. If anything, I'm making fun of myself for admitting to you that I spent any time at all trying to find such a thing myself. Or any other employee that has insisted they just knew there was a secret entrance somewhere because their uncle's, boss's, cousin in Tallahassee said that her friend's mom's 3rd husband heard once that it is true from a guy who used to work for the Max Light Rail. I mean really, what would be the point? Because if there was a point, the airport would have been attacked by now . . . don't you think?"

"True, I'll keep your words in mind. In the meantime, if you hear any whisssspers in the walls, let me know, okay?" she said in a serious tone before she finally cracked a slight smile.

"You got it," he chuckled, as he watched her walk away.

Pahlavi walked over to Officer Lansing, the Port Police officer, and asked her if she could stay with Carolyn. When Lansing looked back at Boulder to check if he heard her, and to approve the command that came from the FBI agent instead of her superior, Boulder nodded his assent. Lansing and Carolyn retreated to a back office to remain out of the way and Pahlavi and Boulder walked away to join the search.

Chapter 30

Green Is For Go

MR. T HAD pushed the big green button. The little room that the shivering group huddled in immediately began moving forward to the wide-eyed astonishment of the group. Not being prepared, they fell sideways in one lump towards the back of the small cavern, caught off-guard by the mysterious motion. Beau caught Crutch by the shoulder of his wet shirt to keep him from falling off the slick bench they were on. Samantha managed to stay on the bench.

Jahnni could feel the bottom of the room being linked to a moving chain-like device because it made a ratcheting sound like a roller coaster chain grabbing onto the track before it begins its ascent to the pinnacle of the ride. It felt like they were ascending. She looked at Beau to see if he noticed it as well. She tried to visualize their underground bearings in relationship to the airport.

Beau pulled back from her slightly and lifted her chin.

"I've kept a running picture in my head of the probable height, depth, and direction we have traveled since our little journey began with the first overhead announcement to exit the concourse. I don't get it, but hopefully all this will make sense, soon."

He stopped talking and encircled whoever he could reach with his left arm, as their shivers traveled like electricity through them. Mr. T was standing by the buttons on the front wall, and hanging onto the handles built into the wall. Beau turned slightly and used his right arm to reach across her and add more warmth for Jahnni by rubbing her left shoulder as she leaned into him. He poked Crutch to get his attention. "You doing okay buddy?"

"Yyyyyeesss," he stuttered, before they all started laughing at his chattering voice.

Mr. T spoke up. "Not too long. We get dry and get warm clothes."

"Wwwhere are we going, Mr. Trrrroooo . . . Mr. tttT?" Samantha shouted over the noise of the 'room' and commotion of everyone grappling to remain on the seat they sat on.

He seemed to have a steady grasp on the wall handle, then he smiled widely and answered Samantha, "I take you to safe place. I tell you before that I take care of you all. I tell you the truth! I take care of you." Then he looked at Jahnni and nodded, "I promise my boy here that I get you all safe."

Jahnni looked at Crutch, then at Sam. "I know you will, Mmmr. T. I know you will. Just tttell us what we can do."

Mr. T, still gripping the hand support said, "Nothing right

268

now. But, I suggest you all sit back, and grab handles above your head. Relax. This will be fuuuuuunnnn . . ." he raised an octave as the little room, that was shaped like a gondola, took a controlled dive downward. Jahnni soon felt a drag take hold of their enclosure but it continued its journey in what felt like a more level course.

"Okay," Mr. T added, "now we will soon climb. Hold on guys! It come soon." Before he finished his sentence, Jahnni felt the bottom once again clang onto a chain that began an ascent. A minute or two later they came to a complete, level stop.

"I know it probably doesn't seem possible, Pops, but . . . did we . . . just . . . go under the Columbia River?" Beau asked as his eyes scanned the little room. "Is this more like a gondola, or train car? Because it obviously isn't a little stationary room, and I'm pretty confident we moved north."

"I knew you had scientific brain, my boy! Why you choose FBI instead of drafting table is mystery to me." Mr. T chuckled.

The door latch began turning of its own volition around and around. They all stared at each other and then at the door as if seeing a ghost operating the mechanisms. Catching a quick glimpse of the others, Jahnni realized that there is absolutely no reason to even think anyone of them understood what was happening. Until they all glanced at Mr. T. He had let go of the handle that kept him steady on the ride to this new destination. He slowly walked towards the hatch with a slight puzzlement on his face and a tentative gait that slowed his movement. The realization of something must have tipped his decision over the zenith of his momentary confusion because Jahnni watched the questioning look on his face change to happiness. Mr. T was now standing in front of the hatch with a very large smile on his face. He groomed his hair down with his hands, slicking it back off his face, and tamping it down at the crown. His hat was lost back in the water feature that churned them around. Standing almost ramrod straight, he held his head high as he adjusted his shoulders in his damp suit, wiggled his arms downward as if being fitted by a tailor and patiently waited.

The hatch door lost the vacuum seal with a sucking release and swung open. Mr. T let out an emotional sigh and grabbed the edges of the opening, looking at the person standing on the other side of the hatch door. He was the first to lift his leg over the edge and immediately grabbed onto the man standing on the other side. They embraced and sobbed through laughter and hugs. They pulled apart, studied each other's face and then embraced again, wiping their own eyes and cheeks with their free hands. The others were silent, watching the scene before them. Jahnni spoke first, breaking the group's frozen gazes.

"Are you, I mean, could you possibly be . . . uh . . ." Jahnni stumbled the words out.

"Uncle Zale?" Beau asked.

Chapter 31

We're Comin' In

DELARAM PAHLAVI WAS just one among the several Port Police and FBI agents taking their places by their respective entrance points to access the secured area. Other Port Police stood guard at the inside doors around the airport, should any of the seven individuals try to remove themselves from behind the secured area.

She looked at her watch and glanced across the baggage pickup area to make eye contact with her team at the furthest access door that was in this area of the green parameter. She gave a hand command to proceed and received the universal okay hand gesture from those that had a visual on her. The Port officer assigned to his or her FBI agent accessed their respective doors with their badges and codes then opened their bypass doors swiftly and quietly, shutting the doors immediately behind them to prevent the alarm from sounding. She grabbed her SAT phone and made clicking noises on a button meant to convey a silent order to move forward to the rest of the teams that were not within sight range. The cat and mouse game was on and adrenaline was high.

Teams were coursing through the bagwell and searching behind bins, machinery, and every alcove. One would signal to the other to cover them and cross the small roadway under the airport, meant for baggage tugs that delivered bags to and from airplanes. They were fanned out, yet most had a visual on the other teams when they had a clear moment to stop and view the entire area of roadways and bag belts. While one was scanning the accessible floor area, the other was pointing their rifle or handgun above them, scanning the belt system that clung to the ceilings and wound its way down again to each airline's baggage sorting area. At various points, agents scaled the winding belts above their head, then signaled with their hands to the agent on the ground that it was clear. As each team arrived at an airline's bagwell, the search included a thorough search of every bag cart. Some sat empty, some were partially or fully loaded with suitcases, duffel bags, backpacks, and overnight cases. A handful of dogs or cats were locked in travel crates, awaiting transport among all the airlines checked items. Agent Pahlavi made a mental note to pass the info on to have the animals checked as soon as the incident was over and the area was clear. She didn't have time to see if they needed water and food, and although their silence was odd, it was welcome. The teams continued their search in the bagwells then began accessing the hallways that branched off like tunnels under the main part of the airport.

"This way," Boulder whispered, more like a silent lip reading, as he led Pahlavi down a corridor that had restrooms, and various doors that led to more offices. In the first, there were long rows of tables with computers lined up in front of its corresponding chair. This caused Pahlavi to assume this was a classroom for training airline ticketing or boarding agents. The whiteboard had a vertical list of words on one side, and what appeared to be a randomly ordered list of answers across from the first list. She read all the words. ARNK, Open Jaw, Direct, PNR, LEO, FLEO, FAM, FFDO. *They sure speak a different language here*, she told herself in her head.

Her SAT phone made a silent vibration and she froze. She squinted her eyes and read the text. Boulder noticed that she had stopped and he turned to glance over his shoulder, then back again to keep his eyes ahead, watching for danger. After Pahlavi backed into an alcove, she reached out and tapped his shoulder. She motioned for him to back towards her into the secure corner. She showed him the text she'd received.

She decided to complete their search in this particular wing under the airport, because she knew that they would eventually meet up with another team very soon as they completed a circle, some teams searching clockwise and others, counterclockwise. When the entire underground north side of the airport was clear, she signaled with the SAT phone that they were coming towards the south side, having cleared their assigned parameters.

She had considered very briefly, backing away from the search after she received the message, but she knew that even if they had a visual on the unfriendly Person of Interest, there still could be hostages secluded elsewhere. In her experience, POI's tended to have a backup plan that generally included bargaining, or something of value to threaten, in the hopes of securing a release. So far, they found no one else anywhere and it increased her fears that they wouldn't find them in time. Her tenacity pushed her forward, refusing to give up or leave any stone unturned. *Hang on guys. We'll find you,* she thought to herself, hoping to will it true.

Other teams had done a perimeter search around the building that included under the bellies of the aircraft that were pushed back away from the ramp when the emergency went into effect. If there was someone hidden, they would have found them. Just like another team had found Perry Prattle. That was the message that Pahlavi received before she continued the search for the rest of the missing people. *POI under observation#holding back#alaska airlines luggage sorting area.*

Pahlavi and Boulder came around the corner and quietly joined the group watching Prattle. Liam, Pahlavi's partner was with another Port Policeman. She nodded to him when they saw each other. She quietly watched Perry, as did the others. Without a care, other than his immediate concern, they observed him scratching and clawing at a large hole in the wall under the area of the fountain, a tool in his hand that looked like a gardening hand rake. He appeared to be trying to access what Pahlavi ascertained as probably plumbing fixtures; if she was to make a wild guess as to what was ensconced in the pillar. His movements were erratic and she couldn't understand what he intended to gain by using his hands and a small tool to scratch and chip away at a surface that was unyielding. On the floor beside him was a tool bag. Sitting on the floor beside the bag was an oscillating multi-tool and several attachment heads that showed use. She observed him long enough to realize that the battery must have died. In his determination, he must have thought he could use his hands to finish the job. That would never happen. He picked up a hammer and began to slam the pillar, trying to breach the heavy concrete surface. After knocking out chips here and there, he again, began using his hands to pick at pieces of loosened paint and concrete chips.

They all watched him for some time, as they kept their cover. The last thing they wanted was to grab him and realize that he was strapped with a suicide vest. Pahlavi knew that they were doing the same intense visual on his movements as she was. They were eliminating that threat.

They could all see that he had a gun tucked into the back of the waistband of his pants and one strapped to his side in a holster, clinging to his wet sweaty shirt. His shirt was half-tucked in, his pants were covered in dust, and his hair was disheveled as sweat poured down the side of his face. They had seen enough. She pointed at two teams to take him down. Always assuming he could also have a weapon at his ankle, they moved in to do a routine takedown and pinned him to the ground, searching and cuffing him. They made no noise other than the scuffling and grunting of energy expended while doing their job. Prattle must not have heard them come upon him, because he froze like a limp doll and rolled with the takedown. He did not resist their force and his face appeared vacant, stunned. The teams remained silent as some were part of the apprehension and some kept a vigil on the area behind them.

At this point, she could see no other direction to take until she questioned Mr. Perry Prattle. She instructed everyone to exit the area and escort suspect one to the Port Police Security Office. She intended to bleed him of whatever information he had on the airline employees and their companions. POI two was still unaccounted for so she assumed he could be holding them somewhere else. But where?

She stared intently at Perry Prattle reading his body language and facial expressions. He stared ahead, saying nothing. His face was like stone, showing no emotion which masked his thoughts. It took a couple minutes to reach their exit point that led back to the carousels in the passenger baggage pick-up area, located near the Port offices. Right as she walked up to the door, the SAT phone that Perry had been using, began to ding. They looked at each other and then to Agent Pahlavi.

"You want us to answer it?" an agent asked.

Pahlavi looked at Perry, "Who could that be?"

Perry turned to answer her. "If you let me answer it, I can tell my friend to bring them to you. The others. He can bring them to you."

"Hand him the phone," Pahlavi ordered. "Keep it brief."

The agent that was carrying Perry's duffle bag held the phone up to Perry's mouth and clicked it on.

"Yes . . . You need to . . ." he said before he paused. His eyes darted back and forth. "Get the key at all costs. Do whatever you must do, to get it. I'm being arrested."

The agent yanked the phone back from his mouth and Pahlavi got up into his face. "What was that all about? You said you were going to have the others brought here. You lied!"

Perry turned his face towards hers, stared into her eyes and with nary any emotion said through gritted teeth, "You know the ones you're trying to save are probably dead, right?"

Chapter 32

Are You . . .?

J AHNNI WAS AS perplexed as a person could be. The day's events were playing on a loop and she certainly didn't see this coming. Her eyes shifted from one man to the other. They stood there embracing, releasing, then embracing and releasing again, looking each other over then laughing jovially with overflowing happiness pouring off their lips in Greeklish. That is the only thing Jahnni could describe it as; a mixture of two languages fighting for dominance when words couldn't come fast enough. Both began to speak then they both stopped and held out a hand to the other to speak first.

Jahnni turned to Beau, posing the burning question. "Wait, this is your uncle?" Then turning to face Mr. T and pointing to Zale she asked, "Then how do you know him, Mr. T?"

Mr. T stood with his arm around the man's shoulder and beamed as he proudly attested, "This. This," he stuttered slightly as he held his tears at bay, "Is my brother. Mr. Zale Baptiste. I thought he was lost to me. I cry many tears of happiness this day."

Jahnni looked at Beau. "So, if Mr. T is your grandpa, then Mr. Baptiste is your, what, great-uncle? So, did you know he was here?" As she arced her arms out as she inspected her surroundings.

"Well, I am pleased to meet you, I think," Samantha said as she reached her hand forward around Jahnni to introduce herself to Mr. Zale Baptiste. "I'm Samantha, and this is my temporary charge, Crutch." Crutch extended his arm shyly, and shook hands.

Zale was staring at Jahnni's lanyard that was hanging around her neck, surprisingly still attached considering the mileage of adventures they had today. She patted her wet clothing and realized that her shirt was untucked. She felt self-conscience when he started squinting as he looked more intently at her badges. One was her airline badge that proved she is employed by First Class Air and the other was the airport SIDA badge that gave her access to the security doors as well as proof, when seen by others, that she has permission to be in secured areas. "Oh. I'm sorry. I'm Jahnni," she said as she reached to shake his hand. Then she added, "I think we need to find something dry to put on. I don't want to die of hypothermia before we have a chance to clear our names . . . back there."

"Forgive me," Zale offered as he bowed to Jahnni. He pointed towards the hallway. "Right this way. There are many sizes, although only one style. Help yourselves. I have two rooms that you can use. One is a large shower/restroom."

They all started walking towards the direction he pointed. Behind them Zale began mopping up the puddle from their dripping clothes. He smiled as he glanced up and caught Jahnni looking back. She felt bad about the puddles, *but what could we do about it?* Beau was silent as they began walking towards the hall. Then he stopped and walked back to Pops and Zale. He gave them both a big hug, and turned back to find the dry clothes.

He stopped Jahnni in the hallway to add in a whisper, "I wondered where he'd been all this time. When I saw that reservation we were looking at, back in your baggage office, I saw his name so I knew the white suited guys couldn't be the enemy. Of course, it shocked me to see his name, but I knew at that moment that things would come together somehow. For what reason, I had no idea. I was so surprised because we haven't heard from him or seen him for many, many, years. Pops has been so sad all these years about losing his brother. I didn't want to say anything in front of him when I saw it. False hopes can damage a heart you know."

Jahnni's voice squeaked as she answered him concerning his damaged heart comment, "I know more about that subject than you think." Her heart had been arguing with her the entire time since she met Beau. *Don't get your hopes up. Get your hopes up. Don't waste your time thinking he even noticed you. He noticed you! He noticed you! False hopes? I think I wrote that book,* her thoughts echoed as they taunted her.

Not catching her meaning, he continued talking to her,

"I don't think Pops thought anyone was going to be here when he brought us here. I guess he thought it was still abandoned. Or I can only assume he thought that, because this place is news to me, as it is to you."

Jahnni glanced back to where she could see Mr. T and Zale talking eagerly in low tones. Zale had given Mr. T a blanket that he was wearing like a teepee. She noticed that he looked relatively warmer, so she put her anxiety about him to the back of her mind. For now. She looked back at Beau and said, "So the underground piping system is real. And Zale, who was the original builder and company owner of the water plant, is still alive. That means Carlton was right. There is a conspiracy theory for everything and everyone, and that some conspiracy theories may be linked to some bits of truth. But we are safe here, with Zale, aren't we?"

"Wait, what? Carlton who? And yes, we are safe," Beau said, as he pulled back slightly anticipating her answer.

"I am freezing! I have to get some dry clothes on," she murmured between chattering lips, not realizing she missed what he said. "We can talk when we all get dried off. You go first." She pointed to Beau.

His smile made his dimples light up. "Uh . . . no you don't. You don't get to delegate me into dry clothes while you stand here and shiver. You go first. Get dry. Sam went in that door over there. Get going . . . and don't argue. I insist on you going in there first."

"Okay Poseidon, but look, there are two doors. Crutch must be changing in that one. I'll meet you out here when we all get dressed. We'll have to figure out how to get out of here after we listen to what Zale has to say."

With that, they disappeared down the rest of the hallway; Jahnni harboring a temporary feeling of safety because she knew that they had to get back to the airport. She watched him walk towards the door that Crutch went in. Conflict raced through her chest like a burning building, but she called out anyway, "Uh, Beau?" *Oh great, what am I thinking? I can't be so forward. This is no time to think about my own issues right now. Our safety and innocence in this whole airport mess is at stake! Oh shoot. He is looking at me and waiting for me to say something. I can't ask about him . . . me . . . us. What if there isn't an us. What if it's his pheromones . . . or, or, or . . . testosterone, or who knows, some type of tritones leaking out of his pores that have me imagining that he might be interested in me. He does look like a Greek sea god. What am I thinking? He is staring at me waiting for a response. I can't just blurt it out! What would I say, 'do you like me? Check the box yes or no.' What is wrong with my brain? I should say . . . something. I'll just say, uh, uh,* "Hope your clothes fit."

With that, he cocked his head to the side and smiled. "Hope yours do . . . also?" Then he turned and pushed on the door, pulling his shirt off over his head before the door even closed.

Jahnni stood there, watching him walk through the door, taking in . . . no memorizing, his physique. She had never in her life felt her knees literally feel like they were going to give out from something besides fear. Her feet didn't seem to understand that she was telling them to begin walking again. *Walk! Let's go! No, this way. THIS door where Samantha is,* her mind commanded her body. She stumbled towards the door she was meant to go into, but she was on autopilot. She pushed on the door. Pausing for one more glance at the door that Beau entered, she felt shivers of ice mixed with fire burning in her veins. *Oh boy, I'm in trouble. I think I'm way over my head . . . for Beau.*

Chapter 33

An Unraveling Basket Can't Hold Water

OH MAN, WRONG thing for Mr. Prattle to say to Special Agent Delaram Pahlavi. She immediately grabbed his arm and began dragging him towards the Port Police Office. The other officer on his right, who also had Mr. Prattle's other arm in his grip had to trot to keep up. Her face was slightly flushed with anger as she glanced once more at his face before shoving him into the private room that Office Boulder had shown her, earlier, should she need it.

"SIT! Do you remember me? Special Agent Delaram Pahlavi, FBI." She flipped open her badge wallet and held it in front of his face, then continued speaking as she paced behind and beside him, "What do you mean, 'They're probably dead?'" Boulder walked into the room and stood there. Agent Pahlavi nodded towards four of her agents and motioned for them to watch Prattle. She tipped her chin upwards towards Boulder, directing him outside the door for a chat.

She stopped pacing and stood with her feet firmly planted as she gathered her notes and her thoughts. "Okay . . . We did a full sweep of the entire bagwell: all offices, elevators, closets, shafts, hallways, alcoves, and even ice makers for heaven's sake. You name it, we searched it. Between your people, my people, we can't find his accomplice. You know we were thorough! No one found the others either. You saw Prattle having some type of episode, you were with me! He was manic, delusional, who knows." Pahlavi was pacing, almost in place as she tried to isolate the facts from her anger at Prattle. "We apprehended him near a wall pillar that appears to be under the general vicinity of the water fountain. He was grabbing, clawing, and exerting a great deal of energy trying to get to what I assume is some type of underground plumbing. That is unless you have some other ideas."

Officer Boulder waited to process what she was saying. He narrowed his eyes and asked, "What makes you so sure he was trying to get into some type of plumbing? Maybe he was trying to gain access to something else? Like, maybe . . . hmmm. Can't think of anything else that a wall like that would lead to. Maybe he is psychotic and thought he was trying to go through a door or something."

"Not likely." Delaram answered. "I mean I would not rule out some type of delusions. Why else does anyone plan crimes? But he has been up to something this entire time. Look," as she began holding up one finger with each point she as making. "He has been the Port Manager for some time. He has finagled his own security cameras in his office. He has somehow created another, or tapped into, the security main access program . . . from his office. He keeps disappearing from us, with no other place he could have been, because we all have searched for him. Then we apprehend him behind security, which means he also used a bypass door BEFORE we figured out that there was a quadrant that was not locked down. Which means that he has had full access, and probably anyone else who knew that their badges worked, this entire time."

Boulder seemed cautious. "So, you are implying that this isn't a random act of terrorism to plant a bomb in the fountain? You are saying this has been an inside job from the beginning? Why? For what?"

Delaram was talking as she also was gathering the different pieces of information to tie them together. "Okay . . . we have a fountain. We have a belief that someone is trying to plant a bomb, which by the way is vehemently denied by the First Class Air's Manager when she was told it was one of her best agents. Told to her by the way, by Mr. Perry Prattle. It has also been brought to my attention by someone who, right now wishes to remain anonymous but that could change later, that Perry Prattle is the son of one of the original water plant scientists that helped develop the original land site here. He intimated that this may have been a long-time plan to gain access to the mysterious piping system that everyone thought was merely gossip and unfounded stories of mystery. Are you with me so far?" she asked.

"Yes," Boulder said, his face showing he waited anxiously for the rest to unfold.

287

"Okay, apparently, as we saw in the playback video, Prattle has two people working for him who we are told, no one recognizes. Possibly private security detail, possibly Port cops waiting for their backgrounds to clear . . ." she added.

"Wait, I have never seen those guys on the video until today. I have met all my recruits and they aren't allowed to patrol or act in an official capacity until their backgrounds are clear, they complete on the job training, and pass all their Port training exams after completing recruitment training and are sworn in. Even transfers must be BC'd again. I sign off on all the background checks and those guys are not on my list." Boulder explained insistently.

"Okay, then they are rogue, working for Prattle. I checked earlier on the one guy, Craigs. Prattle claimed he was assaulted by Jahnni, and he's still in the hospital. His head wound is still under observation. They can't close it until the swelling goes down so he isn't leaving the hospital any time soon. I've sent a detail to the hospital to guard his door. I'm not going to let him disappear on us. That's for sure. But where is the other guy? And who is he? We didn't see him down there. Remember, Prattle gathered one of our cooperative teams together down on the main floor to inform them that this Craigs guy was assaulted by Jahnni and an accomplice. He passed out photos and told us about some bomb plot that Carolyn from FC Air has completely debunked as garbage. She seems sincere, but we will still validate everything. I remember that I saw this other guy when he was standing with Prattle the first time he came down to say he was gathering some 'behind the scenes' info and would bring it to us. I admit that I wasn't zeroed in on him. We also saw video of the back of his head in the replay that showed Jahnni and an older gentleman being strong-armed into an elevator. Which by the way, leads to the floor that Prattle's office is on. So, if this guy has been with Prattle, where is he now? I can only assume he is holding the others hostage somewhere. Because they weren't down there either!"

"But why," Boulder asked, trying to fill in the blanks, "would Prattle go through all this trouble for a fountain that our own plumbing department has access to anyway? It doesn't make any sense."

The two were silent as they thought about that. Then in unison as if one brain was shared between the two of them they said, "Unless there really is another plumbing system."

Delaram smiled. "You know. We can't talk about this until we verify everything. There could be a major security breach happening. Or has happened. The public can't know about this yet. Who knows who will talk anonymously. So please . . . let this be between you and me, and of course my partner Agent Liam Anthony, once I fill him in. That is, until we figure this out. There is always the fact that we could be wrong . . . and we will incite panic if we say anything at this point. Let's be cautious. Let's clear the room and talk to Prattle like we already know everything. Agreed?"

"Why even ask," Boulder said. "Agreed."

With that, they shook hands and proceeded back into the room to speak with Prattle; with a little more confidence than they had a mere fifteen minutes prior.

Chapter 34

Sealing the Leak

THE PIPES WERE large, but not as big as the original intake and outflow that was used to draw water from the Columbia River or the aquifer that was used in decades' past. Mimi and Adrian swam in a single file through the piping system, nodding to each other to verify that all was good. Their small but bright headlamps lit up the area wherever they pointed their heads. Dark water became clear. Dark walls became light. Further up, Mimi pointed to a hatch that they knew was their exit point after they finished the welding project they were sent to do. They swam a few feet more then stopped to remove the small loads. Mimi pulled the equipment off her back and passed the cables to Adrian. He swam back to the hatch on the ceiling of the pipe and opened it to gain access to their power supply.

It was a little daunting to work while wearing the insulated gloves but he was used to it. He just moved slower and with more purpose. He climbed back in the pipe and signaled to Mimi that it was ready and she began preparing the welding equipment to close the large rip in the wall of the pipe. It was almost too big, but they were told to attempt this first.

Adrian remembered that Zale warned them that if they couldn't close off the leak, it would jeopardize the entire foundation of the airport. Maybe not in a week, or a month. But over time, it would erode the earth and cause serious damage. Irreparable damage. Why the airport manager detonated a small explosive device down the water fountain was beyond him. All he could figure was that Perry had some notion that it would create a breach in the pipe and lead him to some secret area. Desperation maybe? Crazy, unworkable ideas?

Adrian was happy knowing that in a little while, they'd be free. Free from schlepping bags, free from watching their backs, free from hiding their highly-trained skills, and free from Mr. Perry Prattle. They had their escape already planned once the pipe was welded and the mere thought of freedom made him smile.

In between the seriousness of the welding job, Adrian marveled at the Aquatic Vent, the breathing device they were using. He was proud that it was invented in their own country, Hungary, and was now being tested at Quantico. Using it, quite successfully he thought, was truly proof of concept. He tested it for a year before the FBI, and the Marines Special Ops, jumped onboard for testing. The swimmers he trained caught on quickly and once they trusted the device, nothing separated them from the fish. Oxygen in the water was converted by the crystals and swimmers could do many more things underwater that normally required tanks. Again, lighter weight. Freedom. Even the welding helmet was a new lighter weight that made traversing their amphibious path much easier than they first thought. Mimi gave Adrian an eager thumbs-up. The job would be successfully completed in no time. At that thought, daydreaming was set aside and focus took over. He watched as Mimi set to work and the bright flash of the underwater welder began its powerfully bright glow.

Chapter 35

The Mystery of the Rock Key

ZALE MOTIONED TO the group to sit around the large wooden table. He brought out a cauldron-looking pan and set it down on a round metal plate designed into the middle of the table. A stack of bowls was passed around. "Might as well eat before we leave. You need energy, am I not right?" Zale said while he handed each person a large spoon. They all took turns using the ladle to fill up their bowls.

"I didn't realize how hungry I was until I smelled something cooking," Jahnni said, to anyone listening. *Ah . . . that must be why I felt a little faint when I watched Beau walk into the changing room.* She glanced over at Beau then admitted to herself, *Nope, that wasn't it.*

"Me too. I'm starving," Crutch said laughing, as he rubbed his hands together. He then waited patiently for everyone to fill up their bowls before he dug in.

Silence took over the room as spoons clanked and lips

occasionally smacked to make sure every morsel and dribble didn't miss the target.

After Beau had consumed most of his stew, he turned to Zale and asked, "Say, before we leave, I need a few minutes to clean my weapon. I know she'll probably fire fine . . . but I want to make sure. Do you have a kit for cleaning guns?"

Zale looked at the gun in the damp leather holster beside Beau. Beau flipped open his soggy ID with a smile. "Can't say much about the money in it, but my ID seems okay. Good enough?"

"Of course," Zale said with a wink and smile. "I'll grab it. In the meantime, fill up. You never know if they'll feed you while in questioning." He added as an afterthought, "You know they will separate all five of you and question you separately, right?"

Beau smiled as he dipped another ladle of stew into his bowl. "I expect it. We just need to tell the truth, leaving out nothing."

"Well, I better decide what I can't live without when we leave," Zale said as he opened a tall olive green filing cabinet. "I believe that once we leave, I may not have the opportunity to come back here."

"Not so fast. You aren't locked up yet," Beau reminded him. "They are going to need you to walk them through everything in the underground plant and show them how the "under the river" ride works. Which by the way, was quite an engineering feat. How did you manage that?"

"Oh, well, my brother here, was one hell of a mastermind

in his own right," Zale said as he nodded his head toward his brother, Arnad. "We took advantage of the river dredging project on the north side of the island at the time to manage our own project. I owned the rights to the island, so that wasn't a problem being seen on the island. Except building projects were not necessarily allowed. The dredging equipment and basically the entire work zone, gave us opportunity to pull it off. They dredged on the north, we built on the south."

Samantha motioned to Jahnni like she wanted her to do something. Jahnni shrugged her shoulders and mouthed the word, *What?* Samantha darted her eyes to Mr. T and then nodded to Zale. Still, Jahnni didn't know what she meant, so she shrugged again then pointed at the important task at hand; eating more stew.

Finally, Samantha cleared her throat and took a big breath. "I know there has to be a story here," she said, breaking the remaining silence. "Baptiste and Tropopoulis are two different names. I mean, for being brothers. And, your name is Harleyman," she added as she pointed to Beau with her spoon. "If I am not mistaken about what I've heard over the course of the day, shouldn't at least two of you have the same last name? I mean, since men keep their father's names. Oh, I'm sorry, is that rude of me to ask?"

"Zale, Beau, and Arnad are strong men of strong genes," Mr. T proudly announced, raising his chin in pride. "Zale and I share same mother, different fathers. Zale's father killed in war."

Zale jumped into the conversation, adding, "My, our,

mother had a tough struggle during the war years, being a widow and a young mother, but she met and married Arnad's father. They had Arnad soon after. But life was still hard. We spent many years escaping invasions of Austria, and then my father's homeland, Greece. He was a very good man, rest his soul."

Zale continued his commentary, "It is a little confusing, but we were raised as brothers, not half-brothers. Arnad, or Mr. T as you call him, stayed with the family after they settled back in his father's village. Arnad's father is also Greek, but he was studying in Austria when he met our mother. Eventually, I left home at 14 to come to America, lived with a distant relative, and went to school. I am the first American in our immediate family. Arnad stayed in Greece."

Mr. T added more explanation, "Then I come with my new wife Konstantina, about six years later after my Daphne was born. Daphne grow up and marry Beau's father, Reginald and here come busy Beau baby!"

The table erupted in laughter. Jahnni looked over at Beau and said, "Hmmm . . . busy Beau baby, huh? Now, that is what we'll call you from now on. Busy Beau Baby." Again, everyone continued to laugh. Even Beau.

Jahnni held Beau's gaze as they continued laughing. His eyes felt like they pierced right to her thoughts and she felt the heat of embarrassment slowly creep up into her cheeks. She knew that her walls had been coming down and her real feelings were surfacing over the course of the day. Doubt told her to hold it in, but something else screamed for her to resurrect them. Then . . . *Oh, damn. That quiver up and down my spine is still there.*

Zale cut in to talk over the laughter, "My beautiful Sue gave me Carlton. She was a wonderful mother to our boy. She died suddenly when he was only fifteen." He paused to smile at her memory. "He grew up and married Juanita. They had many happy years. Until, that is . . ." And Zale got silent.

Everyone waited for what came next, but he had tears in his eyes and just looked at the floor before glancing to some photos on the wall. He took a breath and said, "Carlton's son Monty was killed in action in the Gulf war. It was called, uh, Operation Iraqi Freedom. His helicopter was shot down, but, he handled it long enough for his people . . . his team I mean, to jump out over the river. He is a hero. But he is very much missed by everyone."

Jahnni stuttered as she tried to say something comforting, but she knew too many words were useless. So, she said softly, "I'm sorry."

Beau looked at her with a puzzled look on his face. "What?" Jahnni managed to say.

"You mentioned 'Carlton said that there is a conspiracy theory for everything . . .' Who were you talking about? What Carlton? I mean what does he look like?" Beau interjected with confusion.

Zale looked up at Jahnni. "So, you have met my boy Carlton? He has had immense sadness you know. His mother died while he was so young, lost his boy in Iraq, then his wife Juanita died of cancer. He likes simple things now. Hates war. He is very dedicated to protecting our old interests under the airport." Zale shook his head as he let out his breath. "I have made a terrible mistake. I should have told them, but I thought it was too late. I thought I was going to have another chance to buy back my property so I didn't want to destroy her. Then as the airport project got underway, I thought for sure by this time I could not tell them now. Later, I realized that there is no way I could EVER tell them. I have spent all these years trying to keep the airport safe in case someone finds out about the pipe system under it. Carlton is the only person that I could trust to help me, until now. No one else has known anything except for two others that I have come to trust." Then he looked at Arnad, "I am so sorry brother for disappearing. One day led to many days. Then to months, then years. I wanted to contact you, but I thought it safer to just, hide. Not involve you."

Jahnni looked around at everyone then got up and walked closer to Zale to say, "I am sorry to tell you this, but someone has found out about it. Or something about it. In fact, he has two very bad guys that are helping him. And there are two other people that seem to be looking for these two bad guys and watching the fountain already. To make matters worse . . ."

Zale spoke up, "Ah, you mean Mimi and Adrian. They are the two that I just mentioned. They work for the Hungarian Water Preservation Council and were hired by me to get jobs at the airport and find out just how much people know. You know, the gossip among the workers. They were there a little over a month when they finally made it down to the secret pipes, checking for leaks, weak pipes, testing the water flow, and making sure that no one has found the entrance or tampered with anything. I thought I heard water movement during one of my own inspections but I am too old to be checking inside pipes anymore. I could hear the leak when I was there doing a routine check but it was too much for me to fix now. So, I reached out to the HWPC and Mimi and Adrian were chosen to help."

"Wait, you mean they are for sure . . . good guys? You hired them?" Jahnni asked.

"Well, I know them from my more recent meetings in Hungary. Earlier in my life, I studied with the son of Viktor Schauberger in Austria. We studied the theories of Viktor's understanding of water purification. I opened my water treatment plant . . . many, many years later right here," Zale explained as he pointed with his entire arm in the general vicinity of PDX. "Later, when I had nothing left of my plant, I went back and forth to Hungary to work with the HWPC to improve global water issues. Although they are on the Water Preservation Council, they are also formerly with the Special Forces in Hungary. So, when I heard that . . . Oh, you were going to tell me about . . ." Zale stopped talking to look at Jahnni.

Jahnni thought back to what they were talking about earlier then added, "Oh, ya. I was going to tell you about the Airport Manager and the things Mr. T and I have learned about him."

"Ah, yes, I forgot to mention to you brother, that I met a man named Perry Prattle. Bad man, he is. He want to kill nice Janie and me!" Mr. T said with wide eyes.

"Yes, I know all about this person." Zale looked worried and blurted out loudly, "What do you mean he wants to kill you?" Then he looked at Jahnni, "Please explain this to me."

By this time, everyone in the room was silent and staring at the three while they had their own conversation between them. Beau stopped momentarily to pipe up from across the room, "Ya, what do you mean he wants to kill you?"

"Weeelllll," Jahnni turned towards Beau and answered. "I was going to tell you, but I haven't had time yet to tell you what happened to us when Craigs and Benson dragged us upstairs from the bagwell."

Mr. T stepped forward and placed his hand on Zale's shoulder, "I know I am not a big man, in suit size. But up here," he paused as he tapped his index finger on his temple several times, "I am very, uh, very, very, uh, crafty! Wily, like that coyote fellow! What I mean about meeting him is, well, I guess I know him, we both know him, many years ago, when he was a boy. But now I meet him as a grown man. By the way, he is still a brat."

"He's right," Jahnni said. "If it wasn't for Mr. T's quick thinking, we might never had gotten away."

Crutch finally piped up with eagerness, "Come on Jahnni! What happened while you guys were up there? Tell us everything!"

Everyone was meandering around the room, having finished their stew. Zale motioned everyone to sit back down at the table. Then he nodded to Jahnni and Arnad, his brother, to go ahead, "Tell us what you learned."

Beau interjected almost without taking a breath. "And tell us what you mean by he wanted to kill you . . . I mean, I'll tell you what I would have done if something like that would have happened!" He started mumbling under his breath, "Kill you? He's lucky I am sworn to justice, or he'd meet the other end of my justice here," he said as he looked at his gun he was reassembling. Then he looked up at Pop's worried face. "Don't worry, Pops, I'm not gonna do something rash . . . unless I need . . . or rather, it's protocol for the situation." He finished talking as he glanced back at Jahnni with a smile.

Jahnni and Mr. T took turns telling them all that happened once they arrived upstairs in Mr. Prattles office. Mr. T kept calling him Perry, and Jahnni kept referring to him as Mr. Prattlaaayyy, wrinkling her nose and frowning every time she had to mention his name. When Mr. T got to the part about Perry's plans to get rid of them, he exclaimed, "And do you know that he killed his own father!"

Zale shook his head back and forth. "I suspected that when I read that he died on the Deschutes River. His son was quite a handful. Smart, but a handful. I should have done something earlier. But I waited to see if he was going to try to find a way into the airport underground. I wasn't even sure that he knew about it. When I read that he was appointed the Port Manager, I knew deep down that something was afoul."

Jahnni and Mr. T started talking at the same time. Jahnni motioned for Mr. T to go ahead. "He say he found a key in his father's belongings after he died. I was confused you see, because I do not remember anything about a key. He told us about a rock that had the roman numeral II on it. When I accidentally see it while looking around office, I just took it. Here," Mr. T motioned towards the wall as he took a few steps to the chair. It was in a bundle of blankets and his wet clothes. He pulled out the rock that he had guarded on their journey, safely tucked into a buttoned inside pocket . . . in his brown plaid suit. "Mr. Perry Prattle say it is part of two rocks that work together to open a safe. I don't know of this safe, but he startle me when he said he knew it was under the airport. I didn't know that anyone knew about the old pipes. Just in case, here. You can have it."

Zale accepted the rock, and juggled it up and down with his right hand as if he was determining its weight, or value. He looked over at his filing cabinet and walked over to it. He waited a few moments, then opened the bottom cabinet. It rolled forward and displayed its contents. There were several rocks of similar size, similar also in that they all had markings on them. He pushed a few rocks aside then chose one. The room was silent.

"This rock that I just picked up . . . is the other half of this rock that I hold in my other hand. The others you see here in the drawer are also similar. I chose them carefully myself. Each one has a special meaning to me, as well as the recipient." He walked back to the table where everyone was still gathered. "But it is not a key . . . as you were told. It is a reminder of each large project I have worked on over my career. I always look for one of similar size, and have it cut in half, and a flat section smoothed out so that I can have a number engraved. This one here was a gift to Perry's father, because he was instrumental in the research for our first project together. I had its match made for me. It had a Roman numeral I on mine because I was the lead. Some of my partners have rocks that have different etchings altogether. Like a scientific symbol or the $E=MC^2$. My favorite rock had scroll letters that were written in medieval script that said H_2O. Again, it is not a key. Unless you equate the memories of so many long years ago, of friendship and collaboration in quite a few projects as a key, to this old man's heart. I could not have succeeded without his genius. Or anyone's help. It is just . . . my thing. Rocks are strong and quite beautiful to me."

"So . . . it is not a key to open secret safe? That is what he told us it was for. He said he figure it out. And it must have a number I on other rock. He tell us it opens your secret safe," Mr. T added.

"Well, yes there is a safe, but it is no different than a large safe any household has," Zale answered as he pointed to the safe he had retrieved the second rock from. "It preserves all of my life's works. Articles, lectures, blueprints, copies of contracts. I also have all my court records and testimonies of witnesses when the city forced me to close down my company and sell my land. It has my citizenship papers when I became an American citizen, Carlton's original birth certificate, things like that. Nothing of mystery. Although it is odd that Perry came to that conclusion, it warms my heart that his father saved it all these years."

Jahnni narrowed her eyes, remembering the conversation

in Mr. Prattle's office. "He said he was going to get the original blueprints, actually . . . I think he sent Craigs and Benson to break in somewhere and get them but they screwed up. He entered the water purifying contest using his father's notes and apparently won. So, now he thinks once he retrieves all your stash, he will sell everything to the Chinese and become richer than Bill Gates."

Zale started laughing uproariously. He snorted when he tried to catch his breath and tried to talk but it triggered more snorting and laughing. One by one, they all started to join the laughter because his laugh made them laugh. Finally, Zale began to calm down enough to try to explain.

"Forgive me. But that is like saying, 'I am going to steal your technology for the 8-track player your father developed.'" Then he started laughing until he had to sit. "Oh my . . . oh my . . . I can't stop laughing. He is so stupid. You are right, brother; he is still a brat. A dumb brat."

Samantha and Jahnni were the first to stop laughing so hard. Jahnni didn't quite get it and said, "Wait, what's so funny? You had built that enormous structure and apparently from what I heard, it purified water better than anyone else could."

Zale waited while he caught his breath and stopped coughing. "My dear, there was a time a few decades ago, where my research was groundbreaking. I could have saved, literally saved, millions of lives at that time with my water technology. You must understand that research has always continued. Not only by me, but by many, many scientists in countries all over the world. My research back then is old news now. What took my entire plant to do, can now be done glass by glass with a straw. A STRAW! Now that is research that I am proud to say I contributed to . . . under an assumed name of course. If he would have just asked, I would have given him copies of that water purifying technology for nostalgia's sake. My plant is old, even though I keep her from decay. She is like a beautiful woman that you have been married to for forty to fifty years. She was once a fresh faced young teenager and now, although the lines in her face reveal her age, she is still beautiful. She cannot run as fast, do somersaults, dance the night away, or produce children any longer, but her life is, was, and will continue to be as important as the earth itself. Sorry . . . I get carried away when I talk about her."

"I get it," Beau said softly. "You gave the project everything you had. You ended up, basically, giving it your entire life. You have lost so much. I hope that no matter what happens, we will all stay close now and be a family again."

Zale wiped a tear from his cheek and shook his bowed head up and down. He reached for Beau with one arm, to hug him while he was sitting, and with the other arm he pulled his brother Arnad into a hug. "Yes, I would like that. This is all my fault. No amount of planning can fix this. I'll take you all back to the airport. You can take me to whoever you think will listen. No doubt, there will be someone in charge of the whole scene there. I will explain everything. Of course, I may have to go to jail, eventually. But this has been a good life. I made a difference. I made good water. I have taught the Hungarian Water Preservation Council all that I know, and they teach others, working with communities all over the world."

Arnad said softly, "There is plenty of time to catch up all these missing years, brother. But for now, I have warm heart knowing that I have you back again. By the way, where is Carlton? I have not seen him since we go to Monty's funeral. I knew in my heart that since you were not there, that you must have died. I just hug Monty and express how much I miss you as well. He just hug me back and say nothing about you being alive."

Zale continued explaining, "Carlton has known about this all these years. That is why he worked at the airport after his wife and son passed away. To watch. Keep vigil. We were also afraid that if someone came upon the river entrance then there would be a terrorist attack like none we have seen in an airport. But still, neither he, nor I knew what to do other than keep her secret safe. At first, I thought I was doing right by my family to disappear . . . in shame. When I heard about our dear boy being killed I knew he needed me and I began to think that possibly, I could figure out a way to surface again. But there were so many secrets! Where would I start? Who would I talk to? How could it be fixed? I couldn't take a chance of being seen by old friends or even our family so I didn't go to the funeral. My son needed me and I couldn't be there for him. That tore me up."

Zale began repeating his regrets. "This is a terrible thing I have allowed to happen. In the beginning, I thought I was going to figure out a way to buy back the property. Then construction started, and all the plans were in The Oregonian and

The Columbian. I came here, to what was my off-site hidden office. But time kept coming and coming and passing and passing. I have made a life here," he said as he waved his arm to encompass the underground building, "only leaving when I could safely slip back to land for things I need, or to catch a bus to Seattle when I had to fly to Europe. I mostly went out at night. And I couldn't fly out from PDX because I was afraid someone would recognize me."

Jahnni was still a little confused, "Let me get this straight. We are talking about the same Carlton that works at the airport? The Cart Man?"

"Yes. He knew about what I did and one day he just took it upon himself to keep an eye on the airport. He knew what was at stake. But so much tragedy in his life made him . . . tired. He said he just wanted to be my eyes and ears at the airport."

"So, you have never been back to the . . . to that ginormous building that hides under the airport?" Jahnni asked.

Zale paused and considered his response. Several seconds, almost a full minute of silence passed before he answered, "I didn't say that. Maybe you didn't understand who 'the old woman' was that I spoke of minutes ago. I do go back and forth to check everything. I change lightbulbs, flush the water system. Walk around and tinker with knobs and switches. I owe it to her. The building. To take care of her. Then I come home here until I miss her again."

Crutch smiled at Zale and said, "You are a good man. You seem like the kind of man that my dad would like. I get it though. You do something wrong, and before you can fix it, you do something else wrong. Then you try to think what to do about it and something else goes wrong. Before you know it, it has gotten so bad that you only want to hide."

"You seem like a smart young man. How did you come to such wise understanding?" Zale asked.

Crutch smirked and paused to gather his words, "Well, a few years ago, my little brother just started playing t-ball. I was bored, so I figured I could use his tee for my baseball. I didn't realize how easy it would be to hit a homer from my back yard. I swung, without thinking, and the ball went all the way over the neighbor's house behind us, across the street and crashed through another neighbor's front window. Apparently, some teenagers were driving by at the same time with their music bumping. The neighbor kid ran into his house and told his parents that some kids broke the window, and described a car full of teenagers. So, I didn't say anything when I heard my mom and dad talking about how wild the neighborhood was getting when they were talking about the broken window. About a week later, I decided it was safe to try it again, but I was going to be super careful and only bunt the ball. But . . . it still went flying over the fence and into the next-door neighbor's garage window."

"And you still didn't say anything?" Beau asked.

"No! They started having neighborhood watch meetings and forming groups to patrol the area at night and some people were watching the streets for bad guys. I felt like I had dug a hole too deep to get out. None of the other kids unlucky enough to be driving by when the first window broke were caught . . ."

Zale hummed, "Ahh . . . if you didn't have to speak up, you decided the whole baseball-gate would blow over."

"Ya!" Crutch agreed. "It just got crazy and the more time that went by, the crazier our neighborhood got. I mean Mr. Akiyama went out and bought a huge Great Pyrenees to protect his family! Then the Mills family enrolled all their kids in Krav Maga. I was waiting for my dad to order fly-overs above our house at night. It was so out of control."

"You're a wise young man indeed. Sounds like you learned your lesson," Samantha said as she hugged his shoulder. "You remind me of my little brother. Well, before he got to be 6' 4'."

Jahnni and Mr. T finished telling them every detail of their trip to the Port Manager's office. And they all chipped in to tell Zale about the adventures once the alarms went off and the concourse was cleared. Beau had taken the seat next to Jahnni when they had all sat down. While he was talking, she felt some kind of weight land on the back of her chair. She made a casual glance behind her and saw that he was resting his arm on the back of her chair. She sat frozen, trying to hold back the smile on her face. Then a shiver ran down her spine.

"Are you still cold, Jahn?" Beau asked.

"Oh, that. Uh, No. I'm . . . quite warm. Thanks!" She certainly didn't want to tell Beau that *he* was the reason for that shiver, so she just sat still and enjoyed every second of his gentle attention . . . and allowed herself to lean ever so slightly in his direction. Then Jahnni turned to the rest of the group and joined the conversation about what they were going to do to get back to the airport. Before they were finally done talking about their plan, Samantha added, "If we aren't going swimming again, I'm up for anything."

Zale finished the plan by saying, "We'll head up that stair case over there first. When we get to the top, I'll raise up the boat. Then there is a landing that I always use on the other side of the river off Marine Drive. We'll have to walk to the airport after that," Zale said in a deadpan voice.

"WHAT?" Beau said immediately. "Pops can't walk that far!"

"Oh, come on! I'm joking! Neither can I," he chuckled. "Once I go up, I'll have good reception and I'll pull up the Uber app. I'll request a car, probably something big though with this group," Zale said. "It'll meet us on Marine Drive above the boat landing. I've used them several times before."

Crutch eagerly asked, "Boat? What kind of boat? What do you mean you will raise it up? Is it hidden? How did you hide it? Has anyone ever found it? How big is it? I can drive a boat! Can I drive it?"

"Big enough for the six of us to safely get off the island," Zale answered. "And yes, it is hidden. I built a 'boat garage' that I can raise and lower. The top has dirt, grass and foliage so when it is down, no one can see it. When I use it, the roof raises, a levee is released and enough water from the Columbia River flows in so I can gently motor out to the river. I remotely signal the roof to recede and the canal empties the water back to the river. When I come back, I repeat, but backwards. And no, you can't drive it. The Columbia River is one of the most dangerous rivers in the United States. It is one of the most breathtakingly beautiful, but it's beauty is also deceitful with all the undertows and swirling water below the surface."

"OH, MY GOSH! This is like 007 stuff! Or Mission Impossible! Or even better, Batman! Well, come-on guys! Let's get going! We have an airport to save!" Crutch said as he paced back and forth from leg to leg. "Come on!"

Chapter 36

I'll Be the Good Cop Now

"So, TELL ME Mr. Prattle. Can we get you something to drink? Are you hungry?" Pahlavi spoke softly, hoping he would forget how angry she'd been before.

He sat stoically and stared straight ahead, not answering her questions.

"You know, we are going to get to the bottom of whatever this is. We can do it smoothly and be honest with each other, or we can take days to get to the bottom of this. I am sure we both have the same goal in mind. To keep the airport safe and the people safer." She sat casually with a hip on a counter, and one leg on the floor. "You seem like a man that knows his job well. So, let's just put down the walls and have a conversation."

He still sat there staring straight ahead, barely blinking; his hands handcuffed behind his back.

"Tell you what Perry. I can call you Perry, right?" Agent Pahlavi casually offered. "Why don't I have Officer Boulder remove your temporary cuffs and cuff your hands in front of you . . . for now. It looks like your struggling has tightened them further and you're now bleeding a little."

She nodded to Boulder who glanced at Perry's back. He could only see a couple of inches of his hands, but he did see that his wrists were indeed red and little prickles of blood were making the surface. Boulder gently touched under his arm and Perry stood and turned his back to Boulder so he could work the cuffs, and replace them with regular cuffs in front of him.

"Thank you." Perry uttered, barely audible.

"You're welcome. Now, let's have a little conversation. Okay?" Pahlavi said in a soothing voice.

"Am I under arrest for something?" he said.

"Arrest? Why no, not at this time. We are just being cautious and would like to have a conversation with you. You are a little confusing to us. We thought you were in charge here at the airport. But whenever I looked for you to run some information by you, I couldn't find you. Neither could your Port officers. Are you running from someone? Do you need protection?" She said, somewhat like a teacher would address a student who fell off the swing. "If you could let us know what you know, we can clear up this entire airport fiasco. Just start anywhere you like. I'm all ears."

Perry looked at her in a leery way. His eyes darted left and right as he stared at the floor then finally spoke, "I am looking for two agents that appear to be involved in some type of espionage. For some reason, unknown to me, they talked about blowing up the fountain. I was merely trying to ascertain their motives when the officers mistook my motives as some kind of destructive plan. The pillar had markings on it, like someone had tried to carve it open. I was trying to figure it out so no one could access the large pipe that travels up that wall to the fountain in the common area."

"I see," Agent Pahlavi said as she pretended to agree while she wrote down a couple notes. "Are these the same people you came to warn us about earlier?"

He stumbled his words when he tried to answer. His hands were fidgeting in the cuffs, but he rested them in his lap to answer her, "I think, I mean, I know, that one of them is named Jahnni Dawson. First Class Air. Tricky that one. Has her manager fooled. And the other one is, well I don't remember her name. But Jahnni is armed and plans to blow up the fountain, as I told the first group of officers. She told my security guard that she was going to blow it up and she had a device of some sort to do it remotely. Then they attacked him, hitting him in the skull with a heavy object. He barely got the information to me before the paramedics took him away to the hospital. I believe it is imperative that your FBI officers know that she must be immobilized as soon as they see her. Or they are at risk themselves of being shot. She is armed."

"Ooooh, ya, that sounds bad. I wonder if you could tell me if this other agent was with her when she attacked your security guard. I would like to get a description and any other information about her," Pahlavi said.

"Well, okay. I can do that. I gave their pictures to some officer's earlier. It was the two of them. Yes, it was Jahnni and

317

the other agent that attacked him," Perry stated.

"Okay. Got it. So, no one else barged into your office to accost your security guard? It was just the two ladies? This Jahnni Dawson and the second one?" Agent Pahlavi asked gently while writing notes and nodding her head up and down.

"So, can I go now? I have a lot of work to do to take care of the airport in this crisis," Perry asked.

"Go? Go where Perry? Where exactly would you like to go?" Agent Pahlavi asked as she tipped her head towards him.

He looked confused again and looked from Boulder to Pahlavi. "To do my job of course. What's going on here? I have work to do. You need to let me go!"

"Excuse me for a moment, Mr. Prattle." Agent Pahlavi motioned for another agent to come stay with Perry while she and Boulder went out in the hall.

"He's lying," she said. "Jahnni was with an older gentleman when Craigs and this other security guard strong armed them into an elevator in the bagwell. Hold him for now. Don't place him under arrest just yet. But if he asks for an attorney, stall, but follow the law."

Then she poked her head back into the room like she was peeking in on a toddler taking a nap. "Perry, I do have one more question if you don't mind. Why did you say they are probably all dead? Who is probably dead? And how would they die?"

He looked at her and shrugged his shoulders. He took a breath, then waited. He talked to her without looking at her, "I didn't tell you that. Are you trying to trick me?" He put his head down, and turned his face to the wall, away from where she was peeking into the room. He was done talking.

Chapter 37

Mission Accomplished

MIMI AND ADRIAN were done repairing the breach in the pipe that Perry had blown. They gathered up their underwater welding equipment, strapped it onto their backs and pushed off for the hatch a few feet down the pipe. The water looked dark but for their headlamps. Mission accomplished. They crawled up, out of the pipe and waited while their white waterproof suits dripped off. Underneath the suits, they were warm and dry. They dropped the Aquatic from their mouths and it fell at their necks, held securely by a neck band.

"Adrian, how do you feel?" Mimi asked as she removed her gloves.

He looked up after he shook his head like a dog after a dip and replied, "Great. You?"

"Well," she answered, "I feel . . . I don't know, kinda empty. We have been on this mission for almost two months and it is finally over. Oddest job we have ever done, no?"

"You got that right. Once we get out of here, I'll change our flight reservations when we get to the hotel so we can fly out of Seattle. Zale said to just depart. Send him a report, and take off." Then Adrian smiled before reiterating a previous point that they spoke about, "After we quit our airport jobs that is. With the current circumstances, I don't think he will mind if we do it by voicemail and post."

"Right, let's access the outflow and float out of here. We can't go back through the airport, so the shortcut will be just fine. Down this hallway?" She motioned to the olive-green hallway.

Adrian turned circles, getting his bearings. "Uh, ya. This will lead us back to the outflow. Ready honey?"

"I told you I would follow you anywhere, Addy! I made a vow," Mimi answered with a loving look on her face. "I can't wait to get back to Europe. I miss our daughter. The faster we get home, the better."

After she walked a few feet, she turned and waited for him. Oh, and let's not take another job for a while." She reached up on her tip-toes and kissed him gently on the mouth. Not that it isn't fun working with my husband, but we need a vacation. A family vacation. Paris?"

Chapter 38

Crossing Over the Columbia . . .
Instead of Under It

JAHNNI AND HER little band of escapees crawled up the ladder behind Zale. He motioned for them to hold while he scanned the island for campers, boaters, or the rare river patrol boat. It was clear. He raised the door hatch open and climbed out, turning to help his brother next. They all waited around the grass dome while the hatch closed.

"Wow, that is really cool Mr. Zale. I mean Mr. Bapatiste-aeas. I mean . . ." Crutch said.

"Please Crutch, call me just Zale. And, it's Baptiste. But it doesn't matter. We are all equals," he said as he patted Crutch on the shoulder.

Zale then pulled out his mobile phone. He stared at it, then held it up in the air, turning in circles. "Hmmm," he groaned. "I can't get reception. I was gonna order an Uber to meet us at the dock but I just remembered that it goes by your immediate location. We'll figure it out when we dock. Might have to use a landline and call a regular cab?"

Beau realized what he was doing and said, "Oh, wait. This isn't five miles away from the airport."

"Of course, it isn't five miles. Even diagonally to the airport, as the crow flies, it's a couple miles at most." Zale answered.

"Ya, I forgot to tell you that all cell service is down in about a five-mile radius around the airport. Speaking of communication blocks, did you get our email?" Beau asked.

"Email? I only check my email on my phone or my tablet when I come up from my office bunker. I don't know about any email," Zale said.

Beau turned to Jahnni. "I wonder if my captain got mine. If they aren't expecting us, they aren't going to know who we are when we try to approach the airport. So, just to be safe, don't refer to my weapon or mention I am an FBI agent to anyone. I will do that. I'll put my ID wallet in an outside pocket. My holster is strapped under the breast of our lovely designer frocks but easily accessible. I'll identify myself when we get back on site."

They all nodded. Zale looked around once more and told them to follow him into the shrubbery. He pointed a hand-held device at a grassy knoll inside the dense brush and watched as the grass began to raise up. As it climbed higher, they could see the top of a windshield of a boat. He smiled and arced his arm from the ladies towards the boat. "Ladies, your carriage has arrived. After you. Watch your step, hold the rails."

He slowly began motoring down the canal and slipped into the Columbia River. The boat idled quietly near the shore. Zale turned and hit a button on his device and through the thicket of shrubbery back on the island, they could see a glint from the late afternoon sun hitting the metal edges of the trap door as it lowered into the earth.

Jahnni remarked, "Just like it was attached to the ground by roots."

Zale pointed to the pile of life-jackets. "Put on your life preservers. No one rides in a boat without a life preserver." They each donned one, helped each other tighten them up, then turned as Zale slowly made his way across the river towards the Oregon side. He kept a keen eye out on the water.

"What are you looking for?" Crutch asked.

"Oh, I'm looking for floaters, logs. Sometimes, when you least expect it, you hit one, and it isn't fun," Zale answered him.

"Have you ever hit one?" Crutch asked.

Zale smiled at Crutch before answering. "As a matter of fact, I have. A few years after I settled in here, I was going rather quickly down the river when I hit the edge of a very large snag. The boat bumped and twisted and I was thrown out. I was underwater for longer than I cared to be, as the undertow dragged me down the river, holding me down. As I was on my last second of air, it spit me into a calmer area. I managed to swim towards the sandy beach where some boaters gave me a lift towards my boat. It was floating down the river, a little further down from where I landed on the beach. They waited while I checked everything out, and made sure the engine would start."

Crutch was holding his breath. "I know that feeling. So, what happened after that?"

"I promised myself that I would never get in a boat without putting on a life preserver," Zale answered, firmly.

Mr. T had been silent for some time. He was looking around at the water and watching the shoreline. "This reminds me of the Aliakmon. I miss home."

"As do I brother. As do I," Zale answered, giving Mr. T a warm smile.

The boat silently cut through the water as Zale guided it towards the house boats that were surrounded by an aged, but functional ramp made of older pilings with a newer platform.

"I have made friends with another older man over the years. He told me to park my boat here anytime. He knows that I liked to go fishing, or so he thinks," Zale explained as they neared the dock.

They slowly motored a little further and drifted up against the dock. Beau jumped out and grabbed the rope to tie it off. Everyone waited until they were told to stand, and then one at a time, Beau reached to give them a hand out of the boat. Jahnni shooed her hands at them to insist that everyone go before her. Except Zale wouldn't hear of going before her and Jahnni lost the argument as he motioned in a very insistent way, that she was to go before him. She reached up to grab Beau's hand and he practically lifted her out of the boat through the air, grabbing her to him so she didn't fall back.

"Oh my. I can fly!" she whispered.

Beau just smiled those lovely dimples that made Jahnni melt and forget how to form words. His green eyes searched hers then out of the blue he said, "Let's go boating sometime."

"Oh, uh, I, uh . . . okay," she stammered. "I'll check my schedule. Oh look, it says I'm busy today. We better make it some other day." She giggled. *I sound like a little school girl. I can't believe I giggled. Ugh,* she thought to herself.

Beau grabbed her hand as they walked up the ramp towards some boat houses. "Hang on. Sometimes a wave comes and you can lose your balance." Jahnni didn't answer him, but looked back at Zale to see if he was keeping up. When she turned forward to continue walking, she returned the curled fingers around Beau's grasp, but she was careful not to squeeze too hard for fear Beau might realize he was holding her hand by mistake. She memorized the gentle grip he had on her hand and allowed herself to bask in the protected silence as they strolled along the little pier's squeaky boards.

Ahead, Samantha had hold of Crutch's hand as they walked along. He didn't appear to mind all the mothering. Sam turned and grabbed Mr. T's hand behind her. "You too, sailor. Spit spot. Keep up," she ordered, smiling as Mr. T caught up.

Zale made quick time to pass everyone and arrived at the end of the ramp, or rather the beginning of the ramp if you were arriving from the road. He motioned for them to stop. "I'm going to use my friend's phone to call a taxi. He can be pretty crotchety, so you all better wait here."

"Wait for me. I need to call in so they know I'm coming. There's no way they will allow anyone close to the airport without being, or rather, unless someone from a local field office meets us," Beau explained.

The group mulled around in the same spot, never more than an arm's length away from each other. On one hand, Jahnni felt impatient, anxious, still glancing over her shoulder every thirty seconds. On the other hand, she felt a sense of calm coursing through her, shooting relief into her veins with every heartbeat. When they heard Zale and Beau's voices walking towards them they all turned in unison to hear what they had to say.

"A van is on the way," Beau began, "HRT is at the airport. They already had a close idea of what was going on and who we were. They work fast. They were under the assumption that we may have been taken hostage. We need to clear up some assumptions and fill in the blanks asap. They will meet us at the intersection of 82nd and Airport way to take us to the Agent in charge of the investigation at the airport.

Ten minutes later, a man driving a large, newer taxi van arrived to pick them up. He hurriedly got out to open the van doors for the group. "You said that you wanted to go to the airport, but there is a lockdown of some kind. It's all over the news. You can't get close."

"Well," said Beau, "I happen to have it on good faith that they will let us in. They are waiting for us at 82nd. Just head to the airport and get us as close as you can. If they stop us, I'll do the talking when we get close. I'll throw in a big tip for the trouble. That is, if you accept damp money. My wallet took a dip today."

"Yes, sir. You got it. All aboard? Seatbelts please." And off the van went, with the six musketeers since Zale was now part of the group.

Chapter 39

Slow Motion Pain

ANOTHER AGENT FROM Pahlavi's office walked up to her with a message, "This email was handed to me with specific instructions to hand deliver this to you asap. It comes from the Seattle Field Office. I drove it straight here from our office when it came in."

Agent Pahlavi unsealed the envelope. "Thank you." Then she began reading. "Uh huh, okay, makes sense, that's what I thought, just like they said, uh huh, mmm, good. Glad that's confirmed. Ingenious. An email."

After Agent Pahlavi met with Carolyn and some of her agents one more time, she had made a decision. Not the decisions she originally planned on making, but because Perry was looking so pale and confused, she used her SAT phone and made a call. The next plan for Perry was in progress. His ride would be waiting outside in about ten minutes. She went back to the food court where Carlton was still waiting just like he was told. She sat back down in front of him and asked, "Can you really help me?"

He nodded, "I promise."

"Okay then. Do I need to take anything with me down there?" she asked.

"No, but remember, you promised me that you would hear me out when this was all over before you press charges. You promised," Carlton reminded her.

"My word is good Carlton. I promise I will help you if you help me," she said as she shook her head slightly up and down. "I need to talk to Officer Boulder quickly and I'll be right back. Oh . . . who has the level of clearance that we need for this . . . journey?"

He pointed to Rick, the head of maintenance. "He does."

"Okay then. I'll go talk to him first, then I'll be back in a little while. Do you need anything?"

"No. I'm good. I'll be right here."

Agent Pahlavi walked quickly back to the Port Office where they were holding Perry. She saw Boulder standing guard at the door. She opened the door and walked in with a smile on her face, Boulder right behind her. "Hello again Perry. Do you need anything to drink?"

His mouth had a twitch that she hadn't noticed before. But it fit the profile. He glanced her way before turning back to face the wall again. "No, I am good. But when can I go?"

"Soon, Perry. Very soon. I promise," she answered him in a low tone. She just left out where he was going to go.

She motioned for the same agent that had been waiting with Perry that she was going to remain outside the door a couple more minutes. Boulder followed her back out and pulled the door behind him.

She turned to Boulder, "Did you read my message I passed to you when we came out of the office before?"

"Yes ma'am. Still in agreement. I'll hand him over to Agent McNichols. He knows we are coming out?" Boulder said.

"Yes. I'm not sure if I will be gone by then, but just in case. I wrote the booking codes down so there isn't any confusion on what I'm doing, concerning Mr. Prattle. He is in over his head and I don't believe we can get anything more out of him because of his condition. I am beginning to think he doesn't know the true facts, or know the difference between fact and fiction. I firmly believe he needs medical attention," she whispered.

"I agree, and if you need anything more, I'll be here all night wrapping things up," Boulder said.

"I'm following a hunch that I think will pull all this together. My partner Agent Anthony and I are following up on a lead. We're good?" she asked.

"Still in agreement, Delaram. I mean Pahlavi. I mean Agent Pahlavi," he corrected himself.

"You can call me Delaram in private. No problem. But on the job, it's Agent or Special Agent Pahlavi." She smiled. "Okay, here goes. Just let me handle him."

They reentered the room like a boomerang. "Last time," she whispered. Then she said in front of Perry, "Officer Boulder, would you mind escorting Mr. Prattle to his transportation?"

Perry looked confused. His head whipped around back and forth as his eyes roamed the room. "What do you mean? Aren't you going to let me go back to work? I am very important you know! The seriousness of this emergency must be attended to. I . . . I . . . must find something. I mean someone. Uh, those girls. I need to help find that wayward airline agent! She's d-danger-dangerous."

"Well, Mr. Prattle, since . . ." Agent Pahlavi began to say when Perry interrupted her.

"You can call me Perry, remember? We are helping each other." He paused to see that she was looking at him, then leaned forward towards her side. "We are on the SAME TEAM," he whispered loudly like he was giving her a secret message.

"Yes, Perry. I understand," she said, trying to assure him to keep him calm. "We are. But as I was going to say, since there is so much commotion going on here, I believe it is in your best interest to be taken to . . . a safer location. I'll make sure you are taken care of."

She left the room and walked towards the end of the hallway. Boulder and another agent soon walked out of the office with Perry and down the hallway too. By this time, she was standing in the open area where the carousels were. She waved at some of her team and nodded that everything was good. They stood firmly in their place. The evidence that was gathered when they apprehended Mr. Prattle under the main part of the airport in the bagwell area, was sitting in sealed bags at their feet.

Agent Pahlavi watched Perry being led away, Boulder on his right and her agent on his left. She observed Prattle looking intently at the window, glancing back and forth between where he was being led, and then back at the window. After they walked about fifty feet, he stumbled, bumping into her own agent who was helping to escort Perry. Officer Boulder and the FBI agent lifted him back on his feet and continued to walk. As before, Perry looked fixedly at the window then glanced forward at the revolving doors. Once again he stumbled, bumping into the agent and half falling to one knee. They lifted him back up and continued to walk towards the revolving doors. She turned to the big glass window but assumed he was looking at his reflection. Something didn't seem right. *There's something not . . . Who is that?* she wondered.

Pahlavi looked a couple seconds longer out the window and saw an FBI agent standing by a parked black FBI SUV, holding the back door open for someone as a small huddle of people waited for a man to climb out of the SUV. The agent put one of the SAT phones they'd all been using to his ear as he pushed the back door closed and turned to walk with the group. She looked down at the SAT phone clipped to her belt as it began to vibrate but couldn't take her mind off the feeling that something was wrong. It was a blurred cloud of knowing that she couldn't identify, hovering just out of reach.

She focused back at Boulder, wondering what was off. *Wait. They didn't move Prattle's handcuffed arms back behind his back! I only wanted to loosen them in front of him to buy confidence. They should have re-cuffed him behind his back before they led him out!* she screamed in her head.

She quickly looked again out the window to try to see what Prattle was so intently observing, catching a brief glance of the group calmly walking towards the revolving doors. She looked ahead of her at her agent that was escorting Prattle, Boulder on his other side.

"BOULDER! WAIT!" she shouted, as Perry began to fumble with his hands and sway his body.

Boulder began to turn to see what she wanted. In the briefest second he was turned sideways looking back at Agent Pahlavi, the other agent was trying to keep a grasp on Perry as he faltered.

She watched everything unfold in slow motion. She drew her weapon and took off running. "TO YOUR LEFT BOULDER!"

Perry had grabbed the FBI agent's gun out of its holster, having tested the release during his stumbles. Like slow molasses, his arms yanked upward, in the same instant the agent realized what was happening. The agent tried to grab his gun from Perry, as Boulder was drawing his. Pahlavi got a brief glance of the anger that was stretched over Perry's face when he turned sideways away from her agent, and then shrugged his body back the other direction away from Boulder.

Boulder briefly looked towards the revolving doors to see what Perry was focused on. Perry dropped to his knees and tripped Boulder in the process. The other agent lunged again for Perry's arms which were stuck together in front of him by the handcuffs. Perry raised his hands out of the way and the agent fell sideways in front of Perry and landed on the floor. Then he lowered his arms rigidly straight in front of him and aimed again at the door.

Agent Pahlavi dropped to one knee and took aim. She shouted, "DROP THE WEAPON PERRY!" This finally got the full attention of all the other agents milling around and they drew their weapons. But in the commotion and tumble of people, they couldn't shoot. Too many innocents. Boulder was blocking Pahlavi's shot as he swiftly stood back up. She stood and began running towards them. Her eyes caught a glimpse of the people entering the revolving glass doors and in an instant, she recognized Jahnni's face from the photographs and descriptions. She shouted as she ran, "DROP THE WEAPON PERRY! YOU ARE SURROUNDED!" She dropped again to a knee and took aim, willing a clear shot.

The words coming out of her mouth sounded far off and everything around her just kept moving like sludge. She yelled out as the revolving doors spun out the group of people who started walking into the airport, being accompanied by one of the FBI agents from her field office. "GET DOWN!" she shouted.

The group's attention was immediately turned to Perry as he pointed the gun towards them when they exited the spinning glass doors. "YOU! This is what you deserve! You caused this!" He paused briefly to aim. Then he fired. At that briefest moment before Perry pulled the trigger, Beau drew his weapon and flew sideways in the air, pushing Jahnni to the floor. Mid-air, he fired at Perry. Immediately Beau felt the hot burn of the bullet as it entered his abdomen. When he landed on the floor, he rolled back up into a half-crouched position, weapon aimed directly at Perry. But there was no need. Mr. Perry Prattle lay against the pillar with a dark spot in the middle of his forehead, his dark red blood draining like a seeping, broken pipe. He was dead.

"Put your hands up NOW!" Pahlavi yelled at Beau. He immediately opened his hand to show his weapon was only being held by one finger and he slowly reached towards the ceiling. He was surrounded by several Port Police, and FBI agents before his hands even stopped reaching. They grabbed his weapon and yanked his arms, pulling them behind his back, rolling him face-down, and cuffing him. Pahlavi looked around to see that no one else was hit, then ran to the group.

"Ma'am. I'm FBI Special Agent Beau Harleyman. I have ID in my front right pocket," he said as he lay face down with two Port Police and an FBI agent holding him down with their knees. Pahlavi motioned for them to roll him slightly and patted the front of his olive-green jumpsuit. When she felt the wallet, she pulled it out while the other agents began patting him down at the same time.

"I'm sorry Pahlavi. I tried to call you as soon as we pulled up," their escort FBI agent shouted as he burst forward past the crowd of police and the FBI agents that circled the scene. "I'm sorry! I was bringing them to you. The area was deemed secure." He had drawn his weapon when the chaos began as they exited the rotating door, but Beau had already acted before the agent cleared the glass. He holstered his gun, and held up his arms to finish speaking to the well-armed crowd, "He's one of us. He's one of us."

Pahlavi was turning to Boulder as she flipped open his FBI ID wallet and saw that he was indeed an FBI agent. "Stand him up," she ordered, as she holstered her weapon, noting that there were already a dozen other agents with their weapons already pointing in their direction. The blood on the other agents' hands caught her eye but before she ascertained where it came from, or who it came from, Jahnni gasped, an intake of air loud enough for everyone near to hear.

Jahnni began to pull herself up on her knees. She slowly began to stand, holding her hands up as well so no one would mistake her intentions. Pahlavi noticed that Jahnni had a look of horror on her face as she stared down at the floor by Beau. Pahlavi glanced down to see what Jahnni was looking at and saw blood all over the floor. It was under, beside, and at the front of Beau's clothing; a large splotch of blood spreading out across the front of him and along the carpet like a tide slowly breaching the beach. She yelled for the medics and went to Beau. She ordered him uncuffed and to roll him on his back. His eyes began to close yet his head moved back and forth, looking at those beside him. Jahnni stared at Pahlavi and nodded, as if asking for permission to approach him. Pahlavi nodded yes.

"Beau! Beau! You're bleeding!" Jahnni yelled as she fell to his side. "Where are you bleeding? Someone! Help him.

Find out where he is bleeding!" She started shaking, reaching to touch him, but seemingly not knowing where to set her hands. She finally grabbed his hand in hers and covered both of their hands with her other hand, rubbing his fingers gently. The airport paramedics had been parked at the curb and were there in less than a minute. Pahlavi had originally called them to take Perry Prattle to the hospital's psyche unit for an evaluation. They brushed Jahnni aside and began working on Beau. Scissors came out and they began cutting and ripping his clothes to expose the bullet hole. Blood was still streaming out as they applied pressure and began preparing him for transport. Jahnni was too shocked to cry. She now stood as close as they would allow.

Mr. T came to her and she heard him whisper from behind her back, "Not my Beau. Not my baby Beau."

Sam, Crutch, and Zale huddled in a big hug, as tears flowed down their cheeks, too numb to move. When Jahnni realized Mr. T was behind her, she reached around to hold him. "I'm sorry! I'm so sorry! It's my fault! It is all my fault! I should have just left the concourse. I should have just taken a chance and led us out some other way. But everything kept going wrong. Everything kept going wrong when we tried to . . . I tried to help. I tried to get us out. I should have, I should have just . . ." She now began to cry as she looked down at Beau being hoisted onto the gurney. They moved quickly to strap him down. The IV was set, and an oxygen mask was placed on his face. People started shouting orders to clear the way as they began swiftly wheeling towards the doors.

Suddenly he reached up with his free hand and grasped the paramedic's arm. He pulled off the oxygen mask with the other hand. "STOP. WAIT." His eyes were still closed and he sucked in more air. "Was she hit?" He breathed out, opening his eyes to try to focus as he looked at the crowd all around him. He took another breath. "Is she okay? Was she hit?"

"Who?" the paramedic asked in a curt voice. "We have to roll. Let's go."

Again, Beau found the strength to shout again. "NO! STOP. Is she okay? Did she get hit?"

Jahnni realized who he was talking about. "Beau, It's me. It's Jahnni. I'm fine. I'm fine. But you were shot. You need to go to the hospital. Just go. We'll find out where they are taking you. We'll come as soon as they let us."

"Thank God you're okay. Ya . . . I know. I think I need to go . . . soon," Beau breathed out in a whisper. After one more staggered breath, his head lolled to the side. His chest rose up and down like he was trying to take in short bursts of air. His body began to shake with only the sounds of his gasping for oxygen. His eyes were closed, but his face looked pained.

Jahnni turned to the paramedics as they began to hustle towards the door. "How bad is it? Is he going to be okay?"

"Well, ma'am. He did take a good hit," he answered her as he continued pushing the gurney. "We'll take care of him. But we gotta go. Now."

"Another medic ran up with an ambu bag keeping pace beside the gurney while pumping it, forcing more oxygen into Beau's lungs. They wheeled him faster through the gaping hole that once rotated panes of glass and was now arranged into one large opening. They pushed him quickly to the waiting ambulance at the curb.

Two Agents rushed out from behind the crowd that had gathered around Beau. They briskly walked toward Agent Pahlavi, then stopped right in front of her. They looked down at Perry slumped against the pillar. They glanced around at the scene, then looked back at Agent Pahlavi to see if she remembered talking to them earlier in the security office when they saw Harleyman on the video.

"Oh. Hi," she said in a low tired voice. "So, that was the famous Bullseye Messiah," she said. "I suppose . . . I should be the one to take them to the hospital. We should know more as soon as the doctors take over. Keep me posted with what's going on here. I have to go."

She looked out the windows and saw Jahnni and the others watching the ambulance crew intently; wringing their hands; holding onto each other; and pacing in place. The two agents started to walk away when one of them stopped and turned. Pointing at the clean shot right to the center of Perry's head, he said, "See. We told you."

Chapter 40

Chasing Your Heart

THE GROUP WAS huddled together and watched Beau being loaded into the ambulance. Agent Pahlavi had just joined the group on the sidewalk, in front of the airport. They all watched it start driving away, lights flashing. The inside was lit and they could see the one medic's head moving from the side and back to Beau. Suddenly he jumped on top of the gurney that Beau had been strapped to just minutes before. They could see the medics arms pushing down and pushing down. Two, three, four, five, six, seven, eight, he kept pushing. The ambulance suddenly sped up and began rushing down the road, sirens blaring.

"Oh, my God," Jahnni breathed. "They are starting CPR."

Agent Pahlavi waved Boulder to where she was standing at the curb. "I don't think he's going to make it," she whispered. "I need to take them to him. They've suffered through quite an experience together. I'm turning everything over to my partner,

Special Agent Liam Anthony. He can question these guys at the hospital when he is done here."

Jahnni was standing there frantic, pacing in place. Mr. T was shaking. Zale stood still, frozen. Sam stood holding Crutch in front of her, burying his face against her shoulder, covering his eyes. Everyone was numb, trying to figure out what to do. Pahlavi turned to them and said, "Come with me. I'll take you to the hospital."

She walked quickly towards her car, with the others following close behind when she realized that they could not all fit in her sedan. She lifted her SAT phone and called for another agent to drive the other four, and follow her and Jahnni. "Oh, I forgot," she said into the phone. "There is a gentleman in the far north corner of the food court waiting for me. His name is Carlton. Bring him with you. Tell him I sent you and . . . run!" She hung up and glanced at Jahnni as they walked briskly to the car. "Who are the older gentlemen with you?"

Jahnni wiped her eyes and said, "Oh, uh, that is Mr. T, Beau's grandfather. I mean Mr. Tropopoulis. And the other gentleman is Zale, Mr. T's long lost brother. We sort of found him . . . by accident . . . on purpose. I mean, we were trying to find a way, and we got stuck, but we got wet, and rode a, then went for clothes, and Sam and Crutch, I mean, . . . I don't know what I mean. I can't think right now." Jahnni started weeping silently. "Oh, this is all my fault, I think. We were just, just . . ."

"Whatever you are going to tell me," Pahlavi said as she stopped to pick up Jahnni's hands into hers, enveloping them in a little hug, "I believe you. I may not have all the details yet, but I know about . . . you know, the secret. But let's not talk about that right now. Let's just get you all to the hospital first."

Jahnni reached out to Mr. T and said, 'Things are going to be okay. She is taking us to Beau, but you four must ride with another agent. He is bringing Carlton also. She knows about . . . you know . . ." as she pointed down with her head. It's going to be okay."

The extra agent arrived with Carlton and the group began jumping into the two cars. Flashing lights began strobing as the cars careened away from the drop-off area. "Put on your seatbelt and hold on tight," Pahlavi warned, without turning to Jahnni, "and pray for Mr. Harleyman."

The winding streets of short-cuts almost made Jahnni's stomach queasy. She glanced behind the car to see if the other agent was keeping up. It felt like a NASCAR race. The traffic suddenly came to a stop. The cars at the light were backed up fifteen deep easily. "Oh my, come on cars, move! Move!" Jahnni complained out loud. "Move it!" But the cars, of course, could not hear her. Nor could the other drivers. "What is taking so long! Move! Move! Move!"

"They can't hear you," Pahlavi said a little lighthearted to lessen Jahnni's impatience. "But, they can hear this." She turned on the siren to get their attention. Jahnni could see the driver's heads ahead of their car. They perked up, sitting taller as they glanced in their rear-view mirrors then turned to look behind them. All the cars started parting, pulling to one side or the other. Both FBI cars had lights flashing and sirens blaring. It commanded eye-widening attention and the Red Sea was history. Weaving between the opening, they sped along.

"There's the hospital sign! Are you sure this is the hospital they took him to?" Jahnni asked.

Pahlavi shook her head yes as she glanced briefly at Jahnni. "I heard them say, Providence. Couple more turns honey. Almost there."

Screeching into the ER drop off, she told Jahnni to wait. "Give me a sec." One minute later, she came running back out to the agent's car behind them, then jumped back in. "Okay, . . . He's not here . . . They airlifted him to OHSU. Let's go."

The time slowed to a crawl as Jahnni's tortured thoughts kept telling her that this was completely her fault. She sat there playing through every scenario in her head. *Where could I have made a different choice?* She scolded herself. She stared out the side window, watching life scream by as they hit I-84 west, heading to the Medical Center. They were going so fast, but she didn't care. She turned to look out the back window again to see if the other car was keeping up. Turning back around, she realized she was fidgeting with her hair. It was hanging limp with a slight wave of no particular design. She ran her fingers through her hair to brush it out of her face and behind her ears. By now, the sun was setting and lights were beginning to come on. The Max was running beside the freeway, like it was racing them, but they quickly outpaced it. She looked at the businesses, homes, walls blocking the freeway from the residents. Cement everywhere. Poles. Stairs leading to the Max on the other side of the large metal fence. Birds were swooping away like they were looking for a place to rest for the evening.

She noticed every star trying to peek out and every wisp of cloud trying to block the emerging moon. The twilight of the day was trying to emerge yet the light of the day still hung on fighting to live. People in the cars craned their necks at them as they sped by the other drivers, with lights flashing.

One song kept battering at her like a wooden ram trying to break through a thick fortress door. She started humming it. She kept humming the words as she sat frozen.

Pahlavi said, "You can call me Delaram. That's my first name."

"I'm Jahnni. But of course, you know that, don't you?" Jahnni said softly.

"You like the oldies I see, or rather hear," Delaram said softly.

"Ya, my parents were musicians. My mom's band played Country Rock. My dad was a classical and Spanish guitarist. He also taught music theory. My mom's band played everything from Tammy Wynette to Trisha Yearwood and Doobie Brothers to Fleetwood Mac. Sixty's, seventy's, eighty's, ninety's; basically, any music is my escape," Jahnni said before she continued humming.

Pahlavi asked, "Ah, The Moody Blues. Is there a reason you are humming Nights in White Satin?"

"I don't know," Jahnni said in a tone barely audible at first. "I think it's speaking to me. I . . . I have spent too much of my life trying to be strong." Silence filled the space between them. "I think . . . for the first time in a long, long, time . . . I feel."

"Feel what?" Pahlavi asked after waiting a few seconds.

"For who?"

"I . . . I think for me. But it's more than that. I feel . . . something I haven't allowed myself to feel, for someone else. For . . ." then Jahnni stopped talking. She started humming Nights in White Satin again. Softly she began to sing the words.

Pahlavi swerved around a few cars and took the exit toward Salem to get on I-5 south. Then she got into the left lanes to cross over I-5 on the Marquam bridge following the signs to City Center/Beaverton and onto I-405 north. Once on I-405, she took the 6th Street exit and began many turns. Left, left, right, right and sped forward on what seemed like an endless curvy road. She swerved here and there taking a route that Jahnni didn't know, but Pahlavi seemed to know where she was going.

Pahlavi was at ease driving fast. While they wound through the streets, she asked Jahnni, "Did you know him before today?"

"Who?" Jahnni asked.

Pahlavi didn't answer her at first. She just kept turning and driving. "You know, sometimes, when people go through a traumatic experience together, even if they never knew each other before, it makes you speed past the stages of getting to know someone. You go from stage 1 to stage 10 very quickly.

Jahnni turned to her. "I'm not sure what you mean."

"Traumatic incidents, they show you what is important. It forces people to drop their pretend games and be . . . I don't know. Be real. Be authentic."

Jahnni looked at her then looked out the window. "But

what if your authentic self, isn't good enough?"

"Well," Pahlavi answered, "you have to figure that out. You must ask him. Or tell him."

"If he lives, you mean," Jahnni whispered without looking at Pahlavi.

"Even if he doesn't live, you must to tell him. You have to say it out loud. He will still hear you. And most of all, you will hear you."

Jahnni hummed the song a little bit louder as she thought about what Delaram was telling her, the words truly making sense now.

"We're here . . . Let's go," Delaram said as she slid right into a parking spot. Everyone started pouring out of both cars.

Chapter 41

There's No Room for Regrets

THEY TRIED TO sit in the waiting room on the surgery floor, but they kept pacing. Stand up, pace, sit down.

Mr. T sat on the padded bench seat next to Zale. Zale had hold of Mr. T's hand like a brother soothing a brother. "He will be okay. He's a strong man," Zale whispered lovingly.

Carlton was not speaking for some time, just looking at everyone. He finally walked over to sit next to his father, Zale. "Dad, I hope I did the right thing. I told that FBI agent about it. People were missing, and something was wrong. I was so afraid when I found out that Jahnni was one of the people they were looking for. She is a very special person. Not that no one else isn't, but . . . she's just, special. I've known her for a long time."

"I know," Mr. T interrupted. "Janie is good. She try very hard to keep us safe. She almost get killed for it. My Beau save her too. I mean, she do right by us, and Beau do right for her."

Crutch walked over to Jahnni and sat down next to her. He leaned on her shoulder and sighed. "This place brings back so many memories for me."

Jahnni looked down at him and put her arm around his shoulder, pulling him closer. She leaned down and asked, "You've been in the hospital before?"

Crutch shook his head. "I've been in *this* hospital before. Well, in the children's wing. Doernbecher's. When I was 5. And off and on until I was 12."

Jahnni stared at him for a few seconds before she said, "Can I ask why?"

After pausing to choose his words he just blurted it out. "I had cancer."

Tears began to flow from Jahnni's eyes and trickle down her cheeks. She pulled him closer into a tighter hug. "Are you okay now? Are you . . . in remission?"

Crutch looked up and smiled. "So far. It can come back, but they think they got it all. I've been here a few times, but the last treatment was new. I was in a study. They call me the miracle boy cuz I almost died."

"Oh, my God, Crutch! I don't know what to say. I can't imagine my life, if I never had the opportunity to meet you," Jahnni whispered. Then she changed the subject suddenly. "You need to call your parents! They are probably frantic, worried about you! Let me call my supervisor and tell her where we are and what's going on."

Jahnni patted all her pockets. Not finding a phone she asked Delaram if she could borrow hers.

Carlton heard her and said, "Here Jahn, use mine."

She walked out of the waiting area and into an alcove to call Carolyn, her supervisor at the airport. She filled her in on the basics of where they were, but told her she couldn't talk about what has been happening before they made it back to the airport, but promised she would as soon as the FBI agent said she could. They talked for several minutes before she ended the call.

Jahnni walked over to Crutch and handed him the phone. Your parents are worried sick. Carolyn gave me the number to contact them. Here." She handed him the slip of paper.

"I don't need that. I have everyone's phone number memorized. Everyone I have ever met." Crutch took the phone and dialed his dad. He stood next to Jahnni because she told him that they may need to talk to her.

Agent Pahlavi had already told him he couldn't talk about the day yet, until they all make their statements and had their interviews. She'd told them when they arrived at the hospital not to even talk to each other about the day. Crutch assured his parents that he was 'exactly perfect.' A saying that his mom always said to him. He handed the phone to Jahnni and she gave his dad the basic information but confirmed what Crutch had said to him, that they couldn't talk about it yet, but Crutch was completely fine.

Samantha finally spoke up. "I'm not sure I want to work at the airport anymore, Jahn. I like adventure and all, but this has been, like a 'thousand miles an hour' adventure. Maybe I can put in my notice when we get things worked out."

"I understand," Jahnni said. "But it isn't like this will probably happen again . . . EVER. What are the chances? I don't want you to leave, Sam. But, I know you should do what you feel is right. Hey . . . if you don't work with us anymore, how are you ever going to find out if the kismet pilot is meant for you?"

Samantha's eyes lit up at the mention of him. "Ya, maybe you are right. I mean, it was so weird. When we met, we talked and talked and it felt like we had known each other for a long time. He even asked me if he could kiss me good night. I'm used to guys just plunging their lips over mine like a hoover and having to push them off. He was different. And his accent. OMG. His French accent is hypnotic."

"Better be careful. It isn't like you have a good track record picking out the right guys," Jahnni said. They both laughed at the memories of Sam's dating adventures.

"But he was different. It was like . . . like that saying from the movie Sleepless in Seattle. When he kissed me goodnight, *'it was like coming home. But not like any home I had ever known,'*" Sam dreamily quoted, inserting herself into the line.

Jahnni thought about the song, Nights in White Satin again. It made her feel, like she was coming home after a long time of not feeling. "You know Sam, before you quit, before you turn in your notice, look for him. Don't wait to run into him. Look for him. I shouldn't tell you to do this, but by golly I am. When we get back to work, pull up the crew schedules for all our flights every day that you work and see if he is listed as the captain. Or call Crew Scheduling to see if they can help you. Find him. Go for it. I mean, don't make a fool of yourself girl! But . . . talk to him. Ask HIM out. Coffee, a drink, a walk. Even sit by the fountain, that is if it's still there . . . and figure it out. But whatever you do, DON'T just wait and see. Take action! He might be the one."

Sam was almost speechless. "Wow, that is quite a speech coming from your usual excuses of, 'No, I have to give the cat a bath tonight,' Or 'No, I have to pre-treat my laundry.' What has gotten into you Jahnni? You are acting like, I don't know, like you are a 'grab the bull by the horns' kind of girl suddenly."

Jahnni smiled. "Maybe I am. Someone said something to me today that made me ask myself some questions." She looked over at Pahlavi and smiled. Pahlavi smiled back then shrugged one shoulder.

After three hours, the surgeon came walking towards them, pulling his surgery mask down. He looked at everyone in the room, studied them all then looked right at Jahnni. "You must be Jahnni."

Fear rushed to her face. He wasn't smiling. And he knew her name for some reason. She stood and walked closer. Breathlessly she answered, "Yes. I am."

"I thought so. We were able to stabilize Mr. Harleyman and he insisted on communicating before we put him under anesthesia. He was awake, barely of course, but right before he went under, he described you to a tee, from the top of your hair to the bottom of your shoes. He mumbled, as he was losing consciousness that I was to remind you that you two have a boating date."

Chapter 42

The Calm

THEY TOOK TURNS visiting Beau's room at first, but soon Jahnni realized that as some came in, some didn't leave. The room was too crowded and soon the nurses would kick them out. They had been very lenient with visitors and Jahnni knew any moment they would get booted. Besides, Beau needed to rest.

Delaram told Jahnni, "I have to bring you all in for questioning, so you can give your formal statements. Considering the type of situation we find ourselves in, I will break it up over two days. We'll discuss it when we leave."

Mr. T bent down and kissed Beau on the forehead, lovingly brushing the strands of hair off his forehead. Zale gently touched his hand, then slipped his fingers across Beau's palm, careful not to touch his IV that was stuck in his hand. He gave him a gentle squeeze goodbye and smiled as he released his hand. He backed away, bowed his head to Jahnni and left the room. Carlton winked at Beau when he looked up, then they both smiled as Beau tried to nod although it was done in slow motion and his smile was so crooked that only one dimple popped up. Sam held Crutch's hand as they came back in the room to say goodbye.

"I don't know if I will see you again, Beau," Crutch said, teary eyed as he talked. His lips quivered as he stood by the hospital bed holding the rail with both hands. As a tear trickled down his cheek he added, "I guess the airport will be open tomorrow and they scheduled a flight for me. If everything goes okay, Jahnni gets to fly home with me. Sam was supposed to go too, but she says she can't go. My parents asked Jahnni to stay overnight, but she said she has some important things to do when she gets home."

Crutch looked at Jahnni then back at Beau. He turned again to Jahnni and said with a knowing smile, "Oh, I think I get it."

"Ah, buddy," Beau whispered roughly, "I'm so glad you're okay. And I'm so happy that I've met you. Stay in touch man, okay? When I see you again, we'll go get those BK Whoppers." It was difficult to talk much because of the pain, and the pain-killers made his voice sound like his tongue was double the size.

Delaram patted his foot through the blanket. "I'll turn in the paperwork. You'll need to make another statement when you feel better. Just to be sure your head is clearer," she laughed.

Beau tried to laugh, but it hurt his stomach. He took a breath and said, "Ya . . . I don't know what hurts more, taking a bullet, or getting carved up to get it out. But, for now, the morphine drip is my friend." Then his eyes slowly turned to Jahnni. "Will you be back?"

"Yes. I'll be back to check on you tomorrow. I'll fly Crutch home in the late morning, then I'll be back tomorrow night. Get some rest." She paused as he was closing his eyes then added, "I haven't had the chance to tell you, but thank you. Thank you for saving my life. I'm so sorry this happened to you."

Beau started to smile, squeezed Jahnni's hand, and pulled her down closer to him. She realized he wanted to say something, so she leaned close to listen.

"I . . . I want to tell you," he said in a weak breathy voice. "It was worth it. I lo . . ." but his eyes closed and his head fell softly to the side. His eyelashes flitted and his brows slightly raised up like he was trying to stay awake, but he quickly fell asleep because of the morphine.

Jahnni slowly raised up without taking her eyes off his face. *He what? Lost something? Looked for something? Loaned something?* She touched his cheek and fixed his pillow so his neck was supported then slowly let the back of her hand glide gently down the side of his face as she finished standing back up. She paused to memorize the peacefulness as he lay there, pain momentarily washed away.

They left his room, each sharing their gratefulness that their new friend was going to be okay. Jahnni stopped and looked back at the sliding glass door to his room, *I owe you everything. Thank you.*

Before they left the floor, Mr. T told Jahnni that he wanted to stay behind to be with Beau as he healed in the hospital. "Agent Pahlavi tell me she got permission for me to stay with my Beau. When we first plan to fly, he was taking me home and help me with my house in San Francisco. It need some small repairs I cannot do anymore. My good Beau. He grow to be a good man, but when I see him in hospital bed, all I see is my baby Beau. I stay until he can leave hospital."

The car ride back to the airport was calmer than the ride to the hospital. The agent that helped drive them to OHSU, came back and took Carlton and Zale to Carlton's home. Before they left the hospital, Jahnni heard Delaram remind them that they couldn't talk about this to anyone. But she would secure their formal interviews right away so they can get them over with.

On the drive, Delaram spoke up, "I told my superiors the basic location of all the things Carlton and Zale told me when I did our brief interviews. They need to secure the airport."

"I imagine that there are already some fisherman camping overnight on Government Island not too far from the entrance to his underground home," Jahnni assumed out loud.

"Well, the airport is secure and the maintenance room is under 24/7 guard for now," Delaram assured her.

"I thought we weren't supposed to be talking to each other about all this?" Jahnni asked her before Sam got dropped off.

"Oh, we aren't talking about what happened all day," Delaram explained. "I am telling you about the plans so far . . . for the secret. So, you'll know that it is going to be taken care of and you won't worry about a security breach. And, except for the FBI, at least for now, you can't talk about today with anyone else yet. Or about the secret. That's what I mean by NTK. If anyone asks you anything, just say, 'The FBI says that I can't talk about anything yet.'"

Jahnni got out and hugged Samantha as Delaram dropped her at the employee parking lot at the airport. She held her a little longer than normal, then said, "I'll call you tomorrow. Are you sure you can drive home? Because I can't keep my eyes open so Delaram is taking me home. I'll get my car when I get back from San Fran tomorrow night."

"I'm fine. Tired, but fine. At least we have the day off tomorrow. There is no way I want to go near the airport. I'm sorry you have to take Crutch by yourself."

"No worries. I am happy to," Jahnni said convincingly, even though she herself had just a slight bit of trepidation after the day they had. "I want to. I want to hand deliver him to his parents. It's the least I can do. I told Carolyn that I insisted."

Jahnni got back in the car, waving to Samantha as they drove towards the employee parking lot exit. "It's a wonder my ID badge still works after the big swim," she said, as she watched the security arm raise up so they could drive back out. "I don't know about the airport itself, but they must have released employee access to the lot at least. Hundreds of employees were stuck because you can't get the exit arms to raise unless you swipe your badge. Carolyn said the lot had been locked."

Delaram handed her phone to Jahnni as she drove away from the lot. "Put your address in just in case you fall asleep on the way." Then she headed towards Jahnni's home so she could grab a change of clothes and personal items to take to the hotel by the airport. A male and a female employee had to stay with Crutch in the room since he was stuck overnight in Portland.

"I hope whoever Carolyn sends is not a chatter box," Jahnni said as she climbed out when they pulled into her driveway. "Just wait here. I'll only be a couple minutes gathering up a few things."

After she came back out to the car she opened the back door and set an overnight case on the floorboard. She then closed the door and hopped into the front seat. She turned to Crutch and mentioned, "I hope you like the clothes that the other agent is bringing for you. They won't be fancy, but they will be better than the funky jumpsuits we have been stuck in all day!"

"Ahhh, and I was just getting used to these seventy's threads too," Crutch teased as they all laughed.

Agent Pahlavi dropped them at the front of the Embassy Suites. Jahnni and Crutch checked in, dragged their bodies to their rooms and plopped on the beds. The other agent, Lonnie, was already in the room. The last thing Jahnni remembered was listening to Lonnie read them their itinerary, then Lonnie was waking her up a few hours later so she could shower and get ready for their flight. Crutch was already up, showered and dressed.

"Do you know you snore Jahnni?" Crutch said, teasing her.

"Yep, that's what I've been told," she replied as she stretched.

Lonnie said, "Hey, I'll take Crutch down for breakfast so

you can get ready. We'll be back in about 45 minutes, okay?"

"Perfect." Jahnni replied as she gathered her bag and headed to the shower.

Before she shut the door, she added, "Oh ya, bring me a bagel, crème cheese, and a black coffee."

The morning went by fast and they found themselves back at the airport. Avoiding the baggage carousel floor, Jahnni and Crutch went to the ticket counter, checked in, got their boarding passes and headed straight through security. She blocked everything from her mind and focused only on Crutch; Partly because that was her job, and partly because she just had to . . . to get through the day.

"I can't wait to sit back and cruise at 35,000 feet away from everything. Maybe I can catch a catnap," she told Crutch. "You should too."

Chapter 43

. . . Before the Storm

AT 11:50 A.M., Jahnni and Crutch boarded their flight for San Francisco.

"This is going to be the best flight ever! I can't believe how relaxed I feel. Don't you feel better?" She was trying to stay upbeat for Crutch.

"Yep," Crutch answered her. He turned to Jahnni and just smiled at her, holding her gaze a little longer than normal. "Can we be friends forever, Jahnni?"

"Of course, Crutch. We are friends forever. Your mom and dad pretty much told me that I am family now! So, I guess that makes me . . . your sister."

They both laughed and waited for the plane door to close.

Jahnni and Crutch sat in first-class, a gift from Carolyn and First Class Air. It was almost a full flight, although with the events of the day before, it could have been an overbooked flight. First Class Air brought in a plane from SLC and threw an extra segment in to SFO later that day to accommodate all the passengers from the previous day's fiasco because they had the regular passengers that had reservations on today's flights. Carolyn worried that Crutch needed extra of attention to keep him busy, yet calm, since the events of the day before were so volatile. Jahnni wasn't so sure. He seemed fine.

The flight attendant crew had fawned over him when he came onboard. Carolyn had given him the backpack full of items from the First Class Air's gift shop that she hurriedly gathered first thing in the morning. Pins shaped like airplane wings, mugs, water bottles, mouse pads, pens, t-shirts, hoodies, snacks. It was crammed with so many goodies. The pilots heard who was going to be on their flight, and one of them even presented him with a model of their newest airplane after he opened his backpack full of gifts.

"Hey Thanks! This is the Boeing 737-900ER! I love this plane! I've actually flo . . ."

The flight attendant asked him, "What? You've flown on this plane before? This our newest plane. Just went into service last month!"

"Uh . . . ya. I have," Crutch said. "It cruises so smooth and the flight panel is . . . I mean . . . it's a great plane. I'm glad they got the tail tip issue worked out."

"How do you know about the tail tip issue?" the FA asked him.

"Oh, I just like planes. I've flown a lot of them," Crutch answered him.

"You must travel often. That's great!" he said.

They watched out the window as the plane was being pushed back by the tug.

"Out on time. Perfect since this plane was a STAR flight this morning. This plane has already left and came back today," she told Crutch. "Usually all the RON's are on time in the morning since they came in the night before. They *remained overnight*. That's why they are called RON's. They are ready first thing because we don't have to wait for it arrive from another city. And the first flight is called a STAR flight because if it *starts the airline right* first thing in the morning, it sets the pace for the rest of the day . . . providing no other surprises."

"Hey sport," the FA said as he walked away from their row. "My name's Christopher and I'll be taking good care of you today. But right now, I need to help with the safety briefing. I'll talk to you later, okay?"

Jahnni nudged Crutch to pay attention to the flight attendant's briefing. They were pointing to exits and showing what to do if the oxygen masks are released, and just in case no one had used a seat belt in a while, they showed how it unlatches.

"I already know all that," Crutch told her. "I can say that speech myself," he said as a passing bit of trivia.

Jahnni shook her finger in a joking way at him, "Doesn't matter. We should act like we are listening to it for the first time. It sets a good example for the other passengers." Then she asked him, "So, you must travel with your family a great deal?"

"Oh, I kinda do. I love planes and my dad loves planes. My uncle loves planes. My grandpa loves planes. My great-grandpa loves planes. My great-great grandpa loved planes. Basically, our whole family loves planes. A LOT," Crutch said as he rolled his eyes about his crazy plane-loving family. "You know what? My great-great grandpa knew Charles Lindberg."

"Is that right? How incredible!" Jahnni gushed.

"Of course," Crutch added, "I never met him. My great-great grandpa that is. My dad said his great-grandpa died before I was born. Did you know anyone famous like that?"

"Yep!" My dad used to write music for Walt Disney. I met all the famous people there when I went with my dad to a meeting with Mr. Disney once. Mickey, Minnie, Donald . . ." Jahnni said, smiling with pride.

"That doesn't count!" Crutch said as he laughed, practically doubling over. "They aren't real."

"Au contraire, mon frère!" Jahnni said. "They are as real to me as you are sitting next to me. They helped raise me when I was lonely. Not in the real-life sense of course. My parents traveled. They were musicians. I had every stuffed animal to sleep with. I watched every Disney cartoon and my parents bought me every Disney movie on VHS!"

"VHS! You must be O-L-D!" he laughed. "I've only owned DVD's. And now Blue Rays. I own every Disney movie too! I have a HUGE collection of all kinds of movies. About 400 to 500 I think. When I was stuck in the hospital so long, I had my own collection in my room. The nurses would sit and watch them with me. Guess what my favorite movie of all times is?"

"Oh, I couldn't even guess. What is it?" Jahnni asked.

"Fly Away Home. I think I have watched that movie one thousand times. Do you like that movie?" Crutch asked.

"I sure do!" Jahnni said as she shook her head, remembering. "I always cry towards the end, when she is flying all by herself and the song 10,000 miles comes on. I think it's Mary Chapin Carpenter. Anyway, Amy, the girl in the movie, floats over the land, looking for her destination. Everything is quiet as she cuts through the air. Her geese are following her because they trust her like their mama. She's quietly cruising through the air, guiding her geese to their new promised land. The beauty of the gentle rolling land and calm waters below her is like a quiet strength bidding her well; confirming to her that she did it. As soon as that song starts, I always feel free. My heart hurts, yet it feels happy. I don't know what that means, but I always cry during that song."

Crutch was silent for a few seconds while he looked at his lap. "Ya, it makes me cry too. I watch her fly towards her final destination, her dad looking for her, her friends searching, everyone anxiously waiting. She's being so brave, and I always wondered if that is what it is like when you make it to heaven. Are people who have loved you, waiting for you? Knowing that you are coming? Watching. Waiting. And you arrive, sailing through the air softly and landing exactly *where* you are supposed to, exactly *when* you are supposed to."

Jahnni had watched him talk, tears welling up in her eyes. "You must have wondered about that while you were in the hospital. Were you afraid?"

Again, he was silent as he chose his words. "I wasn't at first because I was so young, I just believed that the doctors would keep giving me medicine until I got better. But about the third time I was put in the hospital, I noticed that my friends there, didn't always 'go home' in the way I thought they did." By this time, Crutch had tears in his eyes and he wiped at one that trailed down his cheek. "My mom would tell me, 'He went home.' Or, 'She went home last night.' I didn't understand until I was older, what she meant."

"I'm sorry you had to go through so much. Life can be so . . . so . . . not what we ever expected, or . . . planned," Jahnni said softly. "What do you feel about it now? Or is that too personal?"

"I'm kinda good with it. I think that is why I loved that movie so much. It helped me know the feeling of freedom. It gave me a taste of, 'You'll be okay.' Now that I'm in remission, I just live with 'I don't worry.' I know that today is a great day. Tomorrow may not be. I do everything I can. Try everything. Yesterday, when everything kept going wrong, I knew. I knew in my heart we were going to be okay. I just went with it. It was exhilarating. And . . . I knew right when it all started. You and Sam were going to make it all okay. Then Beau and Mr. T joined us. Thanks, by the way."

Jahnni had tears flowing down both cheeks now. "Look what you've done . . . you've made me cry!" She laughed as she wiped her cheeks with her thumbs. "I don't think you should thank me. I really screwed up. I am not sure exactly what else I could have done right yet . . . but I keep thinking about it."

"You didn't do anything wrong! You did everything right. You never gave up. You kept me safe. You kept Mr. T safe. You and Sam kept your cool. Beau was there if the worst happened.

Well . . . I guess the worst did happen, huh? But when things went wrong, you didn't stop. You always kept trying. You never quit, even when it was a tiny bit scary . . . like when we went swimming," he said, trying to convince her.

"Thanks. I'm not sure I believe it yet, but thanks," Jahnni whispered.

Crutch kept looking towards the galley. He would turn to talk to Jahnni, then it would catch his attention and he would turn back. "It looks like the food cart rolled itself out," he mumbled, then shrugged his shoulders and reached for his backpack.

A man, averting his eyes, came around the corner from the galley, walked through the first-class cabin and disappeared into the coach cabin. His hat was large and floppy, covering most of his face. Jahnni glanced up but then back down as she fiddled with Crutch's new backpack when he couldn't get everything stuffed back into it. After she put his backpack back under the seat in from of them, she glanced to the galley to see what Crutch had been looking at but she couldn't see quite far enough in there from her seat.

"Maybe they forgot to drop the lock levers when the FAB agents loaded the carts for the flight. I'll let the flight attendant know." Then Jahnni pressed the overhead light to summon Christopher, the first-class FA.

Crutch seemed confused. "Does that guy work for the airline?"

"What guy, honey?" Jahnni asked, turning to Crutch to see who he was talking about.

"That guy that just came from the galley."

"I didn't see someone come from the galley. Maybe a passenger was waiting for the lav and got tired of waiting," she answered.

Christopher was asking the couple behind Jahnni and Crutch what their beverage of choice was. He finished, reached up and turned off the light that called him to Jahnni and leaned down. "Is there a problem? Can I get you anything?"

"Oh, no problem really. I was just wondering, oh, never mind, it was nothing." Jahnni decided not to say anything about the silly cart. "Could I have a Coke and my friend here have a Sprite?" Jahnni asked.

Crutch said, "Hey, I want a Coke."

"Nope . . . not on my watch, Mr.! Too much caffeine. You're lucky I am letting you have anything carbonated," she said laughing. "We'll get a great little snack of cheeses and fruit on this flight in a bit. And warm cookies because we are in first-class."

Soon, the cabin was served and everyone appeared to be happily enjoying their trip. Jahnni and Crutch looked out the window, pointing and discussing what they could still see.

A flight attendant came from the aft and whispered to Christopher, who was in the middle of refreshing beverages in first-class. "Oh. Really? Okay . . ." he said. He traded duties with the her. She took over refilling drinks as he went to the flight deck door, pulling a food/beverage cart forward to block access to the flight deck. The flight deck door opened briefly and Christopher went into the flight deck after the pilot came out and he closed the door firmly behind him. The pilot clumsily placed a tray on the counter in the galley then turned and accessed the lav door. The lock flipped to 'occupied.'

After several minutes, Crutch leaned over to Jahnni and whispered, "He sure has been in there a long time. You think he is okay?"

"Really?" Jahnni said. "I didn't really pay attention. I'm sure he's fine." But it made Jahnni watch a little closer. After a few more minutes, she decided to push the call button.

"Hello. I'm Rochelle and I'll be helping Christopher for a few minutes. Can I get you something?" the aft FA that took Christopher's place asked.

"Well," Jahnni said, "The pilot has been in there for some time. Is he okay? Should someone knock on the door to check on him?"

"Uh, no. At least not yet. They don't like to be bothered if they are taking their time. If we knock on the door, passengers get worried and start staring at the door. Then when they finally come out, they feel like everyone is staring . . . which of course they are . . . but they don't like it," she explained.

"Oh . . . okay. We'll avert our eyes when he comes out," Jahnni said jokingly, holding a hand over her eyes as she turned her head in a mock averting tactical maneuver.

The tone sounded that alerted the flight attendants that the flight deck was calling them. Rochelle went to the phone and answered, turning sideways and covering her mouth as she spoke. Her shoulders went a little stiff and she looked casually around the first-class cabin. She nodded, then hung up the phone. She walked to the lav and knocked lightly on the door. She knocked harder. She spoke softer through the door after he mumbled to her. She went back to the phone to talk to the flight deck. Nodding a few times, obviously humming her answer into the phone, she hung up and walked into the galley. She picked up the used tray that had fed both pilots, and looked all over the remaining food. She used a fork to move the left-over grapes and cheese around as if looking for something. She looked in the glasses that held their beverages, swirling the left-over liquid and ice but seemed to not notice anything unusual so she set them back down.

Crutch watched intently. "What is she looking for?"

Jahnni frowned. "I have no idea."

Crutch craned his neck a little further. "She's like, inspecting the captain's finished plate. Why would she do that?"

"First of all, how do you know it was the captain's plate?" she asked.

Crutch was still moving his head around to get a better look. "I guess I assumed, since it was the captain that brought out his tray as the flight attendant switched places with him."

"But how did you know it was the captain?"

"By his bars of course, silly. He has four gold bars on the shoulder of his shirt," Crutch said. "You don't know that?"

Jahnni acted a little insulted. "Of course, I know that. I was surprised that you knew that."

"I have a pretend jacket at home that my dad's boss gave me. It's a whole uniform in my size. It was a gift the last time I was sick. Mine is a captain's uniform and my brother's is a first officer uniform. He said I earned it."

Jahnni shrugged. "Hmmm. How did you earn it?"

"Just because. I practiced all the time." Then Crutch started looking out the window, leaning his face on the cool glass.

Chapter 44

WHAT?

JAHNNI'S EYES FOLLOWED Rochelle. She knew that the 'D' FA mainly assisted the 'A' or first-class FA when needed. She was having trouble gathering up dishes. She was working very quickly and kept dropping silverware and napkins. *She must be nervous doing everything by herself I guess*, Jahnni surmised. A couple overhead lights dinged but she was so busy she seemed to ignore them.

"Is there something that I can help you with?" Jahnni asked when she passed by.

"Uh, no, not yet. I think I got this. I'll let you know if I do. We are just a little short-handed right now," she blurted out in a whisper. "You non-revers are so helpful when you fly with us. Thanks."

"Oh, you're welcome. We have to make good on our free travel, right?" Jahnni said teasingly.

Crutch was falling asleep so Jahnni left him alone. She

glanced behind in coach and saw the aft FA's working quite quickly there as well. The intercom phone dinged and Rochelle rushed to grab it. She was shaking her head no, slightly, but didn't speak. She started arguing or talking firmly then hung up. Jahnni saw the two aft FA's in the coach aisle with the beverage cart when she had glanced back, so she assumed it was the flight deck that she was speaking with. Rochelle picked up the phone again and the familiar tone sounded overhead. Her face appeared pale and Jahnni noticed it glistened, enough that she took a napkin and began patting her face and neck. She hung up, walked to the galley, and pulled out her manifest, unfolding it and running her fingers down a list like she was looking for someone. She started again at the top of the list, but obviously, as far as Jahnni could tell, she didn't see what she was looking for. She looked up again and moved to the right to look down the aisle. She picked up the mic as she planted a smile on her face and made an announcement to all the passengers onboard.

"Could I have your attention, please? Is there a physician onboard this flight? Again, is there a physician onboard this flight? Please hit your call button to summon a flight attendant if you are a physician."

She glanced down the aisle again but no one seemed to be responding. She brought her mic to her lips and made another announcement. "If you are a nurse, please hit your call button. Again, if you are a nurse, please hit your call button to let us know." Still no one responded. She finally added, "If you have any medical training, please hit your call button."

Gosh, I wonder if I should push the call button. I have first aid training, but I think all the FA's have more than me, Jahnni wondered as she craned her neck again to look back into coach.

Finally, a tiny sweet voice in 6C said, "Sweetheart, I pushed my call button but no one is answering it."

One of the aft FA's heard her speaking to Rochelle and rushed forward to the passenger's seat and asked, "Are you a nurse?"

The sweet voice said back, a little too curtly, "No. I've been trying to call you to tell you that I'm a doctor. What can I do to help?"

"Thank God. I mean, oh, thank you. Please follow me to the front," the flight attendant begged.

Jahnni watched the little lady who was probably in her 60's, grab her purse from the overhead bin and rush forward with the FA. Jahnni realized that she knew the flight attendant as someone who transferred to in-flight from customer service not long ago. *Oh, it's Kristy, I should let her know I can help if they need me to do anything.* The flight attendants and the doctor began speaking in the galley then Kristy shrugged and said to the doctor, "I am sorry, I have to."

"Okay dear, just hurry. I need to get in there!" She raised her arms out and Kristy hand-patted her down, very thoroughly. Jahnni realized that she was doing a hand pat-down search before she allowed her in the flight deck. *But no one goes into the flight deck*, so Jahnni realized that something was definitely wrong.

Kristy knocked on the flight deck door while she was talking into the phone. The door came open and Christopher came out and Rochelle went in with the doctor. The door closed immediately. He turned to look at the passengers before he grabbed the manifest, running his fingers down the seating chart as he and Rochelle had done earlier.

What, or who, are they looking for? Jahnni moaned in her head as she fought off the trepidation that was growing. She smiled at Kristy as she walked past. She wanted to ask questions but her lips seemed glued shut; no specific questions came to mind. Kristy returned the blank yet knowing look, then paused to take a breath as she stared straight ahead at the curtains that separated coach from first-class. She suddenly raised her head and smiled as she opened the curtain, entered the coach section and drew the heavy curtains back together.

Christopher looked at Jahnni and asked. "You are a non-rev, flying positive space? What do you do?"

"I'm a CSS for us at PDX. Why?" Now Jahnni was getting nervous. There were passengers all around them, so she didn't want to show her angst as she waited for the reason he asked.

He motioned for Jahnni to lean closer and whispered, "Our captain is extremely ill in the lav. He told the F/O that if he wasn't back in five minutes, it would be because he can't even stand. He had said that he thought he was going to pass out before he left the flight deck. He's been in there for quite a while. We need all the first-class passengers moved to coach. Weight and balance will be fine so they can sit wherever they find an open seat. But they need to be moved quickly so we can help the captain out of the lav." Christopher glanced around the first-class cabin then leaned back to Jahnni. "They can't see him like this. Our first officer has fallen gravely ill as well. Just don't mention any of this to the passengers. Can you handle that?"

Jahnni took a moment to process what he was saying. She noted that his eyes were wide as he spoke and there wasn't a grin or smile hiding anywhere on his face that would have assured her he was teasing. *Why would he tease about a thing like that anyway? Okay . . . Be Calm. Just jump in and help where you can. First things first. Move the passengers out of first-class,* she told herself in a numb obedient manner.

"So, how many seats are available in back?" she asked.

"There are only ten passengers here in first-class on this flight; only eight need to move since you and Crutch will stay here for now, and sixteen open seats in coach. We're fine," he answered.

"Of course, I'll do whatever you need me to do. What would you like me to tell them?" Jahnni asked.

Christopher looked at her name on the manifest. "2C . . . Jahnni? Oh, *you're* Jahnni? I didn't know that was you. My God! Are you escorting this young man then? How did I miss that? I had only glanced at your last name on my list before, but now I . . . well . . . now I know."

"Yes, and yes. . . but let's get back to the coach thing. What should I tell them?" she asked with laser attention. That seemed to be her nature when she did anything. *Home in and get the job done. Make a decision, then full speed ahead. Don't confuse me with fear,* she ordered him with her mind, trying to remain focused.

"Umm . . . tell them the captain said he needs them to move for, uh, weight and balance issues. To, um, streamline the payload or something that sounds like airplane talk. Then after they get moved, keep smiling then close the drape between coach and first-class."

Jahnni saw that Crutch was sleeping, so she left him to sleep and began introducing herself as a First Class Air Supervisor. "I have been asked to move all of us to the coach cabin. The captain says it is important for weight and balance issues," she fibbed. "Please, leave your items in the overhead bin, but grab your immediate belongings and find a seat anywhere that's open in coach."

"My anywhere, is here in first-class. I paid for first-class honey! I'm not moving," the man refused.

Jahnni said, "I'll come back to you." She moved to the next passengers and continued the process to clear the first-class cabin. She returned to the last hold-out. The feisty man in 3A.

"Okay, Here's the deal. I appreciate the price you paid for your flight. So, to let you know how important it is for you to move back there . . . rather quickly I might add . . . I will refund this portion of your flight when we land in San Fran. How's that?"

"You can do that?" he said eagerly.

"Yes. Yes, I can. What is your name? I'll mark it on the manifest and before the end of the day, I will have this portion of your trip refunded. No charge for this leg of your journey."

She waited briefly while he mulled it over. "But you have to start moving in the next five seconds."

"You don't have to tell me twice," he said as he jumped up with his book in hand.

"Well, actually I did . . . have to tell you twice. Maybe three times, but who's counting she said with a friendly smile. Once he found a seat, she left the passengers to Kristy and the other aft FA and closed the curtain, overlapping it to be sure there were not any gaps for people to see forward into the first-class cabin. *This curtain is much heavier than I thought. Must be some type of noise reduction curtain,* Jahnni noticed.

"Okay . . . now what else can I do to help?" she asked Christopher.

Jahnni listened carefully as she was told how to lay out the seats. "There's a latch that the passengers don't know about. It's right here," Christopher said as he grabbed it. "It will lay out the seats in row 1, like an emergency cot." When the seats were prepared, Christopher handed Jahnni gloves and asked her to help him move the captain out of the lav. He was conscious, but barely had the strength to help hold his head up much less his own weight upright as they guided him to the seat. They laid him down and covered him with blankets.

Then Christopher said, "Now . . . we have to move the first officer out of the flight deck. He's sick too."

"WHAT?" Jahnni said too loudly. Her mind searched for some sort of fact to assure her that she did indeed, hear him incorrectly. "I mean, what? Who's flying the plane?"

Christopher was ashen. He looked Jahnni straight in the

eyes and said, "No one."

"WHAT? I mean . . . what?" she asked again. "Is this even possible?" She felt her stomach begin to roll, making gurgling noises and she heard a ping in her ears as they started ringing. She allowed herself a few seconds to feel the balance in the plane which assured her that they were not heading down, sideways, nor up at a fast pitch. *Okay, this is not the time to be weak. Take a deep breath. In with your nose, out through your mouth. One thing at a time. Stay focused, she again lectured herself.*

"There is no one to fly the plane. It is on auto-pilot. We are winging this as we go," Christopher slowly explained, enunciating every word.

"WHAT? I mean, okay . . . I'll stop saying that. But what are we going to do? We are supposed to be landing in about 35 minutes! Okay . . . let's think about this. Do we have any jump-seaters? Or dead-heading crew? Maybe we have a pilot in the bunch heading to another city to work," she offered as a first thought, or process of elimination.

Christopher shook his head back and forth, "No, I checked and there aren't even any crew members flying from another airline as non-revs. Wait. Unless they are flying revenue. We wouldn't know since they aren't listed as an airline employee from any airline if they are flying as revenue passengers. They'd have purchased regular tickets. Or maybe we have a plain ol' private pilot onboard. I'll have to make an announcement! That might certainly scare the passengers, so I need to word it carefully."

Jahnni said, "We need to get the F/O out here laying down. Unless, can he function at all?"

"No, he is worse than the captain, I think," Christopher answered solemnly. After he paused to stare at the floor, he continued laying out this portion of his plan. "Okay . . . Let's go get him. I'll call in, you watch the door. When they open the door, Rochelle will come out and we will go in to get him. The doctor is in there too. It's gonna be a very tight fit."

Through a lot of maneuvering, they managed to lift the F/O out of his seat and onto the floor in a sitting position. His body lolled to one side or the other, depending on which way was the path of least resistance.

"We have a folding aisle seat in the closet behind first-class. Let's use that," Christopher said.

Rochelle had the same idea and had already grabbed the aisle chair, unfolded it and opened the seat belts, pushing it to the open flight deck door. They squatted down, lifted the officer into the aisle chair and wheeled him out of the flight deck and to the folded-out first-class seats, laying him down. They covered him to keep him warm as the doctor continued attending to him. They had already given her their emergency kit and she did what she could to keep the pilots comfortable.

"I'm sorry. My name is Jahnni. I'm a Customer Service Supervisor for First Class Air at PDX. What is your name?"

"I'm Trinity. Doctor Trinity Robinson. I practice in Vancouver and Portland at Legacy."

"Thank you for helping. Do you know what's wrong with them? Is it contagious? Should we pass out face masks?"

Dr. Robinson responded quickly, "I could be wrong, I don't have any way to do a culture to rule out a virus, but I believe they have been poisoned. Either right before they boarded or soon after we took off. I'll monitor them while you do your jobs."

Poisoned? How could that even happen? The pilots eat separate meals and not even the same menu item. It's specifically for this very purpose so no one could know which meal was for who, pilots or passengers. This is not the time to try to figure this out right now. One thing at a time, she reminded herself again.

"Okay. We have pressing issues to tend to, as you've probably already noticed. But let us know if you need anything else. There is sealed bottled water in the galley if you need it." Jahnni turned to Christopher, who was standing in the galley and Dr. Robinson turned to her patients, placing the stethoscope on their chests, one at a time, and checking their pulses again.

"Jahnni? What's going on?" Crutch said as he blinked and rubbed his eyes, then glanced over the seat in front of him as a delayed understanding started to sink in. "Where is everyone? Why are these guys laying down? What the . . .! That's the captain!" Then he looked at the other guy laying there, but before he could blurt out the obvious, Jahnni reached for him and held her hand on his mouth so she could say, "shhh," and place her finger over her lips.

"We have a problem Crutch. Don't panic, but we need to make an announcement to see if there is a pilot onboard. Just stay calm please. We are doing everything we can," she said in the softest, calmest voice she could muster.

Christopher grabbed the mic and began his announcement, "Good afternoon ladies and gentlemen. With the exciting news of flying in our newly acquired Boeing 737-900ER, we would like to know if we have any vacationing pilots onboard that would like to come forward for a short video demonstration of our new plane. We can't help but brag . . . so ring your call button if you are a pilot."

Dead silence. No one rang. Jahnni realized she was holding her breath waiting for call buttons to begin ringing all over the plane. She relaxed the muscles that she was tensing in her hands as she stood there making fists, tapping her sides in a soothing rhythmic motion. She calmly let out a slow release of the breath she was holding and opened her eyes to smile at Crutch. *Poor baby. Hasn't he been through enough?* she asked the heavens.

Christopher peeked through the curtains but no one looked the least bit interested in his announcement. "Going once, twice, three times . . . Sorry then . . . out of luck. Thank you."

"That was a really smooth announcement," Jahnni said. "Did they teach you to say that?"

"Heck no, I made it up as I went. But now what?" Christopher said in between cracking his knuckles and blinking rapidly. "Who's gonna help us now?"

Chapter 45

No, Really . . . I Can Do This

CRUTCH GRABBED AT Jahnni's shirt and began tugging it repeatedly. "I can help Jahnni!"

"Yes, you can, sweetie. Just stay calm and put on your seat belt. Rochelle is calling control from the radio in the flight deck. We will know what to do in a few minutes," Jahnni said out loud, but was thinking in her head, *if there is anything we can do.* She racked her brain trying to think of a movie, or article that she had read anywhere in her life that had a similar situation. Her brain couldn't think of anything. She remembered that they could refuel some planes mid-air, but that wouldn't help to get a pilot inside the plane mid-air. *That's a dumb thought,* she scolded herself.

"No, Jahnni . . . I can help. Let me up there," Crutch insisted.

"Crutch honey, sit back down and put your seat belt back on, please. Rochelle will let us know."

"Jahnni! I'm serious. I can help," he repeated, his voice cracking a bit in frustration.

Christopher looked at Crutch and tried to smile. "Sure buddy. You can help by staying out of the way and letting us do our job. Okay?" he finished in a chipper high pitched voice like he was talking to a 5-year-old.

Crutch tipped his chin down, and glared up at Christopher. "Look, don't patronize me. I might be thirteen, but I'm not stupid, okay?"

"Crutch! Please, I'm sure he didn't mean to be curt. We just have an emergency and we are waiting to be told what to do," Jahnni whispered, hoping that her soft tone would de-escalate the tension.

"That is what I am trying to tell you!" he said, giving a sideways glance at Christopher like his opinion didn't matter anyway. "I can help. Look, let me in the flight deck. I'll call the tower in San Fran, and they can page my dad. They can bring him to the tower and he can explain that I know what to do."

Christopher's chest was rising out and back faster with every breath he took in. He started to walk away, but stepped back to face Crutch. Jahnni was standing so close that she could hear the air being forced in and out of his nose like a mad bull. He was lowering his hands palm side down emphasizing every stanza of his sentences. "Look kid! I'm stressed out. I am trying to be calm. I'm trying to do my job. You aren't making it any easier by interrupting us while we think. Please, sit down and put your seatbelt on!"

"NO! I CAN DO THIS! I CAN HELP!" Crutch said to

Christopher, emphasizing every sentence he spoke as well. "Call the tower and my dad will tell you I can help! Now!" It appeared that Crutch was not taking no for an answer.

Jahnni was startled at the anger in his voice and wondered where this sudden insistent confidence was coming from. This was a new side of Crutch she had never seen before. Jahnni bent down a little to look Crutch in the eyes. She searched his eyes, trying to understand. "Crutch honey, what are you talking about? Just calm down please, and tell me what you mean. What will your dad tell us?"

Crutch swayed back and forth, looking at the floor before finally looking up to meet Jahnni's eyes. "Remember when Beau asked me why they call me Crutch? Yesterday? When we were sitting in the bag carts trying to decide what to do? I told him I would tell him when we had more time. But we never had more time. I never had a chance to tell him."

"Okay," Jahnni said, I remember.

"It's because of the cancer. All the times I was in the hospital, I had surgery to remove tumors in my legs too, along with chemo. The last time they had to do radiation . . . but that's not the point. The point is, I have been on crutches off and on most of my life since I was three. It's my nickname. The doctors called me that. Look, here's my boarding pass," he said as he dug it out of his pocket. "Don't you remember? My name is Eddie Link . . . the fifth."

"Okay . . . that's nice honey but I don't see how that explains anything," Jahnni said.

"Look," Crutch said as he looked up at the ceiling of the

plane with exasperation in his voice. He looked back at Jahnni, then continued, "I am Eddie Link the fifth. You don't know who I am? Who my family is?"

"I am so sorry Crutch, but I don't really know. You are just Crutch. I just met you yesterday. I don't know your family."

Dr. Robinson interrupted, turning from her patients to join the conversation. "I know who the Links are."

"Will someone please just get to the point!" Christopher shouted in a loud whisper.

"Did you say the fifth, sweetie?" Dr. Robinson asked, looking at Crutch.

"Yes! I am trying to explain that I can help. Why won't anyone listen me?" Crutch whined in a testy voice.

Dr. Robinson stood and faced Jahnni. "His, what, great? Great-great, grandfather invented the flight simulator." She turned and looked at Crutch for clarification.

"YES! My entire family does this. They either develop, improve, or build . . . the flight simulators. Your pilots here trained on the simulators that my dad designs. I can fly all of them."

"Now, wait a second kid," Christopher growled louder while rolling his eyes. "If you think I am letting you anywhere NEAR that flight deck, you are completely out of your ever-loving mind!"

Jahnni stared at Christopher, then looked back at Crutch. She looked at Dr. Robinson then again, back at Crutch. "Hold on. You are trying to tell us that you know how to fly this thing?" Jahnni asked, thinking that it was a dumb question anyway. *A kid can't fly this. I'm not even going to entertain this crazy idea,* she told herself.

"Jahnni . . . please . . . have that lady, the flight attendant, tell the tower that I can help! Tell them my dad's name and to page him to wherever they can take him to the tower. He will tell you. Jahnni, I have flown this simulator, in fact all the simulators, since I was three!"

"Oh, please kid, tell me another one. Did someone serve this kid alcohol?" he mumbled, snickering and shaking his head back and forth.

Jahnni looked into Crutch's eyes, trying to understand and hoping for answers. "What do you mean you have flown them all?"

"Okay . . . I have been sick most of my life. I have been in and out of hospitals most of my life. They had to home-school me and everyone got stuck taking me to work with them. I have been to my dad's work, and my grandpa's work, so many times. I have played in the simulators all my life. They are like a game. Like, a, a, a, PS4 game. I have mastered them like a game. It's not that hard really. Well, not for me anymore. I NEVER crash."

"THIS IS NOT A GAME KID!" Christopher announced, his face turning seriously red.

"Okay Crutch. We can at least make the call," Jahnni said. *This is completely nuts and I can't believe I am even going to talk to Christopher about it. Surely, I'm gonna wake up from this nightmare any minute. Right?*

She looked at Christopher and added, "I know, I know!

I don't know what I believe, but we can at least make a call, right? Maybe we can get some answers."

"If you let me sit in the captain's chair. I will call them and talk to them. You can wear the F/O's headset so you can listen," Crutch instructed.

Silence fell between them and no one spoke. They kept looking back and forth to each other and Jahnni used the time to try to condense what had been said so she could figure things out. Still, she didn't know what to believe.

"Look, Christopher . . . there is no one to fly the plane! It is worth at least a conversation," Jahnni whispered. "I'm out of options, you're out of options. Basically, the whole plane is out of options!"

"Absofreakingtively not!" Christopher said.

Rochelle came out of the flight deck like she'd seen a ghost. She looked straight at Christopher and said very solemnly, "They are sending two F-16 fighter jets. What are we going to do?"

"They are going to shoot us down while we are still over the water if we don't land this plane, Jahnni! That is the rule. I know this. I'm telling you the truth! Please! Listen to me! I can do this," Crutch begged one last time.

Jahnni looked at Christopher and Rochelle. "Guys, you know as well as I do this is protocol for an errant plane. We are dead when they get here if we are out over the water. Let's just talk to the tower."

Christopher's shoulders slumped and he shook his head no, before he answered, "Oh whatever. We are dead anyway,

I guess. Hold the door."

"Okay then. Okay." Crutch grabbed his backpack, then probably realizing he wouldn't need it, he set in on the seat. He took a deep breath and walked toward the door. "Jahnni, you can be my F/O."

"What? I don't know how to fly one of these!" she announced, as if no one knew this fact yet.

"You can just sit there. Trust me, I can do this. In fact . . . if they talk to my dad, I'm pretty sure they'll tell you guys to let me do it."

"Forgive me Lord if I am making another stupid wrong turn," Jahnni prayed out loud, looking up. Then Crutch and Jahnni walked toward the flight deck.

Chapter 46

Benson?

"Just wait right there you damn brat!" a voice said behind them. They stopped and slowly turned in unison, Jahnni recognizing the voice, but not placing it, at first. There, just inside the curtain that separated the cabins, stood a man in a tan floppy hat and holding a very short folded up umbrella, pointing the sharp end on Christopher's neck.

What is this man doing in first-class? I thought I moved everyone. Where do I know this guy from? Work? No. Maybe he works in the airport somewhere? No, I just can't place it. Where, do I. . . . she said in her head, running the ideas through her brain like a computer searching for data before the memory of Mr. Prattle's office burst through the fog of yesterday's events.

"Hey, what is this?" Christopher said when the tip of the umbrella shoved him a couple steps forward, as he placed his arms out to his side and raised them in a sign of surrender.

"Benson?" Jahnni said before she could stop the words

from tumbling out. "I forgot about you. What are you doing? The airport debacle is over and your boss is dead. Give it a rest!"

"I have had enough of your mouth. Now, where is Arnad? I thought he was on this flight with you? Where is the key?" Benson said as the muscles in his jaw appeared to throb while forcing the words through his clinched teeth. His eyes darted around the cabin before landing back at Jahnni's.

"Maybe," Jahnni began as she felt the words spill out of her mouth if for nothing more than to stall while she thought further what to do, "you don't understand. It's over. Perry Prattle is no more. Craigs is under arrest, and for all that is holy man, THERE ISN'T A KEY! There never was a rock key! That rock was a souvenir for Prattle's father . . . from Mr. Baptiste. It was a crazy convoluted idea that Prattle made up out of thin air because of unresolved emotional poppycock. Besides, Arnad, or rather Mr. Tropopoulis, isn't on this flight."

Rochelle was frozen but squeaked out, "Who is this? What key is he talking about?"

Jahnni responded to her but stared straight at Benson, concealing her complete fear of the escalating situation, "This is Benson, one of the . . . terrorists that wreaked havoc over the airport causing the evacuation and ground stop yesterday. He's wanted by the . . . well pretty much wanted by everyone about now," she warned, waiting for his response to her short summary.

Benson stood there not saying anything so Jahnni continued speaking to him, "One thing that I realized by the end of the day yesterday is that you don't have a SIDA badge. Or, if you work at the airport somewhere, your job doesn't allow bypass access. That means no access to the passenger manifests for the airlines either. So, how did you know to get on this flight?"

"Well," he finally spoke, answering Jahnni, "like the incredibly astute and tenacious person that I am, I followed you when I fortuitously saw you walk into the airport this morning and was close enough behind you when you were in line at the ticket counter. I purchased a ticket on the flight you told the agent you were checking in for. I managed to flit right past you when I boarded. Now, really . . . where is the key? I know you're lying to me."

Jahnni stared at him, wheels turned in her head as she tried to take this entire muddled mess and understand it. Exasperated with his lack of hearing, she changed course, "Let me see if I understand this," she said as she lifted her hand to tick off a list . . . as she walked slowly toward Benson. "One, you bought a ticket on our flight to somehow be near the person, or people, you thought had something you wanted. Two, you were the person that scooted past us after hanging out briefly in the galley earlier, aren't you? And three, you think you are still supposed to find this mysterious missing rock key for a boss that is dead? What makes you tick, Benson? None of this makes sense."

"Just stay right there, or I, I'll stab him!" Benson said as he dug the sharp tip deeper into Christopher's neck."

"Oh, wait, did you poison the flight crew?" Jahnni asked,

thinking that the obvious almost went right over her head, "Why would you do that? You'll get us all killed. It escaped your notice that you are still on the flight that you disabled?"

"What do you mean? It was meant for you and the kid. The first two settings of food or drinks are for the first two people . . . isn't it? No one was in front of you, so aren't you the first two to be served? Besides, there's always an extra pilot on-board. A, uh, uh, what are they called?" he asked as he snapped his fingers at Jahnni. "You know . . . the, uh . . . Jumpers? Seaters? Seat jumpers? Oh wait . . . I know this one. Jump-seaters. Get one of those up here," Benson ordered, although his voice sounded quite anxious.

"Are you serious?" Jahnni said. "You think they pack all the flights with pilots in case someone like you decides to do something stupid?"

"Well, they always have jump-seaters and stuff. Right?"

"Oh, sure, and they punch their tickets as they board too! Fly 10 and get one free. Are you really that dense?" Jahnni said, trying to get him riled just enough for confusion to set in. She walked a little closer.

"Uh, Jahnni, I need to get in there. I can see the F-16's out the side windows," Crutch said nervously behind her.

Jahnni heard Crutch, but she wanted to finish the last few words on the train of thought she was on before answering him. She continued speaking to Benson. "You know what Benson . . . I am going to do you a favor. I am going to give you the 'key,' the rock, number two. I can't believe I just said that, but maybe now we can get this over with. I happen to have it with me. Let me get it, okay?" she said, hoping he would believe her lie while she stalled a bit longer. Then she spoke to Crutch without turning around, "Eddie, close the door behind you . . . with Rochelle. But don't touch anything yet . . . Quick."

In two seconds, they flew into the flight deck door that Rochelle had held slightly ajar with her foot, and they slammed it shut behind them.

"Hey! What are they doing!" Benson snarled.

"What does it matter? I am going to give you the key. You want it right now? Or do you want to wait until right before we crash? Cuz, you apparently have poisoned our pilots. I am not sure what you think you can do with the key when you are dead . . . like the rest of us," she said casually, although there was no casual thought coursing through her veins. It was taking all her strength to keep fear from quivering in her voice.

"Wait. Wait, I can't think. I want the key . . . ya . . . then, uh, maybe one of these people can land the plane. I saw on TV once how they can talk you through landing."

"Oh, Benson, you watch too many movies. Here . . . Just be patient and let me get the key for you. I have it. Okay?" Jahnni said without breaking his gaze. She knew that Christopher had been slowly reaching for Crutch's backpack that was left on the seat. It was so heavy from all his gifts from the airline.

Jahnni walked a little closer. "Christopher," she said as she still locked eyes with Benson. "Isn't there something you would like to do right now?"

Benson scrunched up his nose and gave Jahnni a questioning look. "My name's not Christopher."

The backpack came flying around from in front of Christopher and smashed into Benson's head, throwing him down to the ground. He landed on his knees with his face pressed down on the seat. Jahnni grabbed the umbrella as it fell and Christopher leaned down on Benson, grabbing and pinning his hands behind his back. Benson struggled, but Christopher held his arms tight.

"Grab the zip ties in the medical bag," Christopher ordered.

Dr. Robinson reached in to the emergency bag and handed them to Jahnni. Jahnni grabbed the plastic ties and wrapped Benson's wrists as Christopher held his hands tight together behind Benson's back. She used two on his wrists and used two on his ankles for a little extra security.

"You got him, Chris?" Jahnni asked.

"Yep. He's not going anywhere," he said, then looked down at his first prisoner, ever. "Whew. I feel like Matt Damon!"

"Get off me, man. I can't breathe! Do you have to press your knee on me so hard?" Benson mumbled in a breathy voice, most of his face buried in the seat cushion. Christopher allowed Benson enough space to turn his head.

"Where are the FAMs when you need them?" Jahnni asked no one in particular. Turning to Dr. Robinson, she asked about the pilots, "How are they? Are they going to be okay? Do you have any idea what they ingested?"

Dr. Robinson tucked the blankets tighter then said, "They are stable. I don't detect fever, but they are in an extremely deep sleep. They moan and try to talk, then just . . . out they go. I've seen this before if it's what I suspect. I think it is Rohypnol."

"Who is she? How'd she know that?" Benson mumbled, with the side of his head pressed against the seat.

"She's a doctor," Christopher said. "Just you never mind." Then Christopher turned to Jahnni, "When you trade places with Rochelle, I'll have her get everything collected and secured here in first-class and Kristy and Vanessa can take care of coach. Just, call us as soon as there is some kind of plan for the no-pilot issue. Maybe the kid does know something. I'm willing to try anything at this point and since we can't parachute a plane full of people out of here, what choice do we have? We need to land."

"Land?" Benson mumbled as he struggled with Christopher. "I thought you said there weren't any pilots onboard?"

"Oh, this is your lucky day. The kid says he can land the plane. Isn't this game you invented fun? What a great plan you thought through," Christopher said, leaning into Benson's ear.

"You gotta buckle me up man! You gotta buckle me up!" Benson ordered, thrashing his face back and forth across the seat. "We're gonna crash!"

Christopher leaned down again to speak into Benson's ear and said between gritted teeth, "I guess you should have thought of that."

Jahnni called the flight deck. She then traded places with Rochelle, and left it to her and Christopher to keep Benson down and do whatever it is that flight attendants do. She knew they had numerous responsibilities, and coupled with today's mayhem, she knew better than to tell them how to do their jobs. *They'll know what to do. Delegation at its finest, I suppose. Dr. Robinson is taking care of the pilots, Christopher is taking care of Benson. Three FA's left to finish the flight...as long as the flight doesn't finish us.* She took one last look into the first-class cabin then secured the door. The F/O had given the door code first to Christopher, before he passed out, probably knowing no one else could've possibly had it. Against all rules, each of them had inherited the flight deck door code as they traded places for one important reason or another. *I guess it's too late to worry about security procedures at this point. We just want to live,* she told herself.

Chapter 47

Good Things Come in Small Packages

As soon as Jahnni made it into the flight deck, Crutch jumped into the captain's seat and said to her right away, "We're cruising at 32,000 feet." He put on the headset and Jahnni watched as he switched the dial to 121.5.

"What are you doing? What's 121.5 mean?" Jahnni asked, trying to hold back her anxiety at his every move.

"That's the emergency channel. Trust me, I know what I'm doing," Crutch answered quickly.

"First Class 6-1-9, on 121.5 calling you guys in the F-16. First Class 6-1-9 calling the F-16, escort aircraft."

Jahnni put her headset on and turned hers to the same channel she saw Crutch turn his to. Staring at all the instruments, she was dizzy with confusion. Everything was glowing and beeping. *I can't do this!* she thought. *What if he doesn't really know what he's doing? I can't believe I'm sitting here . . . with a kid. Oh, my God, what have I done? What if he doesn't know what channel to put it on? What if he doesn't know who to talk to or what to say? What if . . ."*

"First Class 6-1-9, you need to turn immediately to heading 2-7-0," came the disembodied voice speaking in Jahnni's headset.

Crutch froze, staring at the instruments as his chest heaved up and down. He looked out the windows at the two fighter jets on either side of them. His face turned flushed and he tapped his forehead over and over as if in deep thought. He took a big breath then began talking very forcefully to the person on the other end in a fast pleading voice, "My name is Crutch Link. I mean Eddie Link. I know why you are escorting our plane. I have hundreds of hours, of full-motion simulator time. My dad is Edward Link, our family designs and builds the simulators. I have been flying them since I was three years old. I know how to land this plane safely. I guarantee you that I can do this. Again, I have seven hundred and seventy-six hours to be exact, of full-motion simulator time. Please, please, Don't. Shoot. Us. Down! I can land this plane. I can even put it on auto if they don't understand that I can land safely. If you give me the control frequency I can talk to them!"

"Standby, First Class 6-1-9," came the reply.

The longest ninety seconds of Jahnni's life was suspended in the radio silence as she waited to hear what was going to happen. She could see the pilot in the F-16 out her side window. She stared at him, thinking that she could read some type of body language, but realized that she wouldn't know what to look for anyway.

Suddenly the radio squawked back to life. Crutch and Jahnni both jerked.

"First Class 6-1-9, you may switch to NORCAL 135.15. Do you copy?"

"Yes, I copy. Switching to NORCAL 135.15," Crutch responded before reaching for the dial he used before. Jahnni switched hers after watching Crutch.

Jahnni could see he was slightly more relieved, which in turn brought down her anxiety a notch or two.

"NORCAL. First Class 6-1-9 flight level three-two-zero," Crutch spoke clearly into his headset. Then he waited.

"First Class 6-1-9 NORCAL. Squawk indent."

"This is Eddie Link the fifth. I'm on First Class 6-1-9. I can land this plane, sir."

Again. Waiting. Jahnni felt as though she was waiting for a jury verdict while sitting helpless in the co-pilot's spot. She wasn't sure what words she was waiting to hear, but she knew she would know if it was good or bad by watching Crutch's reaction. Then the voice spoke in the headset, like a head-juror citing their sentence.

"First Class 6-1-9, we understand. Now contact San Francisco approach on 127.15," the voice in her headset boomed. She turned slightly to observe Crutch's face. He simply blinked and turned his lips up in a small smile, and inhaled a deep breath, letting it out with a sigh that certainly sounded like relief to Jahnni.

"Approach, First Class 6-1-9. Three two zero. Descending to one, zero, ten thousand," Eddie informed whoever was on the receiving end.

"Eddie, this is approach. Your F/A spoke with Oakland and we received word that your pilots are disabled. Can you see your escorts out your window?"

"Yes, sir. I know the protocol. I know what they are for and it isn't to escort us. You are going to eliminate the threat of our aircraft over the city. But I can do this! I have seven hundred and seventy-six hours of full-motion simulator time. My dad is waiting in the terminal. He can explain to you that I can do this."

"Eddie, your escorts have spoken to us about your experience and your insistence that you can program the autopilot and land safely. Your dad is being escorted to the San Fran tower as we speak. Standby."

Crutch waited to hear back. Instead of sitting idly, he already began entering the information into something on the center panel. "This is the FMC, the flight management computer, and this is the CDU or computer display unit. Sorta like a little desktop and the computer screen," he mumbled to Jahnni as she sat frozen in the seat next to him. His hands moved deftly around the dash in front of him, then he reached for other things beside him and above him. He worked quietly as his methodical movements took control of the plane.

"Approach, I already programmed the FGC to runway 28 left. Flight Guidance Computer is programmed to 28 left."

"Son, read me the FMC screen," the voice firmly asked.

Jahnni sat still listening to Crutch mention numbers, letters, and directions. She heard the words he was saying as he had explained some things to her and simply spoke others to the person on the other end of the radio, but she did not understand what he meant. Words went in one ear and became jumbled as she sat quietly. She kept glancing out the window at the fighter jet to her right, seemingly tethered to them in the air. She looked out Crutch's side and the other was bouncing sunlight rays into the flight deck. Whatever the numbers and letters Crutch was saying, didn't make sense so she didn't bother to try to figure it out. And she didn't dare speak a word yet, fearful that it would trigger 13-yr-old Crutch back. As she listened to him converse with the professionals on the other end, she felt a surprisingly calm sense of comfort coming over her. Several minutes of silence passed when she realized no one was chattering on the radio to them. Then she felt the plane begin gradually descending.

"First Class 6-1-9 approach," came the voice over the radio to Crutch.

"First Class 6-1-9 go ahead."

"First Class 6-1-9 . . . here we go son. Proceed direct to initial approach fix. Descend to 3,000 feet."

"Already in our descent going direct to IAF." Crutch responded.

"First Class 6-1-9, cleared for ILS two eight left."

"Roger, cleared for ILS 28 left."

Crutch had already told Jahnni he entered everything in the FMC. She assumed by him mentioning things as he did them, was his way of assuring her everything was going to be okay. They sat in silence. Crutch did not look at Jahnni as he concentrated on his job. Jahnni thought he looked so calm and professional, watching his instruments and doing what Jahnni assumed all pilots did.

He is really doing this! she thought with dumb wonder. She caught a sideways glance at him, then answered her own underlying fear. *But I think . . . I'm sure . . . I trust him.*

"Oh, I better . . ." Crutch said as he pressed the PA button to talk to the FA's. "Prepare the cabin for final descent and landing."

Jahnni broke her own silence and quietly asked him how to call the FA's to ask about the pilots. He touched a button on her audio panel and told her to push it when she wanted to talk. After getting an update, she continued sitting stoically, watching the scenery get closer and closer. "Dr. Robinson said they are stable. Still too woozy to make any sense when they talk. Rochelle said she had told someone earlier, when she spoke with them on the radio, they will need an ambulance when, or if, we make it. But I assured her that we WILL land safely and as you probably heard, I gave her the quick version so she can brief the others. Then she said . . ."

The radio squawked to life suddenly, breaking their conversation. It made Jahnni jump and a high-pitched chirp escaped her mouth.

"First Class 6-1-9, contact San Fran Tower 118.7," the voice instructed. "And good luck son. Nice to meet you."

"Copy. Going to 118.7," Crutch confirmed.

"San Fran Tower. First Class 6-1-9 with you on localizer two eight left," Crutch said to whoever would be talking to him from the tower.

"First class 6-1-9. Cleared to land two eight left," came the reply.

"Copy. Cleared to land two eight left. We will need police to remove the passenger being held by flight attendants. Highly Dangerous. Wanted at PDX. We need ambulances for two crew members. They are stable, under the care of an onboard doctor, but will need to go to ER."

"Copy that First Class 6-1-9. Port will meet and detain. Ambulance ready. You get the full meal deal today," Crutch was told.

"Copy," Crutch said.

Jahnni noticed that he had a big smile on his face. *Probably the full meal deal comment,* she thought to herself, smiling at that very comment.

"First Class 6-1-9. Do not taxi," came the same voice over the radio. "Come to a stop, set brakes, and remain in place on runway. We will meet the plane. Again, do not taxi to gate."

"Copy Tower. First Class 6-1-9 staying on runway after landing," came Crutch's affirmative response.

Jahnni sat watching the airstrip come into view and felt the airplane curving toward it. It straightened and began to make the approach. Her chest rose a little faster as her breathing filled with anxiety of the unknown. It looked like they were getting ready to land on something as small as a postage stamp. And the nearby water looked ominous. She glanced out the side windows. The twin escorts were still at their sides as the plane got closer to the runway.

"Are you sure this plane can land itself? Don't you have to do anything?" she asked, trying to hide what was left of her fear.

"We are fine, Jahnni. Mainly, I configured the aircraft for landing. If the approach is loaded into the FMC, it will do almost all the work," Crutch said, now looking at her. He turned back and Jahnni watched him begin flipping and moving different gears, buttons, switches and knobs. His actions looked fluid and purposeful and he said, without looking at her, "I'm selecting the landing flaps and lowering the landing gear."

"Why didn't we just let it land by itself before, when the pilots became sick?" Jahnni asked.

"Because they hadn't entered the information into the FMC. That's the Flight Management Computer, remember? It is my database for entering information into the FMS, the flight management system so it knows what to do. I had to look it up and make sure the FMC had everything correct according to our location, weather, winds, and such. Then once I entered it, it took over. It will brake itself also, if the pilot tells it to," Crutch explained patiently, looking up at her through his long messy hair falling on his forehead. He swung his head to make his hair swish out of his face then assured her once again. "It's okay, Jahnni. This is easy to me. I'm being humble when I just keep saying I can do this."

She smiled at him, feeling any left-over anxiety wash out through her feet.

"Besides, we're even now," he snickered.

"Very impressive, Mr. Link. I can't believe they let a kid

land the plane," she said, shaking her head in disbelief.

"They must have talked to my dad. No one has asked me how old I am yet. I don't know if the FAA had to approve it or what, but at least they didn't make us go swimming in the Pacific," he said sarcastically. "You know, not to brag, but I could have done all this without the auto-pilot. It's almost like I had been preparing for this day since I was three. All those years, I just played on the simulators like it was a game I had to master. Seriously though, once we land, I'll stop the plane and set the brake on the runway. This is a compromised flight so they will all come to us. There will be lots of emergency vehicles so don't worry. Yes! Here we go! I LOVE this part!"

The ground was getting closer and closer as Jahnni looked out the side window. The closer it got, the faster her heart sped up. Then all at once the twin fighter jets ascended steeply and turned out, away from their plane. "Oh! They left us. What does that mean? Oh look . . . we're almost there."

Then the plane's back tires touched down and the nose lowered right afterward into a perfect landing, and she felt it begin braking as Crutch pulled up two levers and the engine roared louder. Jahnni's belt pulled on her as her body leaned forward when the plane slowed even faster. The plane continued slowing *as if*, Jahnni thought, *there were ghosts on the wings braking and slowing it.* When the plane was almost to their first turn to leave the runway, Crutch took it off autopilot and controlled the plane to the spot he was told to remain at. He set the brake and turned off the engines.

He switched his radio selector to PA and spoke to the

passengers. "I need everyone to remain seated with your seat belts on. Again . . . Everyone is to remain seated. We have an emergency onboard but everything is . . . under control."

He looked at Jahnni and raised his eyebrows up at the irony of the situation being under control then continued talking to the passengers and the FA's. "Flight Attendants, please disarm the doors. I see the airstairs being rolled to the plane. Police and medical personnel will be boarding the main cabin door."

He then pointed out the window at all the flashing lights, Port Police, fire trucks, and paramedics. Police dressed in SWAT gear jumped out of vans and circled the plane, while others waited for the stairs to lock up against the plane.

"They're waiting for the FA's to open the doors. It's okay," he told Jahnni. "They know we're the good guys. I'll open the flight deck door when I get the signal."

Jahnni thought about what was happening. What has already happened. The last two days flashed like a movie in her memory. On a loop. What seemed like so long ago, also seemed like seconds ago. Out of all the porridge of words flooding her head, one word kept flashing in the forefront of her mind. *Beau*.

Chapter 48

And Down She Went

"DAD! MOM!" CRUTCH yelled as an officer allowed them into the cordoned off gate inside the airport. "I did it dad! I did it!"

Crutch's mom got to him first and clung to him, tears flowing freely down her face. Dad encircled them both. He finally peeled him out of his mom's arms and hugged him to his chest.

"I would like to say that I knew you could do it, but I have to admit, that I was a little scared. You did good son, you did so good. I think you are right about something. We already discussed it and you have absolutely won the age ol' argument that we have been having for so long," Mr. Link said. "We aren't going to make you wait until you are sixteen to *really* go to flight school. You can start as soon as things get settled. Just remember, you can't fly solo until you turn sixteen. Well . . . besides . . . what just happened. I mean from now on, you can't fly solo."

Crutch was speechless . . . for a few seconds. "Are you serious? I can really start this year?"

"Yep. I think you have proven that you know your stuff so we might as well make it legal. Let's make that ground school official." Mr. Link stopped talking and looked at his wife then back at Crutch. "You know what . . . they still haven't asked me how old my son is. I'm afraid to tell 'em," his dad whispered with a grin on his face.

"No one asked me how old I was either, while I was in the air! Not even when I was talking to the jets that were escorting us. And ground control didn't ask either. So . . . I didn't offer!" Crutch said, low enough to not be heard by anyone else, but loud enough so his dad could have a good laugh. Then he pointed to the group of officials who brought them into the airport using the stairs that accessed the jetway, "That guy over there did, ask me, I mean. He questioned all of us. I kinda told him the truth. I hope that is okay."

"Son . . . rule number one in life. Tell the truth no matter how painful it is. Rule number two. Keep believing in yourself. You have made us so proud today. So proud," his dad whispered as he kissed the top of his head. Jahnni's chest felt tight and the bulge of emotions gripped her heart seeing the relief in their eyes and the love showered on their son.

"Mom, Dad! Here . . . I want you to meet the bravest person in the world! This is Jahnni. She and another lady named Samantha kept me safe and made sure that they got me home sa . . . well . . . as safe as they could before I had to become an instant pilot."

Jahnni extended her hand but both Eddie Link Sr and Janice Link, grabbed her and embraced her as if they had known each other for years.

"Thank you so much for bringing us our boy," Janice said with tears filling her eyes that caused the blue to sparkle. Mr. Link shook his head in agreement with his wife, tears rolling down his cheeks as well.

After the commotion of the plane, the interviews by the FAA, Benson, and the ill pilots were all taken care of, Jahnni and Crutch were given permission to finally leave the area. Mr. and Mrs. Link insisted that Jahnni stay and have a late lunch with them before catching the early evening flight back to Portland.

"Besides," Mr. Link added with an exasperated tone, "there are a ton of reporters on the other side of the security checkpoint waiting like vultures to pounce on Crutch, and us I suppose. They can't wait to see the passenger who took over the flight and landed it safely. Let's hide a while longer and stay inside security for lunch, okay?"

Jahnni agreed, "I'd love to have a nice quiet lunch with you! It's going to be difficult to pry me away from this awesome son of yours when I go home though . . . I can't express how proud I am of him also. He has been an integral part of our successes yesterday and today. I owe him my life."

During lunch, Jahnni tried to avoid talking details about the day before and kept reminding Crutch's parents that they couldn't until the FBI gave them permission. "But I can tell you that Crutch was not harmed. In due time, we can share all the adventurous details. If you want to call it that," she said, making an exaggerated scary look on her face, which made everyone laugh.

They sat for two hours talking about Crutch's life and the cancer that was now in remission. They talked about his family's business, and Jahnni's job at the airport. They covered gardening, sailing, vacations, and adventure novels. Every topic was thoroughly shared as the family became fast friends.

"Oh, I just realized," Jahnni said as she glanced around the table. "I didn't get to meet Crutch's little brother."

Janice smiled and said, "Then I guess you'll have to fly back down soon and stay with us. We originally thought we were just coming to the airport to pick up this guy here," she teased, as she ruffled his hair, "but the day has become quite a to-do! He is with the neighbor."

They all laughed, enjoying each other's company before discussing their plans to stay in touch, visiting each other, and maybe getting Jahnni to take some time off and go with them on their family vacation in the summer.

"Hey! Speaking of our conversation earlier about favorite novels, you can write your own now, Jahnni!" Janice blurted out. "I'll co-write it with you. I have a Master's in English and a Doctorate in Philosophy. I want to retire from the University anyway!"

"And boy, what a tale we can tell!" Jahnni said, as she and Crutch laughed. She looked at Crutch, pausing to make eye contact, knowing that someday they not only had a great story to tell, but they now have a bond deeper than they could have ever expected.

It was time for Jahnni to catch her flight back to Portland. They hadn't left the concourse yet, so they walked her to her gate. She hugged them all goodbye then turned back to Crutch again, grabbing his hands and cupping both of hers around them. "I think there are not enough words to express how to thank you for your courage. Thank you Crutch. Thank you for being the most awesome gift to the world."

"I owe everything to you, Jahnni. Thank you. Tell Beau to stay in touch. Give him my phone number and address when you see him, okay?" Crutch said, waving goodbye as she walked down the jetway and boarded her flight back to PDX. She got settled in her seat in first-class, fastened her seatbelt and began nodding off before the plane was even completely boarded up. Leaning against the window, she readied herself to relax and promptly fell into a deep sleep. The next couple hours were filled with complete oblivion. Until they weren't.

She was running and running, gun shots ringing out and pinging on the ground and rocks around her. She suddenly found herself surrounded by children, and elderly people. She screamed at them. *RUN! HIDE! He's coming!* They all scattered into holes in the ground and flaps on tree trunks. They rolled into the river nearby and disappeared into the dark current. She felt an enormous eagle dig his long sharp talons into her shoulders, pulling her into the sky. He began to shake her like he was going to rip her apart to eat. She saw another eagle carrying someone else away, flying in the distance in front of her. She couldn't see who it was but she knew she had to help them somehow. *No! Leave me alone! Let me go!* she screamed in her head. Jahnni felt her body moving as if being shaken by the eagle again.

She opened her eyes to the flight attendant gently rubbing her shoulder, calling her name in a comforting whisper, "Jahnni, Jahnni, are you okay hon? You seem restless in your sleep."

"What? I, uh, what's . . ." she mumbled as she glanced around the cabin. No one else seemed concerned. "I must have had a bad dream. I was worried about . . . Oh, well. It's nothing. I'll be fine, thanks."

She closed her eyes, and soon felt the plane touch down and begin its taxi to the airport. Jahnni looked out the window as the plane was pulling into the gate. The door could not be opened fast enough. She grabbed her things and exited the plane, walked up the jetway and entered the gate. She stopped to get a better hold on her jacket and small bag, and took in a big gulp of air to calm herself before she began walking towards the concourse walkway. The dream was suddenly behind her. *It meant nothing,* she told herself. *I'm fine now.*

She thought she heard her name and turned.

"Jahnni! Jahnni!" Sam was walking hand in hand with someone. "Jahnni!"

Jahnni went straight to her and embraced her so tight she didn't want to let go. "Oh Sam! What a crazy two days . . . How are you? Are you doing well?"

"I sure am. And . . . I would like you to meet someone." She turned to the man she was holding hands with. "This . . . is Carter. Carter Laurent Mercier."

Jahnni held out her hand, making note of the tall fair skinned man with dark blue eyes. He was impeccably dressed and wore his light hair in a tight faded haircut. "I am so very pleased to meet you Carter. I'm Jahnni Dawson. Sam here is a very special person, and she assures me that you are quite special yourself!"

"Oui! I do know zis. We boz feel veery lucky to meetz. When I find oot Zamantha was a poessible hooztage, I was frantic. I knew she was ma dame spéciale. I mean, my special lady. This . . . it open my eyez. I am not going to let her get away froom me!" Carter said as he laughed and pulled her closer into a tight hug.

Jahnni saw the excitement in both of their eyes and shook her head as she turned to each of them. "You know Carter, you two look good together. I mean, not how you look-look. I'm picking up a vibe. You both appreciate each other. Take care of Sam here. She certainly is a dame spéciale," she said in French. "We need to hang out sometime. I would love to brush up on my French."

"Oui! Je suis impressionné. Par tous les moyens, faisons ceci," Carter answered with wide eyes and excitement flooding into his words.

"Je ne peux pas attendre. Encore une fois, tellement agréable de vous rencontrer," Jahnni answered him, smiling at the refreshing encounter.

Samantha's mouth hung open as she looked back and forth between the two of them. She looked at Jahnni, her lips moving like a fish trying to suck in water and asked, "Wh . . . wh

. . . what was that? I didn't know you spoke French. Why did I not know this? What, you took a speed class between yesterday and today?"

"No, Sam. Six years of classes and a foreign exchange program does miracles for a kid," she explained, laughing jovially. "He said, he's impressed, with my French, and we'll do this . . . all hang out that is. And I told him I can't wait and it was nice to meet him."

"Hmmm . . . Hopefully it won't take me six years to understand him," Sam pondered out loud, smiling up at Carter.

"Well, I have to go see Carolyn and get ready to jump back into the schedule tomorrow. I want to stay busy. I hope to see you two soon. We'll get together!" Jahnni added as she wagged her finger at each of them and began to turn away.

Jahnni walked up the concourse towards her manager's office. Except for the plane ride home from San Francisco, this was the first time she was truly by herself. No Mr. T, No Samantha. No Crutch. No . . . Beau.

I'll get to see him later though! she reminded herself.

Every step seemed to take forever to make progress. Step after step was like walking in sludge; walking and walking and getting nowhere. Her legs felt so heavy, and her shoes made of lead. Voices were echoing around her and she could hear dinging and coughing and announcements being made. Coffee steamers were hissing; luggage was clanking and babies were crying. Colors seemed too bright and the sun's rays shining in the big windows seemed too sharp. She squinted her eyes and slowed her pace. She turned around, trying to decide how to make the noise stop. The floor started rolling underneath her and the walls began to melt. Then she just . . . slipped to the floor.

Chapter 49

Be Still My Heart

JAHNNI OPENED HER heavy eyelids. A soft hissing and beeping that was in the distance was suddenly beside her. She moved her hand to rub her eyes and felt a sharp pinch in her arm. Looking down, she saw a bandage holding a needle in her arm and in the dim lights she began to understand where she was. She tried to sit up but realized that she didn't have the strength to reposition herself. She squirmed and tried again, but it was no use. She felt so weak. Then she heard a female voice speaking to her.

"You're awake."

"Huh? Uh . . . ya. Where am I, exactly?" she said groggily to the voice in her room.

"Legacy Emanuel. Do you remember me?"

"I . . . I don't know. Should I?"

"Yes, dear. You should."

"Oh . . . uh, Dr. Robinson? From the plane?"

"Very good. How do you feel honey?"

"I don't know how I feel. How long have I been here? Why am I here?"

"Well, you've had a pretty tough few days that finally caught up with you. We've been keeping an eye on you while you slept like a bear. Of course, the sedatives didn't hurt. You needed rest. A little R & R. The bump on your head also needed to be monitored."

"When can I go home?"

"Well that depends. I see you don't have family anywhere near. An aunt and uncle from the east coast have been getting updates on your condition, and you have had many friends trying to see you, but we have restricted your visitors until you were better. Is there anyone who can stay with you and help you at home if we release you?"

"Well, I have a couple friends who could probably stay with me the first day and check on me after that. How long have I been here?"

"A week."

"WHAT? A WEEK?" she said very loudly before realizing that it really, really made her head hurt.

"Yes, but you had a very scary fall and we had to keep you until you regained your strength."

"Oh. My head does hurt. What are you putting in my IV? I feel a little . . . tired. Can I take a nap and discuss this later?"

"Sure, my dear. Get more rest. I'll check on you when I do my rounds tonight."

The next afternoon, Jahnni waited in the wheelchair for

426

Sam to get to her room. "I get to go home!"

"I know silly! I'm taking you home," Sam said.

"I know, but I am so excited to eat regular food and get in my own bed that I want to tell everyone!" She turned to the nurse, "I'm going home!"

Thirty minutes later, Sam was driving north over the Glen Jackson Bridge, high above the Columbia River towards Vancouver where Jahnni lived. Jahnni looked out her window to see crystal blue skies and dozens of sail boats spread out over the water. The sky was clear with some faint wisps of clouds hovering against the blue. Boats? Boats. *I never got to go on a boat ride with Beau,* she thought. *I wonder where he is, how he is doing. Did he even know that I was in the hospital? Why did I even think that there was chance with him. He probably didn't even know, or care. No sense bothering Sam with my silly imagination. I'll keep it to myself and keep myself busy. I'm sure in time I'll forget about him. He has probably already forgotten about me.* A tickle fluttered in her heart just picturing him. *His smile. His eyes. His kindness. His gentleness. His toughness. His courage. He saved me. Oh Beau. I don't know what to believe. I shouldn't have danced around my feelings. Agent Pahlavi was right. I should have told him. It's probably too late. I should have been clear about my feelings for him. The real ones, not my stupid fantasy ones.* Jahnni sighed and closed her eyes for the rest of the ride home, the motion of the car lulling her.

Agent Pahlavi came to see her at home and they talked about the underground "manse," as they started to refer to it.

Jahnni couldn't hold it in any longer. "How is Beau

doing?"

"He is healing up just fine. He'll be back to work soon enough. Right now, he is resting," Pahlavi offered. "The others have been presented with a court order like this one. It prevents you from speaking of anything below the airport or Zale's former long-time home," Delaram said, then clarified, "because what started as an airport issue became a county issue. Then it escalated into a state issue and because of Homeland Security, turned into a Federal issue. It's a matter that's being determined in private, behind closed doors, until the outcome is finalized. Plus, public talking points have to be determined so no one says something they shouldn't. We need to protect the airport and the passengers."

"Sure," Jahnni replied. "I get it. We are all pretty much of the same mind anyway. We all seem to be the type who want what is best for each other . . . and our airport."

"Well, I have to get back to the office. Agent Anthony is waiting for me in the car while he fills out some paperwork. I'm glad to see that you are recuperating. I'm sure we will see each other again. Please, don't get up." And with that, Special Agent Delaram Pahlavi let herself out, locking the door before pulling it shut.

A week later, Jahnni was back at work, standing behind the ticket counter helping with the large crowd that was trying to get checked in for their flights. She was glad that Carolyn let her take her time coming back full force as a supervisor. She appreciated it as she still felt a little . . . 'off.' Her body seemed to be healing on track, but her heart ached at a rhythm that felt

428

in sync with her breathing; all day, every day. Even at night, she would wake up thinking about Beau.

"Hello! I can help the next person over here. Welcome to First Class Air. Where is your destination today?" she repeated over and over. After another hour, she decided to help one more person before taking her lunch break. Jahnni waved forward the next person in the Special Services line without looking up, because she bent to check the stalled printer. She checked the paper feed to be sure that the boarding passes would print out timelier then pushed the reset button. She stood back up to help the person that walked up to the counter.

"I am on the San Francisco flight and I am traveling armed . . . oh, and I would like to check a bag also," said the tall, dark haired, handsome, green eyed Adonis standing before her. His face appeared chiseled, and his eyes melted the part of Jahnni's brain that formed complete sentences. All sorts of electrical short circuits were going off in her head . . . and elsewhere. He was sublime, a beauteous specimen of maleness. Absolutely worth the embarrassing open mouthed drool that was beginning to form on her lips.

Jahnni's heart skipped several beats. She stood there motionless, staring into his eyes as she tried to respond, but the letters in her head were not forming words, just pictures. Finally, she answered, "Oh, uh, okay." Then added, for the sake of *the rules*, "May I see your ID please?"

"Sure." He flipped open his wallet so she could see his official FBI ID.

She smiled and began checking him in, continually glancing up as she grabbed his boarding pass and tagged his bag.

"I need to have you fill out this paperwork and sign please," Jahnni said, handing him the AI paperwork concerning his armed status. Her face felt warm because she couldn't break her eye contact from him. Try as she did, she felt a string of hope reaching from her eyes to his. He stood there smiling back at her as well.

Finally, more words formed automatically and spilled from her lips, "You'll need to show this paperwork at security and when you introduce yourself to the gate agent."

After a slight lull in the conversation he said, "I was hoping you could help me with a reservation for the future. Can you do that here?"

"Yes, I can do that. Where is your destination?" Jahnni asked, her fingers resting on the keyboard ready to type in the information. Her heart was pounding and her knees felt feeble as she stood there, three feet of space between them.

"Well, I would like to make a reservation for a beach getaway. What do you suggest?" he asked, as he leaned onto the counter, tracing her face with his eyes.

His smile, his lips. She wanted to reach up and touch his hand, as it rested on top of the counter. Fear of mistaking his intentions made her hold back.

"Okay . . . do you mean like the Oregon Coast?" she asked, trying to remain professional . . . with unprofessional longing.

"No, farther."

"Do you mean like San Diego?"

"No, farther. Quieter."

"Okay . . . Hawaii?"

"Nope, too commercial."

"Uh . . . Cancun, in Mexico?"

"Nah . . . I'm thinking quieter. If you could go anywhere, where would you suggest? It's for two."

Jahnni suddenly felt queasy. The nausea swept over her, choking her heart from feeling any joy in the world. She felt an immediate sense of loss and retreated inward. *Is he going to take someone with him there? I hate her already!* she thought as she kept her smile plastered on her face.

She cleared her throat then asked further, "Oh, uh, well, is this a female friend? I would suggest Bora Bora. I have always wanted to go there. I am sure anyone would love it."

"That sounds great! Then Bora Bora it is. Two weeks. Just her and I. We will block out the world and relax, napping in hammock swings, eating fresh fruit, watching the sun come up and watching the sun go down. I've always wanted to take a walk on a sunset beach, hand in hand along the edge of the water, the soft waves lapping at our bare feet."

Jahnni felt a little flushed. Since the time she saw him last, she had wrestled with her longing to see him again. But her heart began aching so deeply when he said those three words, 'it's for two.' *What was real and what was my imagination? Did I misread any of his friendliness as possibly something more? Have I really been that caught up in my hope that I couldn't see . . . the truth? Oh God, I want to run into the office and send someone else out here to finish up this transaction. I want to . . . cry! Has he even forgiven me for what happened to him?*

To know that he was going to take some lady on vacation was a crushing blow to the hopes and dreams that had lived in her heart . . . since *that* day. That day when he first walked up to the ticket counter. So many thoughts and memories flooded her mind. Still, she realized that her mistake of misinterpreting his intentions was no reason to not do her job. *I'll be profes-sional and make the reservation for him and his . . . whoever,* she painfully decided.

"So, what are the dates for this . . . beautiful, relaxing, romantic, getaway?" she asked, cheerfulness masking the ache of despondent misery.

Beau tipped his head to the side and smiled as those glorious dimples broke the surface. He looked into her eyes and she felt his gaze burn away a part of her that was afraid; afraid of carrying the burden of hopelessness around forever, yet afraid to dare hope for more. As fear began to fade, she realized nothing mattered at this moment except what she felt rising like a tide inside her. Hope. Hope flowing as the world around them faded. *I'm just going to tell him. I don't care if he is planning on taking someone else. I'm going to simply blurt it out and be done with this torture that has me chained to the unknown. Here goes. I'll be clear and to the point. I'm not afraid. I am gonna tell him. I'm just gonna say it. I, I, I lo . . .* She breathed in courage, preparing to say it out loud.

Time ticked slowly before Beau spoke first, interrupting her thoughts in a way that melted away years of waiting and days of longing and wondering. He reached over the counter and gently touched the side of her face.

"I don't know the dates yet . . . you tell me. When's your vacation?"

The End

Acknowledgements

I read a book once that promoted the theme that no one who ever "made it," really did so alone. (Outliers-The Story of True Success-by Malcolm Gladwell.) At first I thought about all the self-made millionaires you hear about, or singers who made it big after being discovered in a seedy bar, singing for pennies. I thought about people I've known who "made millions" or those who simply had a ginormous retirement. What I have come to see is that many people, most people in fact, who have been successful, look back with short memories and think, "I did this all by myself."

They forget about anyone who has loaned them a dollar, gave them their time, or hooked them up with a friend that could help them. They forget about the free used car they received to get to their job, the job that eventually gave them the skills that they used to carve out their future. The tax advice that saved their business, home, or bank account. The free day-care either by a friend, helpful relative or spouse as they forged ahead. Loans when they couldn't pay rent or they needed just a few hundred dollars to get their patent. On-going free advice from significant sources.

Yes . . . the hand up is underrated. And, no one gets there

all alone. In this vein, I accept the fact that I have not done any-thing great without help. That is, if I could even label anything I have ever done, as great. I thought about all the mistakes I've made in life after I thought about a decision and tried to weigh the pros and cons, mulling over every detail . . . only to end up in a worse position for having tried to improve my life or financial situation. In the long run, they were amazing detours I needed, but not for the reasons I had originally assumed.

So, I would like to thank anyone, and everyone who has encouraged me, or helped me with ideas or confirmation about my ideas while writing this book. Most of all, I would like to thank those who made my project monetarily possible. I apologize ahead of time if I have accidentally left anyone out. Freda Gardner, who has been one of my biggest fans and gave me enough of a donation to make me realize I can't give up now! Jeralita Costa, Rietta Costa, Charvette Costa, Traci Fontyn, Madden Strawn, Marlene Tucker, Kelly Hollingshead, Danyelle Prom, Barb and Don Wilkenson, Jo Coila, (did you know I applied some of my tips to my book fund?) Mae Ries, (did you know I applied some of my tips to my book fund also?) and my three anonymous donors. Your gifts are so kind and the reason I could publish. My cheering section and/or idea bouncers, Cindi McNichols, Linda Fleischman, Jill McPherson, Cory Strawn, and Cory Fontyn. To Matt and Carla Christensen and Shane DeLong for being in my cheering section. And especially to all my wonderful grandbabies that seemed to arrive as if a heavenly conveyor belt was connected to our family.

My heart beats for you; Gabriel, Madison, Riley, Brianna, Madalynn, Madden, Isabella, Chenoa, Cheyenne, Sage, and Summer. For you, I can't give up. How can I tell you to chase your dreams if I grow weary of chasing mine? I can't forget Keri Kuper who probably thought I would never finish this book, but never said anything except how she can't wait to read it. Then she had superb suggestions that turned out to be do-or-die scene improvements; those details that slipped by me. James Chesky, who was not afraid to point out some issues with the storyline that I needed to consider in the be-ginning. Valuable advice delivered with fun and chuckles! I'm still laughing.

To one of the greatest pilots, Todd Phillips, who is a master of cutting down the small talk and getting to the point. You are a true teacher and mentor when it comes to the big tin bird in the sky, but I'm not sure I'm a very good learner! Your friendship, time and expertise were invaluable. Thank you!

Special thanks to Laura Kingsley, my editor who did more than edit, she made me dig deeper and had a crisp way of cutting to the chase, which by the way, is refreshingly honest and helpful. (https://laurakingsley.wordpress.com or laurakingsleyeEd@yahoo.com)

And of course, to Cheri Lasota, my formatter, up-loader, and designer for my book interior and covers. She's also an author and editor with mad skills! (www.CheriLasota.com or Cheri@CheriLasota.com).

Thank you ALL!

Glossary

AI—Armed Individual

ARNK—Arrival Unknown (gap in the reservation where the travel isn't synched in the reservation. An *ARNK* in the reservation will hold the rest of the reservation in place without getting canceled. A pause, in the reservation, making no changes below it.

BC'd—Background checked

Captain—Pilot in Command

CDU—Control Display Unit-A small screen with keyboard and touch screen for the plane's FMC/FMS

CSS—Customer Service Supervisor

CTX—Computer Tomography Xray. Explosive detection device that scans luggage and more.

Direct—A flight that may have one or more stops without changing planes

DOT—Department of Transportation

ETA—Estimated Time of Arrival

ETD—Estimated Time of Departure

FA—Flight Attendant-There are forward and aft FA's

FAA—Federal Aviation Administration

FAB—Food and Beverage

FAM—Federal Air Marshall

FBI—Federal Bureau of Investigation

FFDO—Federal Flight Deck Officer (armed pilot)

FGC—Flight Guidance Computer

FID's—Flight Information Displays

FLEO—Federal Law Enforcement Officer

FLIFO—Flight Information

Flight Deck—Front of aircraft where pilots operate the airplane. Also referred to as the cockpit.

Flight Simulator—A machine used to train pilots that recreates an airplane's flight deck, and outside environment through movement, and computer-generated visuals.

FMC—Flight Management Computer-controls the FMS

FMS—Flight Management System-A specialized computer system that automates a wide variety of in-flight tasks. Manages and guides the aircraft along the flight plan using information entered into the FMC.

F/O—First Officer/co-pilot/second in command under the captain

HRT—Hostage Rescue Team

IAF—Initial Approach Fix

ILS—Instrument Landing System

Jump-seater/Jump seat—A select few employees (and select government employees like FAA inspectors) are authorized to ride in a folding auxiliary seat called a jump seat. Usually only pilots from most airlines flying non-revenue, or to assignments when no other seats available. Jump seats in the main cabin are the seats the crew use on the flight and can often be used by flight attendants flying non-rev.

LEO—Law Enforcement Officer

LSP—Lightning Strike Protection

NONREV/Non-rev—any airline employee/family member/guest of an employee that is flying for free or for extremely reduced fare. Non-revenue.

NTK—Need to Know

OJT-On the Job Training

Open Jaw—The departure city is not the return city. On a map, it looks like a triangle without points C and A connecting. Passenger flies from city A to city B and their return trip is flying from city B to city C (instead of back to city A) and the travel is over. (PDX-LAX then LAX-SEA)

OPS—Operations. All airlines have differing duties. Usually they communicate with the pilots coordinating inbound/outbound flight needs. Assign parking spots for aircraft, food and beverage delegation, ordering fuel, tracking flights and relaying information to ground agents and inside agents. Communicates with Tower in an emergency. Investigative research for accurate reporting of flights and their daily history for the airline and to report to the DOT.

PA—Public Address system

PBX—Private Branch Exchange. Used for SAT phones

PDX—Portland International Airport (Portland, Oregon)

PNR—Passenger Name Record, the reservation

POI—Person of Interest

RAC Room—Ramp Action Center or Reaccomodation Center

RON—Remain Over Night

SAC—Special Agent in Charge

SAT phone—Satellite phones do not rely on towers, like a regular wireless but instead transmits signals via satellites that orbit the earth.

SFO—San Francisco

SIDA—Secure Identification Display Area badge-must always be worn visibly in a secured area

SLC—Salt Lake City

SSR—Special Service Request or Special Services

STAR—Start The Airline out Right

TSA—Transportation Security Administration

UM—Unaccompanied Minor. Requires the child 5-13 yrs. old to be in direct possession at every point by an airline employee until the child is handed over to the receiving adult.

UML—Unaccompanied Minor Liaison-Assigned duty to care for the UM's at the airport

About the Author

JL LeGerrette has been expressing herself through writing since she was a child through musical lyrics, short stories, and poetry. Her first self-published book was a small collection of short stories and poems that were written over, and about, many years of her life called The Colors of My Life by JL LeGerrette. Read from front to back in order, you see her grow up . . . with her own set of rules of maneuvering through life and finish with seeing the beauty of her children and a final explanation of her odd sense of "experiencing" life. In her first novel, You're Clear, you see her vivid imagination take you from controlled environment to chaos in seconds. After raising children and gathering grandchildren like a backyard Spring garden, 0-60 is a way of life. After all, what is life without a little adventure?

Follow the author's blog at www.JLLeGerrette.com and sign up to receive the newsletter, latest posts and information on current books, and new releases that will follow. Or contact the author at Jerilynn@JLLeGerrette.com

Made in the USA
Columbia, SC
09 December 2017